ILLUSIVE

VIRGINIA DUAN

Letters to Artax Press

Book cover by Joyce Park
Developmental edit by Jacquelin Cangro
Copy edit by Melody Ip
Cultural edit by Diane Park
Author photo by Susanna Stroberg

Paperback ISBN: 979-8-9901853-0-2
EPUB ISBN: 979-8-9901853-1-9

1st edition 2024

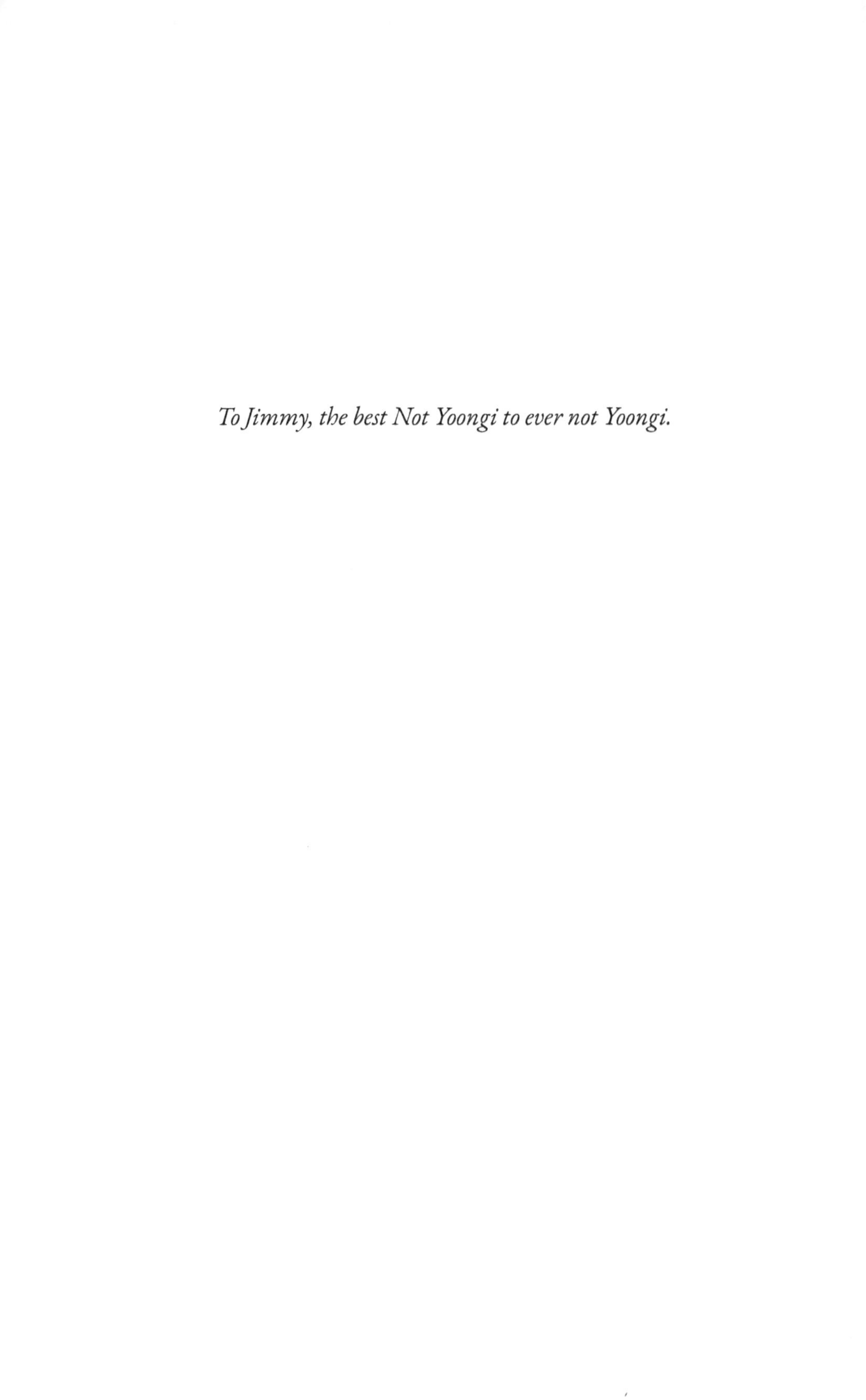

To Jimmy, the best Not Yoongi to ever not Yoongi.

Table of Contents

Chapter 1

October 2021

Twenty-seven-year-old rapper Jung Do-won, who also went by 1DEL1GHT, was mindlessly shoveling the SB Entertainment cafeteria ramyeon in his mouth. Only half-listening to Kitahara Akihiro and Park Dae-jung, two of his Dreams of Youth Eternal Nation (DOYEN) bandmates, Do-won's eyes landed on a bright pink mohawk with closely shaved sides. From there, he followed the sexy curve of a neck, a loose army green tank where hints of ink peeked out and flowed into well-toned arms covered in tattoos of Chinese or Korean calligraphy painting.

Do-won squinted.

Was that Katie Wu?

She looked very much the same despite the new tattoos and yet, even from this distance, he could tell she held herself differently than she had.

He was pretty sure his managers didn't say anything about Katie visiting or returning to the Seoul branch of his agency, but he could have been wrong. Perhaps he'd been working too hard lately. He was still getting used to being a civilian again after serving the mandatory South Korean military service with the Korean members of his band during the worst of the pandemic.

It had been a little unusual for them to serve together, considering they'd ruled the global charts just prior, but the world had seemed so uncertain then. It had made the best sense at the time. Plus, Akihiro had released both a Korean and Japanese version of his mini-album, and their youngest member Choi Soo-min had released an all-English album to keep the interest in DOYEN going.

"Noona," Akihiro called out over the noise of the cafeteria, waving. His fading orange hair floofed as he ran a hand through it in his signature move. "Come sit with us!"

Katie snapped her head in their direction, her face covered with horn-rimmed glasses and a black face mask. Even from this distance, Do-won could tell she was happy to see Akihiro. His noona had always been pretty thanks to her excellent bone structure, and her eye smile only amplified her beauty. She was as breathtaking as ever.

"Noona's back?" asked Do-won.

The two younger vocalists both stared at him oddly. "Good one, hyung," Dae-jung said, chuckling in his low baritone. "You had me for a second."

Do-won felt like he was missing the punchline of a joke and maybe he was. He tugged on the collar of his Human Made distressed T-shirt. Why was Katie here and why did his two band members seem to know, and he did not?

Katie strutted over — quite a feat, considering her tray was particularly laden with SB Entertainment cafeteria's most famous offerings — in particular, the kimchi ramyeon and the egg tarts with the face of Song Byung-ho, the company's CEO, stamped on them.

Do-won felt slow, as if his brain were drowning in water. It had been a common feeling as of late. Perhaps he really had not been taking care of himself as well as he could have been. Being the most famous K-pop band in the world had its downsides, even if they had been out of the game for eighteen months. The pressure to recapture the heights of their previous success loomed around every corner, and Do-won just wanted to get back into the rhythm of idol life.

"Noona, I was wondering when you'd show up at the office," Dae-jung pouted even before she sat down, his regular boxy smile nowhere to be seen. "Why didn't you text us to hang out? That's so mean!"

The older woman just snickered, low and throaty, and Do-won felt it hit his gut. The laugh was so familiar, and he felt a rush of fond memories. He had missed Katie something fierce. It's a wonder that it all just hit him now.

Akihiro hurriedly cleared some room at their table, his numerous bracelets tinkling, adding to the noise of shuffled plates and utensils. Do-won scooted over politely to allow her space instead of forcing her to sit so close to him. It had been years and he didn't want to impose.

Katie set down her tray and stood with her arms open, as if she knew Akihiro and Dae-jung would immediately attack her with hugs and a barrage of questions that left her unable to get a word in edgewise. Though the two vocalists were only a year younger than Do-won, they leaned so often into their cute side that Do-won often forgot they were full-grown men. For a brief moment, her eyes seemed to flash hurt at Do-won, but that would be weird. How was he supposed to hug her with the other two in the way? Besides, why would she be hurt? But as quickly as he had registered it, it was gone.

She plopped down in the open seat next to Do-won and took off her mask. Do-won's breath was knocked out of him. She was still so beautiful and brash.

September 2015

Do-won was exhausted and impatient for the van to pick him up from SB Entertainment's ramshackle offices. He'd stayed late and his managers had arranged for one of the newer managers — newly acquired labelmate Taiwanese pop star Katie Wu's manager, in fact — to take him back to the dingy dorm where he shared a crowded apartment with his six bandmates. When the nondescript white van arrived in front of the office building, Do-won slid into the back and saw Katie completely passed out against the window, her mouth hanging slightly open.

Had she been one of his fellow members, Do-won would have likely thrown something into her mouth. As she was not, he tamped down the puerile urge.

He recognized Katie from when he'd first met her backstage at DOYEN's Taipei concert earlier that year, except obviously, she was now asleep. If he recalled correctly, Katie was born in the year before him, though at the moment, she seemed younger and smaller than she had been on that March evening. Then, she'd seemed to take up so much space, her rush of English words and attempt at Korean greetings and palpable excitement filling the room.

Katie had been so intimidating.

It hadn't mattered that Do-won was one-seventh of the popular K-pop boy band DOYEN. Despite her debuting a few months after their own debut in mid-2013, Katie had exuded a confidence he hadn't really felt until recently. He wondered if it had to do with her being an American, though Soo-min, who was also born in the U.S., wasn't like that. Even so, Americans always acted like they should dominate the conversation — never mind the pop world, even when K-pop was ascendant.

"Thank you, manager-nim," Do-won said politely to a barrel-shaped man as he entered the vehicle, careful not to scuff his cream-colored Yeezys. He pulled his Supreme hat lower across his forehead.

The man grunted and merely said, "Call me Ha-joon hyung."

Do-won appreciated the reminder because he'd forgotten the older man's name and felt bad, but was also too tired to feel too badly about it. He encountered so many new people on a daily basis, it really was to be expected. He slipped an earbud in an ear and listened to the track he'd been working on all evening, discontent with the results.

Sometimes, he envied their leader Park Jae-sung, who also went by King Ja$e, and fellow rapper Hwang Woo-jin, who also went by Lambent. The other two rappers/producers of DOYEN seemed to live and breathe music and were light years ahead of Do-won in terms of music production. He felt the pressure to catch up to the two older men since he didn't have nearly as much experience making music and had only auditioned because he loved to dance.

Do-won was acutely aware that DOYEN's active participation in their music accounted a lot for their global fans. Something about how American fans especially considered K-pop to be less "authentic" despite the fact that American pop stars were also manufactured. And yet, the stereotype about Korean idols persisted, thanks to global racism, that Asians were robots: technically great, but artistically bereft.

DOYEN wasn't huge in their home country, but global fans had buffeted their sales until South Koreans couldn't help but take notice. Not for the first time did Do-won feel intense gratitude for the CHIMERAs, the ridiculously long acronym for DOYEN's fandom. He couldn't even remember the whole thing on most days. Cute Humble Independent Musically Evolved something something? He chided himself for his obvious lack.

Just one more flaw for him to eradicate.

Do-won's mood dipped even further, and he was grateful Katie was asleep, negating the need for him to seem cheerful, chipper, and on-brand with his delightful persona.

After months of traveling for their 36-stop tour, Do-won was sick of people (including his members). All Do-won wanted was silence and zero expectations of setting the mood for his bandmates. Even the human vitamin needed to recharge every now and then. They'd just returned from their first world tour — which had been amazing but also draining. And yet, here he was, immediately jumping back into making tracks for the next album and perhaps the one after that.

He needed a break.

Do-won startled when the van came to a lurching stop in front of a modest apartment complex. He must have dozed off during the drive and felt all the groggier for it.

"Katie-yah," Ha-joon said, "you're home."

"Mmmph?" Katie slurred, still caught at the edge of sleep.

Ha-joon unclipped his seatbelt and turned around in the driver's seat to shake Katie by the knee. She yelped in surprise and when Ha-joon laughed gently at her, she flushed a charming pink. Katie muttered an embarrassed "Thanks, oppa" and as she gathered her things, Do-won watched as she finally realized she wasn't alone.

"Oh," Katie squawked awkwardly, drawing a hand to her chest. "How rude of me," she said in English. "Hello, nice to meet you again. I'm Katie Wu," she said politely in serviceable Korean with a half-bow from her seat.

"I'm Jung Do-won," he replied. "It's good to see you again, Katie-ssi."

"Ah, please call me noona," she said haltingly. "I'm sorry my Korean is so bad, Do-won-ssi. I'm still learning." Katie rubbed the back of her neck and then she grinned, her entire face transformed. Do-won was again reminded of their meeting backstage. She had glowed then, too.

Katie was so, so pretty.

He cleared his throat. "Ah, no need to be so formal, noona, if you don't want to be. Although you are older, so you can set how formal you'd like it to be between us."

Katie's face blanked in confusion. "Uhhhh," she faltered. "Oppa, help!"

Ha-joon sighed. It would seem that Ha-joon was tired, too. Do-won couldn't quite catch what Ha-joon was saying — though he did hear him say "banmal" so Do-won figured Katie's manager was explaining again how she could use informal language with him since she was older.

"I feel rude," she replied before speaking more English that Do-won couldn't comprehend due to the speed.

He'd studied English in school, of course, but he'd never been particularly diligent. Hence, the burden of communicating in other countries mostly fell on Jae-sung, who had spent a few years in New Jersey during his elementary years. Technically, Soo-min was even better at English on account of him being an American, but he'd been so painfully shy in their early years, it had seemed cruel to make their youngest do it. Besides, Jae-sung was so much more articulate, most people thought he was the American member. They weren't the only of his bandmates fluent in English, but Jae-sung was the only one confident enough to use it all the time.

It was yet another reminder of how Do-won was lacking, how he was failing his friend who could only do so much alone.

Ha-joon was likely in the middle of explaining the finer details of Korean language and formalities, although Do-won wondered if Katie was paying attention to her Korean tutors. They should have covered that in the first few days of class. But he had no idea what sort of student she was.

He really knew nothing about Katie.

Do-won tuned out the rest of their conversation, focusing more on how Katie was distractingly fetching despite the lack of makeup and accessories, her open and animated heart-shaped face, and — oh, shit. She was talking to him.

"I'm so sorry, Do-won. I was terribly rude," she said in Korean, her voice husky and rough.

Clearly, Katie had practiced that phrase a lot. It sounded as if it rolled off her tongue quite nicely. And then, Do-won was thinking of her tongue and what else could roll off it quite nicely.

He was an idiot.

As his brain went into overdrive trying to come up with words, his subconscious blamed her voice. It was so low-key sexy that he didn't know how to respond, and Katie was now waiting for his turn in the social dance.

"It's okay, noona," Do-won finally woodenly forced out. "Korean is hard."

She smiled again, glorious and full and bright. "Thanks, Wonnie," she said. "Oh, wait. Can I call you Wonnie?"

He nodded. Do-won tried to rein himself in, but he could not help it. Do-won was completely smitten.

A few days later at SB Entertainment's very tiny offices, Do-won saw Katie again in their shabby conference room. (Really, it was just two folding tables pushed together in the center of the room, surrounded by flimsy metal chairs.) Katie was again beaming — this time, at his bandmates. She nodded as one of his managers introduced him and the other rappers, Jae-sung and Woo-jin, before moving on to introduce the singers Lee Ye-jun, Akihiro, Dae-jung, and Soo-min.

He took in her oversized T-shirt, half-tucked into her baggy gray UCLA sweats, her jaunty pageboy hat, black hair in two braids, and her plain white Adidas sneakers. She wasn't nearly as stylish as he preferred, but she was still cute. Do-won wanted to coo at her except he did not think she'd appreciate the gesture. She was tiny but mighty.

"Thank you so much for your lovely welcome," Katie said politely, her eyes warm and dancing. "It's always a joy to be surrounded by such attractive men, even if many of you are younger than me."

Soo-min, their youngest member, looked as if he'd been hit by a bus and blushed bright pink. Do-won also wanted to coo at the maknae, but he knew for a fact that Soo-min would definitely not appreciate the gesture and that thought made him snort. At his sound, Katie turned to him and winked. All of a sudden, Do-won didn't quite feel so smug anymore.

"I'm so sorry you're being forced to share your studio with me. I promise to not get in your way too often," she said smoothly in Korean. Do-won wondered how long she'd practiced that with her manager before she'd felt comfortable enough to speak as if she were speaking extemporaneously. "If I can ever help you with anything — whether it's English or you need me to play something for you on the guitar or bass, please let me know. I'd be happy to help."

"YAH! Are you saying my guitar playing isn't good enough?" Ye-jun balked, the 23-year-old's arms flapping, exaggerated as always. Their eldest member never acted his age.

Katie grinned, sly and sparkling after Ha-joon translated. "Oh, Ye-jun-ssi," she said in English as she raked her eyes over Ye-jun's body and face, "everything about you is fine — including your guitar playing. However, I'd be happy to help you work on your fingering." She winked and laughed, bright and teasing.

Even Do-won's mediocre English could understand the suggestion in that.

Again, she sounded so upbeat and buoyant that Do-won idly wondered if Katie was real. He further wondered if this was how his members saw him and if she was ever like him: tired but doing her best, because his group depended on him to be their battery.

He wondered if Katie ever got a break since she was a solo artist and had the spotlight on her the entire time. She didn't have other members who could sub in for her or answer a question to which she'd had a difficult time memorizing the answer. He wondered if Katie ever got lonely in Seoul, and then he wondered why he was wondering so much about her.

She seemed too happy and chirpy just now, offering her help if they should ever need it. Do-won wasn't sure if it was her rehearsed phrases or if the relentless good humor was part of her persona, but the more pep she injected into her voice, the less Do-won began to believe it.

Do-won wasn't sure why — after all, it wasn't as if Katie wasn't sincere or genuine. She didn't sound fake, but again, maybe she had been groomed in the most spectacular fashion. Katie had given him no reason to think she wasn't being genuine, but the more she flirted and acted cute, the less Do-won trusted her.

Do-won knew he was being irrational.

After all, this was Katie's first formal meeting with him and the rest of DOYEN in Seoul after switching record labels, thanks to the scandal she'd been involved in — something about her ex? Do-won rarely paid attention to gossip so he couldn't quite remember off the top of his head.

Do-won watched as she continued chatting with his bandmates, speaking mostly to Jae-sung, Ye-jun, and Woo-jin because they were the best at English. (Poor Soo-min hovered on the edge, too timid to jump in.) He noted how she positioned her body, how she angled her head, how she moved her face, and how she attempted to bring Soo-min into the conversation by widening the circle to include him.

It was both a combination of calculated effort at putting his friends at ease and perhaps, her inherent Americanness — but she was most assuredly working. He recognized the effort Katie exerted even if the others did not. Do-won supposed they could've also recognized it and not cared.

Of course, Katie would be on her best behavior. Of course, she was polite and cheerful and wanted to be liked. Of course, of course, of course.

And yet, Do-won could not explain why her demeanor had him in his feelings.

It was as if she had stolen his personality — all the way down to her bright and effusive laughter. And the reason he knew it couldn't possibly be real was because he, too, had faked it until, for the most part, it became authentic. It was well-known among Do-won's bandmates that he'd been a rather grumpy fellow until he adopted 1DEL1GHT as his moniker and imbued his soul with delight, forging himself into who he was today.

If Katie really was that naturally ebullient, then she was another reminder of how far Do-won had to go until he was a more perfect version of himself.

Do-won did not like all these thoughts churning inside him, rendering him quieter than usual. He just did what he did best and smiled — making sure it reached his eyes to sell the lie — and decided he would endeavor to be on his most positive behavior whenever he was around her.

He was a professional, and she would not expose him for who he was deep inside. He'd worked too hard and spent too much of his youth beating his body into that of a dancer (and when that had not been enough, he'd pounded the beats of music making and rapping into himself, too). He'd honed his skills until his imperfections were just a memory. Do-won would not be the first to crack; he would make sure of it.

October 2021

"Katie noona?"

"Hey, Wonnie. You sound surprised. Did you not know I moved back?" she replied cheekily. At his grimace, she cracked up. "Oh my god, Wonnie!! You didn't!" Katie threw her head back, mouth wide open, cackling with her entire body.

Do-won held back the urge to admonish Katie for being so loud amidst all his colleagues at SB Entertainment. Instead, he just waved apologetically at the people who had glanced over with annoyance.

"Hyung!" Akihiro and Dae-jung chimed in judgmentally, joining the teasing. Do-won supposed he deserved it. There must have been a company-wide memo, and he'd just missed it.

He grinned sheepishly. "To be fair, I haven't thought of you in a few years."

Katie clutched her chest dramatically. "A hit! A palpable hit!" she laughed. "Don't you follow my socials? I've posted about nothing else for weeks."

"Hyung doesn't follow anyone's socials," Akihiro supplied helpfully.

Katie pouted. "But that doesn't explain why you two didn't inform him. Don't you guys talk about me? I talked to you two and Soo-min enough through Dae-jung's military service."

"Not as much as you talked to Ye-jun hyung and Woo-jin hyung," complained Dae-jung. His dark eyes smoldered and Do-won wanted to tell him to dial down the charm a notch.

"Well of course not, darlings. We're grown-ups and you're infants."

Do-won wondered briefly if Katie also texted Jae-sung — and if he was the only one to not have ongoing conversations with her. He wondered why that was and if there was something inherently wrong with him that made her not want to chat with him.

He knew better than to go down that road. It would only hurt himself and her.

As if Katie read his mind, she placed a hand tenderly on his shoulder, saying, "Don't feel bad, Do-won-ah. I don't actually talk to any of these idiots very much. It's mostly the babies oversharing — and, by that, I mean it's Aki and Dae sending us every thought they've ever had to me and Soo-min." She paused to mull things over a bit. "I think Soo-min has us muted."

Do-won laughed. "He definitely has our group chat muted. He and Woo-jin both do."

"Yeah, I'm pretty sure Woo-jin oppa has me and Ye-jun oppa muted, too."

"What's that chat like? Junie hyung demanding you tell him he's funny and pretty every five minutes?" Everyone laughed.

"I wouldn't say every five minutes." She smiled. "Maybe closer to once a week. I try to give him his due. It's the only way I can get him to send me his selfies."

Do-won settled into the familiar rhythm of her cadence. It had been so long since Katie had been in Korea that she'd forgotten a lot of words and was switching back to English a lot. It was a good thing all their English had improved even as Katie's Korean had regressed.

"Noona, you're almost as bad as you were when you first got here!" Dae-jung exclaimed, slightly appalled. "How do you even text us?"

Katie flushed. "Naver? Papago? Look, if it makes you feel better, I was struggling in Chinese, too." She slumped in her chair. "I'm never going to sound smart again."

"As if you ever did," ribbed Akihiro.

"I'll have you know that I graduated UCLA in three years — *summa cum laude*, I might add," she huffed.

Dae-jung didn't look suitably impressed. "I don't even know what that means, noona."

This time, it was Katie's turn to look appalled. "I — you —"

"I'm just fucking with you, noona." Dae-jung's eyes glinted with mischief. "What, you think just because I didn't go to college in the traditional sense, I don't know random Latin designations for American universities and their diplomas?"

"Okay, yeah, wow." She raised her hands in peace and Do-won noticed even more tattoos on her inner forearms. "I get it. I'll stop with the U.S. -centric bullshit."

Akihiro grabbed an arm to examine Katie's tattoos more closely. "When did you get these, noona? You never posted them on Instagram or Twitter."

Akihiro swiped a thumb over her left wrist and frowned. "Noona," he whispered.

Katie flinched imperceptibly and her shoulders tightened. Intrigued, Do-won and Dae-jung both focused on where Akihiro was looking. Do-won's stomach dropped. Hidden underneath the lines of a Chinese painted crane were multiple vertical scars indicative of self-harm or suicide attempts. Do-won grabbed her other wrist and underneath a Chinese painted phoenix were matching slashes, giving lie to the hope that the marks were an accident.

"When?" growled Akihiro, tears threatening to spill out of his furious eyes. "Do the hyungs know?"

Katie glanced around the cafeteria, mindful of watchful eyes. She smiled wide and loose. "Not here, Aki," she murmured.

Do-won could feel Katie resisting the urge to snatch her arms back. He could sense her retreating back to herself, hiding in plain sight under the cover of a happy face. He released her and Akihiro followed his lead. She gathered her limbs and resumed her methodical way through lunch.

"We're heading out to New York for our comeback in a few weeks, noona," Akihiro said, offering an olive branch. "You were just in the U.S., right? How is it?"

"It's weird," Katie said in between bites. "Other than seeing more masks than before, people are still acting as if we haven't been in a pandemic. The enforcement of masks and vaccines are haphazard — as if my country couldn't give a fuck that over half a million people died of COVID." She impassionately shoved a bite of kimbap in her mouth. "I felt unsafe the whole time, even after I got vaccinated. I'd forgotten how white people treated Asians, especially since the pandemic."

"But you were born there, right?" asked Dae-jung. "Doesn't that make a difference?"

Katie shook her head. "No, DaeDae. No, it doesn't."

"We should be fine," assured Akihiro. "Our staff will keep us safe."

She merely nodded, as if she disagreed but didn't have the heart to add to their anxiety. "The U.S. should have learned from Taiwan or New Zealand, but arrogance will always out itself."

The conversation veered off on random tangents and lighter topics after that, but Do-won couldn't stop thinking of the heavy scars carved in Katie's wrists. The weight of her pain hounded him long after they'd said their goodbyes, her somber eyes the last image on his mind before he fell into a troubled sleep.

December 2015

"It's no use," Katie grumbled to Ha-joon in English as she collapsed on the wooden dance floor after her dance practice. "I'm just not a sexy person. Can't we settle for cute? I can maybe do cute?"

DOYEN had the compact practice room after Katie's session and Do-won had snuck in early because he'd been compulsively curious about her dancing ability. From his vantage point against the wall of mirrors, he wanted to interject that she could definitely do cute. However, he knew how important practice time was for an artist and held his tongue.

"You'll be fine," reassured Ha-joon. "The filming for your M/V isn't until next week, so you have some time."

"I could have an entire year and still, I wouldn't be able to move the way Wonnie does. Isn't that right, Do-won?"

She was okay considering her lack of dance training, but she was not anywhere close to where she was supposed to be — unless head choreographer and performance director Chun Yu-mi had drastically lowered her standards.

"You're too stiff," Do-won observed. "You're thinking too much."

"If I don't think, I can't remember the steps," Katie said in English as Ha-joon translated for her.

"That's precisely the problem." Do-won was irritated though he tried valiantly not to seem so. Non-dancers just didn't think the same. He plastered a congenial smile on his face, digging deep for patience. "You're thinking of the choreography as a series of steps to execute versus sinking into the movement and expressing the story of your song in one continuous conversation."

Katie's mouth made a slight "oh" after Ha-joon repeated his words in English, but she clearly had no clue how to apply his advice to movement.

"Get up, noona." At least she understood that without her manager.

Katie got up and Do-won pulled her into the middle of the studio floor, idly noting how their reflections repeated infinitely in the mirrored front and back walls. He moved her into the starting position and then sidled up behind her, molding his body into hers.

"This song is about sex, right?" Do-won said in halting English, his voice unexpectedly hoarse.

He felt more than heard Katie swallow. "Um, what?"

He sank low and adjusted her hips so that her ass practically sat on his crotch. "This song is about sex. So, move like sex — not sexy. Sex." Then Do-won wrapped his arms around hers, picked up her hand, and slid it down her body as he moved their two bodies into a coordinated body wave.

"You're still too stiff, noona," he said in Korean. "That's not the kind of stiff we want." Ha-joon choked on his water and lifted his eyebrow at Do-won as a warning before translating only the first part. Do-won just tossed Katie's manager an unrepentant grin.

"Let's try it again."

Over and over, Do-won tried to get Katie to loosen up by making increasingly inappropriate comments. By the time Ha-joon gave up translating, Katie was sweaty, panting, and the two of them had garnered an audience.

"So, this is where you snuck off to, hyung," Akihiro said, his dark eyes all too knowing. "No fair that you get noona all to yourself."

"I'm just giving noona some pointers is all."

The upper corner of Akihiro's mouth lifted, as if calling bullshit. "Right. Then surely noona wouldn't mind me giving some pointers of my own. I am, after all, a professionally trained ballet dancer, unlike some people." He winked and Do-won merely gritted his teeth and moved to give Akihiro room.

"Be my guest," he said.

But Akihiro — that bastard — instead of taking up Do-won's previous spot behind Katie, pulled her in so that his legs slotted between hers as she straddled one of his thick, muscular thighs with a "meep!"

"Um, I —"

Akihiro hooked an arm behind the small of Katie's back to close the gap between their bodies and began to grind, dirty and slow. The speed at which she pushed off Akihiro would have been comical had the jealousy coursing through Do-won not reared its ugly fury. Katie stumbled back so quickly that she tripped over her own feet and crashed onto the hard dance floor.

"Oh my god," cried Akihiro as he rushed to help her up.

When he pulled Katie up by her hand, she yelped and fell back again, only to cry out once more. This time, Ha-joon was by her side, examining her arm as she turned a decidedly unflattering shade of green.

"Oppa," she gasped at Ha-joon, "I'm going to throw up."

Do-won hurried to the corner of the room and dragged the trash can over, thrusting it into Katie's face as she bent over and promptly vomited. After she clearly emptied herself of all her stomach contents, Akihiro handed Katie a bottle of water to rinse out her mouth.

"I think I broke my arm," she said in English after spitting into the trash one last time. "I always throw up when I break a bone."

"How many bones have you broken?" Do-won couldn't help but ask after Ha-joon translated. The poor man never got a moment's rest.

"Including this one? Three." She chuffed ruefully even as she gingerly held her injured arm. "Fun fact: every bone I've broken was in front of a boy I liked. I guess this ends the streak."

Do-won had experienced his fair share of physical injuries from his hip-hop dancing days (and even when training for DOYEN). He understood her need to seem fine in the face of excruciating pain. He could respect her stoicism even as he wished she didn't feel the need to put up a strong front for them.

Akihiro lifted a dramatic hand to his forehead and then staggered to the floor. He was all grace as befitted his classically trained dance background. "Noona, you're breaking my heart!" Do-won was glad Akihiro could help Katie keep her mind off the pain even in this little way.

Katie grimaced as Ha-joon helped her up and gathered her things. "Somehow, I'm sure you'll recover just fine, Hiro-yah." She gave him a one-sided hug. "Now go break hearts, not arms."

Do-won and Akihiro just groaned as she passed the rest of his members filing into the room. Though Katie had put on an unbothered face for him and Akihiro, Do-won did not doubt that her mind was likely churning with worry. After all, if she really had broken her arm, she would have a tough road ahead as she practiced for her debut. Katie could not afford any time off to heal — not with her dancing as it was.

He did not envy Akihiro having to explain to their bandmates what had just transpired with their favorite labelmate.

November 2021

"Noona!" cheered Do-won and his members as Katie entered Woo-jin's familiar open kitchen area. He loved the sleek, mid-century modern lines of Woo-jin's dining furniture and lighting fixtures. It was so different from the loud, bright décor of his own home.

Though they'd all wanted to meet up with Katie earlier, their insanely busy schedules hadn't allowed for it. Plus, she had been equally busy, constantly in the studio, working on her first new Korean album in years. Every time Do-won had trekked down the hall from his studio to pop his head into hers, her headphones had been on, her face glaring at the screen as if it had mortally offended her. He'd always felt as if he were intruding.

"Sorry I'm late," she apologized. "I brought Soo-min's favorite tteok-bokki as penance."

Woo-jin and Ye-jun, the two eldest members, made room between them for her at Woo-jin's polished teak dining table. For some reason, Do-won opened his big mouth and said, "Come sit next to me, noona."

Katie startled for a second as Woo-jin and Ye-jun exchanged delighted glances. "Oh, uh, sure." Her cheeks tinged and she slid into the curved earth-toned upholstered seat Do-won forced Jae-sung to vacate. "Sorry, Jae," she added. Jae-sung only chuckled and whispered something odd like, "Go get your man, Katie." She colored even darker.

Do-won had to be hearing things. Clearly, his bandmates were messing with Katie as much as they enjoyed messing with him.

The conversation swirled around him and the night progressed, though Do-won couldn't have told anyone what was said or remarked upon. His body just thrummed with some energy he couldn't identify, and he briefly wondered if he'd had too much to drink too early on in the night.

"Noona, I'm getting more beer from the fridge — do you want me to get you one?" Soo-min asked as he got up.

"Oh, uh, no. But thank you," Katie replied.

"We have the soju you like, too, if you prefer that instead. Or wine?"

"Ah, I'm good, Minnie. Thanks."

"But we wanted to get drunk with you, noona," whined Akihiro. "It's been so long!"

Katie shifted uncomfortably in her seat. "Ah, about that." She cleared her throat. "Turns out alcohol and I don't go so well together anymore so, uh, I —" Her voice trailed off hesitantly as all conversation stopped.

"Like, you're allergic to alcohol now or..." Ye-jun tried to clarify.

"Like I'm taking a break from it," Katie said. "It's no big deal. I started using it too much to self-medicate and that ended poorly."

"Should we not drink in front of you?" asked Woo-jin. "We don't have to drink."

"Oh, no. It doesn't bother me to have people drink in front of me. It's not a compulsion or anything — at least, not generally." Katie rubbed the scars on her left wrist unconsciously with her right thumb until, all of a sudden, she realized her tell and stopped. "Anyway, there's no need for you to not have a good time just because of me. Besides, you know I've never been fun — alcohol or not."

"You're telling me," complained Ye-jun. "I have to hard carry you and Woo-jin in the group chat all the fucking time."

"Your capacity for self-aggrandizement is truly an achievement, oppa."

"It's a gift."

Do-won was still reeling from Katie's confession about the alcohol. He couldn't believe that Ye-jun was just acting as if everything was fine. As the other moodmaker of the group, Do-won was insulted by the poor execution in judgment from his hyung. Surely the two years he had on Do-won would give him the right to say something to Katie. Do-won could not understand why he was so very furious.

"So, we're just going to pretend noona didn't just drop something extra heavy on us just now? She disappeared for years, tried to kill herself, is possibly an alcoholic — and we're all just okay with this? We're just going to pretend that everything is fine?"

Do-won vaguely registered the horror on the faces of his bandmates. He clearly had too much to drink. He rarely lost his temper or said exactly what he was thinking. He tended to say only good things unless he was acting in the capacity of dance leader — and, even then, he was exacting but kind.

Katie's face was carefully blank, damning in her mild exterior. Though so much had changed in the intervening years, it seemed that some things had stayed the same. She was still an incomparable liar.

April 2016

Almost a year after her scandal with Taiwanese pop star Johnny Chen, Katie Wu's debut Korean album "Shameless" (SB Entertainment, 2016) pulls zero punches. Wu kicks detractors in the teeth with her strong vocals and aggressive lyrics. From the rebellious basslines, the growl and whine of electric guitars, to the evocative melodies, "Shameless" is a proud addition to Wu's discography. Fierce and sparkling, the five-track mini album refuses to wallow in self-pity or sorrow, instead glorying in her power and agency.
- The Hankyoreh, January 2016

Defiantly optimistic.
- The Korea Herald, January 2016

[1] Shameless [3:47]
[2] Good Trouble [4:01]
[3] Joy in the Rain [3:28]
[4] Gristle and Bone [3:52]
[5] Girl on Fire [4:19]
        - Track list, "Shameless" (SB Entertainment, 2016)

Hollowed out my viscera
Stuffed full of your lies
Sucked out my marrow
Spread apart my thighs

Ground between your teeth
You thought I'd just pass through
You cracked me open
Ripped through my sinew

You carved me up
Told everyone I was through
But I'll have the last laugh, baby
I've carved you up, too
        - "Gristle and Bone" (SB Entertainment, 2016)

Akihiro cheered for Katie along with the rest of DOYEN and her team when sales for her January album were better than expected. Not only was he happy for her sake, Katie's success meant slightly more breathing room for him and his group. Though they were still the main source of revenue for their small entertainment company, the success of "Shameless" meant SB Entertainment was that much closer to operating in the black.

Akihiro was happy to see that Katie's loyal fans, newly dubbed the Jezebelles, had proven true. Their fandom name came about after some misogynistic pastor had declared Katie a modern-day Jezebel because of her salacious "Shameless" and "Good Trouble" M/Vs and explicit lyrics. In a fit of pique, his noona had declared on Twitter (much to the chagrin of her management and the delight of her fans) that Jezebelle was now the official name of her fandom.

The Jezebelles coordinated mass buying parties to qualify for intimate fanmeets in either Seoul or Taipei. Not only that, her Jezzies had organized mass donations to various women's rights organizations. All in all, Katie had behaved smug as fuck.

Of course, Akihiro tried to take credit for her success as much as possible. He even demanded she thank him for all his private dancing sessions. (And the good sport that Katie was, she did.) Granted, they mostly consisted of him throwing himself at her and blatantly flirting more than dancing, but it was the thought that counted, right? It had nothing to do with her acute embarrassment and the flare of desire he caught in her eyes.

All Akihiro knew was that fooling around with Katie served two purposes: one, she was hot and kept calling him an infant (she was only two years his senior!) so he wanted to prove her wrong, and two, it really annoyed Do-won.

Akihiro never said he was mature about it.

But beyond the fact that Akihiro was being a punk, he also really liked Katie. In a way, she reminded him a lot of Do-won. The two of them were so incredibly focused, talented, and full of personality. The way every room brightened when Katie entered — she and Do-won were like portable generators, providing that extra bit of oomph when they were totally spent.

Plus, she was so very American.

He appreciated how Katie questioned things where he rarely did, even when he didn't quite understand them. She wasn't disrespectful; she genuinely did not comprehend. While Akihiro didn't mind looking stupid when it came to dancing (mostly because he was naturally good at it and asking clarifying questions made him better), that willingness to put himself out there did not translate to navigating life.

Korean culture was often very different from Japanese culture, but Akihiro had gotten so used to squashing down all his questions during training. There had been no time for long cultural explanations when he'd been too busy trying to learn Korean and figure out school at the same time. Other agencies often brought in tutors for their foreign trainees, but SB Entertainment had been too poor for such luxuries. Without Dae-jung as a fellow student and trainee to help with making friends and doing homework, Akihiro would have had an even harder time.

Even before moving to Seoul, he had just done whatever his teachers and parents had asked of him. He hadn't been class president in middle school for nothing. On the other hand, Katie rarely let things slide and didn't care if asking about what he considered culturally obvious made her look foolish. He couldn't imagine questioning the status quo, and he found her brave for doing so.

When the media publicized her quiet donations to various Korean and Taiwanese women's rights organizations, her sales exploded even as the backlash skyrocketed from some segments of South Korean male populations. It got so bad that SB Entertainment had to double her security team due to the endless death and rape threats streaming in.

Instead of being afraid, Katie joked about the perks of being surrounded by big, beefy men. Akihiro was worried for her, but he was also glad she seemed to be taking everything in stride. Her American-ness was particularly evident when she expressed confusion about why it was such a flashpoint in the first place.

"What's the big fucking deal?" she'd asked Jae-sung in English. "Surely I'm not the first nor the last woman in Korea — famous or not — to care about women's rights?"

Jae-sung had attempted to explain and give context and Akihiro had tuned him out, mostly because the English was definitely beyond his abilities and only partially because Jae-sung could easily turn any subject into a lecture. When Jae-sung had asked why she'd contributed the money in the first place, she'd only said, "I always repay my debts." Then, she'd changed the subject.

When Akihiro finally broke down and read the news articles about the controversy surrounding Katie, he discovered that many of the feminist groups she'd donated to were the ones who had championed her after the scandal with Taiwanese pop star Johnny Chen. The gossip rags, of course, had taken great pleasure in sensationalizing what had happened. From what Akihiro gathered, Katie had been discovered by winning a Taiwanese reality show called "The Singer Songwriter" in late 2013 and had gone on to be a relatively famous Taiwanese pop star in her own right.

But last March, Johnny went on a shock jock radio show and accused Katie of trading sexual favors to rig the contest instead of winning by getting the most votes. It likely would have been written off, except Johnny was also her boyfriend and had been her mentor on the show.

Though Katie and the show had denied the allegations, she had been viciously slut-shamed on Taiwanese forums. Johnny's fans had been particularly vile, though the vast majority were also women. The women's rights organizations had rallied under her banner and defended her, while Katie's label, which she'd shared with Johnny, had unceremoniously dropped her.

Akihiro remembered meeting Johnny backstage at their Taipei concert. He'd been impatient and acted as if he was doing everyone a favor by being there. Johnny gave Ye-jun a run for his money in the looks department and he undoubtedly deserved his fame, but Akihiro had privately thought he was an asshole. Even then, Akihiro had found Katie too good for Johnny.

Though Akihiro found it a bizarre business strategy of SB Entertainment to bet on a disgraced Taiwanese American — especially given South Korea's far more conservative atmosphere, he dismissed his concerns. He figured it had to be because she was wildly talented — that and the fact that Woo-jin had been obsessed with Katie, insisting on somehow bringing her into the SB Entertainment fold.

He supposed he could have just asked her, but though she was open about some topics — too open, actually — Katie was incredibly tight-lipped about her past. She almost never spoke about her family or her time in Taiwan. It was as if she had sprung up in Seoul like Athena: fully formed.

She had no past, only the present and hopefully, a future.

"How does it feel to have another hit album, noona?" asked Soo-min after a long day of promotions and rehearsals. They were in the small common area of the DOYEN dorm and as the youngest person present, Soo-min refilled Katie's glass with more soju. He also poured more into Do-won's, Dae-jung's, and Akihiro's glasses, and Akihiro quickly turned his face away to take another sip.

Katie tapped her index finger on the coffee table in thanks, a habit she said she just couldn't shake. She had once explained to them that in Chinese culture, when someone filled your cup with tea or any beverage, you tapped to symbolize kētóu, the formal bow of respect and thanks.

"I'm happy, of course. And relieved. But if I'm honest, uh, hold on," Katie said as she whipped out her phone to look up how to say what she wanted to say. "If I'm honest, I want to shove it all up Johnny's ass and tell him to choke on it." Clearly, she was several shots deep already and the effects were beginning to show.

Dae-jung snorted a laugh, his blue-tinged hair shaking. "You sure you have that right?"

"Absolutely," Katie replied, her face uncharacteristically ruthless. "I want to fuck him so far up his asshole that it comes out his mouth. It would be nice for something other than shit to come out of it for once."

At least, Akihiro was pretty sure that's what Katie meant to say. It wasn't entirely right, but they all got the gist. Akihiro found it amusing that despite how hard she studied Korean culture, how often her nose was buried in a beginner's Korean book or drilling vocabulary on her phone, swearing in another language was always awkward and unwieldy. He wanted to tell her that he'd been in Seoul for five years and his swearing still never sounded quite right.

"Noona, I meant to ask you before," Do-won said suddenly. "How do you write your songs? Music first then lyrics? Or lyrics first then music?"

Katie tilted her head as she puzzled out Do-won's questions before Soo-min swooped in to translate. "It depends," she said in English and Soo-min dutifully translated. Not for the first time was Akihiro grateful for the English skills of his members. She shrugged. "For me, it's the language I am strongest at — whether it's the language of the lyric or the language of the melody itself. The producer adds the beats, additional music, and all the fun flourishes to my words and topline." She took a sip of her soju and continued. "You know it's a lot of work to take all these disparate pieces and put them together. Producers like mun.light unni make my shit a lot better, honestly."

"Ah, I usually write more of the lyrics to my verses and work on production and beats. I think of what feels good for my body to move to and dance to," Do-won said.

"That makes a lot of sense since that's how you became interested in music." Katie nodded thoughtfully. "I was always writing poems and stories. Lyrics were a natural step after I'd started composing melodies. Of course,

I can't really write any Korean lyrics right now, but I hope to do so in the future."

"I'm sure you'll do great at it, noona," Soo-min said, his eyes wide and sweet. "It took me a year or two before my Korean improved and sounded less American."

Akihiro laughed kindly. "At least you already knew Korean!" he declared. "I knew absolutely nothing!"

Katie flashed him a sympathetic smile. "How long did it take before you felt comfortable, Aki?"

Akihiro thought for a moment before replying. "I could hold simple conversations by the end of the first year, but it helped that Jae-sung hyung and Do-won hyung were also learning some Japanese," he said. "Of course, the fact that no one could really speak Japanese and I didn't have anyone translating into English for me made me learn much faster."

"Well, I'm fucked," Katie sighed after Soo-min finished translating.

"You know what helps?" Dae-jung asked slyly. "More soju!"

Later that evening, when Akihiro discovered Katie still hadn't learned the proper etiquette for alcohol in Korea, he took it upon himself to teach her the finer points of drinking culture as one foreigner to another. Soo-min and Do-won took that opportunity to leave and Dae-jung just looked on in amusement. Akihiro knew he was in for a world of teasing tomorrow, but until then, he knew his soulmate would be a helpful wingman.

Eventually, Dae-jung also tapped out and went to bed, but Akihiro and Katie soldiered on, lining up soju bottle after soju bottle. It wasn't even that Katie had a high tolerance — it was more that she conveniently let Akihiro take two or three shots for every one of hers. *After all,* she complained, *she wasn't a man. Look at his muscles! It was basic human biology!*

Even so, by the time Do-won stumbled out of his and Akihiro's shared room to scold the two of them for being too loud, they were sprawled all over each other on the slouchy sofa. Katie was drunk and warm and pleasantly tucked into Akihiro's side as she tried valiantly to explain in broken Konglish what college had been like. Akihiro wasn't quite clear on what she was saying since he was also on the drunker side, but he knew she was exactly where she needed to be.

Akihiro ignored Do-won's disapproving glance and focused instead on how soft Katie's skin was as he dragged his lithe fingers over her bare arm. He committed her little shiver to memory and wondered how soft the skin of her belly and inner thighs would be.

Akihiro was well and truly fucked.

November 2021

"Do-won," Woo-jin admonished, his dark eyebrows drawn against his delicate features. "Katie doesn't owe us her life story. It's none of our business. Apologize to your noona."

Do-won did not seem inclined to apologize and Akihiro didn't blame him. Though he didn't agree with Do-won's approach, Akihiro was just as pissed and bewildered. He wanted an accounting of the last three or four years, too.

Katie cleared her throat. "It's okay, oppa. I'm sure Wonnie means well."

Akihiro waited for Katie to continue but she did not. It would seem she agreed with Woo-jin that it wasn't their business — and, well, she wasn't wrong. Akihiro didn't know why he was surprised. This was on-brand for her. Open about all the stuff that didn't matter and closed about all the things that did.

"Are you getting the support you need?" his best friend Dae-jung asked, always solicitous. "How can we help?"

"Yes," Katie said, her face placid as ever. "I have the support I need — and I appreciate your concern, but there's nothing to worry about. I'm fine now."

"You know you can always talk to us, right?" asked Soo-min, his big doe eyes filled with concern. Now that Do-won had cracked open the seal, the rest of the members were pressing in.

She sighed. "Yeah, I know."

Ye-jun reached for Katie's hand and she let him squeeze it. "I love you and I'm so glad you're still here, Katie-yah." The rest of his members chorused their agreement.

Akihiro felt his throat close, thick with tears.

"Aish, please don't worry, guys," Katie insisted, somewhat flustered by all the sentimentality. "I'm on a shit ton of medication so I don't constantly feel like throwing myself off a bridge. They don't mix well with alcohol, so that's another reason I've stopped drinking."

"You don't owe us an explanation, Katie," interjected Woo-jin firmly. He wasn't the oldest or tallest, but the group rarely ever crossed him. "If you had wanted us to know, you would have told us. As long as you are getting the support you need when you need it, we are satisfied."

Katie nodded.

Akihiro wasn't sure he believed Katie, but he really, really wanted to.

October 2016

"How was your day?" Akihiro asked as he kicked Katie's ass at Just Dance 2016.

His lean body moved and undulated with exacting accuracy, and Katie could not help but notice how his muscles rippled under his designer shirt and sweats. She normally liked her men taller, but there was no denying the sheer physicality of Akihiro.

"This is unfair," she complained. "You own this game and thus have more chances to practice."

Akihiro leveled Katie with a look of pity. His level of sass was legendary. "Oh, noona. Darling. No."

"What do you mean?" She felt indignant.

"You could own this game and log in hours every day and still — still I would beat the snot out of you."

Katie slumped on the black leather couch in their dorm in defeat. Woo-jin and Ye-jun had left at least an hour ago, and while Soo-min and Dae-jung had dropped by for a few rounds and Jae-sung had popped by to say hello, they had all gone on with their evening.

Akihiro dropped next to her, huffing so his blond hair no longer covered his eyes. "You never answered my question. How was your day?"

Katie scrunched her face. "It was shitty."

"Tell your favorite dongsaeng about it."

"Uh, must I?"

Akihiro shifted to his side and ordered, "You're already here. We might as well have a conversation."

Katie quirked her mouth. He was the most compact member, but definitely the bossiest if he put his mind to it. "If that's the price for being friends with a celebrity, I accept."

"Noona! That's all I am to you?"

"I mean, you have a nice face?" Katie struggled not to laugh. Akihiro could be so easily riled, always so sensitive about his appearance and perceived manliness.

"Tell me everything."

"I spent all morning on my album, but nothing was working. And then, at my Korean class, some white dude bro rushed up to me yelling, 'Oh, my god! Are you okay? Did it hurt?' and I was super confused. I started looking all over my body to see if I was bleeding — stop laughing!"

Akihiro was dying.

"Look, I was really startled, okay?"

"What was the reason?" he wheezed, his eyes disappearing in charming half-crescents. "Did he ask if it hurt when you fell from heaven?"

"Yes! And then he asked me out or something — I don't remember because I was so pissed. Don't laugh — I was really upset!"

"Why? It's super cheesy. What's to be mad about?"

"Well, I was super confused — and it's so terrible — like don't I merit a better line than this? At least say I fell from the vending machine 'cause I'm a snack?" Katie couldn't stop laughing now, either. "Plus, the grammar setup was so bad. It made me angry!"

"I just — you know, it sounds like something Jun hyung would say."

Katie lightly pushed his chest. He was so firm. "Only because he's forced to say it to your fans and be cheesy. All of you are."

"You like it." He leaned back against the sofa, arm draped casually over the back.

Katie took in Akihiro's lines, the way he was so carelessly attractive. "I do not."

"You do, too." He bopped her on the nose and whispered in her ear, "Noona, did it hurt when you fell from heaven?"

Katie's stomach did a little flip. "Please don't ever do that again," she groaned.

"It's not even a little bit romantic?" pouted Akihiro. "Or cute?"

"I don't do romance."

"Why not?"

"It's all lies," Katie said. She knew well the perils of falling for men who were all talk. She had fallen for the ways Johnny had championed and wooed her on "The Singer Songwriter," except it had all been an elaborate deception. Never again. "Romance is to trick you into loving someone before you find out all their nasty, hidden parts."

"You talking about people in general or just yourself?"

Katie hated how Akihiro always caught her unaware; she was constantly lulled by his youth only to have him surprise her with his perceptive observations.

She looked away.

"I'll have you know that I have no nasty, hidden parts and I am offended that you implied otherwise," Akihiro offered as a means to save face.

"Stop trying to convince me to see you naked, Hiro-yah."

"You really should conduct a thorough examination just to be sure."

Katie threw an obnoxiously decorative pillow at him.

"Oh, you're going to regret that," Akihiro cried.

He pounced on top of her, tickling her until she shrieked with laughter. Katie's shirt rolled up and then Akihiro's fingers were all over her bare skin.

Katie wanted.

The moment stretched between them like taffy, sticky and sweet. And then Akihiro kissed her, his lips so lush and shockingly insistent. Katie floated, content to let him claim her with his wet, hot mouth.

They kissed leisurely, despite the fact that Akihiro's bandmates could walk in at any time. Katie's brain went hazy with pleasure as he flicked his tongue along her seam, coaxing her lips apart.

She opened.

"So precious," he murmured reverently as his tongue dipped into her heat. "So sweet."

Katie found herself wanting to please him. It had been so long since she'd been properly kissed.

"Oh, fuck," she breathed. "Want you inside me so bad. Want you to ruin me."

Katie could feel his smile against her own. "Is that right?"

She nipped his neck. "You know you're hot, Aki."

"I know, but it's still nice to hear you say so." Akihiro kissed her again, his breath so warm and inviting. "We should move to my room," he suggested, voice strained. "I can ask Wonnie hyung to bunk with another member."

Akihiro's words sank like deadweight into the miasma of her consciousness.

She was an idiot.

Katie allowed herself one more kiss — he had such plush, sinful lips — and though all she could think of was Akihiro pounding into her, she broke away. "I — I'm sorry," she said.

Akihiro stopped. He smiled softly and cupped her jaw for a brief second before rolling off the couch. "Don't be sorry, noona," he said after collecting himself. "It's only fun if everyone wants it."

Katie sat up and adjusted her clothing and hair, the evening's events swirling in her now whirring brain. It had been so long since she'd slept with — let alone considered sleeping with — a person she genuinely adored and connected with. She had wanted to indulge in Akihiro, to drive him to the brink of ecstasy and shove him over the edge.

Katie had been so tempted to ensure maximal mutual destruction. She still was.

There had been no one since Johnny — well, no one since the string of one-night stands after the scandal had initially broken. But Katie didn't really consider those men worthy of note.

It was a lot to consider in the span of a few heartbeats.

"Noona, stop freaking out," muttered Akihiro. "Let's forget about it and go back to playing Just Dance."

"You're not weirded out?"

"Weirded out by what?"

Katie felt shame pulse through her body and sat up. "I don't go around fucking my friends, you know. I have rules — I don't —," she abruptly cut herself off. "You must think I'm so pathetic. Always throwing myself at a set of abs and a handsome face. Even at dongsaengs."

"Who are all these abs and handsome faces you've been throwing yourself at?" he asked kindly. "Or are you being too hard on yourself again?"

Katie felt his comment hit a little too close to home.

"To be fair, I do have both quite a set of abs and a handsome face — even if I am so much younger than you." Akihiro smiled. "Plus, as your friend, I can't say I terribly mind."

She snorted.

"Noona," he said, his tenor voice a caress. "I don't think you're pathetic. And even if I did, who the fuck cares what I or anyone else thinks?"

"I know better than to fuck around with you or anyone in our industry, Akihiro. Especially since you're — as you said — so much younger."

Akihiro regarded Katie carefully. "I respect that," he replied. "We don't have to let what happened change anything between us. I promise not to say anything."

"Not even to the rest of your members?" she asked, skeptical.

"I don't see how it's any of their business."

Katie was quiet for another few beats. "Okay," she said. "I won't say anything either."

"It will be okay, alright?" At her raised eyebrow, he added, "I would never risk fucking things up with my favorite noona. I promise."

"Alright."

"I'm gonna go take a cold shower now," Akihiro said. "You gonna be okay? You can see yourself out?"

Katie leaned her head against the back of the sofa and closed her eyes wearily. She whooshed out a tense breath. The last thing either of their careers needed was a dating scandal. "I'll be okay."

"Go home now," he ordered after kissing her on the forehead, his oversized Chanel tee gaping to show off his collarbones. "And maybe, if you're lucky, I will let you treat me to lunch tomorrow."

On her way out to the cab, Katie ran into Do-won in the hallway. He seemed flustered and refused to look her in the eyes and, for a moment, she wondered if he'd seen her and Akihiro on the sofa in the common area. She decided not to worry about it. When Katie went to bed that night after a large glass of wine, she fell asleep to thoughts of Akihiro's soft lips and his beautiful hands.

She ached.

November 2021

Katie was spent.

She had known going over to Woo-jin's place for a night of drinking with DOYEN would be a bad idea. She should have planned better, lied better, responded better. Katie's plan of showing up late didn't do shit other than draw more attention to herself. Clearly, she was out of practice being around people who actually cared about her.

Katie wrapped a throw blanket around her shoulders and stepped out on her balcony. She picked up the pack of Marlboro Ultra Light 100s on her patio table and packed it again just for the comfort of the motion. She swiped her brushed steel Zippo lighter and fished out a cigarette with shaking fingers. She held it to her lips, flicked the Zippo and took that first drag, holding the smoke in her mouth and slowly breathing it out her nose.

She sat back and watched the cigarette burn as she occasionally tapped the ash into a Gudetama ashtray.

It had been a mistake to return to Seoul, but Katie didn't know where else to go. She refused to stay in Hong Kong or Shanghai, the memories of Tony still too fresh, too sharp. She didn't want to impose on Alton in Singapore — she'd done enough of that recently, and Taiwan was too full of meddling family members. And America? What would she do in America? If her trip back this past year had taught her anything, it was that America was no longer beautiful and perhaps had never been.

Katie stared at the curl of smoke wisping into the brisk winter sky. Oh, how she wished to float away and disappear, too. But instead, she waited until the cigarette burned its way to the filter and then stabbed it out with more force than strictly necessary.

Chapter 2

K atie sprang up from sleep mid-scream.

She did not know where she was. The bedroom was the one she'd had in Seoul, but she didn't want to hope. Katie didn't want to be disappointed — that would somehow cut more — to allow herself to think for even a moment that she was safe.

The blue blur of early morning terrified her.

Tony had probably just stumbled into her apartment drunk, intent on confirming she was where she was supposed to be. Katie prepared herself for his rough hands, his sour breath, his sloppy thrusts.

Her stomach plunged and she could feel sweat prickle in her armpits. She buried herself back under her blankets, blocking out the light and curling into a fetal position, forcing her heart to slow down. It would hurt more if she was too tense.

Katie knew this, and yet she could not ease the panic building in her gut.

She waited and waited but still, Tony did not come. How drunk was he?

If possible, the fear in her blood spiked even higher. She could taste the metal in her saliva as she waited. All she could latch onto was the inevitable: it was going to be one of those times Tony was too inebriated and couldn't get his dick up. Katie resigned herself to the aftermath of his shame and frustration. She hoped he was taking so long because he had passed out.

That, of course, brought on its own set of difficulties. Tony was easily set off when hungover. She mentally prepared herself for what was to come.

When she finally could not take the suspense any longer, Katie hesitantly pushed back her covers and reached for her glasses. She really should get LASIK but her optometrist said that her prescription kept increasing and she'd need it to stay steady before undergoing the procedure.

Katie put on her glasses and realized that she was, indeed, in her Seoul bedroom.

She tried to puzzle out the pieces. She didn't remember getting here — how much did she drink last night? But if she was in Seoul, why was Tony in her apartment? Some tiny part of her shouted that none of these conclusions made any sense. Nothing made sense. And then Katie remembered snatches of rushing to Alton's private jet, the secret trips to the U.S. Consulate General in Hong Kong, touching down in Singapore, and hiding for weeks.

An iron vise squeezed around her chest, and she could not breathe.

Tony had found her.

He was going to force her back to Hong Kong. He was going to hide her passport again. He was going to punish her. He was going to make her pay.

Katie stumbled out her bedroom door and toward the kitchen, desperate to get to the knife block.

Katie would sooner die than go back. She had to get to those knives before he did. But when she got to the kitchen, the knives were nowhere to be found. How did Tony get here before she did? How was he so fast? With shaking hands, she pulled open drawer after drawer but there was nothing sharper than a butter knife. Not even a good set of kitchen shears.

He was going to kill her. He was going to hurt her. Katie had to hide. She was so stupid — he was toying with her. How could he not hear her with all the noise she had made? The knives were gone. He had taken all the knives.

Katie ran back to her room, grabbed her phone and hid in her closet.

Trembling, she dialed Alton's number. He had contacts at the Gangnam police station, and surely he could send his people from his hotel. They were reasonably close, right? She couldn't think of distances or timing — she could barely think at all.

"Baby, what's wrong?" Alton's sleepy voice asked.

"He's found me, Alton," Katie whispered. "He's here. He's in my apartment right now."

Katie could hear rustling, as if Alton was suddenly sitting up and alert. "Calm down, love. I need you to breathe."

"Alton," she cried, her voice high with terror, "he took all the knives. Shit — I should have taken the pepper spray from my purse. He's going to — I can't go back, Alton. I won't do it — I —"

"Baby, listen to me. I need you to listen carefully to me."

"Alton," Katie sobbed hysterically.

"He will never hurt you again. I swear on my ancestors and everything I own. He cannot harm you ever again."

"You can't be sure, Alton. You can't be sure. You don't know him — he — he's here in my apartment —"

"I know exactly where he is, Mei, and it's not in Seoul." Alton sounded hard and terrifying. She was so confused.

"You can't know —"

"I know exactly where he is, love. Please don't make me say it."

And then more memories flitted through Katie's mind — so fast, so vague — of Alton receiving a call and his face cruel and impassive as he thanked the person on the other end. He then told Katie that Tony would never trouble her again — that he'd taken care of it. She had collapsed onto the floor and Alton had embraced her as she'd sobbed in relief.

"What if it's Mr. Lau's men, Alton? What if they found out?"

Alton was silent for a long while. "It's not Mr. Lau's men, love."

Katie could tell he was trying very hard to be patient. What time was it in Singapore? She could not remember if it was an hour earlier or later there — but it was dawn in Seoul so, regardless, it was early in Singapore.

"Are you doubting me, baby?" He laughed softly. "When have you known me for shoddy work? Don't make me hop on the Lear to show you just how competent I am." His voice dropped low and husky and she found comfort in his familiar rasp.

"I miss you," Katie finally said.

She heard Alton sigh quietly. "You know you always have a home with me, Katie. Just say the word."

"You can't protect me forever," Katie said. Now that her panic had subsided, her reality came flooding back. Katie was embarrassed and ashamed. "I need to be able to do this for myself."

"Just remember that doing this for yourself doesn't mean you have to go at it alone. Tell Ha-joon to move you into my penthouse at Hannam the Hill." Alton's tone brooked no argument.

"Which one?"

"Whichever one you want." Katie almost laughed at how bored he sounded.

Katie would never get used to how wealthy Alton was, and she was used to money. Had grown up with it. Had taken it for granted before she understood the cost it had exacted upon her mother. Before the costs it had exacted from her.

"I'll come visit you soon, baby," Alton said, knocking her out of her ruminations. "Maybe to celebrate your new album?"

"When it's released or when it's finished?"

"Either. Both. Whatever you want. Whatever is easier."

Katie smiled. "How about when it's finished?" she suggested. "I'll be too busy when it actually releases."

"As long as you let me hear it first," he wheedled. "I am, after all, your biggest fan."

"Deal."

"I love you, Mei," he said tenderly. "You're safe now. I promise."

"Love you, too, Ge," she replied. "Sorry I woke you."

"Don't apologize, baby. Always call me. Always."

"Okay," Katie said.

"Okay."

June 2017

Katie was bored out of her goddamn mind. First of all, she hated weddings, especially when she was being tapped as the celebrity host. She couldn't understand why Taiwanese weddings of rich people were so stupid. Why did these spectacles require local celebrities to play emcee to entertain all these pretentious guests, the majority of whom were invited because of their status instead of any relation to the marrying couple?

Katie, in fact, did not know the couple at all. Only that her maternal grandfather had called in a favor and, since he never asked for anything, the least she could do was oblige him. Apparently, the bride was the granddaughter of a business acquaintance and the celebrity they'd hired had gotten sick, so Katie was a last-minute substitute. Katie had happened to be free — or rather, she'd made Ha-joon rearrange her schedule so that she could make it.

Second, she wasn't even being paid, and she'd had to bring a red envelope full of cash, too! Katie's American mind was so thoroughly annoyed, particularly since she was on the clock so she couldn't even partake in the copious amounts of expensive alcohol.

But she was a professional, so she dug deep inside her soul and enthusiastically dispatched her duties. Katie was charming. She smiled. She stopped for endless selfies and listened to people talk all while quietly nodding and making the polite murmurs of the secretly disinterested. She beamed at men, young and old, who could have been better about adhering to her physical boundaries, and she beamed equally at the women, young and old, who were catty and fake.

By the end of the evening, Katie wanted to set the entire hotel on fire.

Katie had just bowed her last bow and escaped into an empty elevator — she was so close to the blessed silence of her suite she could almost taste it — when a warm voice called out, "Please hold the elevator!" She dredged the last remnants of proper upbringing by hitting the "open elevator door" button, and a gorgeous man in a navy suit that was three times as expensive as her already costly designer dress entered the elevator.

He had the most velvety chocolate brown eyes. Katie recognized him from the wedding.

"Thanks," he said in perfect, American standard English.

"You're welcome," she replied in kind.

"I'm Alton Kuang, cousin to the bride. Thanks for emceeing at the last minute. It was super clutch."

Katie tried valiantly not to laugh out loud. "Did you just say 'super clutch'?"

Alton looked mildly offended. "I did."

"Aren't you too old to be using slang in such a manner?" Katie covered her smile with a hand, but there was no way he could miss the way her eyes crinkled.

Now Alton looked mortally offended. "How old do you think I am?"

Katie ran her eyes over the length of his body, making no effort to hide her very thorough perusal of him. "It's hard to say, given that you're Asian. You could be anywhere from twenty to fifty."

"Fifty, huh?" She could see him trying to keep up his offended exterior and failing.

"I guess the only way to tell would be from your stamina and recovery time."

He grinned, his eyes lingering on Katie's mouth. Alton's tongue darted out, wetting his lips. "The only way, hmmm?" He swiped a thumb at his lower lip.

Katie lifted a shoulder in casual nonchalance. "I certainly can't think of any other." She felt the heat of his stare.

"Are you always this forward?"

Truthfully, she wasn't quite sure why she was doing this, except that she was away from the prying eyes of Seoul, sick of being alone, and he was very handsome. Money had a way of elevating a person, but Alton was legitimately hot. Tall, lean, and a strong jaw. Katie rarely needed more.

"Is that a problem?" Katie asked, an edge bleeding into her tone.

"Never."

Katie reached for Alton's tie and pulled him closer so that he caged her against the elevator wall. "Let's not waste anymore time then," she said as she discovered for herself his true age.

December 2021

"Who is this guy again?" asked Akihiro, somewhat possessively. He'd never heard of this Alton Kuang fellow and now Katie was living in his penthouse? Granted, she was now in the same complex as many of their personal apartments, including his, so that was at least convenient.

"A family friend," Katie said, "and when he comes to visit next year, you will be kind and welcoming."

Akihiro just scowled.

He wandered through her quarters and vaguely listened as Woo-jin remarked on the architectural accents and interior design of the place. Ye-jun was ecstatic over the kitchen and lamented that it was wasted on her.

"You don't even have knives!" he exclaimed.

Katie laughed. "I don't cook. What's the point of spending that kind of money on something I won't use at all?"

"What if I want to cook for you?" he protested.

"I'll believe it when I see it. You've been promising for years and have never once followed through," she shot back. "And why can't you cook for me in your kitchen? I'm sure Mina unni won't mind."

"But I want to do so in your kitchen! It's fantastic! Look at all that pristine counter space!"

"Ah, leave it alone, oppa," Katie said.

"I will not! It's my birthday next month — you cannot refuse me. I'm going to buy you the fanciest knife block ever and a set of steak knives and kitchen shears, too." Ye-jun looked inordinately proud of himself. "How can you live in Korea and not have any kitchen shears? It's more essential than chopsticks!"

"Are you saying you want to cut ties with me?" Katie joked.

Ye-jun scoffed. "That's old-fashioned and superstitious, Katie-yah. And if you really feel strongly about it, you can pay me a single won."

Akihiro watched as Katie's face clouded over. "Oppa, that's just a waste of money."

"Are you saying I can't afford it? I could buy a penthouse like your Alton several times over. I can waste my money however I want!" Ye-jun was in fine, blustery form.

"I would really much rather you spend money treating me to food," Katie said.

Akihiro knew a lost cause when he saw one. Ye-jun dug in. "No! This is a housewarming present and very practical because you actually need knives. This way you can think of me every time you use them! I can treat you to food any time."

"I don't want to impose on you and unni —" Katie interjected only to be cut off by Ye-jun's "You know noona doesn't mind me going out with you!"

"I really don't want knives, oppa," she insisted. Katie was clearly getting irritated but Ye-jun, who normally was very astute, was not having it. "Why can't you get me a plant like Jae-sung did?"

"Because it would die — just like the plant Jae-sung gave you like literally a week ago — he's very disappointed, Katie!"

"Ah, Ye-jun." Woo-jin said, failing at playing peacemaker. Do-won was usually much better at it, but Akihiro's favorite hyung wasn't here. Things between Do-won and Katie had been tense since that dinner at Woo-jin's a few weeks ago.

"Don't 'Ye-jun' me, Woo-jin-ah, I'm your hyung!" Ye-jun argued as he was wont to do sometimes.

Akihiro didn't know if the timing of Ye-jun's mood was appropriate, but he occasionally got on a blustery roll and couldn't stop. He loved to insist that he was Woo-jin's hyung even though they were born the same year. Ye-jun liked to argue that he was considered an "early '92" since his birthday was before the Lunar New Year and was thus technically considered a '91-liner. It was complicated and old-fashioned.

"YAH! Who cares about that stuff these days, Ye-jun?" retorted Woo-jin. "Anyway, even if you were my hyung, you're only four months older than me."

"There's no respect these days!" Ye-jun shouted in his typical ridiculousness. "Speaking of which, Katie-yah, I don't understand why you won't let me provide this basic thing for you. It's not a big deal. You're literally letting this man, Alton, provide an entire residence!"

"Oh, so it's okay to be old-fashioned about Woo-jin oppa calling you 'hyung' but not when it comes to giving me knives? Is this some oppa pissing contest? Are you jealous?"

Ye-jun's mouth flopped open like a gasping fish. He drew to his full height, puffed out his broad chest and shoulders, and gesticulated wildly. "I've just never heard of this Alton Kuang before. How good of a family friend is he? Is he your boyfriend? Why does he have an empty penthouse in Seoul? He could be a serial killer for all we know!"

"Mina unni has worked with him before and trusts him. Are you questioning your girlfriend's judgment?"

Ye-jun flushed red at the implication.

"Alton's one of the best people I know, oppa. Please stop slandering his name."

"Only if you let me buy you a set of Japanese knives." Akihiro had to give it to Ye-jun for being stubborn.

"No."

"German ones, then."

"No."

"I don't see why you're arguing — you know I'll just have them delivered —"

"Stop it, oppa! Stop!" Katie yelled finally. In all his years, Akihiro had never seen Katie lose her temper at Ye-jun. "I can't have knives in the house, okay, oppa? It's not safe!"

The shock on his members' faces likely matched Akihiro's own.

"Why can't you have knives in the house, Katie-yah?" asked Woo-jin quietly. "Why isn't it safe?"

"I —," Katie refused to look at them. Her hands trembled. "I can't be trusted with them," she finally grated out.

"You said you were okay," said Ye-jun, an edge of hysteria creeping in. "You said you were on medication, Katie. You said you were getting the support you needed."

Katie still wouldn't look at them. "I am." At their dubious faces, she doubled down. "I am." Her voice was hard and brittle. "It's just sometimes — sometimes, I have really bad days and — and —"

She stopped as if she couldn't bring herself to say anything else. Katie rubbed the skin of her left wrist.

"I — I'm sorry, Katie. I shouldn't have insisted," Ye-jun apologized.

She nodded a curt acknowledgment. "Please, excuse me a moment," she said and headed to the balcony.

Akihiro watched through the glass doors as Katie packed a pack of cigarettes, extracted one, and lit it with practiced ease. He didn't even know she smoked.

July 2017

Do-won felt stupid.

He didn't particularly like scary things and this escape room concept, though not scary per se, wasn't exactly warm or cozy. It was, in fact, a little too dimly lit for Do-won's liking, with ominous music streaming in the background. Plus, all these puzzles and logic games really weren't his strong suit.

He wasn't sure why they were being forced into some team-building exercise with Katie and Na Gyuri noona, the other solo artist at SB Entertainment. After all, he and the rest of his bandmates were just fine — their entire lives were a team-building exercise. Why did the two solo artists need to be added into the mix?

It seemed ridiculous.

It was all the more ridiculous in light of the fact that DOYEN was still preparing for their September comeback. With every comeback, there were just more and more expectations to beat their previous records. There was so much to do, and yet, they were all being forced into this cheesy activity to promote artist interaction and comradery, or whatever bullshit the marketing teams had concocted as content for their label.

Do-won knew his role. He would ham it up for the cameras, act a little more terrified than he was, and just generally be the comedic foil. He was no good at figuring out clues or whatever was actually going on.

"You okay, Wonnie?" Katie asked as everyone got their makeup touched up. "You seem quieter than usual."

"I keep waiting for them to spring some zombies on us or something," Do-won replied automatically, trying to be funny. "I hate zombies."

"Don't say that too loudly, Do-won," Katie smiled. "Someone is bound to hear and incorporate it into future content for your fans. I would hate to see your soul leave your actual body."

"Have you done these sort of escape rooms before, noona?"

"I did a few back in the States. I've never tried them in Seoul, though. I'm not sure I will be of much help given that my Korean is so bad." Katie pulled her Golden State Warriors sweatshirt sleeves over her fingers, forming sweater paws. "But if they have math or if Jae-sung translates for me, I think I should be somewhat useful. I was always good at this sort of thing."

"I just leave all the heavy lifting to Jae-sung hyung, Akihiro, and Jun hyung. They're the clever ones. The rest of us are just here for our personalities."

"Thanks for the tip," Katie said as she squeezed his arm. "I hope you're wrong about the zombies, though. This set is creepy as fuck already."

Do-won glanced around the abandoned asylum set again, taking in the bloodied handprints on the walls and windows. Beds and medical equipment were strewn haphazardly around the rooms and hallways as if the occupants had hastily evacuated. Everything looked dingy and worse for wear and Do-won hated it.

"It is, right? Is it the lighting?"

"And the music. The whole fucking vibe." Katie shuddered as her gaze alighted on the straps of a hospital bed.

"Dae-jung and Woo-jin hyung must be crying inside. We're all such cowards," Do-won admitted. Though, now that they were talking about it, it didn't seem so bad.

"I'll protect you, Wonnie. Noona isn't scared of monsters."

"No? Why not?"

Katie smiled sadly. "Because they're not real, Wonnie. The real monsters are people." She squeezed him one more time and walked back to where Ye-jun and Woo-jin were.

Somehow, Do-won was not much reassured.

"Noona, you are so awesome!" cheered Soo-min, all eyes and eager limbs. "I'm so glad I was on your team. We all expected one of the other teams to win since they had Jae-sung hyung or Jun hyung — but your mind! Pow!" said the 21-year-old as he mimed an explosion.

The losing teams complained good-naturedly, and Do-won realized that though it was a cheesy exercise, he did feel more bonded to his team, as well as to Katie and Gyuri noonas. The various escape rooms, friendly competition, and ensuing meal were good ways to blow off steam, and he was grateful to the staff now that the stress of filming was over.

"Hey, I helped, too!" protested Akihiro, his cheeks puffed in fake furor. "You make it seem like all I did was stand there and look pretty."

"You were both very pretty and very helpful," Katie reassured. "The prettiest and the most helpful!"

Akihiro preened and Do-won couldn't help but coo as he back-hugged his roommate. "Ah, Hiro-yah, why are you so cute?"

Akihiro wiggled in happiness and added, "Noona, I was surprised at how you kept your cool. When the lights went out in that tiny room and they started piping in screaming, I thought for sure you'd lose it, but you didn't."

Katie brushed off his compliment. "I mean, it's all fake, right? You just have to tune it out and get done what you need to do."

"Do you watch scary movies, too?" asked Dae-jung. "I hate scary movies."

"Oh my god, no. I hate scary movies," she said. "They're the actual worst. I used to watch them all the time to prove that I wasn't scared, but honestly, why? Who was I proving my bravery to? The world is horrible enough."

"Did you watch 'Train to Busan'?" asked Woo-jin.

Katie shot him a look. "I literally just said I don't watch scary movies!"

"But that's not scary, at least not in the horror movie sense," replied the older man. "It's a thriller!"

"No. Not even Gong Yoo's handsome face — or Woo-shik's — can convince me to watch."

"I could have sworn you would have watched it in theaters," mused Ye-jun. "You know, to support your faves."

"It's hard for me to watch movies in the theaters," Katie said.

"Oh? Because you're afraid of being recognized?" asked Do-won. "Just wear a hoodie, a hat, and a mask like me and Jun hyung," he suggested.

Katie looked a bit embarrassed but plowed ahead anyway. "Ah, it's because everyone talks too fast and there aren't any English subtitles at the theater."

"But you seem to understand us just fine," commented Soo-min.

"It's nice of you to think so," Katie laughed. "Although, if I'm honest, when you all talk at the same time, I have no idea what you're saying. I just kinda nod and laugh along."

"Don't worry, I still have a hard time every now and then," Akihiro said. "Soo-min, too."

Soo-min nodded. "Gyopo problems."

Akihiro scoffed. "More like foreigner problems, Soo-min," he corrected. "Some of us had to learn Korean from scratch."

Do-won giggled. "If it makes you feel better, I don't think anyone actually catches everything we're saying."

"Your poor editors," Katie acknowledged.

"They get their revenge in the editing," observed Jae-sung drily.

Katie cracked up again. "That they do, Jae. That they do."

March 2022

After a four-year hiatus from the Korean music scene, Katie Wu returns with "Disintegration" (SB Entertainment, 2022). Deviating from her previous albums which, on the whole, pulsed with bold idealism, "Disintegration" delves into the twisted, hidden crevices of the psyche. Proceed with caution — even if you are in a good headspace.

The album is excruciating, the fear and despair palpable. Wu seizes you by the throat and whispers the stuff of nightmares. Standout tracks amidst this stellar album are "A Cluster of

Cells" and "Don't." The former meditates on the inflection point between a cluster of cells and a human, asking us what makes a person a person? What makes us good or evil? What makes us a life worth living? The latter is a heartbreaking plea to choose life — to fight the lies we tell ourselves that oblivion is at least quiet and beyond the pain of the living.

And finally, we would be remiss not to mention the hidden track: an unexpected 23-minute cello concerto that is transcendent.

- South China Morning Post, March 2022

Absolutely gutted.

- NME, March 2022

We're calling it now: hand Katie Wu all the "Album of the Year" awards already.

- Rolling Stone Korea, March 2022

[1] The Rise and Fall of the Roman Empire [4:07]
[2] I Lie All the Time — Even Now [4:22]
[3] Breathe [3:53]
[4] In Space No One Can Hear You Scream [2:39]
[5] But You're So Pretty When You Smile [4:31]
[6] A Cluster of Cells [2:50]
[7] Exsanguination [4:44]
[8] Save Yourself and Come Down [3:28]

[9] Get Your Hand Outta My Pocket [2:26]
[10] You Say Degenerate, I Say Liberate [4:05]
[11] Don't [2:46]
[12] You Don't See Me, I Am Not Here [4:13]
[Hidden track] Home [23:17]
        - Track list, "Disintegration" (SB Entertainment, 2022)

1 then 2 then 4 then 8
At which point did we become too great
And more than just a cluster of cells
More than just a cluster of cells
I really want to know the exact date
We're more than just a cluster of cells
                - "A Cluster of Cells" (SB Entertainment, 2022)

To Alton.
        - Album dedication, "Disintegration" (SB Entertainment,
                                                                2022)

Do-won could not stop weeping. He was hiccupping snot and tears, and his face was an entire mess and still, he could not stop. Beyond the fact that Katie's album had gutted him, it reminded him of just how far he had to go in his own writing. He was glad he was in the privacy of his own studio because he did not know if he had the emotional bandwidth to explain himself to anyone else.

He was relieved he'd waited until after all the schedules of his day before he sat down to listen. There was no way he would have been able to concentrate on writing for his latest solo album if he'd listened to Katie's album first. The creative process was difficult enough dealing with his own emotional state, but to add on the tumultuous feelings from Katie's album, Do-won would have had to call the day a loss.

Woo-jin had warned him — the rapper had warned them all — and Do-won had thought he'd adequately prepared himself, but truthfully, how could he have? How could he have adequately prepared himself when Katie had never told them anything except the bare minimum?

Do-won wanted to lie to himself, to tell himself that Katie's album was just a concept she'd committed to fully. That it did not come from whatever had happened to her these past four years. But even he, consummate purveyor of the positive, could not.

He was reserved, strictly cordoning off his public persona from his private self more than all the other members save for Ye-jun, but he was not a liar.

What had happened to her?

Katie used to rival him for SB Entertainment's sunshine status, determined to one up him in the positivity awards. She had been so ambitious, so full of brio and a restless energy to prove to everyone her talent and music were worth noticing. That she was a contender.

Frankly, Katie had pushed his members to be even more honest in their music and lyrics. She was such a force, her talent so evident.

And then one day, she'd simply left for Hong Kong.

There was no falling out. There was no conflict to speak of with management. Do-won barely remembered what had happened. From what he recalled, Katie had been in mid-album promotions of her latest album and then, she was gone.

She hadn't even said goodbye.

It wasn't until months later that Do-won had learned through the tabloids that Katie was dating a Hong Kong playboy, a Tony Lau, and that it was because of this whirlwind romance that she'd relocated for love.

Do-won had found it so baffling, in part because it was so out of character.

Katie's trajectory had been ascendant, and Tony didn't seem like the kind of man she'd be attracted to — not that Do-won had a bead on her type, other than that Woo-jin had been her bias and Ye-jun had been her wrecker in DOYEN. He'd only known that because before Katie joined their agency, the two eldest had constantly bickered about it. Woo-jin had heard Katie admit as much in an interview, and he had delighted in rubbing that in Ye-jun's face.

His only other reference point was Akihiro, and Do-won had refused to acknowledge that one time he'd overheard her making out with his roommate on their battered couch. He had locked away her desperate panting and begging, focusing instead on the fact that she could be with who she wanted. Besides, he loved Akihiro like a brother. No woman (or man, for that matter) would ever come between them.

It had been a questionable career move, and yet Katie had made it work, pivoting into acting and taking over the Chinese music scene. She was constantly on Tony's arm in glittering function after glittering function.

How had this album come out of that? What had Tony done to her?

July 2018

Do-won wanted to be anywhere but at some gala that Bright Horizon Conglomerate, Tony Lau's family company, was sponsoring in Seoul. Unfortunately, DOYEN had been requisitioned for some special performance and what the Hong Kong playboy wanted, the Hong Kong playboy got.

The grand ballroom dripped with flowers and hanging crystals, the attendees decked in their finest evening clothes. Everywhere Do-won looked screamed new money, the décor garish and the fashion flashy. He loved it all except that all these people looked down on him and his bandmates. All that money and yet, no class.

At least the food was good.

The evening opened with Katie singing a famous Korean ballad Do-won's mother had played all the time on the radio and then an Italian aria that even he recognized. He was reminded that Katie had been classically trained and of how good a voice she had. Of course, it was her job to be a singer, but he had never heard her sing in these styles. Plus, she'd been out of the country for months so it had been a while since he'd heard her sing live.

Do-won found that he'd missed Katie's voice.

"Noona! We missed you so much!" cried Akihiro as the slight man bounced up to greet and hug Katie. Her dress sparkled, the high neck hiding a plunging back. "You almost never text the group chat anymore. Do you not love us now that you're a famous actress in Hong Kong?"

None of them acknowledged that the only reason any of them were attending the function was to ensure that Katie's boyfriend remained happy and would continue to facilitate the roles she had been garnering in Hong Kong and China. Not that Katie didn't deserve the work. It's just that the doors opened much wider for a rich man than it did for musical performers — especially K-pop ones at a smaller Korean entertainment company. Time would tell if Katie would turn these opportunities and connections into bigger and better ones.

Katie flashed a wan smile. "Of course I still love you, Hiro-yah. Besides, you guys are the ones going on world tours and performing at international award shows. I should be the one worrying if I'm famous enough for you seven."

She was right, too. DOYEN had steadily caught the attention of the American media and they were surpassing everyone's expectations, even their own.

Katie hung out with them for a good while, joking around. It felt so much like old times that Do-won was taken aback by how much he'd missed it.

"I see this is where my Katie has wandered off to while I was busy attending business," Do-won heard Tony slur in Hong Kong-accented English. Reeking of alcohol, he staggered toward where she sat next to Dae-jung. "You shame me." He roughly grabbed her by the arm, dragging her out of her seat.

Do-won and his fellow members tensed as they watched Katie's face go blank. "I was just greeting my friends, Tony. They're not accustomed to attending such functions and I didn't want them to feel lonely," she replied in kind.

Do-won wasn't sure if he was glad his English had improved enough to understand them both or not.

"They're the entertainment for the evening, darling. And you're my entertainment — so make sure I get my money's worth, hmmmm? Or did you not like that latest cosmetic line courting you?"

Katie stiffened and then just as quickly, her face became serene. She bowed politely to their table and drew Tony away from them, fawning over the much older man as if to appease him. Do-won just watched as Tony steered her back to their seats, her dragon, tiger, and cyborg rooster tattoos rippling along her beautiful back.

He wondered if Katie liked her new life at all.

May 2022

Katie was trying very hard to be a good sport. The artist management teams at SB Entertainment had gotten it into their heads that she'd been gone too long and wanted to facilitate bonding and artist collaboration amongst her and her labelmates. After all, the younger boyband AQ9 (now popular in their own right) had come up while she'd been in Hong Kong. Though she vaguely recalled them as trainees, she didn't know them well at all.

Once again, Katie found herself at some escape room facility.

It wasn't that she didn't like bonding exercises (actually, she didn't like bonding exercises), but what was SB Entertainment's obsession with escape rooms? Katie figured that they found it hilarious to see superstars stymied by logic and get spooked, while being extra competitive.

Katie dutifully let herself be sorted into a team consisting of Woo-jin, Lee Seul-ki, and Chae Sang-hun. The two AQ9 members seemed a little intimidated by her at first. But after an afternoon of seeing her struggle with some of the Korean and talking shit to Woo-jin while simultaneously trying to encourage them, Seul-ki and Sang-hun seemed to be more settled in her presence.

Katie was happy for that small victory; she didn't like for people to be afraid of her. She knew that feeling all too well. But then, Seul-ki turned on the charm and she decided he could do with a little more fear.

"Noona," Seul-ki pouted, leaning his tall, lanky frame deep into her space, his sinful lips mere millimeters from hers. "When are you taking me out to dinner? I want to become closer. I think you could do with a younger man in your life."

"I'm not taking you out on a date, Seul-ki. I'm old enough to be your mother."

Seul-ki lifted an eyebrow, attempting his best sultry attack. "That doesn't even make sense, noona. Unless you mean you want me to call you Mommy?"

"I —"

"That's not my kink but I could be persuaded."

Sang-hun just groaned and Woo-jin was crying with laughter. Katie caught a glimpse of a masked male staff member walking by when she smelled a familiar mix of iced mango, tangerine, sandalwood, and patchouli.

She whirled around but the man was gone. She could not breathe.

"Noona — are you okay?" an unfamiliar voice asked Katie.

He wouldn't dare. Not when she was surrounded by so many SB Entertainment staff members — but everyone was wearing masks. It would be no problem for him to sneak in. He had money. He had power. He could do whatever he wanted.

The room seemed to swirl, the production lights too bright, too sharp. Katie stumbled back.

He would want her to hide. He would wait to corner her when Katie thought she was safe. When everyone else had gone. But she was stronger now. She would not go quietly.

"Oppa!" she yelled. "Oppa!!"

Katie could feel hundreds of eyes digging into her. Good. The more people who were watching, the less likely he could take her.

"OPPA!!!!" The light was so bright, and Katie's head felt as if it were splitting in half. She crumpled to the ground and wanted to throw up.

"Katie-yah, who are you yelling for?" asked a low, raspy voice.

Katie vaguely registered her friend Woo-jin, but why would he be on set in Hong Kong? When did she arrive in Hong Kong again? Her head hurt and she knew she was missing something. Something important. Did she have too much to drink this morning? Tony was on set and he must have seen that young, pretty boy flirting with her.

Tony must be walking toward her because all Katie could smell was Ralph Lauren's Polo Black and she wanted to scream — she was screaming — someone was holding her down — Tony had found her.

Tony had found her.

"OPPA!!!" Katie screamed as she struggled against the arms holding her down. "OPPA! Don't let him take me, oppa — I can't go back — I swear I will kill myself first —"

"Katie-yah, listen to me," she heard Ha-joon's voice, calm and steady. "He's not here. It's me, Ha-joon oppa. You know me, right?"

Katie was frantic. "Oppa, he'll kill me this time — he knows — he knows I got rid of his baby —" She clung to Ha-joon, burying her face in his solid chest. Her whole body quavered. "We have to hide," she hissed. "If he finds you, he'll hurt you, too."

"Listen to me, Katie-yah," Ha-joon directed. "You are in Seoul. You are safe. Tony cannot ever hurt you again, remember?"

Katie could not stop sobbing. "Promise me you'll kill me yourself if he tries to take me. Promise me, oppa," she pleaded.

Her manager paused a long while until, finally, he said, "I promise."

Chapter 3

SB Entertainment solo artist confesses to an abortion in a meltdown during filming activities...

            - Soompi, May 2022

Authorities investigating Katie Wu regarding abortion allegations...

            - The Korea Herald, May 2022

[+ 200,892, - 201] Add Katie Wu to the "no condom club" — which is hilarious since she used to rep a condom company. Send that whore back to China.

            - Internet user, Pann, May 2022

SB Entertainment star Katie Wu loses it during filming, puts fellow artists and staff in danger...

            - One Hallyu, May 2022

Katie Wu overheard screaming she would rather kill herself than go back to Hong Kong...

           - Koreaboo, May 2022

Singer/actress Katie Wu accuses missing Hong Kong businessman and playboy Tony Lau of abuse...

      South China Morning Post, May 2022

It was madness outside of SB Entertainment headquarters. Do-won had never seen it that crazy — not even when they had topped Billboard for all those weeks last year or when they won all their western media awards.

Along with swarms of paparazzi and reporters hoping to catch a glimpse of her, hundreds of protesters with signs were calling Katie all sorts of names: baby killer, murderer, butcher. They called her heartless, the natural result of feminism gone rampant.

Letters from CHIMERA and AQ9 fans calling for her immediate dismissal from the label poured in from all over the world. Stan Twitter was abuzz and the media just fanned the flames higher. The fan wars between Katie's fandom and other fandoms raged. SB Entertainment's stock plummeted, and calls from shareholders also demanded her departure.

What Do-won couldn't understand was how Katie kept showing up at the office every day, head held high, smile bright, and polite as ever. Somehow, he'd thought she would hole up in her apartment until things blew over, but he supposed this was the sort of thing she had to actively address.

But no statement from her had been forthcoming. SB Entertainment stuck with the company line that it did not comment on their artists' personal lives and that, to their knowledge, no Korean laws had been broken while she had resided in Korea. Since Katie was not a Korean citizen, Korean laws did not apply to her when she was outside of the country.

Katie was shut in meeting after meeting with the CEO and executive teams of SB Entertainment, presumably discussing her future with the company. On the rare occasions she wasn't stuck in an office with her personal lawyers, company counsel — and a few times with Oh Mina, the high-powered consultant who happened to be Ye-jun's girlfriend — Katie would lock herself in her studio.

Do-won didn't know what to do.

He was worried for Katie. That day at the escape room, he had never — not in his entire life — seen someone as terrified as she was. Do-won couldn't even imagine what Katie's life had been like if any of it was true — and he had no reason to doubt her unless, perhaps she was psychologically unhinged (he hated that sliver of doubt whispering in the back of his mind).

In truth, he didn't want to believe her because if she was telling the truth, what sort of friend was he that he hadn't noticed? That he hadn't helped while she was suffering? That he found it preferable to believe she was crazy over accepting what she'd experienced told him everything.

It broke his heart, and Do-won did not know how to help Katie or love her — or if she would even want any of it. The few times he'd approached her, she had just bowed and apologized for being in a hurry to or from somewhere.

He told himself not to take her dismissal personally. Katie had sidelined all of his members — even Woo-jin and Ye-jun. Plus, as Woo-jin had so accurately stated: she did not owe them her life story.

The one time he'd asked his fellow members why she'd stayed if Tony had been so abusive, Woo-jin again had cut in with words of wisdom. "You're asking the wrong question," Woo-jin had said, his voice all gravel. "Why did Tony get to hurt her? And why did no one do anything to stop him?"

Do-won still felt shame coursing through him when he thought back to that moment. Why indeed?

January 2017

"I knew it," Katie sneered even as her face remained pleasant. She never knew who was watching. "I knew you were here to ask for more money."

"Careful," her father growled. Katie forced herself not to flinch. "You forget who you're speaking to."

"And who is that?"

"I'm your father," he scowled. "You should show me the proper respect."

Katie's fury was a banked fire. "I respect those who deserve it."

Her father looked around the restaurant, trying to keep his temper in check. Katie had chosen a public setting in Seoul for this very purpose. She knew better than to tell him 'no' in private. It had been years since he'd beaten her, but that didn't mean he wouldn't again. It was for lack of opportunity, really, and not any rehabilitation on his part. This, she knew deep in her bones.

"Ah, wá," her father said. He had abruptly switched tacks. "I know I haven't been the best father to you."

Katie snorted at the understatement. A tick in her father's face betrayed his agitation.

"I know you sacrificed a lot — and I appreciate it. But those people took advantage of you, bǎobèi," he said. "They were investors, not lenders, and they shouldn't have gone after you. They should know loss is part of business in general. They should not have expected you to pay them."

"That's not what the contracts said," Katie replied.

Her father laughed in a manner that could only be described as paternalistic. "I don't expect you to understand matters of business, wá. Besides, you can't exactly read Chinese."

Katie bristled at the implication. As if she hadn't had her lawyers look everything over and do their own investigations before paying several hundred thousand dollars' worth of money her father had cheated his Taiwanese partners out of. She had only just recently finished paying them back.

Katie told herself to swallow it down, that she didn't always need to fight over every word out of her father's mouth. She forced herself to listen to her brother Mattie and her mother for once and let the old man save face.

"Unfortunately, this time, I am embarrassed to say that I really do need you to pay off actual debts."

"Maybe you should explain it in simpler terms since I'm too stupid to understand." Welp, there went Katie's resolve to swallow it all down.

Katie's father cleared his throat. "I borrowed from the wrong people, Kǎi Tíng-ah."

"I fail to see how this is any of my concern." She would not be tricked again.

"They're threatening our house — and your mother. Mattie is still in college, and we have to pay tuition somehow," he explained.

"I'm already paying Mattie's tuition," Katie said, "and helping with the mortgage."

"These are bad men, bǎobèi."

A twinge of guilt pulsed through Katie. "Then you shouldn't have borrowed money from them."

Her father looked distinctly uncomfortable, a circumstance she'd never witnessed. Thomas Wu was always full of bluster and unfounded confidence. If his words didn't twist you into submission, his height and weight would.

"You don't have to give me the full amount," he bargained.

"How much is the full amount?"

Her father glanced furtively around again. "$1.5 million."

Katie sucked in a breath. Jesus. "I don't have anywhere near that —
not after paying off your other debts. How did you get them to lend it
to you?"

This time, Katie's father had the grace to look ashamed. "I used you
as collateral."

"What?"

"I showed them I was good for it. I told them you were my daughter
— that you had taken care of my Taiwanese problems — and that you
were a dutiful and filial child. They lent me the money on the strength
of your celebrity."

Fuck. Katie hid her trembling hands under the table. "What happens
if you don't pay them back?"

"I don't know." Her father looked afraid, and he was never afraid. Or
at least, he never showed fear that she knew of. He'd never had to; he was
an ox of a man.

"Is there a payment plan option?" Katie did not know why she was
asking, except that she wasn't a monster. She loved her father even if he
was a shit human.

"They want $25,000 in the next few days and another $25,000 the
week after."

"I —" She was at a loss.

Her father shifted in his seat. "Maybe after those good faith payments,
I can negotiate better terms."

"Why can't you ask Ah-Gong?"

Katie's maternal grandfather owned a steel company, but even she
knew that he didn't have a spare $1.5 million to give her father. Her aunts
and uncles would scream favoritism. Besides, he wasn't their blood.

"I have. He refused."

Ah. Likely, her grandfather didn't want to continue throwing good money after bad — especially after how her father had treated her mother. His numerous affairs and poor business sense likely did not endear him either.

"I can wire you $50,000 to buy you some time, but the rest is your problem. I simply don't have the funds."

Katie's father merely nodded and waited for her to pay the bill. She didn't know why she expected any thanks. It wasn't as if he had ever thanked her for anything. Her father had never had to suffer a consequence in his life and, even now, Katie regretted agreeing to wire him the funds. She knew he would be back.

May 2022

Katie was in a bad way.

That was probably underselling it.

Several hundred times a day — any time she looked out a window, really — she saw reminders that she was a worthless human being, that she was a monster. That she should save everyone the trouble and go kill herself already.

More often than not, Katie felt as if she should oblige them.

And then, every now and then, a spark of rebellion would flare inside her. How dare they tell her what to do? How dare they judge her not worthy of being here after all she fought through to survive — no — to live?

But those rare flashes were short-lived.

Instead, Katie started drinking again. She hid it, of course. Just as she had before, Katie only drank as a last resort when sleep eluded her — which was every night — passing out only after making a dent through the handle of vodka tucked underneath her bed.

Some days, Katie nipped a shot before heading to work, too. But on the whole, she was afraid of Ha-joon smelling the vodka on her and intervening. She stayed at work as long as possible. She told herself she would never drink while on the clock; she was a professional, after all.

And now, with sponsors dropping left and right, Katie and her team were wracking their collective brains to make sure she made up that lost income. No one would hire her for acting or modeling work right now — not at the height of her controversy anyway.

When Katie had expressed her surprise that SB Entertainment wasn't forcing her to quit or dropping her from the label, Song PD had merely commented that they knew what they'd signed up for when they chose her in the first place. "It was right after your scandal with Johnny, after all," he'd said. "We saw the wisdom when Woo-jin insisted we scoop you and your talent before you got snatched by another company. Our point of view has not changed."

It had been news to Katie that Woo-jin had been her champion then. She had made a note to ask him about it in the future when she was no longer hiding from them. She knew the guys wouldn't judge her, but their pity would be worse. It was better if she kept her distance. Besides, Katie knew that what one artist did reflected on all the other artists at a label. It wasn't fair, but that's the way it was. She had too much to answer for, and she was not looking forward to it.

"Besides," the avuncular CEO had added, "you're part of the original SB Entertainment family and we leave no one behind. You're ours. Always."

"Oh," was all Katie had been able to choke out. She was unconvinced that she deserved such faith and devotion.

No, she could not let these people — people who loved and supported her and were risking their company on her — know that she was drinking or thinking suicidal thoughts again. How could Katie disappoint them when they hoped so much for her?

And, thus, despite Katie's incredible reservations, she agreed to a KBS interview. She did not know how she was going to lie through her teeth to survive it, but she supposed she'd had ample experience these past few years. After all, Katie would do anything to protect the people she loved, too.

November 2017

"Firework" (SB Entertainment, 2017), Katie Wu's third Korean entry, is a solid follow-up to her sophomore album, "Rusty Lanterns" (SB Entertainment, 2016). "Firework" excels at bright, infectious pop — a sonically joyful celebration of summer, young love, and the inevitable end of both.

Wu intersperses the album with club bangers like "Bubbly" and "Starburst," slinky R&B tracks like "Gunpowder and Sex," and introspective ballads like "The More I Grasp, The More You Slip Away." Once again, Wu proves herself to be a musician's rock star, deftly writing hits in multiple genres.

- Taipei Times, August 2017

The perfect summer album.

> \- The Chosun Ilbo, August 2017

[1] Intro: Spark [1:47]
[2] Gunpowder and Sex [4:03]
[3] Bubbly [3:26]
[4] You Shine From Across the Room [3:42]|
[5] Sling Me Out Into the Big, Wide Open [3:50]
[6] Interlude: Shot [2:01]
[7] Starburst [3:34]
[8] Pop Goes My Heart [3:28]
[9] In Bloom [2:53]
[10] The More I Grasp, The More You Slip Away [3:29]
[11] Falling Embers [3:16]
[12] Outro: Smoke [1:17]

> \- Track list, "Firework" (SB Entertainment, 2017)

Pop, pop, pop goes my heart, heart, heart
You were only supposed to be a lark, lark, lark
But you're kind and funny and smart, smart, smart
Your heart-shaped smile is pure art, art, art

> \- "Pop Goes My Heart" (SB Entertainment, 2017)

Katie didn't want to admit it, but she was really excited to see DOYEN perform at the MNet Asian Music Awards (MAMA) Hong Kong show. From what she'd seen of their rehearsals, it was guaranteed to be an epic performance. The way all seven of them were going to kill that stage during the dance break for their latest hit, "Ready or Not" — she could not wait. The body rolls alone would kill her along with the rest of her fellow CHIMERA.

Katie had tagged along with the staff because why not?

She would never have been invited to the show on her own, but she could take advantage of all the arrangements and use it as time to network with other artists, Korean or otherwise. Plus, she wanted to get another tattoo and her favorite tattoo artist in Hong Kong serendipitously had an opening.

SB Entertainment had scheduled a few low-key fan meetings for Katie and her Jezebelles, and she was excited to perform an acoustic set of a few songs off the album she'd dropped in August. She was pleased that each successive album seemed to garner more rave reviews and sell better than the previous one.

Not only did it prove to SB Entertainment that she'd been the right horse to bet on, it also relined her thinning bank accounts.

Of course, Katie still had to be cautious of the various mens' rights activists who constantly stalked her. These anti-feminists hadn't forgotten her blatant support of feminism — quite possibly because her albums were all unapologetically pro-women. She often wished men were optional in her world, and the insecure bastards couldn't stand it.

Katie also ignored the fact that her father was merely a half-hour drive away in Shenzhen. After he'd taken her money in January, he hadn't made any other attempts to get more. When Katie had asked her mother about the house, she had only said they'd taken out a second mortgage on the home and had maxed out the home equity line of credit. Katie had figured he was using the value of her parents' Bay Area home to make the rest of the repayments.

Katie couldn't bear the thought of her mother losing her home. She started making additional monthly mortgage payments for them, even though she knew it was almost the same as giving her father additional funds. She felt the pressure to push out more albums and tours, as well as start looking into more endorsements and acting and modeling roles.

She was in the bathroom washing her hands when her phone rang. She dried her hands and checked the caller ID. It was her father. Katie knew it had been too quiet.

After ditching her security, Katie got out of the taxi, walked into a fancy restaurant, and gave the hostess her name. She dutifully followed the person past the regular seating and briefly wondered if her father had chosen a private room to protect himself from any witnesses. A prickle of fear slunk down her spine.

When she entered the private room, she was a little taken aback by the presence of several people around her father's age, in addition to her father. The men and women all looked very serious, clad in extremely expensive suits. The sole exception was a younger man maybe in his twenties or thirties. He was reasonably attractive, his obvious wealth a big help.

Katie felt sorely underdressed in ripped black skinny jeans, a graphic tee, and a leather jacket. Hong Kong's weather was a lot warmer than Seoul's, and she had taken advantage of the warmer clime.

"Baba, I didn't realize we had company. I would have dressed up," she said in English, and then bowed and politely greeted the guests in Mandarin.

Katie took the seat her father indicated next to the younger man.

"This is Mr. Lau, bǎobèi. He owns the Bright Horizon Conglomerate company, and this is his son, Tony."

Katie nodded. From the little she knew of Bright Horizon Conglomerate, she knew they owned a lot of shopping centers and popular commercial real estate in Hong Kong. She'd seen their billboards all over the city.

Katie's father continued. "These are Mr. Ng and Ms. Fong," indicating a man with a wicked scar near his temple and a severe-looking woman. "They're Mr. Lau's executives."

Were these people her father's friends or unscrupulous business partners? Katie was leaning toward the latter because her father seemed uncharacteristically muted. She wondered if he was actually anxious or just pretending to be to get more cooperation from her. With her father, it could be either; it could be both.

Katie wasn't sure if her father just wanted to introduce her to these people or if he wanted to back her in a corner by requesting in front of them something she didn't want to give. Helping her family save face had been ingrained in her since she was a child. She knew better than to deviate from that narrative.

Katie attempted some basic small talk with her neighbor as they all waited for the dishes to arrive. Tony was a few years older than her, had attended her rival school, USC, and the two of them mentioned old LA haunts and favorite Hong Kong clubs. He was courteous and polite, and she was grateful for his presence.

Finally, after most people had eaten enough, Mr. Lau addressed her directly.

"Katie, I know you've experienced some success in Taiwan and Korea as a singer," Mr. Lau said. "But Thomas mentioned to us that you are interested in breaking into the Chinese and Hong Kong markets — in particular for acting and endorsements."

"Did he?" she hummed noncommittally. It was news to Katie, but in all negotiations, it was best not to seem too eager. And she'd made no mistake; this was an opening salvo. She just wasn't quite sure for what yet.

Mr. Lau bared his teeth in a devil's smile. "My son Tony here is a big fan of your work, Ms. Wu. And due to our close friendship with your father and my great affection for my youngest son, we at the Bright Horizon

Conglomerate, would like for you to consider being one of our latest ambassadors."

Katie swallowed.

"Ah, thank you so much for your most generous offer, Mr. Lau. I am honored. But I cannot enter into any agreements without my manager or my agency, SB Entertainment, present." She made a face of extreme embarrassment. "Had I known earlier of Baba's intentions, I would have ensured my manager and counsel were also present at this lovely father-daughter lunch."

Mr. Lau chuckled. "The rose has thorns, I see." He tossed Tony a bemused glance. "Careful you don't prick yourself, son."

"Don't worry, father. I have a prick of my own," Tony replied, his eyes merry.

Katie sat up straight as a warning clanged through her consciousness. *Pay attention*, her gut screamed. *Pay close attention.*

"I'm afraid I haven't been entirely honest with you, Ms. Wu," said Mr. Lau, his smile oily like an unguent. "You see, we're in somewhat of a tough position. We want to continue our business relationship with your father, but unfortunately, Thomas has run into some difficulties."

"Shame," she murmured. At that moment, Katie caught Tony's eye and he subtly shook his head. It had been too long since she'd walked on eggshells in the presence of powerful men. She chided herself for being so sloppy.

Mr. Lau went on as if she hadn't spoken. "We are hoping that you would consider signing on as a partner with us in your father's stead."

"With all due respect, Mr. Lau, I'm not sure what my father's situation has anything to do with me."

The older man nodded at Mr. Ng, and the scarred man said, "We would hate for your father to experience any unnecessary harm in the course of our daily business activities."

Shit. "Again, my father is an adult. He made his choices," she said as bored as she could.

"You're a cold-hearted cunt, aren't you?" Mr. Lau snarled.

"Yes."

"I wonder," drawled Mr. Ng, "if you would feel the same if an unfortunate accident would befall your mother or younger brother — Mattie, is it? Computer engineering in his third year of university?" Mr. Ng cleared his throat. "It would be such a shame for Mattie not to reach his full potential."

Katie was aghast. She checked her father, but his face was impassive. He didn't even have the courtesy to look outraged or afraid. He just seemed satisfied.

"Ah, Mr. Ng," Tony cut in smoothly. "There's no need to threaten violence. Perhaps Ms. Wu would be more amenable to the situation if she had time to think about our offer and discuss it with her management team. Surely, Ms. Wu wouldn't be able to sign any contracts without her agency's approval."

"I — I would appreciate that," Katie stammered. She was still reeling.

"Truthfully, Katie — may I call you Katie?" At her nod, Tony continued. "Truthfully, my father neglected to mention that we can open many doors for you here in Hong Kong and China. We would love to find a way where all our interests can align and mutually benefit one another." He smiled, all warmth and trustworthiness, and Katie wanted to be convinced. "You would break into a new market and we would get properly indemnified."

Katie noted how Tony purposely elided that her family would remain safe, but the underlying message was still the same. He was not on her side. She would do well to remember that.

June 2022

*"All the rumors are false," claims Katie Wu. "The gossip rags
have been watching too many dramas."*
                                    - Apple Daily, June 2022

*After a thorough investigation into abortion allegations, Seoul
authorities declare Katie Wu did not violate any Korean laws.*
                              - The Korea Herald, June 2022

*The Lau family is offering an award for any information
leading to the whereabouts of missing Hong Kong businessman
and playboy Tony Lau. Local Hong Kong and Vientiane police
are asking the public's cooperation for locating Lau, who disappeared in late August 2021 while on a business trip to Laos.*
                        - Hong Kong Financial Times, June 2022

*International pop star Katie Wu tells authorities she and
boyfriend Tony Lau parted ways on friendly terms at the end
of 2020. "The pressures of work and our separate careers took its
toll," she said, expressing concern for his safety and well-being.*
                        - The Wall Street Journal Asia, June 2022

Do-won wondered if Katie's face hurt from how hard it was working
to seem effortlessly pleasant. Her first and only exclusive interview with

KBS was airing, and the members of DOYEN were avidly watching in the swanky SB Entertainment artist lounge. They all sat in one of the modern slate gray couches that lined the perimeter of the spacious room.

He was impressed at how authoritative and sure Katie sounded despite likely feeling anything but. It helped that she was dressed in an understated pink cashmere sweater paired with navy pinstriped pants. She looked both soft and professional — far from the hellion she could come across as in her work. He wondered how much money his company had thrown at KBS for this fluff interview.

"How long did noona practice?" asked Do-won.

"She was holed up with Mina noona for at least a week." Ye-jun shuddered as he got up. Even he knew his girlfriend was formidable. He crossed the room to grab himself a drink from the fridge their staff kept stocked with everyone's favorite beverages. "If Katie could make it through that, these interviews will be a breeze."

The bandmates grunted their agreement. Mina was terrifying in the best way. If Do-won was honest with himself, he was still a little bit scared of her. He reverted his attention back to the screen.

"What actually happened on set that day, Katie-ssi?" asked the journalist, clearly ramping up for the hard-hitting portion of the interview.

"To tell you the truth, it's been a long time since I've worked this much." Katie flashed a sheepish smile from her seat. "I was working in Hong Kong, of course. I modeled and acted in movies and shows, which are difficult in their own way, but it has been years since I did a full Korean music comeback. Releasing Chinese features and official soundtrack singles cannot possibly compare."

"I'll say," grumbled Ye-jun. "Nothing like a comeback to make a person feel energized and exhausted all at the same time."

Do-won agreed wholeheartedly as the journalist nodded on screen. "So, what? You were stressed out?"

"Spectacularly," Katie laughed self-deprecatingly. "I hadn't been sleeping or eating enough. My body broke and so did my brain in a very loud and public way. Frankly, I'm embarrassed."

"How so?"

"Some of it is pride — like, come on! My labelmates DOYEN and AQ9 experience way more pressure than I do, and here I am, crumbling and adding to their worries." She flushed endearingly. "Some of it is because I caused a lot of trouble over nothing at all. My poor team and agency are busy enough — and I made everything a hundred times worse when all I had to do was take care of myself a little better."

Do-won had to admire Katie's answer. It was likely all true, which made her answer such a convincing lie.

"What about the rumors that you wanted to kill yourself? Or that your boyfriend Tony Lau was abusive? Or that you had had an abortion?" The journalist clearly had taken off her gloves and had gone with the heavy questions.

Katie paused, as if to gather her thoughts, as if she hadn't rehearsed the answer a million times. Do-won could see why she'd done well as an actress. Katie was very believable.

"Well, first of all, Tony is an ex-boyfriend. We broke up at the end of 2020, and it was a really tough time. I'm sure we both felt our fair share of hurt as a result. And as for everything else, it sounds kind of like a K-drama, doesn't it?"

Do-won could tell the journalist wasn't buying it. "So you're saying people lied to the media?"

Katie shrugged. "It wouldn't be the first time or the last," she said. "I don't pretend to know the motives of people who do so."

"So you're not suicidal? Your ex wasn't abusive? You didn't have an abortion?" pressed the journalist.

Do-won watched as Katie rubbed her left wrist over the sleeve. Even though he knew the interview was recorded several days ago, he still willed with all his might that she would stop.

"I would be lying if I said I've never had thoughts of self-harm," Katie finally said quietly. "I wish I didn't. I wish my job — despite its many benefits — didn't also bring a lot of criticism and cyberbullying with it. I'm still a person. What people say on the internet does hurt me, no matter how I try to ignore it."

"Have you been experiencing an uptick in cyberbullying?"

Katie looked incredulously at the journalist. "You could say that. It's not that I wasn't already used to the death threats and rape threats — but also, how does a person get used to that?" Her dark eyes shone with unshed tears. "And then to read all these other lies on top of the constant messages that I should kill myself? It's a lot."

As a lone tear leaked from her beautiful eyes, Do-won recalled that Katie had always been able to cry at the drop of a hat. It had been an entertaining party trick of hers back in her early days at SB Entertainment. He wondered how much of that tear was calculated and how much was a happy coincidence.

Do-won decided that with Katie, there was no such thing as coincidence.

He could tell the journalist understood that any further hardball questions would brand her as incredibly unsympathetic, so she lobbed a lot of easy questions at Katie instead. The rest of the interview was neither informative nor salacious and, thus, Do-won tuned the rest of it out.

He wanted to find Katie and comfort her and tell her that she didn't have to lie to him or his members, but even Do-won recognized that for the fantasy it was. Katie was hiding from them and he didn't know how to bridge that divide. He didn't know if he deserved to.

April 2018

Pardon the pun, but Katie Wu's latest mini-album, "A Murder of Crows," (SB Entertainment, 2018) soars. Just the right mix of intellect and sentiment, Wu weaves fables and hunting terms with scientific and congressional ones to tell stories of community, individualism, and how quickly both can advance or devolve.

Wu's fierce acumen is displayed to great effect in her lyricism while her musicality is obvious in every track. Her instrumentation, melodies, and intricate rhythms are a feast for the ears while her vocals haunt, soothe, and provoke. The chill-inducing "Call a Quorum" is sublime in its aggressive demand for change, and "Flight" is all that is exhilarating and expectant without venturing into cliché territory. But the absolute favorite will no doubt be "They Tell Me You're a Clever One" for its incisive sarcasm and terrifying call to examine the shackles with which we willfully bind ourselves.

- Consequence, February 2018

Absolutely remarkable. Katie Wu is no vapid pop star. "A Murder of Crows," slays on all fronts, rivaling the leading philosophers and thinkers of our times but in song form.

- Dong-A Ilbo, February 2018

[1] Terms of Venery [1:34]
[2] Call a Quorum [3:01]
[3] They Tell Me You're a Clever One [3:48]
[4] Good Hunting [3:16]
[5] A Pitcher Full of Pebbles [2:50]
[6] Blotting Out the Sky [4:29]
[7] Flight [2:42]
- Track list, "A Murder of Crows" (SB Entertainment, 2018)

With this ring, I thee wed
With this ring, I thee dread
I do
I said I would and so I will do
They tell me you're a clever one
And it's true, it's true
You've got me saying, "I do"
I do
When every red flag screams
I should be running, adieu
  - "They Tell Me You're a Clever One" (SB Entertainment, 2018)

To Mattie.
  - Album dedication, "A Murder of Crows" (SB Entertainment, 2018)

Katie should have seen this coming. She had prided herself in being clever, and yet for all her cleverness, she was still here.

In retrospect, it was inevitable. How could she have reasonably expected to stay in Seoul while conducting so much new business in Hong Kong? She could not and yet, she was still baffled at how she had been so thoroughly manipulated even as she'd known she was being maneuvered.

It was humiliating.

After the initial meeting in Hong Kong with her father and Mr. Lau, Katie had returned to Seoul to put the finishing touches on her album, "A Murder of Crows." At the very last second, she swapped in "They Tell Me You're a Clever One" which, on reflection, pretty much summed up how she felt about herself and her utter foolishness.

But she had made her bed, and she would lie in it.

SB Entertainment had understandably been reticent regarding her relocation. Their cut of all promotions and deals outside of Korea was a fraction of what they would have received had she stayed in Seoul. But with Tony's promise of endorsement deals and minor roles in various Chinese dramas, they had reluctantly hired Tony as her manager in Hong Kong at her insistence.

Tony was as good as his word. He ran interference between his father's people and Katie as she worked out contracts and repayment plans. He and his staff set up all her Hong Kong arrangements, and she finished her latest Korean album and its accompanying promotions. It was easy to be lulled into complacency.

And then, Katie moved.

She didn't say goodbye to anyone except Ha-joon, who was briefly re-assigned to some of the trainees. Though he must have resented the temporary demotion, he was still kind and sweet. When she hugged him goodbye at the airport, he told her that she could call him anytime. He would always be available for her.

Katie had tucked that small comfort into her heart, and then she got on the plane.

Tony had immediately made himself indispensable. It was his job as her manager — but also, Katie knew it made her vulnerable. And still, because she was a soft, useless sort, she let him, because the alternative was too hard.

Before she knew it, Katie was fully and wholly trapped.

And then, Tony stopped being nice.

July 2022

Akihiro and Woo-jin opened the door to one of the recording studios only to be startled by Katie screaming in the recording booth. Or at least that's what it looked like she was doing. They couldn't exactly hear much. But Akihiro considered himself a smart man with reasonable powers of deduction. When he glanced at Woo-jin, the rapper seemed to have reached a similar conclusion.

"Should we come back?" he asked Woo-jin. "Or should we check on her?"

Woo-jin mulled it over but his response died on his lips when Katie opened her eyes and saw them through the soundproof glass. She immediately turned her back to them to gather herself.

After a few moments, Katie exited the vocal booth. "I didn't expect anyone to come in so late," she said in lieu of a greeting. Her voice was hoarse and her eyes damp. Akihiro's heart broke a bit.

"Got inspired last minute for my album," said Woo-jin nonchalantly. "I may need your vocals, too. You and Akihiro would sound good together."

"I didn't know you were making another one."

Woo-jin threw his notebooks on the desk. "Surprise," he remarked drily.

"I wasn't able to record for hyung's last solo album so he made sure to include a track for me on his new one," Akihiro offered.

Katie grunted. "I'm afraid my voice isn't in the best shape right now, oppa."

Woo-jin shrugged. "We all need to scream sometimes," he said. "Stay anyway. Wanna know what you think of the track."

Katie sighed and sat on the couch.

"I can't sing this, oppa," Katie said. She sounded furious.

Akihiro was baffled, and from the look on Woo-jin's face, he was, too. Woo-jin had written a sweet, tender love song, and Akihiro was crooning the hook in his best honey voice. Katie's clear tone would complement his vocals perfectly.

"Why not? Is it too high? Does your throat hurt?" Woo-jin asked solicitously.

"I thought you were an honest artist," Katie accused.

Woo-jin just stared at her with his cat-like eyes. "Um, I am? Excuse you?"

Katie scowled. "Then why are you still writing this bullshit?"

Oh, shit. It seemed to Akihiro that Katie was spoiling for a fight.

"Love is not bullshit, Katie-yah."

She snorted in contempt. "In what world is a man sweet and tender in love? In what world is a man gentle?"

"We're sweet and gentle, noona," Akihiro replied softly.

Katie's face embodied derision. "Is that right?"

"It is," Akihiro insisted.

"How nice for you." Katie did not sound as if she meant it. "This song is cruel," she spat. "It's cruel because it's a lie men use. And when it no longer serves them, they show their true face. But by then, it's too late."

"Not all men are Tony, noona," Akihiro finally said.

"Yes, all men," she grated out, her face warped with rancor and rage. "If not yet, then it's just a matter of time."

Woo-jin regarded Katie carefully from under his dark fringe. "You know that's not true. You know we would never."

"Do I?" Her voice dripped in violence. All the fight left her as she slumped in her seat. "It must be me then." Katie's voice hitched. "There's something wrong with me then."

Akihiro rushed to sit next to Katie on the couch, but she recoiled so hard that he stayed back. "No, noona. There's nothing wrong with you."

"Then why did my own father sell me to a monster and leave me there to die?" she asked plaintively.

Katie sank her face into her hands and shattered. This time, when Akihiro and Woo-jin held her, she let them.

Chapter 4

January 2020

"I thought it was you," Katie heard a sleek, cultured voice say. She turned and saw one suave Alton Kuang sidle up next to her at the bar. She tried not to panic.

Katie glanced around to note Tony's location and calculated that she had about five minutes to politely extricate herself from the conversation without alerting her boyfriend. She didn't want to cause trouble for a family friend, but moreso, she didn't want to deal with Tony's temper after the event.

"Hey, Alton. Fancy meeting you here," she said, polite and distant even in the tease. It was safer that way. Katie had only slept with Alton the once and had kept in touch sporadically due to her schedules. Nothing had ever come of it.

Alton smiled equally politely. "When Tony inevitably comes to make a fuss, make sure you emphasize that we're old family friends and that my family expressed interest in working with Bright Horizon Conglomerate."

"What?" She wasn't quite sure she heard him right.

"Our company is called the Empyrean Group," added Alton, "and, in particular, Empyrean International Hotel Management Ltd. is interested in doing some deals with Bright Horizon."

"What?"

Katie normally wasn't so slow on the uptake, but she'd been steadily drinking all evening so that she could endure another event. She usually tried to make as many connections as possible for Tony and herself — not that he ever noticed — but she was still recovering from a bad bout of food poisoning and taking a break (though it did not stop her from drinking).

"We met when you were five and I was seven. You were visiting Kaohsiung and now you're practically my little sister, okay, Mei?" Alton melted into a jovial older brother before her very eyes. "Tony's coming this way now. Play along and call me 'gē.'"

Katie pushed the confusion from her face and played into her bratty, pouty side.

"Ah, I finally get to meet Meimei's boyfriend — I can't believe she didn't see fit to introduce us earlier."

"You would just try to scare him away and say mean things about me."

"I would never." Alton reached out his hand to shake Tony's. "Don't think Shú Gong hasn't been hounding me to make sure I get Tony into our good graces for the last year and a half, Mei."

"Tony, darling," she drawled, "surely you know Alton Kuang of the Empyrean Group? I think we stayed at their hotels when we went to visit Malaysia and Singapore a few months ago."

"A pleasure to meet you," said Tony gruffly. "How do you know my Katie, Alton?"

Alton burst into a hearty laugh and clapped Tony on his thick back. "I've known Katie since she was a child — she's always been an insufferable brat." He leaned in conspiratorially, oozing charisma. "I can't believe she's conned someone of your caliber and discernment into being with her."

"Hey, now. That's uncalled for, Ge. Don't make me complain to Ah-Gong so that your shú gong can scold you," Katie grumbled.

"My granduncle and her grandfather are good friends," Alton confided to Tony. "It's actually why I'm here tonight, Tony — to prevail upon our families' friendship." He crooked a lopsided grin. "Mei, surely you don't mind if I steal your man from you for a bit? We big kids have important business to discuss. It'll likely go over your head entirely — unless you suddenly got smart."

Tony cracked an indulgent smile. "You're welcome to join us, Katie. You might learn something."

"Oh, god, no," she protested. "I leave all that thinking to the two of you, Tony. You know I have no head for business. I'll just be here, decorating the bar."

"We'll catch up later, okay? Maybe we can all meet for lunch?" asked Alton unassumingly. "If that's alright with Tony. He's the one I actually want to sit down with."

"I'll have my assistant check my schedule," Tony said, "but you two should still meet."

Tony gave Katie a meaningful glance. She knew he wanted her to play upon her family connections to his benefit. All he saw were dollar signs when he looked at Alton, and Alton wasn't even trying to play hard to get. It was a tactical mistake he was unlikely to make because it would cost the Empyrean Group millions, and yet, Alton was making it anyway.

"Why bother including me at all?" Katie groused. "Just have lunch with Tony, Alton."

He threw her his best shit-eating grin. "I promised your ah-gong I would check on his American granddaughter. I have to at least go through the motions, right?"

"Whatever," Katie huffed.

"Maybe you could also invite some of your actress and model friends for drinks after?"

Tony snorted as she rolled her eyes. "I knew there was a reason for your unusual friendliness."

"You know how I love models," commented Alton, eyes playful and bright. "Preferably two at a time."

"I'll introduce you to a few, Ge."

"There's a good girl," Alton tossed over his shoulder as he finally steered Katie's boyfriend's stocky body into a private corner.

Katie narrowed her eyes at their collective backs. What was Alton up to?

"Excuse me, miss," the bartender said, interrupting her thoughts. "The sir left this for you."

Katie looked up and the man slid a tiny black Chanel clutch to her. She almost laughed but instead, she surreptitiously put the heavy little purse into her larger one.

The next day after Tony left for the office, Katie slipped into the bathroom with Alton's gift and found an envelope with HK$50,000, $10,000 USD, a SIM card, and a burner phone. With shaking hands, she turned on the burner phone and noted three pre-programmed numbers in the contacts saved merely under the ordinal numbers of 1, 2, and 3.

Katie checked the numbers; 1 had Singapore's country code, while 2 and 3 had Korea's country code. She recognized 2 as Ha-joon's but she wasn't sure who 3 was. She proceeded to memorize the numbers just in case she should have the need. She split the money and hid everything throughout the apartment.

Katie stared at the raised scars on her wrists, and then, she waited.

July 2022

Akihiro had never heard a person cry like Katie. Weep seemed too soft a word. Weep did not adequately capture the way she had sounded, as if her heart had been shattered and she was choking on its pieces.

Katie curled up, so tiny and small, and Akihiro, who had always been the epitome of grace and beauty, felt clumsy and oafish. He mostly just sat next to her on the couch in the studio and held her with Woo-jin. Akihiro was grateful his hyung did most of the heavy lifting of comforting her and murmuring the right words.

When she finally gathered herself, Akihiro could feel her sliding back into her public mask and found that he could not stand the idea of Katie hiding again.

"Don't," he said quietly.

Katie looked at him with doleful eyes, still shining with tears. "What?"

"Don't hide anymore, noona. Please."

Her eyes hardened. She folded more into herself. "Being out is the privilege of the safe."

"You're safe now," Akihiro said.

"You make promises without any idea of what is possible or true, Aki." Katie's voice was biting.

"How can we if you don't tell us?" he insisted. Woo-jin sighed a bone-weary sigh as he glowered at Akihiro.

"You don't want to know, and I don't want to tell you. I refuse to be an object of pity."

"But, noona —"

"Leave off, Aki-yah," Woo-jin snapped, cutting him short.

Akihiro scowled. He knew he had no right to Katie's story, no right to force her to divulge what she did not want them to know.

Of all his hyungs, Woo-jin was the one who cared about hierarchy the most except when it served him to annoy Ye-jun. Akihiro knew better than to test him, except — "But, hyung —"

"Do not take more than what she has already given, Hiro-yah. Especially when so much has already been taken." Woo-jin softened his tone. "Knowing the specifics of what Katie endured doesn't change the fact that she was abused and abused terribly. It just makes it more real to you, but it was always real. Only now, you're making her relive it for your sake."

Akihiro's face flushed with shame. "I — I'm sorry, noona. I just feel so helpless and angry. I hate this for you."

Katie nodded in acknowledgment.

The three of them sat in awkward silence for a bit until finally, Katie said quietly, "Thanks for holding space for me." She got up abruptly and headed for the door only to stop.

"It got so bad that I was almost always drunk when I wasn't working," she whispered. She rubbed her left wrist over her oversized hoodie. "After one particularly bad night, I remembered that the two-year suicide clause on my life insurance policy had ended. I was so drunk and distraught that I thought killing myself was my best option to get my father out of debt and for it all to stop."

Shit.

"Alton got me out. I barely knew him — and he got me out with manager-nim and Mina unni's help. I owe them a life debt that I can never repay."

Katie was right. Akihiro had not really wanted to know.

"Thank you for trusting us with part of your story, Katie-yah," Woo-jin said softly as Akihiro bobbed his head in agreement. "I'm grateful to them, too. And I'm grateful you're here."

Katie dipped her chin and paused as if she wanted to add more, but then she seemed to change her mind and left.

"Shit," Akihiro said, this time out loud.

"Does knowing make it better?"

Akihiro hung his head. "No."

"Yeah," sighed his old friend, "me neither."

March 2020

"Why didn't you say anything sooner?"

It was a perfectly logical question, and yet Katie couldn't help but bristle. She already felt like a fucking idiot. She knew Oh Mina, top SB Entertainment consultant and Ye-jun's new girlfriend was just doing her job, but it was really difficult all the same.

Katie straightened in her seat. "I didn't want to be a burden. It was my fault — my father. It did not seem fair to bring the company into this, especially since I was costing so much money already." She stared at the wood grain on the conference table. "I know I'm nothing compared to DOYEN. I know the only reason the company has thrived these past few years was because of DOYEN and their success."

"Is that why you accepted the relationship with Tony Lau?"

Katie winced. Jesus, Mina did not mince words, did she? "Yes," Katie admitted. She burned.

What did this Oh Mina know of desperation or fear? She was the youngest person ever to make partner at KSI Consulting and intimidated even SB Entertainment's odious head of marketing Lee Mal-Chin. In fact, this woman was the only person to take that fucker down on a consistent basis and, for that alone, Mina was a hero in the office. (Katie, coward that she was, had studiously avoided Mal-Chin as much as possible.)

"I told Song PD to cut you loose, you know," said Mina.

"What?"

Katie knew this had been a bad idea. Mina's client was SB Entertainment, not her. She should have never agreed to this meeting. She should have stayed quiet. She was going to have to find a new agency, but who would want her? Katie would be stuck with Tony forever or have to disappear and start over.

Just disappear and die of shame in a hole somewhere. At least that would be useful.

"You're in Hong Kong and haven't put out a full album in almost two years. Rumors say you're always drunk and your boyfriend is both powerful and dangerous. Yet you just act as if you're fine." The older woman made a moue. "You are obviously not fine."

"If I wanted to be insulted, I could just stay with Tony." Katie got up. This was a waste of time and a risk to her safety for nothing. Alton was mistaken.

"Sit down, Katie." Mina's tone allowed for no dissent. "We're not through."

Katie sat down. "You seem pretty through with me."

Mina sighed and pinched the bridge of her nose. "I told Song PD and Ha-joon-ssi that I was the wrong person to talk to you. Don't worry, Ye-jun knows nothing about this. But neither of them will listen. They think that because I also lived and went to school in the States, I could be helpful to you."

"And you don't?"

"Believe it or not, I'm on your side."

"I can't afford your rate to be on my side."

Mina inhaled a deep, cleansing breath. "I get it, Katie. Your old agency fucked you over with the Johnny situation. Your father is a piece of shit and has betrayed you, just like many of the men in your life. You have no reason to trust me except maybe that Alton, Ha-joon, and Ye-jun trust me. Is that about right?"

Katie grunted in acknowledgment. She knew better than to let the expensive Armani suits, sophisticated bob, and heavy jewelry distract her from the truth. Mina was too keen for her own good.

"You need help, Katie."

"Wow, they pay you the big bucks to state the obvious? Isn't that why I'm here?"

"Beyond this current situation, I mean. You need professional psychiatric or psychological help."

Katie suspected Mina was right, but still, who the fuck did Mina think she was? "I'll take that under advisement. I'm already seeing a psychotherapist. They made me after my last stint at the hospital."

"When you made an attempt on your life? Ah, yes. You just sit there counting seconds and look as if you're expecting the most mild-mannered middle-aged man to murder you or something."

"He's bought and paid for by Tony. How do you know all this?"

"It's my job to know everything concerning this company and its artists."

"You are terrifying."

Mina glowed. "Thank you."

"It wasn't a compliment."

"Sure it wasn't." The older woman huffed a low, husky laugh.

Katie found herself oddly aroused. No wonder Ye-jun was with Mina.

The consultant softened her tone. "Let's make a deal."

Katie raised an eyebrow and gestured for Mina to continue.

"I will do everything in my power to protect you from your father and the Lau family — specifically Tony," she explained, "and in exchange, you will at the very least start taking the appropriate medication and stop drinking."

"Aren't you supposed to protect me anyway?"

"I'm supposed to protect SB Entertainment, an important distinction as you so astutely observed earlier. But I could be persuaded to slightly shift my priorities with the right motivation."

"This is blackmail. I should know. I'm intimately familiar with its machinations."

"Ooooh, machinations!" Mina clapped in delight. "Ye-jun was right! You really do study your Korean!"

"It's a work in progress."

"Katie, Katie, Katie. Blackmail is such an ugly business. Just think of me as a personalized employee incentive program."

Katie couldn't help but snort in amusement. "Alright, sajangnim."

"Call me, unni."

"Alright, unni. Anything else?"

"Yes, actually," Mina said. "I want you to be absolutely clear on something. You were very clever, Katie. You made a way where there was none and protected the people you loved."

Katie's vision blurred. "Oh," she croaked.

"You did the best you could and your best was fine until it wasn't. But unni is here now. And unni will destroy anyone who ever tries to fuck you again."

Katie nodded, unable to speak.

"Alright. Glad we got that settled. Any questions?"

Katie had only one. "Unni, will you please do me the greatest honor and marry me?"

Mina laughed and laughed and laughed. "You're going to be just fine, Katie. I promise."

Katie desperately wanted to believe Mina. But then, COVID-19 happened and the world stopped.

November 2022

Something was up with the DOYEN members. Despite just coming off of their incredibly packed and emotionally charged world stadium tour, they prioritized meeting with Katie individually and as a group. Katie didn't understand. It was like they were taking shifts to make sure she wasn't alone.

"We missed you, that's all," Akihiro said when she confronted them one night when they'd brought jjajangmyeon over to her studio. She always complained that the Korean version of the dish was too sweet, but she always finished her portion.

"I'm not fragile," Katie insisted from her spot on the floor. She was eating over her coffee table, having ceded the available seating to him and his bandmates.

Ye-jun slurped up a bunch of noodles then ruffled her hair even though he knew she hated it. "Who said anything about you being fragile, you fool?" he said, his mouth still full. "We missed you. Why can't we be greedy and take up all your time? What were you doing anyway?"

At Katie's guilty start, Ye-jun laughed. "I knew it," he cackled. "You were doing nothing."

"That's not true," Katie protested and set down her chopsticks. "Someone had to keep Mina unni company while you were gone."

"You know, I'm not too sure how I feel about you and noona being such good friends."

"Please," Katie huffed, "as if we waste any time talking about you."

"That's so strange," mused Ye-jun. "I'm so handsome though."

"I'm surrounded by handsomeness — it's like we're in entertainment, oppa. You're nothing special," she taunted. She lied though. Ye-jun was a cut above even the most attractive men in their business.

"Not nearly the same," the older man brazened as only a man who'd been scouted off the street could. "What do you two talk about then?"

"Honestly? Mostly VISION's Choi Gyeong-gu."

"What?" spluttered Ye-jun, his lips wet with noodle sauce. Katie resisted the urge to wipe it for him.

"He's her bias, you know." Katie grinned wickedly. "I introduced them a few weeks ago. I'll note that you never did unni a solid and used your connections to do so — oh, my god, oppa. Are you okay?"

Ye-jun had turned a bright shade of red, and his bandmates were all in various states of collapse at his distress.

"Did she not tell you?" Katie asked meekly. "I mean, nothing happened. She may have squealed like a little girl and cried a little — ah, fuck. Oppa, please breathe."

"I have to go," Ye-jun squawked as he bolted from the room, leaving his unfinished dinner. "Don't think we're done, Katie," he called on his way out the door.

Katie raised her eyebrows quizzically as the rest of Ye-jun's members succumbed to yet another round of hysterical howling. Do-won and Woo-jin were wiping tears from their eyes.

"Noona, this was the best thing we have ever witnessed," exclaimed Do-won, his brown eyes dancing. "I wish someone had recorded it on video."

"I feel bad," Katie chortled, clearly not feeling remorseful. "We generally talk about books and business."

Jae-sung's interest piqued. "Really?"

"None of that pretentious shit you like, Jae. Strictly romance novels and sci-fi fantasy."

"Noona reads that?"

"Not remotely! But I do and we talk about the ideas in the books. Or we talk business."

"So you don't really talk about Gyeong-gu hyung?" asked Dae-jung, his unreal features arresting Katie for just a moment.

"I didn't say that."

Soo-min sighed happily. "I missed you, noona. No one gives hyung as much shit as you do."

Katie mocked a little bow and fluttered her lashes appealingly. Her soul felt light and she was grateful for such moments of grace.

October 2020

Katie was late.

She had texted Alton, the Contact 1 on her burner phone, and was trying not to panic (and failing miserably). How could she be so careless as to overindulge in alcohol and likely vomit up her birth control? Clearly, the constant barfing and her recent bout of stress-induced diarrhea — seriously, it was a really big problem that had started a few months after moving to Hong Kong — had fucked with her birth control.

At least that's what Katie's frantic Googling in incognito mode had led her to believe.

It was a wonder this was the first time it had happened.

The worst part was that she couldn't even buy a home pregnancy test without tipping off Tony. She was always being watched and she didn't dare ask a friend. Katie had no idea who was trustworthy and who was dependent on Tony's beneficence.

By her online calculations, Katie was about five or six weeks pregnant because — get this shit — apparently during her first two weeks of pregnancy, she wasn't even pregnant! Turns out, the first day of a woman's last period is just part of the pregnancy timeline, which means conception doesn't take place until the end of week two. This greatly concerned Katie since this gave her even less time than she thought to get an abortion.

There was no question of Katie keeping it. She could never allow such a thing to happen. It would be cruel. She would be tied to Tony forever; she would never be able to escape. Tony might be able to let her go — but not if she took his child with her. There existed no scenario where Katie would consider leaving the baby behind. How could she protect such a tiny life from such a malevolent force as the Lau family?

She had to leave Hong Kong. Katie wouldn't be able to get an abortion in the region. No doctor would sign off that the pregnancy threatened her physical or mental health — the only allowable instances of abortion save for fetal defect. Buying such a diagnosis would require massive amounts of money that she didn't have; and even if she did, the Lau family would hear of it.

Katie somehow had to get to Shenzhen in a pandemic and get access to a hospital that would prescribe her the abortion pills before she hit nine weeks. Otherwise, she would have to go to a clinic or hospital for a surgical procedure, and that would be a lot harder to hide.

The clock was ticking and so much time had already passed.

Even though Shenzhen was just a half-hour away, Katie would have to somehow shake her guard and hide the outing from Tony, assuming he would even allow her to leave. He had her passport locked away, and she needed it to enter China proper.

Katie's only alternative would be to escape Hong Kong altogether for Singapore, where she could get an abortion up to 24 weeks. She had no idea how she would hide the pregnancy until then, but she supposed she would cross that bridge when she came to it.

But first things first. She needed to obtain a pregnancy test and somehow take it without alerting Tony.

A week after texting Alton, Katie entered the Louis Vuitton store by appointment and browsed lazily with a glass of champagne in hand. After spending a good ten minutes examining the goods, a young salesperson strong-armed her into buying a bicolor monogram Onthego MM purse.

Katie asked to use the restroom — too much champagne, you know — and brought the new purse in with her. She took out the pregnancy tests hidden in her new purse and peed on several sticks of different brands. She exerted extreme self-control when she saw the double lines appear on one and a plus sign appear on another.

Katie buried the tests in the trash and exited the store. After a few more hours of shopping, she returned to her apartment, locked herself in the bathroom, and texted the results to Contact 1 on her burner phone.

She resisted the urge to lash out. Someone was always listening.

After only two weeks, Katie got bored of her LV purse and made an appointment to check out the Saint Laurent profferings. She eventually was convinced by another knowledgeable salesperson to purchase a small, tasteful saffron-colored, quilted lambskin puffer purse. Thanks to the looser COVID restrictions in Hong Kong, she went out to lunch with her model friends, drank a little too much, and begged off more shopping, citing PMS. She complained to Tony about how awful her cramps were and canceled her dinner.

Katie went home, shut herself in the bathroom, and took the first pill. She resisted the urge to drink a fifth of vodka due to possible interference with the medication. If she'd learned a lesson, it was to not fuck with medication.

The next day, she took the second pill and a few hours later, she was wracked with the worst cramps she'd ever experienced, despite predosing with a ton of ibuprofen. Katie climbed into bed as she bled into overnight pads for the next day or so and obediently took her antibiotics. Katie told Tony her period was heavier than normal and that she was miserable. He tuned her out as she'd expected, saying he would be staying at his apartment for the next few days until her period stopped.

Katie knew he was likely with one of his mistresses — probably Jing Jing, his current favorite. As always, she did not know whether to feel relieved for herself or sorry for the other woman. Both, she decided. She could be both.

November 2022

Akihiro startled awake. A quick assessment of his surroundings reminded him that he'd fallen into a drunken stupor on Katie's very comfortable sectional after coming over with chicken and beer. Katie had passed on the beer but she'd eaten her fair share of chicken wings, forcing all the drumettes on him. He noted that she'd covered him with a bright marigold chenille throw.

He staggered to the banging sounds in the kitchen. "Noona?" he groggily called out as he entered the room, only to briefly register her flying across the space and slapping a hand over his mouth. She had a butter knife in the other shaking hand.

"Quiet! He'll hear you," Katie hissed. She sounded out of her mind with terror.

"Who will hear me, noona? There's only me." Akihiro tried to get the knife from her, but her grip was too tight and he didn't want to hurt her.

Katie pulled him close, her entire body trembling. "You have to be quiet, Aki-yah," she whispered in his ear. "If he finds you, he'll kill you. I'll distract him while you sneak out, okay? Can you do that for me?"

Akihiro's brain frantically tried to keep up. "Do you mean Tony? He's been missing for over a year, noona. He's not here."

"He's found me — we have to hide." Katie panicked. "I won't let him hurt you. I promise. Please, just do as I say," she begged.

"Let me call Ha-joon hyung, noona," suggested Akihiro as he fished his phone out of his pocket. "He'll know what to do."

Katie dragged him under her kitchen table, trying to shield him with her body.

"Manager-nim, it's Akihiro. I'm so sorry for calling so late —"

"Oppa," Katie cried as she pried the phone from him. "He's here, oppa. He's found me." Her voice edged perilously close to hysteria. "He's going to hurt Akihiro — he'll think —"

Akihiro caught snatches of what her manager was saying to her. Something about Alton taking care of Tony already and that she was safe in Seoul. After a few fraught minutes, Katie finally stopped arguing with Ha-joon and calmed down.

"Sorry for waking you, oppa," Katie said abashedly. "I — I thought I was getting better." She paused to listen to whatever Ha-joon was saying. "Don't tell Alton, please. I don't want him to worry." She passed Akihiro the phone. "Manager-nim wants to talk to you."

"Yes?" Akihiro answered.

"Don't leave her alone, Aki-yah," said Ha-joon. "I'll be over right away."

"I can stay with her, manager-nim," he said. "She'll be safe with me, hyung. You forget. I know kendo and aikido."

"Are you sure this is wise?"

"She's my friend, manager-nim. I'll protect her."

Akihiro could hear Ha-joon sighing on the other end. "Okay. I'll come by in the morning before her schedule so you can get home and change." He paused. "Thanks, Akihiro. I'm glad you were there."

"Of course, hyung." Akihiro ended the call and turned to Katie. "It's your lucky night, noona. You get to keep me company until I have to go to work tomorrow."

Katie flashed a wan smile. "I'm sorry, Akihiro."

He crawled out from under the table and stretched his hand out to her. "It's nothing to be sorry for, noona."

Katie grabbed his hand and let him pull her out. And then she hugged him so tightly he couldn't breathe. "Could you stay with me?" she asked shyly.

"Didn't I just say I was?" he teased.

"I mean," she cleared her throat, "could you hold me until I fall asleep?"

Akihiro had no idea how much it cost Katie to ask. She was such a proud creature. "Of course, noona," he said.

He barely heard her whispered thanks as he followed her into her room. Akihiro stripped down to his undershirt and boxers and slid under the seafoam green gingham duvet. Katie was adamant about not having his outside clothes on the bed. She and Do-won were so similar sometimes it was startling. He tucked himself around the curve of Katie's back and lightly stroked her hair until her sobs subsided.

Akihiro kissed her on the crown of her head and breathed her in. She smelled like tangerines and bergamot. Katie released one last soggy breath and relaxed into his warmth. "Thank you," she murmured again before she fell into a restless slumber.

"YAH, Akihiro!" snapped his long-time in-house producer Mun Chin-Sun, who also went by mun.light. She looked annoyed and somewhat frayed around the edges. There were dark circles under her eyes, and despite her outfit being her classic black on black, coffee and food stains were still visible. The two of them had been trapped in the recording studio for too long today.

"I know you worry about a sophomore slump, but if you don't like the direction of your album, just say so," mun.light said. "Don't zone out and waste everyone's time."

"Sorry, producer-nim," Akihiro replied contritely. "I'm thinking maybe I changed my mind. I don't know if I want to focus on the keywords of identity and true self anymore."

Mun.light leveled her steely gaze at Akihiro and seeing his hangdog expression, she melted into a puddle of fond exasperation. "It's okay, Aki-yah. It happens. There's no hard deadline for your album, and maybe if we hit on a theme you're more excited about, we can move more quickly."

Akihiro appreciated mun.light's understanding, knowing it's why she'd meshed so well with DOYEN and their team for so many years. Though she didn't join SB Entertainment until after "Fight 4 U," their first song that hit number one on the music shows, mun.light had felt like family right away.

Something about her intensity and compassion during the creation process made her a safe harbor. She took their musical aspirations seriously and genuinely viewed the songwriting process as a collaboration. Mun.light was a breath of fresh air in a business where producers acted like tiny gods, unable to take feedback or consider their artists' vision.

"Is there a direction you're thinking of instead?"

In truth, Akihiro couldn't stop thinking about Katie. He kept harkening back to that night when she'd fallen asleep in his arms, her scent of citrus and bergamot wrapping him in a pleasant haze. His arms had felt too empty and cold since then, and he wondered if she was laying in the arms of someone else. Then he felt unreasonably upset about the prospect.

But of course, he couldn't make an album about her. That would be weird. Except, maybe he could in a more oblique way?

"Actually, producer-nim," Akihiro voiced tentatively. "I was wondering if we could form an album around the keyword 'obsession.'"

Mun.light tapped her chin pensively. "Like from a fan perspective and you're the object of the obsession?" She sat up straighter in her ergonomic chair. "Or you are obsessed with someone?"

Akihiro replied, "The latter. Like, I can't stop thinking about them and want them even though they may be bad for me."

"Do they want you back?" she asked, taking notes on her notepad.

"I don't know," Akihiro said.

"Okay," said mun.light. "I can work with that. If you want to veer darker, some of these lyrics we were considering about identity and revealing our inner selves can still be used, too. We can also repurpose the beats and toplines you liked."

Excitement thrummed through Akihiro's blood. Maybe he would eventually make an album about identity and his true self, but right now, it didn't speak to him. He wondered if not wanting to show himself in that manner said anything — made him less vulnerable. But then, wasn't it vulnerable of him to admit to obsession?

Akihiro decided he could be real in whatever contexts he chose.

"Maybe we could explore all these different aspects of obsession? Like, in addition to not being able to get someone out of your mind, we can explore when obsession goes wrong — when you want to possess or own someone instead of letting them be their own person," Akihiro suggested.

"Okay, that's definitely darker." Mun.light nodded some more and hummed approvingly. "You sure you want your fans to see you in this light?"

Akihiro paused, considering it more. "I might have a baby face, noona, but I'm not a baby," he decided. "If the fans can't stomach more mature subject matter, they don't have to buy it." The more he thought about the possibilities, the more Akihiro vibed with the new concept. "Maybe we can have songs about loving someone so much that you try your best to help them heal — even if it's hard for you. Even if it causes you to suffer."

"As in you ignore all their red flags? Maybe you think you can fix them even though it hurts you?" the producer confirmed.

"True love looks past people's faults, noona," he insisted. "Love covers all things."

The older woman flicked her dark brown eyes at Akihiro and pinned him with her exacting stare. "Tell me more about this, Akihiro."

Akihiro thought about how his parents had gone through a rough patch when he was a kid, how he'd found his mother crying over their mounting bills when his father had lost his manufacturing job.

"My mother always taught me that if you love someone, you love their whole person, faults and all. She stuck by my father when money was tight and they were constantly fighting about it," he shared. "My father was depressed and not at his best, but she did everything she could to make his life easier anyway. She sacrificed and ate a lot of shit until he finally found a job a year later. She taught me how to love."

"No offense, but is that obsession or love?" mun.light asked delicately.

"It's love, I guess, but can't obsession be the starting point of love?" Akihiro said. "I want to portray how someone can get under your skin, into your blood, and all you want is to consume them. Make them a part of you." He thought of Katie and the scars she'd hidden on her forearms. "You see how they are and how they could be, and you want to heal them. Make them better. Make them see how amazing they are — that they're worth sticking with through thick and thin."

His producer continued examining him, as if she could peer through his soul from staring alone. He wanted to shift, as if he had to defend his point of view. It was a tactic mun.light occasionally resorted to in order to provoke her artists into revealing even more of their thoughts and feelings to incorporate into lyrics or capture in the music.

Akihiro had always found it extremely disconcerting, but he couldn't deny its results.

"You think she'll figure it out when she hears the album?" mun.light asked.

Akihiro was thrown. "Who, producer-nim?"

She snorted. "You think you're so slick," his producer observed. "I'd tell you that it's a bad idea, but you won't listen. You guys never do. She's like catnip to men like you."

Akihiro felt his face heat up and, this time, he did squirm despite his best efforts not to.

He only hoped he was that easy to read because mun.light knew them both. His reputation was at risk if people realized who his album was about, but he was determined to prove Katie wrong about men. After all, did not Alton and Ha-joon both exist? Surely Akihiro could be added to their ranks.

November 2020

Katie was in the shower when Tony arrived on a night she hadn't expected him. While that in and of itself could be mildly alarming, Tony loved to show up suddenly as a means to keep her honest. But since only a week had passed since her trip to Saint Laurent, a sense of misgiving slithered its way into her mind as she finished her ablutions and stepped out of the shower.

Katie should have paid her body more attention when without warning, Tony had her by the throat with a meaty, manicured hand.

"Funny thing happened today," he said, his voice so placid and smooth. "I finally realized what had been bothering me these past few weeks."

He loosened his grip so she could gasp in a breath, but he was just so much stronger than her. So much bigger. Katie knew fighting Tony would just make him hurt her more, so she willed her body limp.

"I likely wouldn't have noticed, but Jing Jing — you know Jing Jing — she wouldn't stop complaining how I hadn't visited her in over a month and I thought, that's strange. You're normally very regular." Tony squeezed as he pushed Katie down to the floor. "But then, a few weeks later, you had an unusually painful period."

What little oxygen that made it to her quickly fuzzing brain gave Katie just enough awareness to know without a doubt that she was absolutely fucked. He knew. Tony knew.

Again, Tony let go just enough so she wouldn't pass out. "I would have chalked it up to stress, but it just didn't sit right with me." His hand tightened once more. "I did a little asking around and wouldn't you know it? After a little incentive, a shopgirl at Louis Vuitton recalled two positive pregnancy tests in the trash when she'd emptied it a few hours after you left."

Katie was so stupid. She knew she should have kept the tests and thrown them out somewhere along the way while running the rest of her errands. She had been too upset to think clearly — and, frankly, too scared of getting caught with the positive tests on her person. She had naively hoped that whatever Alton had paid the attendant would have been enough.

Katie should have known. Once purchased, a person was relatively easy to sell to a higher bidder.

"That wasn't enough proof, though," mused Tony, "and so I found another shopgirl — at Yves Saint Laurent this time — confirming that she'd packed a purse full of pills on the weekend you canceled dinner with me."

Katie resigned herself to her fate. Perhaps in her next life, she could do better.

"I confess, I was a little shocked," Tony said, his voice a silken caress. "I thought you couldn't possibly be so stupid as to take what was mine and rob me of my own flesh and blood."

Katie braced herself.

"I was wrong, though." Tony's fist made contact with her jaw and Katie refused to cry. "And now, I'm owed an eye for an eye, a tooth for a tooth."

Katie thought of her mother and brother and hoped the $100 million policy she'd taken out on her life would be enough to keep them safe. Her body vaguely registered the pain as Tony's hits landed, but her mind had long since dissociated. If she were alive at the end of this, Katie knew she had time enough to feel it in the aftermath.

Her vision slid into darkness.

February 2023

Reviewing a Katie Wu album always requires one to be on their A Game, and "Threading the Needle" (SB Entertainment, 2023) is no exception. Deeply intellectual, Wu's latest Korean release mines all the usages of the idiom "threading the needle," from American football to billiards to business to diplomacy to an actual needle and thread. Wu expounds and expands upon the knife edge each turn of phrase depends, literally and figuratively threading the needle with her music and lyrics.

Of course, heady subject matter does not guarantee good music — and sly bangers don't guarantee depth of verse — but Wu delivers both. Wu flips genres on their head, freely intermixing opera and classical memorably with trap and boom bap beats. The hard-hitting performances are more akin to rap, but somehow, it works.

"(Fr)Agile" lives up to its name by being both delicate and deft, surprising as it explores the balancing act of compromise as a verb and being compromised as an adjective. "But Who Will We Be After?" wonders at the interplay between free will and fate, and ultimately scuttles the question, choosing instead to contemplate the aftermath of what we will become instead. Are our choices worth it, and can we ever recover if we choose poorly?
- IZM, February 2023

Rich in metaphor. No skips. Masterful.
- The Korea Times, February 2023

Katie Wu's "Threading the Needle" should be required listening for all statespeople — aspiring or seasoned alike. Wu exemplifies nuance and keen perceptivity of the state, its roles and its wielding, and most of all, its perfect execution.
- The Diplomat, February 2023

[1] Break Shot [2:34]
[2] Duplicity [2:22]
[3] A Bull in a China Shop [3:51]
[4] Here's Where It All Goes to Shit [3:09]
[5] Failed State [2:42]
[6] Easier for a Camel [3:25]
[7] Backstitch Through Leather [4:14]
[8] Velocity and Vectors [4:27]
[9] The Straits of Messina [4:18]
[10] (Fr)Agile [3:59]
[11] Complicity [4:08]
[12] But Who Will We Be After? [2:43]
[13] Tipping the Scales of Justice [3:05]
[14] The Prince of Talleyrand [3:26]
[15] Diplomacy [4:23]
[16] Like Water [3:39]

- Track list, "Threading the Needle" (SB Entertainment, 2023)

You told me to be shapeless
You told me to be formless
Like water, like water, like water, you said
Like water, like water, like water, you said

And so I became shapeless
And so I was formless
I became water, like water, like water, you said
Like water, like water, like water, you said

So I drowned in the water
Led myself to a slaughter
I was only your daughter
You were only my father

And when I circled the drain (the drain, the drain)
Washed to sea in the rain (the rain, the rain)
You ignored all my pain (my pain, my pain)
Cuz you had nothing to gain (no pain no gain, you said)

I became water, like water, like water, you said
Like water, like water, like water, you said
                    - "Like Water" (SB Entertainment, 2023)

To Unni.
- Album dedication, "Threading the Needle" (SB Entertain-
                                        ment, 2023)

"Noona!" Akihiro exclaimed happily as he peeked inside Katie's studio. He had been on his way to the fifth floor to bother Do-won, and since his, Jae-sung, and Woo-jin's individual music studios were all grouped next to Katie's on the same floor for ease of collaboration, he'd hoped Katie would be in. She was sprawled face down on her deep-seated tuxedo sofa, face buried among the decorative pillows. He'd always liked the abstract painted-on geometric shapes on them, the jewel tones complementing the teal of her couch.

Katie did not lift her head and merely mumbled into the pillows what Akihiro supposed was a greeting.

"You're going to get makeup on your pillows," he observed as he entered the room.

At Katie's rude hand gesture, he considered jumping on her like he would have with his fellow members, except he didn't particularly want to be murdered today. He decided to sit at Katie's mini baby grand piano instead, bypassing the more comfortable matching oversized chair.

Akihiro plonked a few of the keys absentmindedly as he complained, "I haven't seen you properly for weeks."

"Sorry, Aki-yah," she rumbled quietly as she propped herself up. "You know how it gets."

Akihiro did know how it got.

Katie had just released a new album and he knew intimately the exhaustion from the whirl of promotions. She was either in hair and makeup getting ready for a schedule or she was on her way to or back from one. If she was lucky, Katie would be able to grab a few meager hours of sleep between fittings, album signings, and filming like she had been doing when he'd barged in.

Katie repositioned her weary body into one that was more appropriate for company. Her shock of blue hair was pulled back messily into two short ponytails nestled at the nape of her neck, and her makeup was still mostly on her face. The setting spray her stylists used was top-notch.

"It's okay, noona. I've been busy, too," he said.

She flashed him a tiny smile. "I don't know how you and your members do it. I think you performed at every major award show these last few months," she observed. "The rehearsals must have been brutal."

Akihiro nodded. Their end-of-year show stages were often upward of fifteen to twenty minutes long — not to mention that they tried to switch up the performances so that fans wouldn't get bored. His body was still recovering.

"Didn't you have to fly to New York City for the New Year's Eve broadcast?"

Akihiro nodded. "Yeah," he answered, "Do-won had offered to go by himself or with a subunit since we were so tired, but we couldn't do that to our fans."

"Mmmmm," Katie hummed in acknowledgement. "I hope my fellow CHIMERA know how lucky we are."

"'We,' noona?"

"Hmph," his friend snorted. "Of course 'we,'" she grumbled. "I may be a friend, but I'm also a fan."

It didn't matter how often Akihiro fished for compliments about his group, it still meant the world to him how Katie had been a fan first. He loved how she supported DOYEN even when she was so busy herself.

"How are promotions going?" he asked.

Katie shrugged. "They're going. I don't think people really get what it's about though."

"Did you really think they would?" he wondered, genuinely curious. Akihiro didn't consider himself a stupid man, but "Threading the Needle" had completely gone over his head.

"I mean, yes?" she replied, making a face.

Akihiro merely quirked a questioning brow and she sighed.

"Okay, I didn't think most people would get the diplomatic references, but I thought for sure in 'Like Water' they'd catch the subversion of the Chinese idea that women are stronger because they are like water," Katie explained. She pulled out her two ponytails, ran her hands through her hair, and then pulled it back into a loose bun. "Water has no shape or form. It's adaptable, always taking on the shape of the container. It's the strongest substance because water can wear down even the tallest mountains — you just need enough time."

"Uh, and it's subversive, how?" Akihiro asked, adding, "I'm asking for a friend."

"Because in the song, being like water is not a strength — it's her undoing," Katie replied exasperatedly.

"Ah," Akihiro intoned.

It was sounding familiar the more Katie went on about it. Jae-sung had said something similar when Akihiro had asked him to explain a bunch of the concepts after he'd listened when the album first dropped.

"My mother used to tell me I had to be water," she continued softly while tucking her feet under herself. "She said that water could absorb a punch, that it could get into cracks and wear down even stone." Katie pulled the sleeves of her UCLA hoodie past her fingers. "It's such bullshit though. Why do we have to be patient and tolerate men who would punch us?"

"You shouldn't have to," he agreed. Katie looked so fragile that Akihiro longed to reach out and enfold Katie in his arms.

These tiny glimpses into her soul were why he preferred spending time with Katie in her own spaces, why he often conned his way over to her penthouse after work. She was much quieter and more subdued than Akihiro had expected, but he also understood that the life of a public person could drain even the most blatant of extroverts, which he knew she used to be.

Often, he'd find her watching the latest K-drama with Chinese subs (she claimed it helped her study two languages simultaneously) or actively studying Korean. If he had been half as diligent with his English studies, he would've been at Jae-sung's level already. But Akihiro just didn't particularly care about learning English. Korean had been hard enough. There were always interpreters and translators who were so much faster than he could ever hope to be.

If he swung by particularly late, Katie would sometimes reek of cigarettes and every now and then, he'd catch a whiff of alcohol on her. On those nights, he never pressed. He would know to be extra gentle with her, and sometimes — sometimes — she would let slip these bits of herself and he would fall just a little deeper for her.

"I just want to be loved," she continued forlornly. "There must be a love that doesn't require accepting pain."

Akihiro wanted to say that he could love her like that, that he would never hurt her — that he could be good for her — but he couldn't bring himself to. Katie was in the middle of album promotions. She did not have time for what she would surely consider an unwelcome complication.

"Wanna grab dinner?" he asked instead, noting how Katie still seemed a little disoriented.

He'd gotten used to dragging her to dinner with him on days he went into the SB Entertainment headquarters. This usually consisted of him either ordering too much food and whining until Katie agreed to help him finish it or of him whining until she agreed to eat with him in the cafeteria. Either way, he whined a lot. Akihiro wasn't too proud to abuse his status as a dongsaeng. He knew Katie could rarely deny him, Dae-jung, or Soo-min anything.

On the occasions Akihiro had wheedled his way over to her penthouse after work, she either had dinner waiting for him or if he was late, some sort of sustaining snack instead. Since she had no useful knives, she always ordered in despite her insistence that she knew how to cook.

"Ah, I wish I could," Katie said regretfully. "Alton's coming over after he's done for the day. He should be here any minute."

"Oh, hyung's in town?" Akihiro hoped he sounded casual enough. "Wasn't he just here for Seollal?"

Katie's eyes softened, taking on a dream-like quality. "Yeah, he's looking for a celebrity collab for his boutique hotel. Maybe I should mention it to Woo-jin."

Akihiro laughed. "Can Alton hyung afford Woo-jin hyung's brand ambassador rates?"

"More like can Woo-jin oppa pass up an opportunity to discuss architecture and interior elements with a fellow nerd and get paid to do so," she quipped back.

Someone knocked politely on the studio door and Katie bounced up, her entire countenance brightening. "That must be Alton!" she exclaimed and let the older man in, immediately launching herself into Alton's embrace and melting.

Akihiro took in Alton's three-piece suit, polished shoes, slicked back hair, and expensive watch. He observed how possessively the tall businessman held Katie — as if she was his — and Akihiro felt, at best, extreme agitation.

"Hey, Mei," Alton murmured. He gently kissed Katie on the crown of her head and she sighed happily.

Akihiro found himself hating Alton for being able to elicit such a transformation in her. He knew it was selfish and ridiculous. She was allowed to love other people and have other friends. He did not like what this said about him.

"Oh, hey, Akihiro," he added belatedly in Korean upon realizing they weren't alone.

"Hey, hyung," Akihiro greeted.

"Ah, what did I say, Akihiro," Alton protested in badly accented Korean. "Call me Alton. No need for formalities."

"If you're really going to learn Korean, you need to stop bullying people into your cultural preferences, Alton," Katie scolded in English. "Don't be a cultural imperialist."

Even though Akihiro adamantly refused to improve his English, he clearly had spent enough time with Katie and Alton together to pick up some of their banter. They had this conversation every time Alton visited because of Akihiro. He didn't know why he could never remember not to call the foreigner 'hyung.'

"I should just practice my Japanese with you, Akihiro-san," Alton said in Japanese. Akihiro begrudgingly conceded that Alton's Japanese accent was much better than his Korean one.

Before Akihiro could respond, Katie scolded Alton again in English. "Hiro is a person, Alton! His existence is not just to improve your terrible language skills."

"Actually, his Japanese is pretty good, at least from the pronunciation standpoint," Akihiro said in Korean, waiting for Katie to translate into English. "You must do a lot of business in Japan," he added in Japanese.

Alton grinned, wide and friendly. "Thanks, I do!"

It honestly was difficult to hate the man (which was partially why Akihiro did). He stayed a bit longer, chatting in Japanese with Alton for social appearances and also to annoy Katie, who didn't understand any of it. Then, Akihiro excused himself. He wasn't an idiot. He knew when he was extraneous.

All he could think about as he headed to the artist lounge was that Alton was in Seoul again and Katie was living in his penthouse. He wondered if she still had nightmares and if Alton would comfort her. The idea of Alton possibly holding her at night when she was blurry with the edges of sleep made Akihiro stabby.

When he entered the brightly lit room, he was surprised to see that Soo-min was already there, sprawled on a butter yellow easy chair, and playing what was most likely Mario Kart on his Nintendo Switch.

The younger man barely looked up but still remembered to ask, "What are you doing here, hyung? I thought you were going to grab dinner with Katie noona."

Akihiro did not bother preventing the grimace that crossed his features. Soo-min was just as protective of Katie as Akihiro and the rest of his members were.

"Alton hyung's in Seoul," he said dully.

Soo-min glanced up briefly to shoot Akihiro an understanding look.

Akihiro had thought Soo-min would tease him about his attitude, but the maknae likely knew he didn't have much of a leg to stand on. Everyone, including Soo-min's girlfriend Myung-ok, was well aware of the huge crush Soo-min had had on Katie when she'd first transferred to Seoul. The crush had lasted for years, and sometimes Akihiro wasn't sure it had entirely disappeared.

"You know Alton hyung and noona aren't fucking, right?" Soo-min said as Akihiro rifled through the kitchenette cabinets by the lounge entrance.

Akihiro grabbed a pack of roasted seaweed and a diet soda before flopping down on a couch by Soo-min.

"I fail to see why you're telling me this." Akihiro ripped open the pack of seaweed and ate a few pieces.

Soo-min's delicate Cupid's bow pursed in bemusement, his silver lip ring glinting in the light. "He's with some Singaporean model. Has been for the past few months already. They're very happy and hyung's smitten."

Akihiro cracked open his soda and downed half of it. "Again, I didn't ask."

Soo-min threw down his Switch and pointedly swept his gaze over Akihiro's face, a spark in his anime eyes.

"If you have something to say, just say it." Akihiro would not stand for this disrespect.

The younger man just flashed his pearly white teeth. "You don't have anything to worry about with Alton hyung. He's not your competition."

"Why would he be my competition?"

"Right," said Soo-min as he picked up his game and resumed playing. "I'll just leave you to your sulking then."

Akihiro found that he didn't like the maknae's tone — or that smirk on his face. The youth these days didn't understand how to properly treat their elders. "I don't need this aggravation," he grumbled, getting up to leave.

Soo-min waved him off with just a bit too much insolence for Akihiro's tastes. "Have fun not obsessing about noona with Alton hyung!"

Akihiro flipped Soo-min off and left the lounge to the sound of Soo-min's mocking laughter. He stewed all the way home.

November 2020

When Katie came to, her apartment was in shambles.

Tony was convinced that she had a secret phone and secret accounts — and he'd found them. She'd made sure he found a prepaid phone and some random envelopes of cash, too. Katie had hidden them in the obvious places: a cut in the mattress, taped under the nightstand drawer, and behind a shelf.

If he wanted to find something, he'd find it and hopefully stop looking for the real items.

He'd made her unlock her phone and quickly read through her emails and various text message threads, finding only business-related communications with Ha-joon and vapid texts with her model and actress friends.

Katie resisted the urge to immediately check if her things were still in place. How foolish would she be if in her haste, she led Tony right to her burner phone or her emergency money? She'd already paid for her previous folly. Her pride couldn't handle being dumb twice in a row.

She told herself she'd get up from the living room floor eventually. She was just catching her breath — which hurt. Her ribs were probably broken and she'd likely identify more of the injuries in the coming days. But at the moment, her entire body screamed in pain so it was not exactly providing useful data.

In fact, Katie's body could do with being a little less informative and a bit more mysterious, but alas, her pathetic heap of flesh was not taking directions well.

She decided to close her eyes again and deal with thinking later. She was so very tired.

Later, when Katie had finally hauled herself off the hard wooden ground, she found and charged her dead cell phone, then texted Ha-joon about some pressing business matters. *Manager-nim, I forgot to buy Jun oppa a present. Could you send him 501 bags of jelly candies by his birthday? Hopefully, you can get it in before the Christmas rush since his birthday is so early in the new year?*

501 bags? You sure? came Ha-joon's quick reply. *That will be difficult to do.*

501. If not, it's ok. As long as it's before Seollal. Anytime after and I'm afraid it will be too late.

Okay. Anything else? Classic Ha-joon. Always going above and beyond.

Thx, oppa. Sorry for all the trouble.

You are never any trouble.

Katie resisted the urge to cry. She desperately clung to the hope that one day, she could make her miserable life worthy of her friends' efforts. But until then, she just had to make it to that day.

Chapter 5

As expected, Akihiro of DOYEN shatters streaming and sales records with his second solo EP album "Obsession" (SB Entertainment, 2023). The album chronicles the rise and fall of an obsessive romance and is the much-awaited follow-up to his debut solo album "Home = Prison" (SB Entertainment, 2021).

Akihiro opens with the light and buoyant "First Sight," a brief and rapturously happy intro reminiscent of the giddiness one feels when first encountering someone magical. The mood continues up, ramping more and more hype in tone and feel, filled to the brim with love and expectation.

The optimism takes a sharp left with title track "See Me," a pleading ballad begging to be noticed and have their love returned. "See Me" is sublime, full of throbbing bass, quivering strings, blaring brass, and pulsing synths. From there, the songs descend into despair and fury, exploring the dark and heavy feelings of unrequited love (and perhaps commenting on the unbalanced nature of fans to their artists). "Regret" is heavy,

*the overwhelming wall of sound leaning into madness instead
of contemplation.*

- Billboard, April 2023

Sultry and disturbing. We're obsessed.

- The Guardian, April 2023

[1] First Sight [1:16]
[2] Fire [2:42]
[3] Heartbeat [3:01]
[4] See Me [3:09]
[5] Love Me Tender [3:12]
[6] Crash and Fall [2:39]
[7] Regret [2:35]

- Track list, "Obsession" (SB Entertainment, 2023)

I hate the sun
The way that it kisses you
And anyone
If they get to hear your voice
Say their name
It isn't fun anymore, no

You were the one
I was willing and waiting to
Give the sum
Of my all and my everything

Played your game
It isn't enough anymore, no

I want to be only you and me
We, we, we, only you and me
Can't you see you're killing me
I love you so much that it hurts and seethes
Tenderly
Tenderly, even so
                    - "Love Me Tender" (SB Entertainment, 2023)

To all the lonely hearts.
     - Album dedication, "Obsession" (SB Entertainment, 2023)

Akihiro could not stop thinking about what Soo-min had told him. It had been weeks, and despite his imminent solo album release, he could not get Katie out of his mind. He supposed it didn't help that "Obsession" was literally about her (or at least, the idea of her).

It wasn't even that he'd thought Katie and Alton were fucking — just that Alton occupied a space in her heart that no one else could possibly fill. Although Akihiro supposed that would be true for anyone in general, it seemed especially evident when Katie was around the Singaporean chae-bol.

When Alton was in the room, she constantly oriented herself to him — as if she were lost and he was her Polaris. Katie normally seemed so self-contained, so self-assured, so self-confident. But around Alton? The only word he could think of was that she melted. She became so soft, so pliable around him — so much younger than her 29 years — it was as if she trusted her entire being with this man.

This state of vulnerability was what Akihiro found himself envying. What would it be like to be Katie's person? What would it be like to be the one to whom she turned for protection and safety?

Akihiro decided he would try and find out.

"Noona, are you free for dinner tomorrow?" Akihiro asked from his seat on the overstuffed sofa in Katie's music studio. He hugged one of her accent pillows to his chest, needing to ground himself as he waited for her answer.

Katie looked up from the Korean novel she was reading on the other end of the sofa and blinked. "Of course, Akihiro. You know I always have time for you." Katie paused. She slid in a random napkin to mark her page and tossed the book onto the scattered notebooks strewn all over her coffee table. "Wait, don't you have rehearsals for your solo comeback all this week? What's this about, Akihiro? Are you stressed out or anxious about the album?"

"I am, a little. You know how there's always worry about a sophomore slump," Akihiro acknowledged.

Katie's face melted into concern. "I suppose the Japanese version of your first album doesn't count as a second one, but from the snatches mun.light unni has shown me, I don't think you need to worry."

"Well, I need a break anyway," Akihiro said, "and I miss you."

"We're literally hanging out right now," she retorted. "If you just want to play hooky like you are now, you don't have to ask me so formally. We have dinner all the time."

Akihiro was normally a lot smoother. He would have something flippant or full of innuendo to say and, of course, he was also a DOYEN member. That always helped. But truthfully, he was flustered. Plus, Katie had caught him, too. He was playing hooky, and he also loved spending time with her. It was all true at the same time.

He had to make his intentions more obvious.

"It's not like that, noona," he scrambled. "I wanted to ask you to dinner — like a date."

Katie eyed him quizzically. He could feel Katie's bewilderment radiating from her. He had hoped she would be pleased.

"I asked for tomorrow because I'd already asked for the time off and I checked with manager-nim to see if your schedule was clear," he explained.

"Wait, what? Like a date?" It seemed as if Katie's brain finally caught on to what he had said. He was wondering when it would register.

"I really like you, noona," he said. "I was hoping you could learn to like me, too."

"I like you just fine, Hiro-yah."

Akihiro sighed. "I was hoping you could learn to see me as someone other than a dongsaeng."

"Didn't we do this already?" Katie's face was suddenly a closed book. "I feel like we did this already."

"Not really — unless you count making out once."

"If you just want to have sex with me, Akihiro, I suppose we can do that. Finish what we started a few years ago and satisfy your curiosity?" Katie flushed and shifted on the couch. She leaned over and shuffled her notebooks into a neater pile. "I don't know if it will be as you expect. It's been — I don't know if I even want sex anymore. But I'm willing to give it a shot. You seem like a good lay."

Akihiro was horrified. It must have shown on his face because Katie quickly backtracked.

"That sounds awful, doesn't it?" she said, her voice breaking. "I really don't know how to talk about negotiating a friends-with-benefits situation anymore. Maybe I never did."

"I'm asking you on a date because I want to be with you, noona. Because I really like you." Akihiro paused for a second. He had a feeling he had one chance to get it right. "Of course, I find you sexually appealing and want to have sex with you if you wanted — but it's not required of you. You don't have to fuck me just because I want you to."

Katie refused to look his way and instead stared at the framed Batman poster on the wall. "What if I never want to, Akihiro?"

"Then, I suppose we'd have to cross that bridge when we get to it." Akihiro scooted closer to her and turned her chin so he could look her in the eyes. "Sex is important to me, but I'm willing to wait and discover with you your comfort levels."

"I tried, you know," Katie said, pulling back abruptly. "I've had sex with people since Tony. A lot, actually. I mean, not as much as you —"

"Noona...," Akihiro whined. He wasn't ashamed of his past, he just wasn't expecting her to bring it up so baldly.

"Oh, am I supposed to pretend you didn't fuck your way through the last decade?"

"Well, no," admitted Akihiro. "I just —"

"I don't care about your body count, Akihiro. I merely meant to say that I tried. I slept with a lot of people — and no one could — I —," Katie sighed. "I didn't enjoy it. Not anymore. And then I stopped trying to see if I would."

"Have you tried by yourself?"

"Are you asking me if I've gotten myself off, Hiro?" The corner of Katie's mouth lifted just a fraction.

Akihiro felt his face burn. "Maybe?"

"A few times just to see if I could. I never particularly found it worth the effort. The doctors said it was likely a side effect of my medications," she said, pointedly not looking at Akihiro again. "They even offered to adjust it for me. But honestly, I had just found a dosage that didn't make me feel crazy. I really didn't want to go through the effort again just so I could come."

"I feel like we're doing this dating thing backwards," Akihiro confessed. "Doesn't this usually come up later?"

"I believe people should have all the facts before jumping into something ill-advised. You still want to date me?" Katie asked, somewhat incredulously.

"I told you, noona. I really like you. I really, really like you." Akihiro leaned into Katie's space just enough to make his intentions clear. "That's why I'm asking you on a date."

"Oh."

He could tell she didn't believe him. "You have no idea your effect on me, do you?" he asked.

"Um, no?" Katie folded her hands into her lap. "I swear I'm not fishing for compliments."

"I don't mind telling you," he said softly and resisted the urge to grab her hands. "I mean, of course, you're super hot — but everyone in our industry is. You're not special in that sense."

Katie rolled her eyes. "Thanks. Forget I asked."

Akihiro sensed embarrassment and shame roiling from his friend. He had wanted to assure her that it wasn't just because she was gorgeous, but that had backfired. "Noona, that came out wrong."

"It's fine, Akihiro. I don't think this is a good —"

"You're brave," he cut in, this time grabbing one of her hands with both of his. His thumb rubbed lightly over her knuckles and she shivered involuntarily. "You're smart — like so fucking smart — maybe Jae-sung hyung smart or smarter." Akihiro thought he saw the corner of Katie's mouth lift again in amusement. "And you're funny, clever, kind, and talented — and just — you're amazing, noona. You're amazing."

Katie's eyes widened and stared at him in wonder. "You're not just saying that to make me feel better?" she asked, her voice hesitant and small.

"I swear," Akihiro replied huskily. "I can't stop thinking about you."

She regarded him warily for a few beats. "I suppose you expect me to pay since I'm the noona," she grumbled.

"Is that a yes?" He grinned as endearingly as he could muster. "And don't be ridiculous. I asked so I'll pay." He could tell she was still flustered from the entire conversation and secretly exulted that he still had his lethal charm.

Katie sucked in a steadying breath. "Okay," she replied.

"Great!" he exclaimed and squeezed her hand tightly. "I'll pick you up at eight." He couldn't wait.

September 2025

"Wonnie!!" Katie exclaimed as she got up from her seat at her workstation and rushed to him, enveloping him in a hug. "What brings you back to the office? I thought you were supposed to be on vacation with Ae-cha for at least another few weeks."

"Ae-cha wanted to come back early," Do-won said, shrugging. He pulled off his Supreme beanie and tucked himself into the teal easy chair near the studio door.

Katie flashed a wicked grin. "She's got the right idea, though. Staycations are way less stressful. Are you re-christening every surface of your apartment?"

"Ah," mumbled Do-won, flushing. "Not exactly, noona."

Katie frowned. "No offense to Ae-cha, but is she stupid?"

"Noona," he said warningly. "Let's not exaggerate."

Katie crossed over from her desk setup and leaned down toward him. She grabbed him by the chin and stared deep into his eyes. "You are a magnificent man, Do-won. When I first found DOYEN, I thought you were the visual. Your looks were so striking, and your jawline was so sharp. And the way you moved — Jesus."

Do-won swallowed. Katie was just a bit too intense for his comfort level, but he appreciated her attempt at affirming him.

"I know what I am," he said instead. He knew he was the least attractive of all the DOYEN members. He had long since resigned himself to this fact.

"I suppose you probably thought it was unhygienic." Katie sighed as he smothered a laugh. She put aside some of her throw pillows and sat on the couch next to his seat. "You're not wrong, but there's something fun about fucking in every corner of an apartment. It's not comfortable by any means, but it's definitely fun."

Do-won raised a doubtful brow and Katie deflated.

"Okay, okay. It's not actually fun and as far as ideas go, it's great in theory and terrible in execution." Katie leaned back toward him and squished his cheeks. "You always call me on my bullshit, Wonnie. I've missed you."

"I didn't even say anything!" he protested.

"You didn't have to. It's all over your face."

Do-won didn't know how he felt about that. He used to pride himself on keeping his face camera ready, always well within the confines of certain acceptable ranges of emotion. He knew better than to have his real thoughts shine through. Perhaps it just meant that he was finally more himself and unbothered about what people could read from him. Or perhaps, it took a faker to recognize another.

Do-won hated himself for that last uncharitable observation. He'd thought he'd grown past these assumptions about Katie.

There was nothing wrong with having extremely defined and established boundaries between public and private personas. And Katie — Katie was definitely extremely private.

He wondered, though, if maybe she would open up more to someone who also extended her that same courtesy. For a few months before she and Akihiro had started dating, Do-won had felt Katie slowly unfurl, the delicate petals of her trust particularly fragile.

At the time, he had felt a surge of bitterness that he wasn't the only one she was allowing herself to be vulnerable with, that it was any of the DOYEN members who happened to be present. But now, Do-won realized it wasn't any less precious just because Katie happened to include him within a small circle of trust. Now, he recognized it for the honor it had been.

"She wants to take a break," Do-won said.

Katie's face broke into sadness and sympathy. "Oh, Wonnie. I'm sorry."

"She said that we got serious too fast and too soon. And that she was caught up in the excitement of it all." Now that Do-won had started, he couldn't stop. "But now that we're two years in, the realities of my fame are too much."

"Oh, Do-won."

"She says she wants to take a break, noona," Do-won said as he sank his face into his palms, "but I think she wants out."

Do-won started to sob and he couldn't stop. He vaguely registered Katie squishing in next to him and hugging him, murmuring comforting words and shushing him as if he were a child. He supposed he was blubbering like a child so at least it seemed fitting.

He cried for a long time and when he finally looked up, Katie's face was wet with her own tears. For some reason, her sadness on his behalf made him feel shame and comfort all in one. Do-won knew in the grand scheme of things, his current pain was small and dumb, but it was still his. He was grateful she was willing to take on part of it with him.

"I'm sorry, friend."

Do-won sniffled. "Yeah, me, too."

April 2023

Katie was having a crisis. "Alton, help!" she whined into her phone as she FaceTimed her dear friend. "I don't know what to wear!"

"I thought you were just having dinner with Akihiro?" he asked, his voice full of mirth.

He was at least half a bottle into his favorite merlot and already in bed. She recognized the understated gray and white striped linens and his navy and dark leather headboard.

"I am!"

"So what's the big deal? You've had a million dinners with Akihiro." Alton turned and fluffed his pillows before turning back to the screen. His face was kind and curious.

"I —," she paused.

Katie really didn't know why she was freaking out over what to wear. The man had literally seen her in various states of casual dress — including her ratty pajamas and even her go-to period clothes when she was just a giant bloated mess swathed in sweats and a low-sitting baseball cap.

"I don't know! It should seem special, I guess? Because it's a date? I don't want him to feel bad that I didn't take it seriously." She stared blankly at her neatly hung dresses and jackets. She eyed the rows of her displayed shoes.

"You've gone on dates before, Mei. Just wear what you'd wear to one of those."

"I suppose you're right," Katie replied as she continued scanning the organized shelves of her walk-in closet. After a few more moments, she wailed, "Nothing! I have nothing!"

Alton sniggered and she hated him for it. "Why don't you wear that silver halter dress? The one with the super low back?"

"It's not too slutty?"

"Nothing wrong with slutty," he parried. "Wear it with your black moto jacket with all the studs and combat boots if you're worried about it."

"I'm going to look like a female version of Soo-min," she grumbled.

"According to all the fan fiction I've read about Akihiro and Soo-min, that might be just the thing."

Katie grunted. "If the fans only knew," she sighed. "Assuming I go with your Femme!Soo-min look, what jewelry should I wear?" She angled her phone so Alton could see into one of the jewelry drawers set in her custom island. She pulled out a few more so he could see the breadth of her options.

"Do you want to continue with the tough girl image or do you want to soften it up?"

"I don't know. I don't care. I just want to stop thinking about this ridiculous farce of a date." Katie slammed the offending drawers shut and looked at her watch selection instead.

Alton was quiet and she mentally counted to see how long he could resist from commentating. She made it to sixteen before he broke in.

"I don't think Akihiro cares what you wear, love."

"That's almost worse, Alton. I'm just going to end up disappointing him."

"Then why are you going on a date with him?" Her friend sounded exasperated. Alton sipped his wine and set the glass back onto his dark wood nightstand. "Why are you doing this if you don't actually think it will work out?"

Katie stopped and forced herself to really think instead of constantly reacting. "Because if I just tell him it's a bad idea, he won't believe me. But if I give it a shot, and he experiences it firsthand —"

"Wait, are you sabotaging this? On purpose? He's a good guy, Katie. I don't think he likes me, but don't do this. This is beneath you."

Shame pulsed through Katie. "That's not what I meant, Alton. I don't fuck with people's emotions like that."

"Then what did you mean, love? Surely, you don't think that just being yourself will eventually convince him you're bad news?" At her sudden lack of response, Alton looked so sad. "Meimei, Akihiro would be lucky to date you. You know this, right?"

Katie slunk back into her bedroom and threw herself onto her bed. "It's a lot, Alton. I'm a lot."

The plaintive tug of his lips sent a spike of guilt through her. "You're worth it, Katie. I wish you could believe that what happened to you — what you chose was not your shame. The shame is all your father's and Tony's and his family's. You — you are a marvel. You survived."

Katie was quiet for a long time. So long that the silence stretched awkward and thick. She was grateful Alton was used to her silences and just let her breathe.

"I'll make you proud one day, Alton. I will make up for all the sacrifices you made for me."

Alton sighed, impatient and annoyed. "You already make me proud. Live your life, love. You owe me nothing."

September 2021

Katie didn't want to go.

The prospect of returning to Seoul terrified her after nine months of constantly moving and hiding, but she was determined.

When she'd visited the States back in April for her COVID vaccine and to see her mother and Mattie, two bodyguards had accompanied her at all times. Katie was grateful that her mother and brother had also been assigned guards, though Alton had assured her their safety had been guaranteed through whatever deal he'd managed between Empyrean International Hotel Management Ltd. and Bright Horizon Conglomerate.

Alton had even bought her father some measure of safety, but Katie had not cared to hear it once Alton had promised that her father wouldn't contact her. She never wanted to see her father again.

Katie had tried to make sense of the details but her memory was shit of late. There were holes in her mind, and all too often, she couldn't recall information she'd just heard or read.

She hadn't even recalled telling her college roommate Ellie Poon that she'd be home for a few weeks. When Ellie had insisted on visiting from Los Angeles, Katie had been too ashamed to say no. Katie knew she'd let their friendship fall to the wayside when she'd moved to Hong Kong, because it had exhausted her to lie all the time. She'd chosen to drop off the face of the earth instead.

Her guilt had compounded when Ellie had screamed and enveloped Katie in a bone-crushing hug after years of absence. She'd taken one look at Katie and demanded the whole sordid story. Katie, feeling emotionally overwhelmed, had acquiesced and given her a bare-bones version.

Ellie had been one of the only people Katie'd told, and even then, that had taken too much out of her. The mixture of pity and helpless fury on Ellie's face had convinced Katie not to share with anyone else. She had not wanted to impose, to change the way her friends saw her. She had not wanted to be recast as a victim.

So when Katie visited Danny Chen, her best friend from elementary school, and he had asked about the bodyguards, she'd fed him some bullshit about stalkers and people she'd pissed off. She supposed it wasn't entirely a lie. He'd seemed concerned but ascertained from her noncommittal responses that she'd not wanted to discuss it further. Out of deference to her feelings, Danny had changed the topic to old memories. Except when Danny had changed the subject, Katie had no idea what they were talking about. Katie had just laughed and nodded along.

Katie's brain still felt as if it were wrapped in a persistent fog despite the anti-anxiety meds she was taking. Every movement seemed to be through molasses and she just couldn't keep up. Even her bones were exhausted.

She did not know how she was going to get her shit together. SB Entertainment would take one look at her and know she was a fraud. She was a shell of a person.

Alton, dressed impeccably, as always, in a designer white tee under a royal blue blazer with distressed jeans, found her vomiting into the toilet when he'd come home to accompany her on his private jet. "Ah, love. This could all be avoided if you just married me instead."

"What would your model friend say if you did?" Katie snorted. She rose from the floor and rinsed her mouth in the sink. She felt dowdy and grimy in her loose linen pants and old UCLA hoodie. The taste of bile in her mouth did not help.

"She'd be disappointed," he said, "but would ultimately move on to the next rich man in her life. Marry me, Katie."

She pinned him with a glance, fully aware how ridiculous it was to be having this conversation in his bathroom where she'd been bent over his toilet not five minutes prior. "What, Alton? So we can hate and resent each other in a few years?"

"I love you, Katie."

Katie was going to cry. Why was he doing this? "I love you, too, Alton."

"Then why?"

Alton looked gutted, and she was responsible for him being this way. If Katie could only just give him this one thing. Instead, she brushed past him into the hallway and briskly walked to his sitting area full of sleek, modern furniture. It was cool and collected just like Alton.

She did not belong there.

"You know why. I owe you a life debt — one that I can never repay." Katie tried to soften her voice for him. "I — I can't tell if I love you because I love you or because I owe you. And I can't live that way, always beholden to you."

"You know I would never use it against you," he insisted, his velvety brown eyes imploring.

Katie wound her way past the round, gunmetal coffee table and the cream-colored silk sofas. She shielded herself behind the furniture even though she knew Alton would never hurt her.

"You would resent me," she said. "Don't you want to be loved for who you are and not out of some misplaced sense of obligation or gratitude?"

Alton took a step toward her, but then stopped as if needing the distance, too. "My love for you is intertwined with who you are and what we've been through. Why can't it be both? I accept both, why can't you?" His normally genial visage twisted. Katie didn't know what to do.

"Why did you save me, Alton? You barely knew me." She gripped the back of his couch.

"Because he was killing you, and I couldn't stand by and watch."

Katie didn't understand. She had always meant to ask, but she had been afraid. "You had no obligation to me. None whatsoever. Why did you help?"

She could feel it when Alton's resolve broke. "Your grandfather," he said. "He'd heard rumors from his other business associates and begged for help from Shú Gong."

Katie was mortified. "But why you?"

"Who else could?" Alton shrugged. "Shú Gong said your ah-gong lent us money at a crucial time. That without it, we would have been wiped out." Alton ran his capable hands roughly through his dark hair. "When our family got back on its feet, your ah-gong refused to let him return a penny more than he was owed." He flicked an imaginary piece of lint off his sleeve. "Everything we have is because of your grandfather. We, too, owe a life debt."

"That hardly sounds the same at all."

"Correct," he agreed. "Your ah-gong saved my whole family and asked us only to save you. We are still in your debt."

Katie knew Alton had told her to absolve her of any obligation — but his words had the opposite effect. She felt, instead, the ponderous weight of families linked by money and blood.

"I made you do horrible things, Alton." Katie's voice was barely above a whisper. She dared not speak any louder. She did not want to acknowledge what he'd done to protect her.

"I would do it again in a heartbeat." He swallowed hard. "Stay with me, Katie. Let me love you and keep you safe."

Katie let herself go to Alton. She wrapped her arms around him, squeezing him as tightly as she could. "Let me go, Alton, and if it's meant to be, I'll come back to you."

Alton kissed her lightly and let her go.

April 2023

Akihiro didn't know what he was expecting, but it was not this. "You look like a girl version of Soo-min."

Despite knowing her door code, Akihiro stood awkwardly in the hallway of Katie's apartment complex, waiting for Katie to invite him in. He had wanted the night to feel like a real date but, in retrospect, perhaps that was too much to expect.

"Excuse you, I'm much prettier than he is." Katie pouted fetchingly even as she opened the steel reinforced door wider to let Akihiro in.

"That goes without saying, noona," Akihiro said politely as he entered her apartment. She wasn't wrong, but neither was he. He felt overdressed all in Yves Saint Laurent from his button-down to his trademark black Chelsea boots.

Katie's face fell. "Should I change?"

Akihiro went into damage control mode. He handed her the bouquet of pink peonies he knew she loved. "You look amazing and hot and you absolutely should not change."

Katie clearly did not believe a word out of his mouth, but she went into the kitchen, found a vase, and set the peonies in water. Then she grabbed her purse and followed him dutifully out of her apartment. The rest of the date did not fare much better.

First, the restaurant couldn't find his reservation. Though Akihiro was one of the most recognizable faces in all of South Korea, the maître d' did not give any shits and was brutal in his dismissal.

Katie tugged on his sleeve, eager not to make a scene. "Akihiro," she whispered, "it's okay. Let's go somewhere else."

Akihiro scowled and had he not remembered his behavior reflected on the rest of his group, he would've likely given the man what for. But as he was always cognizant of his public image, as well as trying desperately to impress Katie, he did not.

"I like oppa's restaurant — and they always make room for us," she suggested.

Still in a terrible mood, Akihiro took Katie to Heiwa, the Japanese restaurant co-owned by Ye-jun and Ye-jun's older brother. At least the food was authentic enough.

Then, he ordered hot sake without thinking and remembered belatedly that Katie didn't drink — or at least, still kept the party line of not drinking. He knew there were some bad nights where she'd indulged in the handle of vodka under her bed. He'd never said anything and had allowed her her secrets.

Akihiro apologized profusely and Katie apologized back for the inconvenience.

He was miserable.

The date went from bad to worse. He burned his tongue and then bit it. He spilled sake all over the table and in his attempt to clean that up, he spilled hot tea all over Katie. He forgot how to converse like a human and their conversation was strained and full of awkward silences.

To top it all off, he'd forgotten his wallet. Katie was a good sport and paid, joking that it had clearly been his plan all along and it was her duty as noona to pay for dinner anyway.

Akihiro drove Katie back to her apartment in fuming silence, barely able to utter a word. He hovered at her door, unsure if he would be welcomed in her home. Katie merely arced a concerned eyebrow and waved him inside.

"Do you want to stay the night?" she asked. "I'm not going to have sex with you, but you're welcome to stay over." She guided him to her living room, pausing only to smell the peonies sitting on the console table in the hallway.

After the evening they'd had, Akihiro couldn't believe what Katie was offering. "You sure?" he asked dejectedly.

Katie tossed him a wry grin and sat him at her L-shaped sectional. "I'm going to get ready for bed. I have extra toothbrushes and you can always use my products if you want." She leaned over and kissed him lightly on his cheek. "Please stay, Aki-yah. I don't want the night to end yet."

Akihiro swallowed. "Okay, noona," he said.

This time, Katie flashed him a happy smile and went off to change and wash up for the night. By the time he was ready for bed, she was already scrolling on her phone under the covers.

"You going to join me or are you going to stew a bit longer?" Katie asked lightly.

Akihiro wanted to cry in frustration. "I'm sorry, noona. Tonight was a disaster."

Katie set her phone on the bedside table and swept back the blankets, patting the space beside her. "Don't worry about it and come to bed, Aki-yah. At least it was memorable," she reasoned, a smile tugging at her lips.

Clad once again in only his undershirt and boxers, Akihiro reluctantly climbed into bed next to Katie. Before he could curl around her, she turned so that he was the little spoon instead. She tucked her chin over his shoulder and kissed him softly on the curve of his shoulder.

"Let's start over tomorrow, okay, Hiro? As the Chinese say, don't put it on your heart."

Akihiro sighed and sank into the solidity of her body behind him. "I wanted tonight to be perfect for you, noona. You deserve some perfection."

He felt the puff of her breath against his neck as Katie tutted affably.

"You have no idea how appropriate tonight was, Aki-yah. I am a disaster — and it's better for you to know up front."

"You're not —," Akihiro started to protest.

"Ach, Akihiro," she scolded. "Let's not start off with a lie, hmmm? You know why I agreed to a date? Because you already know I'm a mess and you still want to try anyway."

Akihiro stilled. Somehow, he heard the truth of what Katie was trying to tell him. "I can be a safe space for you, noona. I want to be a safe place for you."

"I'd like that." Katie kissed him again, this time at the base of his neck. "I see how kind you are to your fellow members and staff, how you listen to them and provide comfort when they need it." She placed another kiss on his neck, this time a little higher. "I see how you tell your fans that no matter what happens in their lives, they will always have your support." She kissed him just below his ear, soft and warm. "I see how you go out of your way to make sure I eat and that I'm not alone too often." She placed her lips right at the shell of his ear and whispered, "You are lovely and sweet, Akihiro, and I'm glad you asked me on a date."

Akihiro let himself feel the truth of Katie's words. He let her kisses soothe him and he drifted. He couldn't help but feel that as far as first dates went, tonight hadn't been so bad after all.

October 2025

"Hey, noona," Do-won said as he entered Katie's cluttered studio.

It was a far cry from his own meticulously tended space of equipment, collectibles, and ambient lighting. Notebooks and closed boxes of what must have been her lunch littered her coffee table. Empty water bottles were lined up on her desk along with piles of more books and notebooks. The light was bright and warm.

"I was wondering if you had time to help me out a bit," he said.

Katie looked up from her reading and took off her reading glasses, smiling with welcome from her easy chair. "Sure, Wonnie. What's up?"

"I was wondering if you could teach me how to write songs."

He did not understand why he felt so sheepish and embarrassed. He was a multi-award-winning artist and, like Katie, a full member of the Korean Music Copyright Association (KOMCA). And yet, he felt like a child in comparison to her and some of his bandmates. He sat on her sofa and awaited what he hoped would be a positive response.

"Whatever for? You're already so good at it. Your tracks were my favorite on the last few albums. I still listen to 'Fog of War' at least once a day."

"Really?"

"Really. The change up in your flow and the funk guitar, man," Katie commented. "Oh, and you can't forget that high swinging bridge. Best shit ever."

"I — I just thought that I would have more respect as a producer or songwriter in the industry by now." Do-won felt naked and petty. He didn't understand how even after a mixtape and two solo albums of his own, no one ever approached him for anything more than a feature. "And not that I am jealous of Jae-sung hyung or Woo-jin hyung. They're both amazing and have been producing for much longer than I have, so I'm not trying to be better than them...," Do-won trailed off. He didn't know exactly what he was trying to say, but he felt foolish.

"Ah," Katie said. "Personally, I don't think you need my help. I think you're a fantastic producer and songwriter already."

Do-won's spirits drooped. He hadn't expected her to agree, but he also had hoped —

"But, okay," Katie said. "Maybe you don't exactly need to learn how to make a song, but perhaps you would just like to learn a different way to approach writing music and lyrics. Like a different tool in your toolbelt. Not everyone can be like Woo-jin oppa and write a song a day. That man's a machine."

Do-won had worked with Woo-jin for fifteen years and he still didn't know how he did it.

"Yeah?" Do-won was elated and got up to hug her, his favorite sun necklace grazing her hair. "I — I can't thank you enough, noona."

"How's this? I'll teach you my process and maybe you could return the favor and teach me how to rap?" Katie seemed unusually timid.

"You want to rap?"

Do-won never figured Katie for a rapper, but her lyricism, meter, and ferocity were already present in her work. If she could figure out flow and delivery, then she would be an amazing rapper.

"I love hip-hop. I grew up on it and love how good hip-hop engages the mind — that it grew out of activism and ideas. That rappers could say something revolutionary and change culture." She picked up a hot thermos from the floor and sipped. "That's what I want my music to do."

"Your music already does, noona," Do-won said.

Katie acknowledged his words with a hum. "You may be right, but I still want to rap. You guys look so fucking cool doing it. I want to be cool like that, too."

Do-won laughed. "Cool people don't try to be cool, noona. That ruins the entire point."

"I suppose I'll never be cool enough then," she pouted.

Well, he couldn't have her think that. "You're amazing, noona. Your albums are so cohesive and I always feel so stupid when I listen. I know I'm missing more of your deeper meanings."

"I don't want you to feel stupid. That's the last thing I want." Katie frowned.

"I don't know how to explain it." Do-won twirled his bracelets. "You know how we have the Dreaming Universe, and CHIMERAs have all these theories about it?"

"Oh my god," she groaned, "you don't even know how much I've tried to harass your creative team to tell me what the fuck is going on in that thing. Like, please, just tell me what happens. Why is it 2025 and I still don't know? It's been twelve years!"

Do-won felt inexplicably warm inside. Katie really was a CHIMERA through and through. He was pleased to know that she had been so invested in his band from early on and that she knew their discography and mythos so intimately. Katie was not only a friend but a fan — and not a casual fan at that.

So much of his life was wrapped up in his work and it felt comforting to not have to explain much to Katie. He could reference a song or an era and she would know and understand because not only was she a colleague, she had experienced it from the other end, too.

Do-won often felt as if he couldn't understand Katie or her actions — but he knew CHIMERAs. There was at least one part of her that he could relate to — could know — without worrying that he would inadvertently trip on a wire. She was like a minefield, and her CHIMERA status was like a strip that was mercifully cleared.

"That's how your music makes me feel — that there might be entire layers I've missed because I'm not educated enough to know what I don't know," confessed Do-won.

"Do you know that I go to so many fan translation sites every time DOYEN releases an album? I did that for your mixtapes and solo albums, too." Katie giggled. "I have to watch so many explainer videos on YouTube and scour Twitter because there is no way I could catch the nuances of your songs, Do-won. You're already at whatever level you think I'm at. You've actually far surpassed me. You should probably just make it known that you want to produce and send out songs to other artists like Woo-jin oppa does."

"Don't try to get out of helping me, noona. I'm on to your tricks," Do-won teased. "You're stuck with me for a while."

"Please," Katie scoffed. "You couldn't possibly get rid of me. I'm going to ask you so many questions about rapping that you'll beg me to leave you alone."

"You free tomorrow?" Do-won never believed in procrastinating. Hard work never betrayed.

Katie checked her phone calendar. "It's pretty packed in the afternoon, but I could come in the morning."

"You'd do that for me?"

"Of course. I'm starting work on my next album anyway." Katie grinned modestly. "You'll find that much of my process is glaring at a blank notepad, giving up, and then watching stupid TikTok videos all day."

Do-won cackled. "I see we have a lot in common already."

"I knew I shouldn't have given away that secret so soon," she laughed, joining him. "Now you won't teach me how to rap."

Do-won felt a thrill rush through him at Katie's happiness. For a brief moment, she had seemed to be as she used to be — alive and animated — and he was proud that it was because of him.

"How come you don't ask Woo-jin hyung to teach you, noona?"

"I probably will," she mused. "But you came in at the perfect moment, Wonnie. And you're a magnificent rapper. You have such a unique and powerful delivery and performance. It is no hardship to learn from you first. Maybe some of your swag will rub off on me."

Do-won furrowed his brow and made his infamous triangle mouth of disapproval. "Oh, noona. That's cute that you think you'd know what to do with my swag."

Katie cackled delightedly, her mouth wide and uncovered. "We're going to have the best time," she stated, her eyes bright with mischief. "They won't know what hit 'em."

July 2023

Katie was happy and she did not know what to do with that emotion. She was also exhausted, so that perhaps accounted for her bewilderment.

After that first catastrophe of a date, things with Akihiro had proceeded a bit more normally. He had asked if he could drop calling her "noona" as many younger men did when dating an older woman. Katie didn't see the big deal, but it had seemed important to Akihiro. When Katie had asked, Ye-jun had explained it was something about righting a perceived power imbalance. But when Katie had pointed out that Ye-jun still called Mina "noona," he'd merely shrugged.

She hadn't minded. As a foreigner, the age thing hadn't ever mattered except in terms of not offending people. Maybe that was how Akihiro felt about it, too.

They had gone on a few dates in between preparing for her twelve-stop world tour and his busy schedule. He'd been fun, and very little had changed between the two of them except that she'd actively chosen to see Akihiro as more than a friend.

It wasn't too difficult. He was Kitahara Akihiro of DOYEN after all. Funny, attractive, and when he focused his entire attention on her, absolutely unnerving. It was ridiculous, actually. How could someone she'd known for so long do this to her? Katie didn't like it at all, and she was grateful that Akihiro did not push her for more than she was ready to give.

Katie went on her tour.

She had been surprised that so many of her fans had still been willing to pay money to see her. Though all the venues had been small theaters, it was still more than she had hoped for. She'd forgotten the rhythm of performing and posing endlessly with fans for photos at high-touch events, but when they'd tearfully expressed how her albums had provided comfort during difficult times, Katie had found it all worth it.

She'd made room for nightly calls with Akihiro during her tour, and though he'd still texted her a lot more than she'd texted him, Katie had tried to make an effort to make him feel as if he was important. It was more fun than she'd expected.

She should have known it would not last.

When Katie returned to Seoul, Akihiro was soon sleeping over most nights. Again, she didn't particularly mind, except that she missed seeing Woo-jin, Ye-jun, and the other DOYEN members as much in her off hours. Though Akihiro had said it didn't matter to him who she spent her free time with, it clearly did. Eventually, the other DOYEN members stopped dropping by after work entirely.

Katie was annoyed that even though she didn't really need to accommodate Akihiro's unspoken preferences, she also didn't want to disrespect him, so she followed his lead. Except, Katie had not expected him to be so clingy, and it chafed. It reminded her of Tony, and though logically she knew Akihiro and Tony were not the same, it felt identical to her panicking brain.

She could not help but feel as if Akihiro was trying to control and trap her.

Katie started lying to him, saying she was too busy to hang out even though she was not. Sometimes, she would drive the Sowol-gil up Mt. Nam in the heart of Seoul and park at the top until late into the night. Other times, she would take the Bugak Skyway and wind up Mt. Bugak.

Katie would sometimes stand outside of her car and wonder what would happen if she lost her footing and tumbled down the mountain. How long would it be before someone realized she was missing? How badly injured would she be? How quickly would she expire? Would it be fast? Would it be slow?

Something was wrong with her and she did not know what it was. A beautiful and kind man adored her, was patient and interested, and all Katie could think was that she was choking to death.

By the time she got home, Akihiro was usually in her kitchen, drinking himself steadily drunker as he worried, waiting for her despite Katie telling him not to come over. She would apologize, tell him she was caught up in something, and he would not call her on her obvious lie.

Sometimes, he would head to bed. Other times, he would watch from the kitchen as she headed to the balcony and lit cigarette after cigarette.

It was untenable.

And then, one night, it exploded all around her and Katie only had herself to blame.

Chapter 6

July 2023

Katie opened the door to her apartment as quietly as possible, not wishing to disturb Akihiro if he was asleep. She didn't hear any signs of life and all the lights were off, but years of habit were difficult to break. She moved silently in the dark, peering into the empty kitchen, the empty sitting area, and her empty bedroom.

Katie turned on the light and whooshed out a sigh of relief.

"Looking for someone?" She heard Akihiro's tenor voice cut sullenly through the stillness.

She shrieked and clutched her heart, only to whirl around and see Akihiro's wiry silhouette in the hallway.

"Jesus Christ!" Katie cried. "Don't do that, you fucking bastard!"

Akihiro staggered unsmiling toward her. "Sorry," he threw out casually, clearly not sorry. "I forgot."

Katie eyed him carefully. How much had he had to drink? She was instantly alert, resisting her increasing alarm. "Hiro-yah, you startled me, that's all," she crooned instead, voice placating and sweet. "Come to bed."

Akihiro glowered and her heart thundered.

"Where have you been?" he asked, voice thick with alcohol. "You're never home anymore."

Katie swallowed and willed her words to come out viscous, like honey. "Hiro-yah, have you missed me?" She forced herself to slink up to him, plastering her body against his. She mouthed up the column of his neck and whispered hot into his ear. "Don't be mad, darling. I'll make it up to you."

She pulled him down and kissed him, slow and full the way he liked it. Katie bit and soothed his plush lower lip. She flicked her tongue into his mouth and teased. The two of them hadn't slept together yet, but they'd spent enough time making out for her to know what got Akihiro hot.

Akihiro maneuvered her against the wall, caging her between his sculpted arms and powerful thighs. She gasped. She made all the right sounds and forced her body pliant.

Katie's mind whirled a million calculations.

How much did she have to give up physically to appease him? What would be enough? Would he press for more, thinking she felt guilty? When would this all be over?

"I missed you," he breathed against her mouth, chasing her tongue. "I missed you so much."

He sounded so sad that, for a moment, she thought perhaps she'd misread him entirely. Guilt lanced through her. Katie hadn't wanted to hurt him.

"I'm right here," Katie replied, pitching her voice to pacify and seduce — but not too much.

Akihiro swept his tongue hungrily into her mouth, pressing himself more intently into her and against the wall. She could feel his arousal and she desperately tried to quell the spike of adrenaline warning her to flee. She had done this for years; she could do it again.

"Want you so much, Katie," Akihiro confessed, hot and wet against her skin. "I like you so much. Why do you always hide from me? I feel as if I can never quite catch you."

He sounded so vulnerable that Katie held his face a second between her hands to look at him — really look at him. Akihiro had tears in his eyes and she was the cause of them. In an instant, her fear dissipated, leaving only crushing shame.

Katie had done this. She'd hurt this beautiful man by pushing him away, hiding herself and keeping her past a secret. She made a split-second decision and caressed the hard length in his pants.

"You've caught me, baby," she said breathlessly. "Now what are you going to do with me?"

Akihiro's pupils blew out. "Everything, Katie. I want to do everything with you."

"Then do it."

He leaned in to kiss her again, sweet and full of yearning. "Are you sure this is what you want?" he asked, worried. "I thought you didn't —"

"I want this," Katie said, not exactly lying. She knew the shape of things. She knew the steps to this dance. "I want you."

Katie grabbed his hand and led him back to her room.

Akihiro wasn't a huge man, but he was still a familiar and not unwelcome weight on top of her naked body. Katie vaguely recalled loving that feeling from before, from before she lost interest in such proceedings. As such proceedings went, Akihiro was quite proficient. He was attentive, pursuing not only his pleasure, but hers.

Which would be great, except it was doing nothing for her.

Katie had known this would happen, of course. She had known, but a tiny part of her had hoped this time would be different. It would be different because she knew Akihiro, cared for him, and objectively knew he was the embodiment of sex.

And yet, despite all these facts — Akihiro naked, Akihiro's hands all over her body, Akihiro's tongue in her mouth, Akihiro whispering filth, Akihiro's heat and hardness, Akihiro's smell — Katie was going by muscle memory alone. When Akihiro seemed disappointed that she wasn't wet, she merely told him that she took a while to warm up and found the unused lube in her nightstand.

When he stroked her with his wet, slippery fingers, Katie lied and sighed, instructing her body to melt.

"You like this okay?" Akihiro asked breathily. "Tell me how you want it."

"Whatever you want — just want you to be happy, Akihiro," she replied. At least that wasn't a lie. She did want to comfort him in a way that he could understand. In a way that he could feel.

He frowned momentarily. "But I want you to like it, too."

"I like it, Akihiro. Now hush and kiss me some more."

Katie found a condom in the nightstand and hoped it hadn't expired in the intervening years, slowly sliding it down Akihiro's cock.

"You sure about this?" Akihiro scraped out. "We don't have to do anything more. I just want to be with you."

"I want this, Aki-yah. Want you inside me," she whispered.

Akihiro thrust into her. She sucked in a breath as the prior incarnation of her would have. Katie used to love that moment when a man first slid home. She moved as he moved. She panted and she moaned in all the right spots. Her mouth said dirty words and exhortations. She kissed Akihiro as if she wanted to eat him.

After enough time had ticked past in her mind, Katie ramped up her breathing. She let her gasps get more ragged, groaning as she cried out his name in wispy sobs. Akihiro followed her soon after, covering her with kisses.

The two of them cleaned up after themselves and he held her tight against him, his chest still slick with sweat.

Part of Katie felt guilty for continuing down this road, but she also knew it wouldn't matter if it was now or some other time. She just wasn't wired that way anymore. Better to get it over and done with. And then maybe, maybe Akihiro wouldn't feel so neglected or shut out.

Maybe, if she gave him her body, he wouldn't ask for the rest of her.

October 2025

When Do-won knocked on her studio the next morning, Katie was already there with an iced Americano for him at the ready and a giant tumbler of hot tea for herself.

"Noona, you didn't have to get me coffee! I should have gotten you something first."

Katie grinned at him and said, "You can get the next round. I have my stash of Earl Grey here, but I hear the hot water at SB Entertainment is top-notch." She threw him a cheap, generic notebook and a pen.

He sat next to her on the comfortable tuxedo sofa. "Is this where we stare at the blank pages for a few hours and get angry and sad?"

"Almost, Wonnie. That's for later." Katie laughed and winked at him. "I didn't get a chance this morning, but I try to start off my days with morning pages."

"Morning pages?"

"Yeah, it's based off of this woman's book, 'The Artist's Way,' and I was obsessed with it in college. Basically, you write three pages first thing in the morning — whatever you want — even if it's 'I have nothing to say' — as long as you write three pages. I hated it." Katie grimaced. "It was difficult because I wanted to make sure I did it right."

"Were you?" Do-won sat and took a sip of the iced Americano.

"Yes? No? Maybe?" Katie shrugged. "It doesn't matter. Who was going to check? Who has the right to judge my pages?"

"So, you're telling me to do something you hate every morning? Is this like some extended metaphor of how art is pain and suffering?" Do-won wasn't sure where she was going with this.

Katie leaned into him and giggled. "Not remotely. I quit the practice when I was in college. It was horrible. But I picked up the habit again a few years ago," she said. "I realized that my problem then was that I was too worried about perfection and following the rules. Doing the pages called attention to that and I couldn't push past my discomfort."

Do-won nodded. He knew all about the drive for perfection and the fear behind it. "And now?"

"Now, I can. But it's harder for me to make it through the pages without picking up my phone and getting distracted. I've gotten better though." Her mouth pulled upward. "Not *much* better, mind you. But better."

"We just write about whatever?" Do-won wasn't sure how he felt about this. What if his whatever was wrong?

"Yup. The idea is that you clear your brain of all that noise floating around, and if you do it often enough, it will unleash your creativity or some bullshit." Katie took a sip of her tea. Do-won idly wondered how much tea she consumed. If it was on par with his coffee problem, it was likely a lot.

"And it works?"

"It's not magic and I don't want you to think that this will always happen," Katie replied, as if she understood his skepticism. "But on occasion, I use some of my raw thoughts in lyrics or they become the inspiration for a song — or once, an entire album concept."

"Which album?"

"'Disintegration.'"

Do-won could not resist asking. "What was the raw thought?"

Katie's eyes hazed over for a moment before she shook herself. "I thought I was coming apart at the seams and I didn't know if I would ever be put back together again," she answered quietly.

"Ah," replied Do-won. "I still can't listen to that album without sobbing like an idiot."

Katie looked at him like he was crazy. "Why would you listen to it then?"

"Because it's a masterpiece." Do-won cleared his throat. He sipped his Americano to buy himself some time to formulate a more cogent thought. "Especially that hidden cello track. It hurt even more when I realized you were the one playing. I sometimes just put it on repeat when I need to cry."

Katie stared at him some more. "You're very strange, Wonnie."

"Hey, sometimes, you just need a good cry, noona," he defended.

She made as if she were going to say something and then thought better of it. "I think I've cried enough to last a lifetime," Katie said instead. "I never want to cry again." She shuddered as if to clear whatever ghosts haunted her. "Come on, let's try some morning pages, shall we? I'm sure you didn't come over to hear me be overdramatic."

She opened her notebook and Do-won wondered what sort of words she wrote in there now. He hoped they were words that no longer made her cry.

July 2023

"You're in a good mood," observed Dae-jung before dance practice the next morning. "I take it the talk went well with noona last night?"

"Yeah, you could say that."

Dae-jung cut his brown eyes to Akihiro. His judgmental image repli-cated infinitely in the mirrored walls of the dance studio. "You look like the cat that swallowed the canary. Spill."

"I'm not one to kiss and tell," said Akihiro as he grinned and raised his eyebrows suggestively.

"What a load of shit. You totally are the type. You know how I know?" scowled Dae-jung. "I'm the one you tell. Now 'fess up."

Akihiro's eyes crinkled into happy crescents at his friend. He looked around to make sure none of the staff or his other members were listening. He pulled Dae-jung into a more private corner of the large room. "Katie and I finally, you know, finally."

"No, I don't know. You finally what? Told her how hurt and worried you've been?"

This time, it was Akihiro's turn to scowl. "Well, no. We skipped that part and straight to the makeup sex. It was amazing."

Dae-jung just raised a thick eyebrow at Akihiro's comment. Akihiro refused to be intimidated by his best friend's sultry good looks. He told himself he was immune to Dae-jung's piercing monolidded eyes after over a decade in his presence.

"It was!" protested Akihiro. "I even made her come because I am a sex god."

"I thought you said she doesn't have a sex drive anymore?" asked Dae-jung. At the fallen expression on Akihiro's face, Dae-jung request-ed gently, "Tell me exactly what happened, Hiro-yah."

"Why can't you just let me have this?"

"Because it's not real."

Akihiro sighed and threw himself against the wall next to Dae-jung. "I was drinking by myself in the guest room when she came home late, as usual. I don't even know where she goes."

"Why were you in the guest room? Don't you usually sleep with her?"

"I don't like being in her room alone. It makes me feel too pathetic, and I was sick of solo drinking in the kitchen. I wanted a change of scenery." Akihiro put his head on Dae-jung's shoulder. It felt like home. "I'd be worried about her cheating on me but she doesn't even look at me — let alone other men."

"I thought you were a sex god." Dae-jung nudged Akihiro with his arm in a friendly gesture.

"Shut up, Dae," said Akihiro without any heat. "I asked her where she'd been, and then she was on me and, you know...," Akihiro's voice trailed off as he mentally connected the dots. He sat up. "Wait, do you think she's cheating on me? Was it all a distraction? Did she fake the whole thing to get me to stop asking?"

"You said she wasn't into sex, right?" asked Dae-jung soothingly. "She probably wasn't lying about that. I doubt she's not having sex with someone else."

"What?"

Dae-jung sighed. "You know what I mean. She probably isn't going out of her way to have a relationship with someone else only to not fuck them and then fuck you to get you to stop asking her about the other guy." His friend ran his large hands through his soft brown hair.

"This is all very confusing." Akihiro swept his hand over his face.

"It wouldn't be if you just told her how you were feeling."

"I tried!"

Dae-jung rolled his eyes. "Maybe you should try again — but this time sober."

"I wasn't drunk," Akihiro argued. "You know I can hold my liquor." He paused, full of uncertainty. "You think she slept with me so she wouldn't have to talk to me?"

Dae-jung hesitated as if he didn't want to hurt Akihiro's feelings, his normally expressive countenance carefully neutral. "Obviously, I'm not noona. But it seems like it?"

"You think she pretended to have a good time?" Akihiro felt like a fool. How could Katie play him this way? "No one has ever faked an orgasm with me before. This is going to take some getting used to."

Dae-jung scoffed. "How do you know?"

"I just know," insisted Akihiro. He would have known, right? He had checked in with her multiple times. Had made sure she'd wanted it. Had made sure she wanted him. "You think she faked the whole thing?"

Dae-jung shrugged. "People fake it all the time during sex. Haven't you ever pretended to nut so you could go to sleep? It's not like they're checking the condom after."

"I have never." Akihiro was appalled. "You've faked an orgasm?"

"Of course. I've definitely been too tired or concentrated so much on not shooting early that the effort to get back into it seemed too much trouble." Dae-jung chuckled. "Not all of us are sex gods like yourself."

"I didn't even realize it was an option." He slid down the wall and slumped onto the polished wooden floor.

Dae-jung joined him and put a comforting hand on Akihiro's thigh. "Well, now you know."

Akihiro's mind raced. "If she — if she didn't want it — did I — do you think I hurt her?" He swallowed as the edge of a horrifying thought crept in; Akihiro did not want to acknowledge it. He tried anyway. "Does that mean I ra—"

"Whoa, whoa, whoa! That's not what I meant to imply at all, Hiro-yah. You can only go by what she told you." Dae-jung hugged Akihiro. "I'm sure you asked a few times if it's what she wanted, right? Listened to what she liked or didn't?"

Akihiro nodded. He was too devastated for words.

"You can't read her mind, and she can't read yours. Just talk to her." Dae-jung pulled Akihiro in for another hug. "This could all have been avoided if you and noona actually spoke to each other. Like grown-ups."

"When did you get so wise, DaeDae?"

Dae-jung held Akihiro's face between his hands and kissed his forehead. "Since always, friend. Since always."

Akihiro let himself sink into Dae-jung's love and care for the rest of rehearsal. He went about his company schedule after and texted Katie, asking if she was free that evening to chat. He tried not to freak out when she left him on read.

October 2025

Do-won wasn't exactly sure what the morning session with Katie would entail or how it would work out, but it went surprisingly quickly. The writing exercise wasn't terrible and he felt a little less buzzy in the brain. The two of them discussed a lot of what she had in mind for the next album, and he was surprised when she didn't want it to be personal.

"I thought that was what made your music yours, noona. You always inject so much of yourself into it," he commented.

"It's exhausting," Katie confessed. "And I don't want to write a cliché breakup album. I'm just not in the right headspace. My last few albums were a little too intimate and I would like not to feel scraped raw at the end of the process. I don't want to sing about heartache for the next six to eight months."

"You're not worried about being inauthentic?"

"It's not inauthentic just because it's not deeply personal. They can be true and not eviscerate me in the process, right? You guys do a really good job of that. I want to do more of it." Katie chuffed a sad little sound. "Besides, if it's fake, then I've faked so much of my life, it will be a relief to go back to it."

Do-won didn't know what to say to that. Except, maybe... "Sometimes, I wonder who I really am outside of DOYEN. Outside of being in the spotlight." He played with the strings of his hoodie. "Is this Jung Do-won who writes music, eats, sleeps, practices, dances, and lives for the stage — is that the real Jung Do-won? If so, is he a ghost? Does he ever actually live?"

Katie flicked her gaze to his, empathy and gratefulness filling her dark irises. "What did you discover?"

"I thought I had gotten it during our 'War' era. But then the pandemic happened and I joined the military. And then, well, each time I think I get a grasp on who I am, something shifts. I'm discharged. My girlfriend dumps me during our anniversary trip."

"Who are you, Jung Do-won?"

Do-won felt the unexpected wonder weighted behind Katie's question. "Just a man, noona. Just a man."

The moment stretched between them, delicate and fragile. She was so strikingly beautiful that he did not dare breathe. Katie shifted her regard and checked her phone.

"Ah, shit," she exclaimed. "I'm going to be late to class. I'm surprised Ha-joon oppa isn't here yet to pick me up."

Do-won was surprised. "You're still taking classes?"

"It's not really a class but for some reason, I call it that?" She blushed. "It's a dance therapy class. I think the official name is Dance Movement Therapy."

"Oh? Is it to help with your dancing? I didn't realize you still danced."

Katie shook her head. "No, I don't really dance anymore. It's supposed to help heal trauma by rooting you in your body — to remind you that your body can feel pleasure." Her face turned an even deeper crimson.

"Is that something you forgot?" Do-won wanted to kick himself for the bluntness of the question. How could he ask her something that deeply personal?

Thankfully, her manager Ha-joon chose that moment to enter the studio to pick Katie up. "Feel free to stay in my studio as long as you want, Wonnie," she said on her way out. "I trust you not to break anything."

"Sure thing, noona. Are you attending Akihiro's birthday party tonight?" he asked.

"Oh, is that tonight? Am I going?" She glanced at Ha-joon and he nodded. She pouted a sad smile. "I guess I will see you tonight then." Katie left with Ha-joon and Do-won heard her murmur, "You sure he said it was alright for me to go?"

Do-won wanted to kick himself again. He kept inserting his foot in his mouth and was an insensitive ass. Even though Katie and Akihiro had acted as if everything was fine and still cared deeply for each other, he knew that Akihiro was still deeply brokenhearted about their breakup. But the way Katie carried on, Do-won often forgot that she was likely also hurting.

Akihiro had insisted it wasn't her fault — that it wasn't anyone's fault, really. Sometimes, things just didn't work out. But somehow, Do-won didn't think Akihiro had told him everything.

Akihiro had been crazy about her.

And Katie? She had always seemed a little too aloof. Do-won had often wondered if she had even cared about Akihiro at all, but that wasn't fair of him. He wasn't privy to the inner workings of their relationship. It would do Do-won well to remember that.

Sometimes though, Do-won wondered if he had loved his ex half as much as Akihiro had loved Katie — if he'd ever really known Ae-cha and she, him. He was sad about the breakup, of course. But if Do-won was honest with himself, he wasn't really that upset. His pride hurt, but shouldn't his heart hurt more?

He was beginning to think that though they were together for two years, it wasn't a real relationship. He wondered if he was broken somehow — that he was unable to open up to another person. That maybe the problem had been him all along.

July 2023

"Katie, we need to talk," said Akihiro as soon as Katie walked through the door of her penthouse.

She took in Akihiro standing in her entryway wearing his pajamas, his serious mien. She wondered if she could delay the conversation any longer. Maybe it would be for the best if Akihiro broke up with her now before he got much more invested. Before he realized she was inherently fractured.

Yet, Katie could not bear it. She could not bear failing so early on in a relationship — not with someone as kind and loving as Akihiro. Who else would love her if not him?

"Talk like yesterday, you mean?" she teased lightly.

It was slight, but Katie noted hurt flickering across Akihiro's countenance. "No, Katie, that's not what I meant."

"I wouldn't mind if it was," she said. "Just give me a moment, and I'll be all yours, Hiro-yah."

Katie winked at him, but it fell flat and stale.

"I'll wait for you in the sitting room, Katie." Akihiro just looked sad.

She hurried to her room and berated herself. She didn't know why she always immediately turned to sex to fix things — well, she knew, but she didn't want to think about it. Though Katie didn't mean to say what she'd said, it was out, and she had to follow through. It was all she knew how to do.

She finally gathered enough courage to return to her sitting area and chose a spot opposite Akihiro on the sectional. She resisted the urge to stroke her wrist. He held a pillow close to him as if to shield himself from her. As if to keep a respectable distance.

"You wanted to talk?" Katie made herself ask. Might as well tear off the bandage and not prolong the inevitable.

Akihiro seemed small and miserable. Katie wanted to hug him but didn't know if she was allowed. "Are you cheating on me?" he asked.

Of all the things she expected Akihiro would say, that was not it. "What?"

"Are you cheating on me?" he repeated.

"Of course not," she replied. "Why would you think such a thing?"

Akihiro huffed, aggrieved. "What am I supposed to think, Katie? You're never home and you never give a straight answer about where you've been."

"I wasn't aware I owed you a daily itinerary."

"Well, I wouldn't need one if you would just tell me where the fuck you've been."

Katie flinched at Akihiro's tone, but she would not be controlled by a man ever again. "Maybe it's none of your fucking business."

"Maybe I just worry about you."

She seethed. "I didn't ask you to be worried about me."

Akihiro's hands clenched, and her stomach dropped.

"What am I supposed to do?" yelled Akihiro. "You don't come home at night and Ha-joon hyung doesn't know where you are. What am I supposed to think?" He stood and took a step toward her, raking his hands through his hair. He looked angry enough to hit something.

Fear coursed through Katie's system. Akihiro had never seemed like the type to be violent — but what did she really know about him? Rumor had it he used to have a temper. What did anyone ever really know about a person until they hurt you?

Katie did the only thing she knew how to do.

November 2025

Writing music and lyrics was generally lonely work — at least the way Katie did it. She knew other groups and singers wrote in music camps, locking themselves with a bunch of producers, writers, and lyricists into a room for a week. Whatever came out of that session was smashed together and workshopped, and that was the album.

Katie had never worked that way. Not even when she was just starting out.

Sure, her first album or two in Taiwan had other writers. A lot of her songs had been written by Johnny, but none of it had been collaborative. They'd usually been finished songs that she sang or ones she'd written that the label's in-house producers had polished and made marketable.

In the intervening years, Katie had written a few songs or helped out on the lyrics or topline for some of the newer SB Entertainment groups. But again, she had just sent in her parts, and they'd been accepted or not. She had never worked closely with another person from beginning to end.

So to say that including Do-won in the process over the last month was a weird experience for her was underselling it. It was a lot weird. Not bad weird, just different weird.

He had so many questions. How did she come up with concepts? How did she come up with lyrics? How did she decide a topline was the topline she wanted? How did she decide what was in English or Korean or sometimes even Chinese?

Katie tried to break down her process into words, but it was much harder than expected.

At the moment, Do-won was asking whether Katie, when composing with counterpoint, preferred a tonal or modal approach when it came to voice leading. Since most composers couldn't even agree on whether or not the approach was relevant, Katie asked him to answer his own question while she stalled for time. That shut him up a bit as they both contemplated their thought processes. When he asked again, Katie got annoyed and threw one of those squishy stress balls at him.

It hit Do-won square in the face.

His shocked triangle mouth sent Katie into a fit of hysterical laughter. The next thing she knew, Do-won was throwing everything that was remotely soft in her studio at her. She hadn't laughed that long or that loud in years. When Do-won finally stopped pummeling her with random objects, the two of them collapsed on the floor, completely spent.

"Whatever your concept of your next album is, noona, it should be happy."

"Like optimistic? Overcoming challenges and triumphing over hardship?"

"No, just happy," Do-won replied. "You don't really do happy music. You have up-tempo music — like hype music — but so little music that is happy."

Katie pondered his words. "I'm not really a happy music kinda person though, Wonnie. I don't know if you've noticed, but I skew sad and mad."

"You do," he agreed. "You have such an infectious laugh though, noona. I'm curious what your version of happy music would sound like."

"I don't even like happy music — what does that even mean?" she pushed back.

"It's just a feeling the music gives you, right? Like that Pharrell song, 'Happy.'"

Katie made a face. "I hate that song. Like legit despise."

"Really?"

"I may have liked it for, like, a day when it first came out — what was I in? Middle school?" Katie tried to do the math. "Whatever. They played it so much I hated it. I always skip if I can."

"This explains so much about you," Do-won observed gravely.

"What, that I have taste?" she defended.

Do-won's face was comically stunned. He took off his brown bucket hat, threw it to the side, and then propped himself against her sofa chair. "You hate all happy songs?"

She laughed and got up from the floor. "I don't know about that — but I hate all songs that sound like 'Happy.'"

"You don't like that Trolls song by JT?"

"Nope," Katie answered as she picked up his hat and put it on her own head. Do-won always had the best accessories. "Hated it on first listen. I despise disco pop."

"Wait — you despise disco pop?" he asked.

Shit. "Uh...maybe?"

"Our hit 'Party Up' was disco pop," said Do-won. "We broke so many world records for a K-pop act with that track — the least of them being eight weeks at number one on the Billboard Hot 100."

Oh, fuck. "Was it?" she replied.

"The track 'Baby, Baby' after that was, too — or kind of like that — super happy and cheerful." Do-won sounded a little too suspicious for his own good.

"Hmmmmmm," was all Katie could respond.

Do-won lurched upright. "Oh my god, noona. Did you hate 'Party Up' and 'Baby, Baby'?"

"Ummmm," she dodged. She fidgeted with his hat, using her phone as a mirror to angle it just right. "Hate is such a strong word..."

He slapped his knee, squealing and giddy. "Ohohohoh, noona. You didn't just hate them — you loathed them, didn't you?" He howled.

Katie wanted to crawl under her coffee table and die. He was absolutely onto her. She detested those songs with every fiber of her being, but she had never said anything because who wanted to be that person? Who wanted to drink the Hatorade? Also, she couldn't believe she just thought, 'Hatorade.' What was she — some stupid frat boy from 2010?

She decided to sidestep the question entirely. "I like some happy songs!"

"Like what?" challenged Do-won, disbelief written clearly all over his face and the way he angled his torso and arms.

Katie thought a bit. "I mean, 'WAP' makes me happy. That song is fucking brilliant — and that video! It makes me so happy."

"You think 'WAP' by Cardi B and Megan Thee Stallion is a happy song." Do-won just stared and judged her.

"Yes?"

"'WAP.'"

Katie grinned. "I mean, if I had a WAP, I'd be pretty happy."

"Noona!!" Do-won winked and shot a finger gun at her. "I like the way you think!"

Of course, after this revelation, the two of them had to watch the video, and the rest of the morning was eaten away by the rabbit hole of YouTube. They snickered and cheered through a ton of Cardi B and Megan Thee Stallion videos, which led to other songs that made her happy, like "Living on a Prayer," "Industry Baby," "I Want It That Way," "It's Gonna Be Me," "Bang Bang Bang," and "Ring Ding Dong."

"In conclusion, you are a very strange person, noona," Do-won observed, throwing a companionable arm around her.

"Don't I know it," she smiled.

"Don't think I've forgotten your feelings about 'Party Up' and 'Baby, Baby,'" he ridiculed. He stuck his tongue out at her and, for a moment, Katie's mind flashed to all the things he could do with that tongue.

Katie gulped. "I just have other songs that I prefer, that's all."

"What DOYEN songs make you happy, noona?" Do-won asked as he moved back to her sitting area.

"All of 'Shadows and Light,'" she answered, relieved at the easy question.

"Really!"

"Too many to count, really," she added. "Your new stuff is good, too. But they haven't had time to sink into my bones yet."

Do-won nodded affably, his heart-shaped smile a balm to her soul. "'Shadows and Light,' huh?"

"That album is unparalleled." Katie remembered screaming to Ellie about the album when it had come out. Those were simpler times.

"We were miserable when we cut it. We were so tired and broke."

"I know. Woo-jin oppa told me. But it's in my top three of your discography anyway. It reminds me of when everything in my life seemed to be going according to plan," Katie said as she leaned against Do-won dreamily. "I had just won 'The Singer Songwriter,' started dating Johnny, and I was on an upward trajectory of fame. I was so happy — all my dreams were coming true. It seems unreal now, knowing what happened after."

The two of them were quiet, her confession permeating the room.

Do-won sighed. "You really have a talent, noona."

"Yeah?"

"You somehow manage to link even happiness with sorrow."

"It's a gift."

All of a sudden, she was swooped into the air by an overzealous Do-won. "It's a good thing I'm your delight, noona."

Her face split into a wide grin. "You sure are, Wonnie. You sure are."

July 2023

Even though Akihiro knew his timing was bad, he had to talk to Katie as soon as she entered the apartment before he lost his nerve. All he could think of was his parents' raised voices when they had thought he and his two younger sisters were asleep. He really hated having difficult conversations, especially if it meant finding out the truth about last night.

Quite frankly, even though he knew intellectually that he'd done nothing wrong, he was still ashamed of himself.

But Katie had tried to flirt with him as soon as he'd brought up having a talk, and Akihiro knew — he knew — she was trying to distract him. It hurt.

He was so upset and flustered that after, everything spewing from his mouth came out totally wrong. He didn't know why he was arguing about whether or not she was cheating on him. Akihiro knew she wasn't cheating on him. He didn't care about her schedule or where she was. He just wanted to know she was safe.

And yet, Katie's response stung.

Katie made him out as if he were some insecure, jealous, controlling prick, and he was none of those things. Akihiro felt as if he'd been plenty patient and understanding. He was allowed to be a man, wasn't he? He had feelings, too.

Before he knew it, he'd lost his temper and then she was wrapped around him, saying, "Aki-yah, I'm sorry. You're right." She sounded repentant and remorseful, but he wasn't sure how she'd gone from furious to apologetic so quickly.

And then, Katie was kissing him, so pliant and soft. So appeasing. So distracting. He was still mad but his brain was hazing over with desire. But then, he remembered his conversation with Dae-jung that morning, which had the effect of a cold shower. Akihiro stepped away.

"Stop," he said. "Please stop, Katie."

Katie peered up at him, eyes large and shining. "Did I do something wrong?" she asked, voice wavering.

"Why are you doing this?" He didn't mean to sound as accusatory as he did, but it was too late. He couldn't retract it even if he wanted to.

Katie pulled him back in by the waist. "Doing what, Aki-yah?" Her voice was sweet and innocent, but her eyes were wary, though she tried to hide it.

"Why are you kissing me?" he clarified.

She lifted her hand to stroke his face. Her hand was trembling.

Akihiro suddenly realized with a shock that Katie was afraid. She was afraid of him. It would have never occurred to him that she could be afraid of *him*. What had he done?

He tenderly sat her back on her sofa. He softened his voice. "Katie, are you scared of me?"

The way she carefully made her face blank of all expressions told Akihiro everything he needed to know. He wasn't sure if he was heartbroken or insulted. He decided he could be both.

"I would never hurt you, Katie," he said cautiously.

"Maybe," she finally said. "But men always say they 'would never' right before they do."

Akihiro flattened. "I don't know what happened exactly between you and Tony, but I'm not him. I don't hit women — and I don't force myself on them, either."

Katie lifted her chin just a fraction in stubborn defiance. "I was never forced. Don't make assumptions about what he was like — what I allowed to happen," she hissed. "You know nothing about him. You know nothing about me."

Akihiro wanted to scream. "How can I know if you never tell me, Katie? I don't know what I did to make you afraid of me. I don't know what I did to make you lie to me about where you've been, or why you avoid me — or why you slept with me last night even though you didn't want to." His voice broke. "Why are you even with me if you can't stand being around me? If I make you afraid?"

Katie was trembling even more now, and Akihiro didn't know how to help.

"Do you want me to leave?" he asked. "I can call Ha-joon hyung to come over to be with you."

She shook her head. Katie looked terrified.

"What do you want me to do, Katie?" Akihiro was so tired. How could he prove to her that he was a good man? It didn't seem as if it was something he could ever win. "You seem really upset and I don't know how to help. I seem to be making everything worse."

Something in his voice must have reached Katie because she stopped shaking.

"I drive the Sowol-gil or the Bugak Skyway," she said finally, fingers digging into her palms.

That's what she was doing? "Oh," he said, more to encourage her than anything else.

"I drive as fast as I can take the curves in the dark, and then I just sit at the top of the mountain." Katie's breath stuttered. "Sometimes, I wonder what would happen if I threw myself off the side. I wonder what would happen if I took a turn too fast or too sharp. I wonder if it would hurt and who would miss me and if everyone would be better off."

"Katie," he gasped. His heart ached.

"I don't really want to die," she whispered, "it's just really hard sometimes. I don't say anything because I don't want anyone to worry — but I suppose you worried anyway."

Akihiro had no idea how much it took for Katie to tell him even that much. "Thank you for telling me."

She dipped her chin and willfully avoided his gaze. "I feel like I'm suffocating," Katie said cagily, shifting in her seat. "Every time you ask where I am or what my schedule is, I feel trapped."

"I — I had no idea." Akihiro felt gutted.

"Tony used to show up unannounced at my apartment or when I was supposed to be out with my friends. He said it was because he liked to surprise me — that he missed me. But it was really because he controlled every aspect of my life in Hong Kong. I don't know why he bothered dressing it up as anything else."

It never crossed Akihiro's mind to keep tabs on Katie in such a manner. No wonder she was like this.

"I don't want to control you, Katie," explained Akihiro. He wanted to scoot closer to her, to envelop her in his arms. He did not move. "I just — I just really like you. I want to spend as much time with you as possible."

"He tracked my cycle, you know? That's how he knew I was pregnant." Katie's voice was so low he could barely hear her. "He laid a trap for me and I walked right into it." She laughed, heavy with bitterness. "I thought I was so clever. But he was just biding his time."

Katie abruptly stopped and he waited for her to continue but she didn't. Akihiro was completely out of his depth.

"I'm sorry. I'm so sorry." He knew he should leave it alone, but he couldn't. Akihiro didn't know when she would be willing to talk to him so candidly again, so he asked anyway. "Did I hurt you last night?"

The question clearly surprised her. "No, Akihiro. You didn't hurt me."

"Did you —," he felt too embarrassed to finish his actual question. "Did you enjoy it?" He was a masochist, clearly. "Please tell me the truth."

Katie opened her mouth to speak, but then shut it. "I — no. Not really." Her cheeks were inflamed. "It's nothing personal, Akihiro. I — I just don't care about sex anymore."

"Then why did you sleep with me? And why did you lie about it?" He felt as if he took advantage of his girlfriend. He hated that.

"I —," she had the grace to look ashamed. "I'm sorry."

"I don't want to have sex with you if you're not into it."

Katie looked so forlorn and guilty. "I'm never into it, Akihiro. Are you going to be celibate until you can't stand it anymore and break up with me? Somehow, you don't strike me as someone who has ever gone without." She sighed and stared at her hands. "I don't mind having sex with you, Akihiro. I don't care if I don't come."

"But I care, Katie. I care."

"Why does it matter?" she argued. "You get off, and I get some cardio."

Akihiro's pride was nettled. He knew it was mostly his bruised ego, but he couldn't let it go. "I've always made sure my partner came."

"You're joking, right? That's exhausting." Katie's shoulders slumped. She grabbed one of her golden throw pillows. "It's not a critique of your skills or whatever, Akihiro. It's a side effect of my medication, and I don't really miss it."

Akihiro didn't know how he felt about that; the idea of Katie pretending to enjoy something just because he wanted it felt anathema and cruel. "I don't want to use you."

"You're not using me if I offer myself to you, Akihiro." Now she sounded exhausted. "You have needs and I'm okay with meeting them. It's not horrible."

"That's what every man wants to hear," he said caustically.

Katie's eyes flashed. "You're telling me you've never fucked someone out of obligation? You were always 100% present and into it? You've never been too tired or not in the mood, but because you cared about the other person, had sex with them anyway?"

He bristled at the implication that he wouldn't take care of his partner. "Well, when you put it that way, I guess I have — but I eventually get into it."

"Do you always come when you fuck?"

"Yes? Maybe? Usually?" Akihiro was starting to think he wasn't normal.

"Oh."

If possible, Katie looked even more dejected than she had before. And then, Akihiro had a moment of self-revelation.

"Maybe it's because I've never been in a long-term relationship?" he offered. "I've never been with anyone longer than a few months. We never get out of the phase where all we do is fuck. You —," he paused, unsure of whether to say what he wanted to say. "You're the only person I've ever waited this long for or saw a future with."

"I'm sorry, Akihiro." Katie flicked her eyes at him. The sorrow and regret her eyes held made his stomach churn. "This is probably not what you had in mind."

"No, it's not." Akihiro was honest and though it would hurt her, he knew the two of them had had too little honesty of late. "It's not what I had in mind, but what I imagined wasn't real." He scooted closer to her and tipped her chin so Katie could look at him. "You're real, Katie. And I want you — the real you."

Katie's chin quivered as tears spilled down her cheeks. "Oh."

"Do you want me, Katie? Not in a sexual way — we can figure that out later." He lightly thumbed the tears off her face. "I'm willing to try if you do. But if you don't, just tell me. Don't tell me what you think I want to hear. I don't think I could bear it."

"I want you, Akihiro."

Akihiro started to examine her face for the lie, but decided he would trust her instead. "Okay," he said.

"What about the sex, though? I know it means a lot to you."

"We don't have to discuss it now. I just — it's more important to me than I thought, is all. But we'll figure it out." He started to reach for Katie and then stopped. "Is it okay if I hug you?"

At her assent, he pulled Katie into a snug embrace.

"I'm sorry, Aki-yah. I really am," she mumbled into his chest.

He kissed her lightly on the head. "I know, love. I know. I'm sorry, too."

Akihiro told himself it would be alright. Hadn't he been determined to become an idol and then became one of the world's most famous people, thanks to his team? Surely, if Katie tried alongside him, the two of them could make it.

CHAPTER 7

Katie was miserable. Absolutely fucking miserable.

She wanted to crawl into bed, pull the covers over her head and disappear into whatever dark hole she prayed would open up and end her pitiful existence. Katie felt as if she had a low-grade flu with the way she was dizzy, constantly nauseated, experiencing chills, and exhausted.

The fucked-up part was: she couldn't even sleep, and when she did, she was plagued with nightmares.

On top of it all, Katie would get brain zaps — as if some sadistic fuck had opened her skull and shocked her gray matter with an electric current.

Forget working on her next album, Katie couldn't think her way out of a paper bag. She was irritable, her brain was in a fog, and she wanted everyone to fuck off and die if she didn't murder them first.

And Akihiro?

Akihiro was miserable watching how miserable she was — which, in her uncharitable moments (which was all of her moments), she thought was the least he could do since this was all for his benefit.

Well, technically, it was for both of them. Katie was a week into switching antidepressants to see if she could find a treatment that wouldn't leave her with a negative libido. Her psychiatrist Dr. Im deemed her depression and anxiety symptoms too severe to safely go off meds, so she was gradually tapering off her current medication as she gradually increased a new one.

Being in the mere vicinity of another human being made Katie want to stab them with many sharp, pointy objects, so being in the presence of Akihiro long enough to fuck him was not really in the cards.

"I'm no fun to be around right now, Akihiro," she said one night after a tense dinner. "I feel like warmed-over garbage."

Akihiro's normally sweet and mischievous brown eyes filled with guilt. "I'm sorry, Katie. Is there anything I can do to make it better? Do you have a headache? Or is dinner not agreeing with you? I can go grab some painkillers if you're out."

He got up and began to clear her dishes into the deep, farmhouse sink. It was difficult to be annoyed at him when he was trying so hard to be accommodating, but Katie found a way.

Katie did have a headache, but what she wanted wasn't more medication. Medication was what had gotten her into this mess in the first place. She just wanted to be alone so she could wallow in peace.

"You should go home," she said. "You've been here at least a week. I'm sure I'm keeping you from things you have to take care of."

"I want to be here with you though, Katie," Akihiro insisted as he started rinsing the dirty dishes and loading them into her dishwasher. "I hate seeing you like this."

Katie sighed. Loudly. And perhaps with a lot more frustration than she normally would have allowed to leak through, but she was tired and had stopped giving a fuck about three days ago.

"I appreciate that — really, Akihiro," she said as calmly as she could contrive. "I'll be fine by myself, I promise." At Akihiro's worried expression, she added, "I'm not a risk to myself — I don't feel any urge for self-harm or whatever."

The real risk was that Akihiro would break up with her because she was so odious to be around during the cross-tapering process and, thus, render the whole needlessly excessive folderol useless. Katie had to get him out of her house as soon as possible.

"It's no hardship," he repeated, stubborn as always. "I want to be here. I want to be with you and take care of you."

She lost it. It had been a week of this persistent détente of Katie stating her very real needs and Akihiro stampeding over them out of his alleged concern and love.

"You can support me by leaving me the fuck alone!" she yelled in frustration. "Every time I see you, I think it's your fault that I'm in such a shit mood even though I know it isn't — that it's just my brain being an asshole. But also, I was just fine not giving two shits about sex, and now I want to climb out of my own skin just because you want to fuck someone who wants to fuck you back!"

Akihiro's stricken face would have made Katie feel terrible, but she was already feeling terrible, and quite frankly, she did not care.

Akihiro left, half-washed dishes still in the sink.

Katie texted Dr. Im because calling seemed like too much effort. She reassured Katie that what she was feeling was completely normal. The serotonin discontinuation syndrome would pass generally in two to four weeks. Ideally, her brain would then adjust to the new medication.

She wasn't sure if she'd still have a boyfriend in two to four weeks, but she instead screenshotted the thread and sent it to Akihiro with a terse apology. Then Katie changed from her daytime pajamas to her nighttime pajamas, turned off all the lights, climbed into bed, and pulled the covers over her head. No black hole opened up to swallow her whole. No end to her pitiful existence was forthcoming, and no merciful sleep bringing oblivion appeared.

She was miserable.

January 2026

Do-won was in his studio fiddling with the track he was working on. Ever since he had started shadowing Katie's album-creating process, he had become obsessed with creating beats and songs that fairly burst with unbridled happiness. He didn't know what to do with any of them since none of them fit DOYEN's current concept. Perhaps he would shop some around, as Katie had suggested, or save his favorites for his next solo venture.

He knew he should just ask for specific guidance from Woo-jin. It wasn't as if his bandmate would be stingy with advice or even about his process. The older man wasn't like that — especially with his fellow DOYEN members. In fact, Woo-jin would likely connect Do-won with some of his contacts and put feelers out on his behalf. Except some part of Do-won felt ashamed, like he wasn't adequately grateful for how far he'd come already, that he was too greedy for personal accolades apart from the group.

Somehow, it had seemed easier to admit to Katie. Do-won didn't know if it was because she had always been solo and ambitious in a different way than his group members had been in their early days. He envied how she seemed to do what she wanted when she wanted and how she wanted. (He knew that was an oversimplification, particularly given the entertainment industry. Except, Katie had always been known for her musicianship, and he wanted just a little bit of that renown for himself.)

Katie was curled up on the black leather couch of his studio, and on the occasions he glanced over, she was grumbling about the needlessly opaque text of some book Jae-sung had recommended years ago. Her Korean had only now progressed to a level where she could possibly read the thing. She generally hated Jae-sung's recommendations, but still, she dutifully read as many as she could.

After her tenth complaint, he interjected. "Why do you bother reading his suggestions if you and Jae-sung hyung clearly have very different tastes?"

"How else can I prove to Jae that he has execrable taste in reading material?" she retorted. Katie then rubbed her palms together, adding, "Besides, someone has to take him down a notch or two, and that someone is me. He's not the only intellectual in this friend group."

"Oh, so it's pride, is it?" giggled Do-won from his Herman Miller Embody gaming chair. "I should have known. You and Jae-sung hyung deserve each other. Two of the smartest idiots I know."

Katie's mouth dropped open, outrage painted all over her features. "I am not an idiot."

Do-won raised a doubting eyebrow. "You spend hours a week reading books you hate when you could be reading books you love — for what? To prove to hyung you're smart? How is that not idiotic behavior?"

"I —," Katie shut her gaping mouth with a click. "Okay, fair," she acknowledged, her dangly earrings jangling as she tossed her hair. "But also, it's so much fun to fuck with Jae. He does that jaw-clenchy thing and I can't decide if it's hot or terrifying or hot in a terrifying way."

Do-won laughed. "Well, in that you are definitely CHIMERA through and through. They have so many YouTube videos about it."

"Oh, trust. I know."

Do-won's brain whirred and then finally caught up, snagging on her comment. "Wait, are you into Jae-sung hyung?"

"What?" Katie furrowed her brow and pulled the sleeves of her Golden State Warriors hoodie over her hands. "That's quite a logical leap, Wonnie."

"It's not at all," he insisted. "You spend all this time trying to impress him and to evoke a response that you find hot."

Katie wasn't buying it. "I mean, all of you are hot. Just because Jae-sung has dimples and got all buff and big doesn't mean anything other than

I have a functioning pair of eyes. I'm not into any of you." She huffed. "Besides, I've already gone down that road."

"YOU HOOKED UP WITH JAE-SUNG HYUNG?!?" Do-won shrieked.

"WHAT?!? NO!" She was aghast. "I meant I already dated one of you! Isn't that violating some 'Bro Code'?"

"Uh, not really? It's not like we haven't hooked up with the same people before," Do-won shared. "There's seven of us. There are bound to be overlapping attractions."

"I'm not talking about fucking, Wonnie. Of course, you've fucked the same people — maybe even at the same time — not that I know or have thought about this in detail or —," Katie abruptly cut herself off.

Do-won found he quite enjoyed her discomfort. She had never been a prude, so the novelty of Katie being embarrassed about sex was quite diverting. "My lips are sealed, noona."

"Oh, Akihiro already told me all about it."

Of course, he did. "Well, if you know, then what's the problem?"

"I don't homewreck — and after me and Akihiro, wouldn't that be a little like homewrecking?"

Katie was probably right. It was bad form to date an ex of a friend. "It's all theoretical anyway, noona. Jae-sung hyung just started seeing someone, Jun hyung is married, Dae's engaged, Soo-min might as well be married, and I think Woo-jin hyung is into someone —"

"OH MY GOD, WHO?!?" she cut in, angling her body more toward him. "I think he is, too, but he won't tell me. That fucking bastard."

Do-won smirked. "Unlike Akihiro, I don't tell our secrets. Woo-jin hyung will tell you when he wants to."

She sighed. "Woo-jin oppa is supposed to be one of my soulmates. How could he do this to me?"

"You can't get in the way of DOJIN, noona," he said, referencing the portmanteau of his and Woo-jin's names. "We won't allow it."

Katie flipped him off and returned with a huff to her reading. She was adorable.

"Do you want to go to Jun hyung's birthday party together, noona?" Do-won asked a few hours later. "I can drive you."

Katie looked up from her book and blinked owlishly at the younger man through her reading glasses. "Is that tonight? I thought it was on Thursday."

"Today is Thursday."

Do-won clucked in bemusement. She never knew what day of the week it was now — let alone month. Katie never used to be this way but after her two years in Hong Kong? After, she was different in more ways than just this. Do-won shook himself of the gloomy thought.

"Ah," she replied, "of course it is. Uh, sure? Can we swing by my place first though? I left his present at home."

"Sure thing, noona. What did you get hyung?"

"You know, I'm not quite sure. I bought it a few weeks ago just in case I forgot when it got closer to his birthday. The irony, of course, is not lost upon me." Katie tilted her head as she tried to recall. "I think I chose to go with absurd and ridiculous?"

"Did you get him your own merch? Please tell me you got him an acrylic stand of yourself."

Do-won wished he had thought of that. He'd bought Ye-jun a very tasteful leather messenger bag that was useful, but not very fun. It was unlike him to be so austere in his accessory game, but he was sick of Ye-jun not using what he bought him.

Katie chuckled. "He should be so lucky! It might have been a Costco-sized box of his favorite ramyeon?"

"How could you forget such a present?" he asked.

"Well, the problem is that I might have opened the box and eaten one — but I can't remember if that was my own Costco-sized box or his."

"Noona, you really are in a class of your own. You should totally give it to him with one ramyeon missing," he suggested.

"Oh, I plan on doing so if it's the case." Katie's eyes gleamed. "Just the thought of his indignant yawping fills me with joy, especially since I doubt I wrapped it."

"It reminds me of that year when you sent hyung several boxes of jelly candies. That was so random," Do-won reminisced. "The boxes took up so much space at his barracks — it was hilarious. Hyung sent us so many pictures. He was so confused."

A look of shock crossed Katie's face. Do-won watched as she tried to cover her surprise by plastering an amused expression over it.

"Do you not remember?" he asked gently.

He was worried her memory was too patchy lately — perhaps she needed to get it checked out? Fame and fortune were great, but not at the expense of health.

Katie seemed torn.

Do-won lamented that he could never hold his tongue when it came to her. He was normally so much more circumspect, but with her? He always wanted to know her secrets.

"I didn't realize manager-oppa actually sent the jellies," she said softly.

"What do you mean?"

"It was, um —," she inhaled sharply.

"It's okay, noona. You don't have to tell me," he said quickly, but he was dying to know.

Katie flashed him a sad smile. "No, no. My therapist said I needed to let safe people into my life, that many of my problems with Akihiro stemmed from me not telling him what happened, so he had no idea if he was triggering something."

Do-won's heart leaped at being considered safe even as it plummeted hearing about the breakup from her perspective.

"It was a code," she finally said. "I didn't think oppa had followed through on the present, but I suppose he did just in case Tony was watching."

"What was? The jellies?" Do-won was confused. "Was hyung supposed to do something? I've never heard of a code with jellies."

Katie shook her head. "I'm explaining it wrong." She pulled her hair into a ponytail in frustration. "I'd texted Ha-joon oppa that I wanted to get 501 jellies for Jun oppa's birthday. 501 was the code for 'mayday.'"

Do-won was still confused.

"It's a play on words," she explained. "'M'aidez' means 'help me' in French, and Americans changed it to 'mayday.' Plus in Europe, May Day is a spring festival celebrated on May 1st."

"Ah, 501 as in: May 1st." It finally clicked. "You were asking for help?"

"Yes," Katie said.

He frowned. "Why didn't you just call hyung? That seems unnecessarily complicated."

Her hands were clenched and her breathing seemed faster.

"Are you okay, noona?"

Katie took a deep breath and held it. "I'll be fine in a moment."

Do-won gave her a few minutes to control her breathing.

"It was, uh, right after he — Tony was tracking —," She stopped again. "I'm sorry, Wonnie. I have to — I —," she apologized as she scrambled for her things.

"Noona, it's okay. I'm sorry I asked —," he blurted out, desperate to calm Katie down, but it was too little, too late.

Katie had fled.

September 2023

It had been eight weeks and Katie was not getting much better. The nausea and general flu-like symptoms had eased, but she still felt completely out of control. Her emotions were on a hair trigger and almost anything could set her off.

Outwardly, she had come up with ways to cope so that she didn't chase Akihiro and all her friends away, but she was still fucking miserable. Her psychiatrist had even upped the dosage, but nothing was working.

On top of that, she had gained ten pounds, and she was pissed. Katie didn't see how that was possible given that her appetite had dropped. But here she was: two months and ten pounds later.

Even if Katie hadn't been a celebrity, gaining ten pounds in such a short time would have upset her. But the fact that she was dating arguably one of the most beautiful humans alive made it all the worse. Despite Akihiro insisting he didn't care about the weight — that he couldn't really tell and whatever other lies he spun — she was not comforted.

She hadn't felt this despondent in years.

Katie begged Dr. Im to switch her to another drug, though the doctor had said this particular one didn't cause weight gain. Katie could not possibly give it any more time. She was terrified she'd burn her entire life down if she didn't.

She reluctantly texted her manager to book her time with the in-house trainer. Katie had just turned 30, and Dr. Im had intimated that perhaps her metabolism had slowed. She knew it was the fluctuating brain chemistry talking, but when Dr. Im had suggested such blasphemy, she had perhaps hated her doctor a lot and wished her to detonate into the sun.

"You look like someone just told you your dog died," Mina commented as Katie slid into her friend's silver S-Class. "You sure you're up for dinner?"

Katie sighed and pulled the strings of her hoodie tighter, the hood constricting around her face. She was severely underdressed compared to Mina, who had just come from work. Mina looked pristine as always, resplendent in a crisp navy Armani pantsuit paired with a gold and cream Hermès silk scarf and dark sapphire earrings. Her long black hair was pulled into a low chignon and she smelled expensive — like figs, coconut, and cedar.

"I feel like that dog died in my mouth," Katie grumbled.

Mina pulled a face. "That's disgusting."

"Sorry," Katie said, not really meaning it. She stared glumly out the window and watched the streets of Seoul pass by. "I just feel like shit." She sighed. "It seems like I always feel like shit. I'm not really good company these days."

Mina checked her mirrors and made a left turn. "You and me both, friend," she murmured. "I feel like shit all the time, too. We can be grumpy together."

"Wanna talk about it?" she asked, hoping that the older woman would tell her more. Katie desperately wanted to feel like a good friend, even if it was to listen to someone just as miserable as she was.

"You know Ye-jun and I have been trying to get pregnant, right?" Mina said casually, as if it wasn't a sore topic for her. "Well, they have me on these hormone injections and I'm bloated, my boobs hurt, and I feel like barfing. Oh, and I'm moody as hell."

Katie felt a surge of gratitude for Mina's candor. She hated feeling like she was a broken thing to be pitied, like she was an anomaly in a world full of happy, shiny people.

"That sucks," Katie commented. "How long do you have to get these shots?"

This time, it was Mina who sighed. "I guess every cycle until I get pregnant or we have to try another treatment."

Katie let out a long breath. "Why is it always us women who have to deal with this bullshit?" she complained lightly. "Like, can you imagine Akihiro or Ye-jun oppa having to deal with it?"

Mina snorted. "The volume — in both quantity and sound — of Ye-jun's assorted ranting would be legion," she said, adding, "although, he would likely do it in as ridiculous a way as possible to make me laugh and not feel bad."

"Yeah," Katie said. "Oppa is kind that way."

"He is," Mina agreed.

Katie settled more into the passenger seat and turned on the heated seat to relieve some of her aches. She felt old and sat in silence as Mina carefully drove through Hannam-dong.

"You'll be such a great mother, unni," Katie said, breaking the peaceable quiet.

Mina acknowledged her words with a hum. "You think so?"

"I do. You and oppa both will be such good parents," she added.

"Sometimes, I think I'm too brusque to be a good mother," Mina confided as she pulled into a parking structure. "I'm not a nurturing kind of person. I don't coddle folks, and though I don't mind children — I even love Ye-jun's niece — I don't strike myself as a maternal sort."

"You don't need to be coddling or some fake sweet thing to be a good mother, unni," Katie said. Katie let Mina concentrate on backing into the parking space before continuing. "Personally, I think there are lots of ways to be a good mom and you have those in spades. You listen well, you're nonjudgmental, and you fight for the people you love. Why wouldn't that translate into being an excellent parent?"

Mina shifted her Mercedes into park and then looked at Katie. "Do you — and feel free to not answer if it's too personal — but do you ever feel as if your body is broken somehow?" The normally cool and collected woman's voice hitched and Katie grabbed her friend's hand, squeezing it tightly. "I feel like such a failure, Katie. We've been trying for so long, and who has such a hard time getting pregnant? It's like a woman's only fucking function for fuck's sake."

Katie knew that Mina knew women were more than just baby incubators. She had heard Mina go off on the sexism in her industry and knew how hard her friend had worked to start her own boutique consulting agency. Katie knew Mina was not in need of trite affirmations.

"All the time, unni," she said instead. "Like how hard is it to enjoy fucking a hot man or like, have knives in your house?" Katie chuckled wetly. "We're a sorry lot, aren't we?"

Mina was quiet for a moment and Katie seized it to get her emotions under control.

"Akihiro is pretty hot for a baby," Mina observed finally. "Don't tell Ye-jun I said so, though. He's still upset about you introducing me to Choi Gyeong-gu."

"Oppa is so dumb. Like you would leave him for just any hot guy."

"Gyeong-gu is really fucking hot, though," mused Mina, "and I've never changed his diapers."

Katie doubled over cackling, pleased that her friend joined her. "I mean, some people are into that, I guess," she choked out, wiping a different sort of tear from the corners of her eyes. "I still can't believe you've known oppa all his life and that you've kept so many embarrassing stories about him to yourself. Frankly, it's upsetting."

Mina made a big show of looking around surreptitiously, as if anyone could overhear them in the car. "One time when Ye-jun was a toddler, he ran up to me and wanted to give me something. I held out my hand and he put what seemed to be a very warm, partially melted chocolate with a dusting of powdered sugar on it. I almost ate it — please keep in mind I was around 6 or 7 at the time —"

Seeing where this was going, Katie shrieked, "No, unni, no! Please tell me it was a chocolate!"

"It's a good thing I stopped to double-check." Mina's voice broke. She covered her mouth and guffawed.

"NOOOOOOOOOO!!! I'm never accepting chocolate from oppa ever again!" Mina's eyes danced and Katie felt something inside her ease. "Thanks, unni."

The older woman just smiled and grabbed her Hermès Birkin bag from the footwell of the backseat. "You ready for dinner, Katie?"

"Yeah," she breathed. She was still generally miserable, but she was grateful for any reprieve she could get.

January 2026

When Do-won picked Katie up for Ye-jun's birthday party, she waved off his apologies and concerns and instead confirmed that she was indeed giving Ye-jun a case of his favorite ramyeon, minus one serving. She had even wrapped it.

He indulged her need to appear as if everything was normal — and he supposed it was normal for her. Perhaps she was triggered regularly through the course of her day, that she was used to not being able to tell her story because the memories were too hard to endure.

Do-won mourned, both for who she had been — the woman he had met ten years ago and had befriended and loved like family — and for the woman she was now, navigating the perilous waters of her mind.

The gathering was a small one. Woo-jin was the only other DOYEN member present due to everyone else having other plans. Ye-jun's older brother Ye-sung and his wife Younga were also there with their little girl. Katie greeted everyone quickly and then beelined to Mina and hugged her tightly. When Katie finally let go, her eyes shimmered with unshed tears.

Do-won watched as she and the two other women disappeared into another part of the apartment. He inclined his head and asked, "What happened?"

"Ah, Wonnie. Mina is pregnant. With twins," Ye-jun replied, his eyes also misty. "We were going to wait until after dinner, but I guess noona already told them."

"Oh, sh— I mean, wow!" Do-won enthused, shooting Ye-sung and his daughter a guilty glance. Thankfully, Ye-jun's niece was busy watching a children's program on the big screen TV. "Congratulations, hyung!"

"Thanks," Ye-jun grinned. "We've been trying for a long time and it finally took. It's been really rough on her."

Woo-jin practically glowed with joy. "Do you know what you're having?"

"One of each!" crowed Ye-jun. "We chose to implant one embryo of each and they're both viable and healthy. It's been a tough first trimester, but the doctors think noona is out of the danger zone now."

Do-won hugged his hyung and willed his elation to radiate from his bones to Ye-jun's. "I'm so happy for you both, hyung," he whispered.

Do-won was happily humming to himself as he drove Katie back to her penthouse.

Ye-jun had outdone himself. He'd cooked up a veritable feast, and Do-won had dug in, indulging in the rich foods but taking it easy on the soju. Even though Katie had offered to drive him home so he could drink more, Do-won had refused.

"Did you have a good time, noona?" he asked as he tapped the leather steering wheel.

She startled out of her reverie. "I did, although my ears are still ringing from the ruckus oppa kicked up about the ramyeon."

Do-won could hear the grin in her voice. "That was awesome," he agreed. "But the best part of the night was still finding out they're having twins!"

"It's great news. They've been trying for so long," she said softly. "Unni will be the best eomma and oppa will be such a fun appa."

"It makes me want to have kids," Do-won sighed wistfully. "My sister's kids are so cute that my mother keeps hounding me to give her more."

Katie chuckled in commiseration. "Same. Mattie already gave my mother a grandchild — I don't see why I have to be involved in this."

"Do you want kids, noona?"

She flinched slightly. "I don't know, Wonnie. I don't think I would be a very good mother. I completely lack maternal instinct."

Do-won paused to consider her words. "I don't think that's true at all, noona."

Katie looked out the window instead of acknowledging his comment.

"You're patient and encouraging when explaining and teaching me about your approach to songwriting. You're fun and kind, and you are very thoughtful even when trolling us," Do-won said. "I don't think you give yourself enough credit."

"Hmmmm" was her only response. She continued to gaze out the window at the passing lights. After some time, her voice broke the silence. "Akihiro didn't think so."

"What?"

She cleared her throat. "Akihiro didn't think so."

"He said that to you?" Do-won refused to believe it.

Katie hesitated. "Not in so many words. But that's what he meant."

"How do you know?"

"I know." She exhaled. "He asked if our children would have to constantly walk on eggshells around me — that they would have to figure out really early what would set off my panic attacks or me disappearing for hours at a time."

Do-won wondered if his heart would ever get used to breaking after one of Katie's casual revelations. "Oh, noona." Even in the dark, he could see the silvery tracks of tears down her cheeks.

"I would ruin them, Wonnie. How could I be trusted with babies when I can't even have knives in my own home?"

He did not know what to say and so he said nothing, except a part of him rebelled at her bleak self-assessment. Do-won reached over and squeezed Katie's hand.

November 2023

Akihiro was miserable. Absolutely fucking miserable.

The last few months as Katie adjusted her medication were complete nightmares. Between his guilt of seeing Katie at the mercy of random chemicals in her brain, the guilt of sometimes hating her, and the guilt of still wanting her to pursue the drug changes so that he wouldn't feel like a predator when the two of them were physically intimate, he was constantly feeling as if her distress was all his fault.

Her misery was why Akihiro was currently snuggled in Dae-jung's comfortable bed with his friend. Katie had kicked him out of her apartment, and he hadn't wanted to be alone in his own.

"Why are you still with her if it's so horrible?" Dae-jung asked into Akihiro's hair from his official position as the big spoon of their friendship.

Akihiro glared into the soft blue linen pillow and said, "What would you have me do? I can't abandon her after all she is doing for me."

Dae-jung turned Akihiro around to look at him, his tan face downcast. "You don't owe her anything, Aki-yah. Be with her because you care about her and want to be with her and not because you feel obligated." He slung an arm around Akihiro and pulled him into an extremely awkward hug. "Noona made her own choices — and maybe she can't help how she's treating you or maybe she can — or maybe it's all a mix."

Akihiro pushed himself out of the hug and made to protest, but Dae-jung cut him off with an irritated cluck of his tongue.

"You didn't force noona into anything. You are allowed to have wants and desires. You are allowed to want sex with her to be mutually satisfying and welcomed," his friend said. Akihiro resisted the urge to look away. "You are allowed to be tired of her behavior and be unsure which noona you're going to get at any given moment."

A tiny sob escaped Akihiro's mouth. How did Dae-jung always know what to say?

"You're allowed to be frustrated and angry and disappointed. You don't have to be with her — no matter what she's doing for you or your relationship," Dae-jung said.

"Are you sure?" Akihiro asked, so quiet. So tentative.

"Absolutely."

Akihiro merely folded himself back into Dae-jung's embrace, crying until he cried himself out. It was good to be with someone who let him be himself and loved him all the same.

January 2026

Katie sat across from Dr. Choi in her plush office, trying desperately not to fidget. The walls were painted a cheerful yellow, the carpet was gray-blue, and pale, airy curtains framed the windows. She noted a delicate writing desk on one side of the room with some files, a laptop, a desk lamp, and a few tiny succulents in cute pots on the surface. Katie was with Dr. Choi in the sitting area that was delineated by an oval rug, two floral wingbacks, and a loveseat in a neutral linen color.

Dr. Im and Katie's regular therapist, Dr. Hong, had recommended Dr. Choi to her, and despite knowing that Dr. Choi was one of the preeminent practitioners of Eye Movement Desensitization and Reprocessing (EMDR) in Seoul, Katie was still incredibly nervous.

"Could you tell me more about what brings you to me, Katie-ssi?" Dr. Choi asked.

"Didn't Dr. Im and Dr. Hong tell you?" she responded defensively.

Katie wanted to kick herself for starting off with such a combative tone. She couldn't help it. She didn't know Dr. Choi. She was new — and though Katie had done her research and trusted her two other doctors — Dr. Choi was still new.

Dr. Choi smiled kindly. "Would it be easier if I switched to English, Katie-ssi? I did my doctorate and initial training in America." At Katie's nod, she continued. "It's understandable to be a little anxious. And yes, to answer your question, I did receive patient notes from both doctors. However, I find that it is often helpful for patients to verbalize to me directly what they hope to get from our sessions."

Katie scolded herself and screwed up her courage. She couldn't be a coward forever.

"I — I was in an abusive relationship for years. His name was Tony." She could do this. These were just facts. She could spew facts. "He was also my manager in Hong Kong and the youngest son of a man my father owed a shit ton of money to. My father was an abusive fuck, too. I would've let him rot, but they threatened my mother and brother."

It was getting hard to breathe. Katie abruptly stopped.

"Ah," Dr. Choi said softly. "Would you like some water?"

At Katie's nod, Dr. Choi got up and grabbed a bottle of water out of the mini-fridge by the wall behind her desk. Katie took her time cracking open the lid and sipping the cold liquid. She set the water bottle on the tiny round end table between her chair and the other matching one.

She proceeded to give Dr. Choi a quick summary and tried not to feel like a pathetic victim; she tried to feel strong instead of the stupid fool she was and had been.

"Why do you want to try EMDR, Katie-ssi?"

"I've been on antidepressants and in therapy for years," Katie revealed. "And while they help, I still get panic attacks. They said it would get better with time, but it hasn't. I mean, it's gotten better, but not — I — my boyfriend left me. He — he said I was too much for him — that it was too hard to be with me. That random things triggered me all the time and he couldn't live his life like that anymore." Tears streamed down her face.

"Do you feel like you're broken?" asked Dr. Choi.

"Yes," she whispered. "All the time."

Dr. Choi nodded. "Did Dr. Hong explain to you what the process of EMDR looks like? What it does?"

"Yes," Katie said. "She said we would target specific memories and you'd reprogram my brain or something as we go over it. That you'd shine lights while doing it."

"Not exactly," smiled Dr. Choi. "We'll be tapping into your instinctive mind as you recall a traumatic experience. I will give you a little buzzer for each hand and while you're thinking about the memory, they'll buzz. I'll ask you some specific questions about what your body is feeling as you try to explain it. We'll try to process the trauma in your body and teach it that you're safe and in control of your feelings."

"Does it really only take a few sessions?" Katie asked.

"Well, it can take about six to eight sessions, but sometimes, really traumatic memories may take a little bit longer," Dr. Choi explained. "It all depends on how you're doing, and if you need us to stop. You'll probably need to take it easy after our time together and maybe the day after."

Katie's body tensed in fear and Dr. Choi's keen eyes missed nothing.

"But before we begin, I want you to know that we can stop anytime. If you feel as if it's too much for you to handle, tell me. We will stop immediately. The purpose isn't to retraumatize you, okay?"

"Okay."

Dr. Choi looked down at her notes and then back to Katie. "I want to first make sure that your safe, calm place is still the same as what you established with Dr. Hong."

"Yes," Katie replied.

"Could you tell me about it?" Dr. Choi requested.

Katie sighed. She always hated these exercises. They generally worked, but she always felt so weak and stupid when she had to resort to them. All the same, she cooperated.

"I usually picture the ocean. I'm sitting on an outcrop of boulders, looking out at the ocean. It's a bit nippy, but the roar of the waves is loud and the call of seagulls is soothing."

"Okay, great." Dr. Choi smiled reassuringly. "From my discussions with Dr. Hong and that questionnaire you filled out, I think a few key moments stand out from your history, but I would like to get your opinion. Out of all your experiences, what would you consider the most negative and triggers you the most?"

She could do this. "Probably when Tony nearly beat me to death after he found out I got an abortion."

"Can you tell me what happened?" At Katie's sharp intake of breath, Dr. Choi added, "You don't have to discuss this with me if you don't want to. Mostly, it's important to visualize it in your mind," reassured Dr. Choi. "But if you can talk about it with me, it can help me identify some of the negative beliefs you think about yourself when you tap into this memory."

"I — I'd prefer not to. Not if you already have the notes from Dr. Hong and my questionnaire." Katie took another sip of her water. "It was hard enough to tell Dr. Hong," she explained shakily. "She's the only one I've ever told in detail."

"That's fine, Katie-ssi," said Dr. Choi gently. "How do you feel when I ask you about these memories?"

"Like I am on the edge of panic," Katie said softly. "Like Tony is just around the corner, just outside my awareness and about to take me back."

"And how do you want to feel after? What are you hoping will happen?"

"I — I just want to feel safe," she said. "I want to feel like Tony will never hurt me again — that if he tried to, I would win."

"What do you mean by win?"

"That he can't outsmart me. That he can't touch me — that nothing he can do can reach me." Katie's voice was hard and unyielding.

"So you want to feel in control, powerful, and clever?" Dr. Choi asked.

"Yes," she replied. "I'm tired of feeling broken. I'm so very tired."

"Alright, Katie-ssi, we have enough time to start the first desensitization session if you would still like to continue," Dr. Choi said. "Or we can end early and try next week."

What Katie really wanted to do was go home and drink a fifth of vodka, but she was afraid that if she delayed it any more, she would never come back into this room. Better to do it now while she was here.

"We can start," Katie said.

"Great," Dr. Choi said as she handed Katie two tiny buzzers. "I want you to hold one in each hand. As I guide you through the memory, the buzzers will alternate buzzing to ground you. If at any point it becomes too much, just let me know and we'll stop, okay?"

"Okay." Katie wanted to throw up.

"You can close your eyes if you want to, Katie-ssi."

Katie closed her eyes. Her right hand buzzed.

"I want you to think about the experience with Tony. In your mind, go over what happened that night," she directed. "If you want to tell me, you can. Or you can just think about it."

Katie remembered Tony coming in as she showered, and her chest tightened. She replayed him grabbing her by the throat, the calm way he spoke to her, all the while squeezing the very air from her trachea.

She went limp. She became weightless as he threw her around like a rag doll.

Her left hand buzzed.

She felt separated from her own body, observing silently as he beat the shit out of her with fists. It hurt to breathe. Everything hurt.

Her right hand buzzed.

Katie was going to die, and part of her welcomed it while another part — that wild, inhuman monster within her — screamed and raged. She didn't want to let him win, but she was so very, very tired.

Her left hand buzzed.

Dr. Choi's voice cut through her memory. "What feels like the worst moment?"

Katie thought of that sick anticipation right when Tony entered her bathroom and she was naked in the shower. Before she knew if he was there on one of his cursory surprise inspections or if he'd already known what she'd done. Everything else after — that was painful and awful — but it was the dread right before that was the worst.

Her stomach churned. Her right hand buzzed.

"Can you tell me what it is?" the doctor asked.

Katie inhaled a deep breath. "When I first see him from the shower," she whispered. Her left hand buzzed.

"What do you see in that moment?" Dr. Choi's voice was a steady, sure presence.

"I — I see Tony through the shower steam and glass walking into the bathroom." Her right hand buzzed.

"What's a negative thought or belief about yourself that goes along with that picture?"

"What have I done? I'm so fucking stupid," Katie grated out. Her left hand buzzed.

"Are you okay, Katie-ssi? Why don't we take a quick five-minute breather?" offered Dr. Choi, "and then you can let me know if you want to go on."

Katie nodded and gathered herself. She leaned against the wingback and tried to even out her breathing. She focused on the inhale, held her breath, and then focused on the exhale.

After what felt like far too little time, she heard Dr. Choi ask, "How are you doing, Katie-ssi?"

"I'm okay," she said, voice fainter than she would have liked.

"We don't have to continue, Katie-ssi. You already did a lot of heavy work today, and I don't want to retraumatize you. Let's reconvene next week, okay?"

"Okay," she replied, relieved. "Okay."

Katie was spent.

After Dr. Choi had waited what had felt like an eternity for Katie to get out of that chair, Ha-joon drove her home and she crawled under her covers to sleep for the rest of the day. For the first time in ages, she slept through the night, too. When she woke up the next morning, Katie felt inexplicably lighter, as if some unknown ballast in her body had been cut loose.

She didn't care if it was just a placebo effect; she would take the feeling for as long as it lasted.

The next week, Dr. Choi picked right up where she'd left off. She guided Katie through the memory again and her hands buzzed left and right repeatedly. Before Katie knew it, she was right back at that image of Tony entering her bathroom.

This time, Dr. Choi pressed on. "When you're in touch with that picture and the negative thought or belief about yourself that accompanies it, what do you feel now when I'm asking these questions?"

Katie's throat went dry. "I — I feel shame. Overwhelming shame. How could I be so fucking stupid? How could I let myself get pregnant like a fucking idiot? How could I let him catch me getting rid of it?" Her right hand buzzed. "I feel a little panicky, too," she admitted.

"You're doing so well, Katie-ssi," said Dr. Choi. "When you're in touch with that picture and the negative thought or belief about yourself that accompanies it, and when you notice the feelings that come up when I ask you these questions, what do you notice physiologically going on in your body?"

Her left hand buzzed. "I want to throw up," Katie said. "I want to scream. There's this build up of pressure and panic in my chest," she continued, "and I feel sweaty and antsy — like I had too much caffeine."

"Ah," Dr. Choi said. "That's normal, Katie-ssi. Let's take a breather for a few minutes. I want you to imagine your safe place with me," the doctor's clear voice instructed.

Katie thought back to the ocean, how the waves roared and didn't expect anything from her. They just did what they had done for time out of mind, beating inexorably against the shore. She was nothing — and it was a comfort.

"How are we doing, Katie-ssi? Are you okay to continue?"

She inhaled one last deep breath. "Yes," Katie said.

"Okay, I'm going to set off the buzzers for about twenty to thirty seconds, and while that's happening, I want you to notice what surfaces," said Dr. Choi. "It could be nothing, it could be a random thought or word or another memory. Don't force anything to come up; just pretend you're watching scenery pass you by."

Her right hand buzzed.

Katie's mind flashed to Tony's black socks as he finally walked out of her bathroom, leaving her on the cold tile floor as he ransacked her flat.

Her left hand buzzed.

She heard him panting, winded from his exertion. She smelled his cologne, wet and sharp, activated by his sweat.

"What came up?" Dr. Choi asked and Katie told her. Dr. Choi listened, took a few notes and repeated the process.

Her right hand buzzed.

She remembered his hair, mussed and dripping. His tie loose and shirt sleeves rolled up.

Her left hand buzzed.

Katie remembered Tony dragging her into the living room and gloating, calling her a stupid bitch, telling her that she would never get rid of him. That he would hound Katie until the day he found her and killed her himself.

"What came up?" Dr. Choi asked again.

Katie told her again. And then she felt her chest crack open as she started to wail and couldn't stop. It was as Katie had always feared: she had begun to fall apart and she would never be put back together again.

November 2023

Katie was miserable.

She didn't care what Jae-sung and Soo-min said — working out sucked. It particularly sucked since she was at that very moment, stuck in the SB Entertainment gym with lead physical trainer Beom-soo, trying not to collapse as he watched her do burpee after burpee with an eagle eye. At least no one else was in the gym at that ungodly early hour to witness her humiliation.

"PT-nim, this is cruel," she gasped.

"You'll thank me when you're in the best shape of your life," Beom-soo commented.

Katie scowled and muttered, "Lumpy's a fantastic shape. Imagine a rude, bossy man trying to tell me lumpy isn't the best shape."

"What was that?"

"Nothing," she grumbled.

"Hmmm, if you can breathe enough to complain then clearly, I'm not working you hard enough," observed the sadistic fuck.

"Ah, hyung," she heard Akihiro's teasing voice say, "you're doing it wrong if the ladies don't like the way you work them — especially when you're hard."

Katie's eyes lit up as she watched her boyfriend, clad in a clingy Under Armour shirt and baggy gray sweats, saunter into the gym. Things had settled down lately as her new medication finally kicked in. She felt less out of control. For the first time since the cross-tapering had begun, she felt human. The jury was still out on her sex drive, but at least she wasn't tempted to bite off Akihiro's admittedly very pretty head every time they were together.

"Fuck off, Hiro-yah," retorted Beom-soo. "Your training session isn't until later this afternoon. What are you doing here? I can't have you distracting your girlfriend. I only have another few weeks to get her ready for her album shoot."

"Don't be mean to Katie, PT-nim. She's already sexy. She doesn't need to work out," Akihiro defended.

Katie counted off her last set of burpees and then dropped to the floor. "Burpees are evil," she panted. "They serve no purpose in life."

Akihiro threw her a bottled water, which she sucked down readily. "Poor Katie," he lilted, "maybe I should join your workouts so you have someone pleasant to look at."

He winked and lifted his shirt to show off his abs as he bodyrolled while twirling around in a sexy dance move.

Katie choked.

Akihiro cocked his head and considered her carefully, his trademark Chanel earrings catching the light. He slowly swiped his thumb over his plush lower lip and smirked an impudent grin. "See something you like?" he growled roughly.

She blamed the surge in her temperature on the inhumane number of sets Beom-soo had just needled her into doing.

"Looks can be deceiving, Aki-yah," she shot back, "and I prefer to squeeze the merchandise before buying."

Akihiro arched a delighted eyebrow. He slunk his way to her and turned around, sticking his perfect ass in her face. "Go ahead and give it a squeeze. Try not to hurt yourself."

"Oh for fuck's sake, children," Beom-soo said exasperatedly. "Katie-yah, wipe the drool off your face. I'm going to take a piss and when I get back, you'll have resolved this foreplay or whatever this is, and I can get back to doing my fucking job."

The older man stalked out of the gym. Katie and Akihiro were alone.

Quick as a flash, Akihiro was on her, crushing her beneath him on the floor. His hands and mouth were everywhere and she was only half-protesting. "Aki-yah, I'm all sticky and sweaty," she gasped. A pressure urgently built up in her gut. Was this desire?

"Tell hyung you need to go home right now," Akihiro purred, his voice molten liquid.

Katie's senses were so overwhelmed with Akihiro's clean, powdery scent, his hard body on hers, and an undercurrent of fear. "Aki-yah, what if — what if we get back and it's gone? What if —"

"Shhhhhh," he breathed as he devoured her mouth. "If that happens, that happens. But if we don't leave soon, I'm going to take you on the floor right now."

Raw need shot through her veins. "Oh my god, Akihiro. You can't just say shit like that to me." Katie squirmed. "I think I'm wet," she whispered. "I — this hasn't — maybe it's sweat —," she babbled senselessly.

"You can't tell me not to say shit like that to you and then tell me you're wet," Akihiro growled. He abruptly got up and hauled Katie to her feet. Her eyes were immediately drawn to the outline of Akihiro's dick in his gray sweats. "Get your things, Katie."

Katie scrambled to comply. She couldn't meet Beom-soo's gaze when she passed him as Akihiro dragged her out of the gym at record speed.

"Katie isn't feeling well, hyung," Akihiro said, his voice rough.

"Right," replied Beom-soo, clearly not buying any of it. "Get out of here before you two idiots commit an act of public indecency — Jesus."

Katie's face was on fire, but nonetheless, she followed Akihiro to his SUV. Her entire body was alight. Maybe she and Akihiro would be okay after all.

February 2026

Katie was back in her Hong Kong flat, Tony's huge palm a vise around her throat. She couldn't breathe. He was going to kill her.

Her left hand buzzed.

Suddenly, Tony was on the floor and she had a bat. And then Katie was smashing into him, small and naked though she was. Katie — covered in bruises, blood, and triumph — beat Tony into a pulp. He sobbed and begged for mercy, but she gave none.

Her right hand buzzed.

"What came up just now?" Dr. Choi asked.

"I was beating Tony into smithereens," she said, eyes wet.

"How did that make you feel?"

Katie hardened her voice. "Good."

She was back in her Hong Kong flat. Katie could see herself, naked and battered on the bathroom floor. She knelt gently by her body and gathered herself into her arms, weeping. "I'm so sorry," she sobbed. "I'm so sorry I didn't protect you better."

Katie's body refused to look at her.

Her left hand buzzed.

"What came up?" she heard Dr. Choi ask.

She was back in her Hong Kong flat. Katie could see herself, naked and battered on the bathroom floor. She knelt gently by her body and gathered herself into her arms, weeping. "I'm so sorry," she sobbed. "I'm so sorry I didn't protect you better."

Katie's body lifted her arm and caressed her cheek, full of love and tenderness. She pulled Katie down and kissed her on the forehead in benediction. She curled into Katie's lap and let Katie stroke her until she slept.

Her right hand buzzed.

"What came up?"

Katie heard her father calling her a stupid whore. She heard Johnny laughing at her on Taiwanese national radio. She heard her father telling her that he was throwing all of her things out into the street because he no longer had a daughter. Katie was a disgrace.

Her left hand buzzed.

"What came up?"

Katie tried to set the scene for Dr. Choi, to give her context.

"It was right after the scandal with my ex Johnny. He told the Howard Stern of Taiwan that I won 'The Singer Songwriter' by fucking the judges." It had been over a decade. She was over Johnny, and yet, her father's words still haunted her. "Johnny basically called me a harlot on public radio and implied I was into all sorts of foul, depraved sexual acts. It was great."

"How old were you?"

"I was 21? 22?" Katie paused to think. "It was March 2015? So I was 21."

"Did your family defend you?" Dr. Choi asked.

She shook her head. "What could they possibly say that wouldn't draw more attention to it?" Katie sighed. "I was so hurt and ashamed — I didn't expect my family to do anything."

"What happened with your father?"

"I called home to break the news to my mother before my aunts could tell her or she could see it on the Taiwanese news," she answered. "My father picked up the phone instead. I didn't realize he was home."

"What did he say?"

"He told me he had no daughter. That I had made him a laughing-stock to his peers — and that his business in China would suffer." Katie sniffled. "'Who would want to do business with the father of a whore?' he screamed."

Dr. Choi took a few notes. "What feelings surface when you think of this moment?"

"Shame. Crushing shame," Katie replied quietly.

"Is that all?"

"I'm mad," she added. "I feel super pissed off."

"Tell me why," Dr. Choi asked.

Katie paused, a little unsure. "How dare he? How dare he use me? He threw me away until he needed me — and what do you know? It turned out it was really convenient he had a whore for a daughter after all," she spat.

"Do you think you're a prostitute?"

Katie looked at Dr. Choi, eyes empty. "I am what my father made me."

Katie saw an image of shrimp shells strewn in her lap and her năinai begging her father not to hurt her.

Her right hand buzzed.

"What came up?"

"I saw my father," Katie said.

"Oh?" replied Dr. Choi. "Tell me about it."

"We were having dinner and I didn't want to eat the celery. I hate celery." Katie made a garbled sound of disgust. "I still hate celery."

Dr. Choi nodded encouragingly at her.

"My father ordered me to eat it, and I just refused. Next thing I knew, he had pushed my plate of shrimp shells into my lap, and I was trying to clean it up. My nǎinai — my father's mother — was trying to help me and — it's a bit of a blur." Katie paused to recall a bit more. "I think he cornered me in the kitchen as I was throwing things away and my nǎinai tried to get in between us, and then I fled. I ran upstairs to my room and locked the door."

"Where was your mother?" asked Dr. Choi.

"She wasn't home. I think she was working late? I'm not sure," Katie replied. "Anyhow, he kept banging on the door and I remember worrying that he'd break the door down and then beat me. I really didn't want him to break my door so I remember thinking, 'Well, he's going to kill me anyway,' and opened the door."

"Why did you think he was going to kill you?"

"I don't know," Katie said. "It was probably just teen angst and overdramatics. I must have been about 14 at the time."

"I didn't ask because I thought you were overdramatic," clarified Dr. Choi. "I was just curious why you thought that and still opened the door."

"It was inevitable," Katie said. "There was really only one way for that to end."

Dr. Choi paused and then asked, "Is that how you felt about Tony?"

Katie shrugged. "I guess I have no sense," she quipped. "Was always too stupid for my own good."

"Why do you say that?"

"Well, if I had been smarter like my brother, I would have just eaten the fucking celery. I wouldn't have always antagonized my father and made him angry enough to hit me." Katie felt sweaty and uncomfortable. "If I had sense, I would have never agreed to whatever deal Mr. Lau negotiated with me. I would have never agreed to move to Hong Kong and let Tony control me. I knew this would happen — and still. Still I chose it. I should have never — I should have —"

"You should have what, Katie-ssi?"

Katie clenched her hands. "I should have told my label sooner. I should have gone to the police. I don't know — but I was just so stupid. So fucking stupid." She shoved her fists into her eyes, as if pressing them could prevent the tears from leaking out.

"Were you afraid? Afraid that they would hurt your mother and brother?" Dr. Choi asked gently.

"Yes, of course! I'm not a monster, Dr. Choi. I would rather go through it a thousand times more if I could keep Mattie safe."

"Are you angry at Mattie for needing you?"

Katie was horrified. "No. Not ever."

"Were you angry at your mother?" she pressed.

"I —," Katie choked on a sob. "How could she?" Katie whispered. "How could she marry a monster like him? How could she stay with him after all he's done? Why did she always choose him? How come she never chose me?"

Katie did not think she had any more pain left in her body, and yet, she was an endless font. Each time Katie thought she couldn't be cracked open wider, her heart surprised her.

She went home after that session and didn't resurface for days.

"Noona, are you free this Saturday?" Do-won asked as he stuck his head into Katie's studio.

Katie looked up from her book, blinking. Do-won really hoped it was something she actually wanted to read instead of whatever god-awful thing

Jae-sung recommended, mostly because he didn't want to hear her constant complaints about it.

"Maybe? I think so?"

"Great! My parents wanted to have dinner with the whole family and they mentioned they missed seeing you. I'll pick you up at 6:30."

"Oh," she said. Do-won carefully observed her as she processed what he'd said. He could tell she did not want to go, but couldn't think of a good reason not to. "Um, do I need to dress up?"

Do-won's entire face lit up. "Nah, I think it's at our actual house."

"Okay. Did you want me to give you your birthday present then? Or did you want me to give it to you later?"

"Noona, you remembered!"

Katie had been so focused on her therapy sessions lately that Do-won would have understood if she'd forgotten. It was in great part why he was inviting her to his family birthday celebration. She needed to be surrounded by people who loved and cared about her — and ever since he started dragging her to his parents' house regularly, her spirits had seemed to rise.

She hmphed with no small irritation. "I've only known you forever, and I was a Cute Humble Independent Musically Evolved Radical Aspect before I ever met you!" She huffed indignantly. He couldn't believe she knew the entire acronym when he'd tried his hardest to forget. "Give me some fucking credit, Wonnie."

"Bring it to dinner," he said, "unless it's inappropriate for a family setting."

She glared at him. "Who's the dongsaeng here? I'm not a savage! I can behave! And I'll have you know: parents love me!"

Do-won just side-eyed her.

"Okay, that's not true," Katie muttered. "But when I try, they do, and I am pretty sure your mother loves me."

She was right. His parents adored her and despite some glances his mother had sent his way, they mostly did not tease him about her. They knew she had dated Akihiro for years.

It would do Do-won well to remember that. "Yeah," he breathed, "she really does."

Katie smiled, brilliant and open. He was so fucked.

November 2023

Katie and Akihiro barely made it through the front door of her penthouse before Akihiro was all over her again. His hands hadn't left her body the entire drive. Now they were omnipresent and she couldn't get enough of him.

Was this how she used to be? Wild and full of want?

"Akihiro," she pleaded, "Akihiro, please."

"What do you want, baby?" he rumbled in her ear.

A fire lit in her veins and her pussy throbbed. "Hiro-yah," she whined. "Need you inside me."

"Here?" he asked as she pulled his sweats down and scooped his hard cock out. He hissed as she palmed him. He was so velvety and smooth.

"Please," Katie begged. Her voice sounded foreign to her own ears. She hadn't been this needy in years and she wanted to rush just in case it was a fluke.

"I don't have a condom, baby," he chuckled. "You think you can make it to your room?" He kicked off his shoes as he tucked himself back into his sweats. "Nevermind. Let's go," he said as he threw her over his shoulder and laughed at her surprised squeak.

By now, Akihiro was a familiar weight on her body. Despite him saying he didn't want to sleep with Katie if she wasn't into it, at the end of the day, he was just a man with needs. Katie had promised not to fake it, and he'd promised to accept what she was offering in good faith.

Normally, by the time the two of them were naked, Katie was trying desperately to connect to her body, trying to be candid, and paying more attention to Akihiro's body and what would bring him pleasure.

But today, she was voracious. Her body was screaming with desire and need, and she could not get enough of him.

Akihiro naked. Akihiro eager. Akihiro reverent. Akihiro, Akihiro, Akihiro.

"Want you in me already," Katie complained, "why aren't you in me yet?"

"Slow down, baby," he rasped. "I won't last long if you keep this up."

Katie forced herself to slow down, to truly root herself in the experience. She watched as he rolled a condom onto his cock and she held her breath in anticipation as he slid his hardness through her silky, wet folds.

She writhed, her body tingling with sensation and want.

"Please," Katie whimpered. "Please, Akihiro. I beg you, please fuck me now."

Akihiro grinned, eyes glinting with joy. "As you wish, Katie. As you wish." He slowly thrust into her open heat, making her feel every inch of his thick, long dick.

"More, Akihiro," she demanded. "More."

He leaned over and tongued Katie's ear and she cried out as prickles of pleasure bloomed down her face. "Such a greedy little thing, aren't you?"

"Yes," she whispered, "yes."

Katie could feel him smile against her skin as he intentionally pumped slowly into her. It had been so long since she felt sexual desire. It had been so long since her body was a source of delight.

Akihiro leaned his forehead against hers as he continued to work deeper and deeper into her. "Want to learn what makes you feel good, Katie," he murmured fervently on her lips. "Want to make you feel as good as you make me feel. Want you to feel loved and adored."

Katie anchored herself to the beautiful man on top of her and was grateful anew as sensation and feeling flooded her senses. She let Akihiro explore her body and her tells as she remembered what she liked and what she didn't. Katie let her conscious mind float and reveled in instinct and biological imperative.

Her body was honest for the first time in years.

"Akihiro," she breathed, "I think I'm gonna come soon."

"Tell me what you want, love," he replied. "How do you want me?"

"Faster, Hiro-yah," Katie panted. "Want to feel you deep inside me."

"Yeah?" he grunted. "Want me to fuck you so hard you forget your name?"

At her ragged "yes," Akihiro upped his pace and rolled his hips in such a way that drove Katie wild with stimulation. All the while, he praised her, telling her she was beautiful, that she was the only woman for him, that he loved her, that he wanted to be with her and only her, that she held his heart, that she was everything he wanted and more.

And when Katie's body finally exploded in ecstasy, she was carried away by Akihiro's love and kisses, his love as tangible as the stars.

The two of them canceled all remaining plans for the day and stayed in bed, exploring each other's bodies as if for the first time — and, in some sense, it was. Akihiro had only ever had a vague sense of what Katie might have liked, in as much as she could feel when her sex drive was blunted. He was eager to make up for lost time.

As for Katie, it was one thing to know Akihiro's body from calculated study; it was another entirely to get aroused by his pleasure. Akihiro unleashed was an experience unlike any other, and she hoped for many more.

She had forgotten so much.

Currently, Akihiro was wrapped around her, and even though she generally hated being held for so long — the heat usually became unbearable — she allowed it. Akihiro seemed to need it, and Katie? Katie marveled that her body could finally enjoy sex and that she could come.

She wondered if it was a fluke or if it was a harbinger of a new normal. Katie used to have a reasonably strong sex drive; would it be like that again? Or was it yet another rhythm and pace of her body that she had to learn through trial and error?

Katie forced her mind to calm and think of other things, to not allow anxiety to rob her of what she'd reclaimed, thanks to altering her brain chemistry.

She focused on how she felt safe and cared for in the arms of a man who had spent the better part of a year with her despite her being a terrible partner. Katie did not deserve him, but she would try her damnedest to in the future.

Katie chose to trust that together, Akihiro could be real with her and she could be real with him, that he was safe enough to hold her and keep her. That they could build each other up instead of break each other down.

For the first time since Katie and Akihiro had started dating, she allowed herself to imagine a life with him in it — a rich life full of babies, laughter, and joy.

For the first time in years, Katie allowed herself to hope.

June 2026

As the months passed, recalling the various traumatic memories became less and less intense for Katie during each successive EMDR session. Katie began to think maybe she wasn't as doomed as she had thought. She paired the weekly EMDR sessions with her weekly therapy sessions with Dr. Hong, and continued attending her dance movement therapy sessions, too.

Katie pursued healing as if it were her full-time job and her career was just a hobby.

One day, as Dr. Choi asked Katie what came up as she thought of her trauma, Katie realized that those memories no longer had power over her. She was in control of her emotions. They could no longer hurt her.

At her last session with Dr. Choi, Katie wept in gratitude and hoped for a future free of panic and fighting her own mind. She took comfort in the fact that, if needed, Dr. Choi could help her again.

Katie was clever. She was strong. She was healing. And maybe, maybe that would be enough. Maybe, just maybe, Akihiro would take her back.

CHAPTER 8

April 2024

Katie Wu's most recent Korean album "Détente" (SB Entertainment, 2024) continues in the same vein as "Threading the Needle" (SB Entertainment, 2023) and further explores what happens when tensions ease between states and people. Whether taken as a metaphor for relationships or literally between countries, the album showcases Wu's penetrating lyrics and signature brilliance.

The album starts with the hopeful "An End to Hostilities" and ends with the less confident "Uneasy Truce." Hands down, the best track is "Modern Pharmacology." The song is a trip — the highs are so high and the lows are so low. The switches in meter and time are unparalleled and exciting, and the hook is mesmerizing. Phenomenal.

- JoongAng Ilbo, April 2024

Deftly alternating between English, Mandarin, and Korean, "Détente" (SB Entertainment, 2024) uses varying language,

*melody, beats, and music genres to illustrate just how difficult
it is to de-escalate and reconcile broken hearts and people. Out-
standing.*

                                        - Taiwan News, April 2024

[1] An End to Hostilities [2:14]
[2] Heavyweight [3:10]
[3] The Elephant in the Room [3:27]
[4] Modern Pharmacology [3:45]
[5] Peripheral Vision [2:51]
[6] A List of Demands [3:16]
[7] Uneasy Truce [4:09]
                    - Track list, "Détente" (SB Entertainment, 2024)

You might as well be another universe
Though our edges touch and intersect
Though we invade each other and swallow
We are foreign bodies; we are not the same

Parley is impossible — and so is parlay
Why would you bet on us when we can't even speak
You say I demand too much but maybe it's just my due
Maybe it's me, but maybe it's you (maybe it's you)
                    - "A List of Demands" (SB Entertainment, 2024)

To manager-nim.
    - Album dedication, "Détente" (SB Entertainment, 2024)

A kihiro was happy.

The past few months had been a whirlwind of sex, sex, and more sex. They did do things other than each other, but Akihiro had figured that since the upcoming year would be full of touring on both of their parts and that the beginning of their relationship had been so bereft of satisfying sex — well, it couldn't be helped, really.

Didn't they deserve a little bit of amazing fucking?

According to Akihiro's members, though, it was a bit much. What did Dae-jung say? Something about it being hard to breathe around them because the sexual tension was so thick?

Surely Dae-jung had to be exaggerating.

Besides, Katie hated public displays of affection. In fact, it was one of Akihiro's greatest joys to annoy her with hugs, hand-holding, and sneaky kisses. She was trying to let him be more touchy with her, but it was hard. It would hurt his feelings more, except in private, Katie couldn't keep her hands off of him.

That was definitely a soothing balm to Akihiro's ego.

Lately, however, they rarely saw each other. Katie was busy in rehearsals, costume fittings, makeup tests, video filming, photoshoots, and doing press for her album and tour that was starting at the end of the month. Though Akihiro mentally understood that even if Katie had been free, he was also preparing for his own worldwide tour with his band members and stuck doing his own endless list of activities.

It was less than ideal.

He still missed her but didn't want to seem clingy or incapable of being an independent person. Akihiro knew from experience that Katie hated having tabs kept on her — but even he could be forgiven for wanting to spend time with his girlfriend. They were both so busy and exhausted, he sometimes wished they were just a normal couple rather than two famous

K-pop stars. He missed when they'd done the normal couple things like going on dates, eating out, watching movies, and hanging out at her home.

The truth was, Akihiro was perhaps a little concerned that Katie's latest album seemed so apprehensive and wary. Granted, it was written around the time of her trying to find the right anxiety medication — but still. It didn't sound very hopeful at all. And now they were going to be spending several months apart? It all seemed portentous.

Plus, he didn't want to be an egotistical asshole and think that he'd somehow transform Katie's very personality or worldview just by being her boyfriend, but maybe he had thought that she'd at least write happier music? That being with him would somehow bleed into her art — that she could at least be less sad?

Akihiro knew that he was being ridiculous. He knew all about how albums had concepts and that songs captured moments in time. Just because she felt one way before didn't mean she still felt that way now.

Except, he was just never brave enough to ask her. He couldn't bring himself to ask how Katie was actually feeling about her relationship with him — or even about life.

Akihiro was a coward.

He found that he didn't really want to know. He was just so tired, really. He was still tired from when she was trying to get that right balance of medication and sex drive — and he didn't know if he could bear to break the seemingly good thing they had right now.

It seemed as if Katie's album hit a little too close to home after all.

There was only one other tiny thing that bothered Akihiro in all this sex and physical connection — and Akihiro would have never even noticed if Dae-jung hadn't mentioned it. He still couldn't shake that feeling of always being on edge around Katie. They were a year in and yet, Akihiro didn't feel as if he knew Katie any better than he ever did.

She was still a closed box.

Yes, the sex was amazing — oh god, was it amazing. Katie did a certain tongue thing around his cock that always made him come so fast, and she was always down for whatever outrageous thing he suggested. (Dae-jung perhaps knew a little too much about Katie's sexual proclivities, but she didn't seem to mind. She knew who they were to each other.)

But now that sex was no longer the huge obstacle it had been and Katie had finally found the right balance in medication, Akihiro found it strange how little things had changed.

Katie was still prickly and skittish. She still clammed up, lashed out, or panicked. She still disappeared sometimes for hours. She still went out to the balcony and lit cigarette after cigarette, watching them ash out in the tray. She still had nightmares.

She still had no sharp knives.

When Katie started the Asia portion of her two-month tour a few weeks later, Akihiro missed her something fierce. He was surprised he'd even had time to since he was still deep in his own preparations for DOYEN's new album and upcoming tour.

He likely wouldn't have been so needy if he'd known ahead of time that she wasn't going to be joining him on the American leg of the DOYEN tour as he had initially assumed. Though they hadn't discussed her joining him, Akihiro had thought it was a done deal. One of Dae-jung's previous partners had done so for the European legs of their tour right before the pandemic. But right before she'd left, Katie had sprung the news that she'd accepted the role of being a judge on "The Singer Songwriter," the Taiwanese show she'd won at the start of her career.

He would have suggested that she come for the few weeks between the end of her tour and the start of the show, except her younger brother

Mattie was getting married. As a result, she was going to spend some time in America with her family instead of returning to Seoul. She had mentioned something about being stressed because her father was going to be in attendance, but had deflected Akihiro's questions about why. He hadn't even realized she wasn't speaking to her dad.

Again, her staying in America instead of coming back to Seoul wouldn't have been a problem except that Akihiro's world tour was starting before she'd get back. He didn't understand why she wouldn't rush back to Korea to see him before he left.

Part of him felt a little miffed that Katie didn't even ask him to attend her brother's wedding as her boyfriend — or that she didn't seem to want him to meet her family. Akihiro had met her mother and Mattie once when she'd first moved to Seoul and maybe one other time. She'd met his parents several times in the last year when they'd visited from Tokyo, though she had never seemed to feel at ease.

She had claimed it was due to the language barrier and always needing Akihiro as an interpreter, but that didn't quite ring true in his mind. At least Katie had started to learn Japanese for his sake, but it was slow going given how busy she was.

Logically, Akihiro knew that meeting up was impractical and not at all about him.

Katie's baby brother was getting married. Of course she would stay in America. Not only that, she'd be exhausted after her tour. To fly back to Korea for what little time Akihiro could spare between photoshoots, fittings, and rehearsals for his own tour, and then fly back to America for the wedding? That would be stupid.

Akihiro knew he was being an ass. Dae-jung agreed.

"What exactly do you want noona to do?" Dae-jung asked after Akihiro had complained again during a break in their rehearsals. They sat on the soft benches lining the hallway where all the dance studios were housed.

Akihiro sighed and waited for a group of backup dancers to pass by. "I don't know," he pouted.

"You know you can't attend the wedding," Dae-jung observed. "Not only do we have a shit ton of rehearsals and comeback preparations, you can't attend openly as her date. The pictures would get out."

"I know." Akihiro scowled. "Although, I'd just like to say that I'm almost 30. It's ludicrous for fans to think I'm supposed to be single and a virgin."

"I'm pretty sure literally zero CHIMERA think you're a virgin," said Dae-jung. "And honestly, we don't have dating clauses. Jun hyung already got married so it wouldn't be a big deal, but noona is still considered controversial and it's right before our tour, Aki-yah."

"I wouldn't be able to meet her in America anyway," muttered Akihiro dejectedly. "But she could have asked. She didn't even ask."

"Yes, she could have asked," Dae-jung carefully repeated.

"Is Katie ashamed of me?" Akihiro asked.

Dae-jung regarded him with sympathetic brown eyes. "Why do you think she would be?"

Akihiro voiced a thought he'd never spoken out loud. "I don't think she's told her family about me," he said.

"I'd ask you why you think that, but I'm sure you have your reasons," Dae-jung said. He picked up his energy drink from the floor and drank from it. "You should ask her."

"It's silly, right?" He hated how insecure he felt about her. "We're going on a little over a year. We're stronger than ever."

"I don't think it's silly."

Akihiro hugged Dae-jung. His best friend was always so good about validating his feelings.

"Maybe I'm just not sure what to expect from a relationship," Akihiro said. "It is the longest I've ever dated someone." His heart panged again. "Why didn't she ask?"

Dae-jung just looked sadly at Akihiro. "Maybe noona didn't want to make you feel bad when she knew you couldn't go. Maybe it didn't occur to her. Maybe she didn't want you to go." His soulmate hugged him tightly again. "You won't know unless you talk to her."

Akihiro supposed he could ask. He knew he should ask.

"Why don't you want to ask her, Aki-yah?"

Akihiro appreciated Dae-jung's gentle prodding. Akihiro knew his best friend already had his suspicions; in fact, he'd told Akihiro his opinion on many occasions. And yet, still, even now, he showed restraint.

"I don't want to upset her."

"Why do you think it will upset her?"

Akihiro curled himself into Dae-jung's side as they both leaned against the wall behind the bench. "That's the thing: I never know what will upset her! Once, I walked into the bathroom while she was taking a shower and she freaked out. Katie's not even a modest person, but she just completely shut down and refused to talk to me after."

Akihiro had never entered Katie's bathroom again without knocking. Even then, he generally tried to avoid her bathroom unless he was expressly invited.

"Katie didn't seem right for days after," Akihiro commented quietly. "But when I asked her about it, she said she was fine. And when I asked if I had done anything wrong, she got even more upset."

Dae-jung quietly stroked Akihiro's mint green hair. "That must be hard," he murmured.

"One time, I brought her a new Louis Vuitton purse — it wasn't even available to the general public yet — and she wouldn't touch it." Akihiro scrunched his face. He was still puzzled. "She thanked me but she never took it out of the box. I don't even think it's in her penthouse. I don't know where it went."

"Maybe she sold it on eBay."

Akihiro cracked a smile. "Maybe."

Akihiro hadn't bought her a present, a purse, or anything LV since. He didn't know what he would do when Katie's birthday hit in August. He supposed he'd figure something out. He loved giving presents. It was his thing. He felt hamstrung.

"Are you happy, Akihiro?" Dae-jung asked after sipping on his energy drink. "Do you like being with noona still?"

"I can't break up with her when she's on tour, Dae," Akihiro replied. "She just started!"

Dae-jung's hand stilled in Akihiro's hair. "That's not what I asked."

"Oh, right," Akihiro said contritely. Why had he rushed to that conclusion? "I — I think I just miss her."

Dae-jung hummed. "It's been a whole week without sex. How are you even alive?"

Grateful for Dae-jung's change in subject, Akihiro pushed himself off the bench and laughed. "It's been rough, man."

"The phone sex is probably good though, yeah?" leered Dae-jung as he raised his brows suggestively.

Akihiro chuckled. "She's filthy." Except, sex really wasn't the problem — or was it? He didn't know anymore.

The conversation moved on, but later, after rehearsals were done, Akihiro couldn't help but wonder why he'd defaulted to breaking up. They had surmounted so much. He felt guilty for even thinking about it. He reminded himself that he loved Katie so very, very much, and of course, people in love had to make compromises. Love didn't count the costs (or if it did, people in love bore it willingly).

Akihiro told himself he was willing. Katie was worth the cost.

July 2026

"What are you doing, noona?" Do-won asked, trying desperately to remove the judgment from his voice.

The furniture of her studio was pushed to the edges and Katie was stopped mid-move where her coffee table normally was. She turned bright red. "Um, twerking?"

"Oh, no. No," Do-won's voice dripped with disappointment. "No one would ever call that twerking."

Katie wilted. "You know I'm terrible at this stuff," she sighed. "I just feel like an idiot doing sexy shit like this."

"What are you twerking for anyway?"

"Does a person actually need a reason?" she replied.

Do-won knew his triangle mouth of disapproval was a bit too prominent, but it just pained him to see such an abysmal showing — especially since he knew Katie could do better.

"You do if you're going to desecrate a club staple such as that."

Katie seemed uncharacteristically embarrassed. "Yumi unni thought it would be fun to have a dance compilation for 'A Near Thing' on the new album and suggested a bunch of old and current sexy dances for me to do." Katie shrugged and gesticulated vaguely in the air. "I don't know what she was thinking."

"That seems unusually cruel even for choreographer-nim," mused Do-won. At Katie's hangdog face, he took immense pity on her. "Come on then, noona. Can't have you looking like a sad, middle-aged woman."

"I *am* a sad, middle-aged woman."

Do-won gasped. "Oh my god, you are! This is worse than I thought." At her grin, he continued. "Good thing I have plenty of experience breaking in the hips of sad, middle-aged women."

"Is that right?" Katie rolled her eyes dramatically.

He pushed up the long sleeves of his Human Made tee, momentarily wondering if he should remove his puffer vest. Instead, he stalked over to Katie and bent her over, tucking himself around her body, her ass flush against his crotch. Do-won flashed to a memory of doing something similar over a decade ago and was amused at how even after all this time, some things still remained the same.

"Ready for me to break you in?" he rumbled into the crook of her neck.

A low trickle of want threaded through him as Katie shivered. Do-won promptly ignored it and gave himself over to his dance teacher persona. He was a professional and so was she. That frisson of desire was a natural reaction to such a blatantly sexual dance move — nothing more.

"You always think too much, noona," he commented as he concentrated on relaxing Katie's body and reminding her of her natural rhythm. "You're actually good at this if you just chill the fuck out."

"I can't help it if I'm an intellectual, Wonnie," she replied wryly.

"Hush, noona," he admonished. "Feel the way your body wants to move instead of telling your body how to move. Your body remembers how it's supposed to go. Trust it."

He could feel Katie sigh as she attempted to stop thinking. It was not going well at all. And then, Do-won had an idea.

"Hold on a sec," he said as he slipped away from her.

He dimmed the lights in her studio and bumped up the volume of her new track. Then he slid back into position and curved his arms possessively around her. He pushed Katie down, reminding her to lower her center of gravity, and then Do-won did what he did best.

He danced. He tempted. He caught the curve of her ass in the curve of his pelvis and rocked Katie to the dirty beat he had created for her.

"Open yourself to me, noona. There you go," he rasped in approval. "Just like that."

This time, when that trickle of desire flared into full-blown lust, Do-won let himself sink into it. If it helped Katie with her work, then he'd go all in. Never let it be said that he wasn't fully committed to perfection.

"Do-won-ah! YAH, here you are!" exclaimed Ye-jun as he burst into Katie's studio. The oldest band member stopped short, taking in the dim lighting and Katie and Do-won dancing suggestively together. "Figures you'd be here instead of your own studio. You're late for lunch and grinding on Katie because...?"

Do-won resisted the urge to push Katie away and create an immediate distance. That would just fuel Ye-jun's merciless teasing later.

Katie saved him the trouble of replying. "Oh, don't be gross, oppa," she lobbed at Ye-jun as she stopped dancing. She turned off the music and turned on the lights. "Do-won is just helping me with my dancing. Don't act like you wouldn't kill for our dance god to give you pointers."

Ye-jun smirked at Do-won knowingly, his dark eyes glinting with mischief. "Gross, huh? You think our Do-won is gross? Take that back, Katie-yah. I'll not have your slander!"

Do-won could feel the heat creep into his face and was thankful Katie was still puttering around her studio instead of looking his way. "Hyung," he warned, but his friend blithely ignored him.

"Katie-yah. Apologize to Do-won. Tell him he's incredibly hot and delicious and that it was an honor for him to be rubbing himself all over you," Ye-jun teased brazenly as he plopped himself on the sofa chair in Katie's studio.

"First of all, the way you phrase things, oppa. It's repugnant," protested Katie. She sniffed in disgust as she tied her dark hair back into a loose bun.

"Second of all, Do-won doesn't need to hear me tell him he's yummy. Unlike you, he doesn't need people telling him he's pretty every five seconds."

Katie was only sort of right. Do-won didn't need her to tell him he was yummy, but he wasn't opposed to it, either.

"YAH! I don't need people to tell me I'm pretty — it's just a fact. I am the most handsome man you will ever meet, and every day, you must resign yourself to the fact that I'm happily married." Ye-jun was all in a lather now. Katie always knew how to wind the man up. "I happen to like hearing people tell me I'm handsome because then I know their faculties are intact and I'm not around liars!"

"Are you calling me a liar because I haven't called you pretty today?" Katie asked, clearly trying to suppress the mocking in her voice and failing.

"Well, now that you mention it, yes," Ye-jun rejoined, his handsome face scrunching into fake disappointment. "To make it up to me, you will join me and Do-won for lunch. I ordered way too much food and because Do-won rudely kept me waiting, I am treating you to his share." He flapped his arms and waved his hands around in wilder and wilder gestures, his purple hoodie strings flying around with each movement. Do-won was greatly endeared in spite of himself.

Katie pretended to consider Ye-jun's offer and then narrowed her eyes at him. "Why are you at the office anyway? Shouldn't you be at home with Mina unni and helping with the babies? They're what — two months old? What are you doing here?"

Do-won smiled just thinking about Ye-jun's twins. They had come almost a month early and were so tiny and cute. His hyung was constantly flooding the group chat with pictures of the first DOYEN babies.

He decided he would join in on the good-natured teasing. "Yeah, I think the best thing you could do for your family is leave the food here with me and noona, and you order new food for Mina noona." The more Do-won yammered, the more he felt as if he was onto something.

"YAH! The disrespect!" crowed Ye-jun as he laughed along. But then, his face crumpled. He wiped his hands over his face. "Ah, the truth is, I'm so tired and I would just like a moment to be with an adult who is not Mina noona, our parents, or the nanny. Besides, my parents are watching the baby so noona can go to the jjimjilbang with Younga noona."

Katie cooed sympathetically and reached over to pat his bandmate on his leg. "Going to the spa does sound nice. Unni did tell me she's exhausted and feels like a cow."

"Oh, that reminds me. She found that cow-patterned nursing bra you gave her hilarious," Ye-jun shared. "It also makes her boobs look amazing."

Do-won put out his arms and hands, stumbling back as if he could physically stave off the image. "Too much information, hyung," he groaned.

"Don't act like you haven't looked at Mina noona's boobs!"

Do-won stared at Ye-jun. "I — I honestly don't know how to respond to that."

"It was neatly done of me, right?" Ye-jun grinned, feral, his eyes taking on a disturbing sheen. "If you have, then you're a pig. If you haven't, you're insulting her boobs!"

"I'm pretty sure that's not how that works, hyung," Do-won frowned.

Katie took one look at his troubled face and laughed. "Oh, Do-won, you're so cute when you're judgy." She threw her arm around Do-won's waist, pulling him into a side hug. "Ye-jun oppa, I really wish I could join you, but I have a session with PT-nim and then a photoshoot fitting later."

Ye-jun nodded understandingly. "Can't be stuffing you full and then sending you to Beom-soo hyung and then the coordi-noonas. That's just asking for trouble."

"Seriously, hyung," Do-won scolded, "do you even listen to yourself? How does noona stand you?"

"Well, Mina noona enjoys me stuffing her full — that's how we got twins!" Ye-jun was a menace. "Wait, that's not true. We got twins from science — but it wasn't for lack of trying on my part!" he cackled.

Katie was cracking up so hard she was bent over and holding her stomach. "Oh my god, make it stop," she gasped, tears streaking down the side of her face.

"It's not that funny," grumbled Do-won, though eventually, he gave into the inherent absurdity and laughed deep from his belly, too.

After a few more minutes of good-natured laughing and banter, Do-won suddenly heard Ye-jun's voice blaring, "YAH! You think I got this far by being handsome?!" on loop.

Katie lurched toward her desk and grabbed her phone, scrambling to turn off what Do-won surmised was an alarm.

"Is that my voice as your alarm?" Ye-jun asked incredulously. He wasn't fooling anyone. Do-won could tell the man was inordinately pleased. "Did you get it off one of my livestreams?"

"Uh," stammered Katie, "yes? It's very, uh, motivating?" Her face started to color. "Oppa, you're one of the hardest working people I know," she explained bashfully. "If anyone could coast on their looks alone, it's you, but you never do. I find you inspiring."

Ye-jun's face burst into happiness. "You hear that, Wonnie? Katie finds me inspiring."

"Technically, I find all of you inspiring. I always hear Do-won insisting in my head that hard work never betrays, but the audio of that is not quite as annoying as yours," Katie continued as she put her phone in her army green crossbody bag. Do-won loved how she had random limited edition DOYEN enamel pins intermixed with her own official pins dotting the bag.

At Ye-jun's indignant squawk, Do-won laughed again. "Come on, hyung. Noona has to go to PT and you've held my lunch hostage long enough." He extended an arm and hauled Ye-jun up with minimal effort. "Thanks for letting me help, noona," he said as he dragged Ye-jun out the door and then down the hall to his own studio.

Do-won had hoped that Ye-jun had forgotten all about him and Katie dancing, but alas, his hyung started on him as soon as they got to his studio door.

"So, what's this thing between you and Katie?" Ye-jun asked even before Do-won had a chance to slip off his shoes on his Takashi Murakami smiling flower doormat.

"I don't know what you're talking about," Do-won replied.

He turned up the ambient lighting of his studio, knowing Ye-jun loved the way the lights lit his skin in a warm glow. He idly noted the fine layer of dust on his Mr. DOB figurines and Futura collectibles and decided he needed to take better care of his possessions. Do-won shuffled to his black leather couch, sat down, and promptly started to unpack the lunch Ye-jun had ordered onto his glass coffee table. Not only was there dak galbi, kimchi fried rice, yuk-jeon, and bulgogi, his bandmate had also ordered kong guksu, and mul-naengmyeon.

"Hyung, you got both kong guksu and naengmyeon?" he asked in an effort to change the subject. "Couldn't decide which cold noodles you wanted?"

"When in doubt, choose both," Ye-jun replied diplomatically from Do-won's Herman Miller Embody chair. "Man, I have half a mind to steal this for my gaming room, Wonnie," he said randomly before continuing. "Besides, I was hoping to get Katie to join us — and not only because I missed her company."

"I thought she goes over to see Mina noona and the babies every week!" Do-won opened the containers of naengmyeon and dak galbi first and immediately began shoveling tangy cold noodles into his mouth, stopping only to add pieces of spicy marinated chicken, sweet potatoes, and tteok. The rice cakes were just the right consistency and hit the spot.

"Ah, but she goes to see the babies and not me," the older man pouted. "And from what I've seen, you've been hogging Katie at the office. Tell hyung what's going on."

Ye-jun rolled the gaming chair over to the coffee table and opened the rest of the containers. He hummed happily while stuffing his face full of kong guksu and bulgogi. Do-won was suddenly reminded of the millions of times he and his bandmates had eaten together. A sharp pang of nostalgia ran through him. Back when he was a poor trainee, the idea of ordering so much food at one time just for the two of them would have appalled him. Though Ye-jun had come from a wealthier family and had often subsidized the group's food budget with his own money, Do-won would have still felt guilty.

His own father had been a teacher and his mother had been a home-maker, but she had occasionally cleaned the homes of elderly neigh-bors, and his father had taken on extra tutoring to afford Do-won's dance lessons. He never forgot how much his parents had sacrificed for his dream. As soon as he'd been able, Do-won had started sending money home, though he'd later found out they'd set it aside in another account for him, just in case. Now, his parents bought things with his credit cards without worry — especially since his older sister Seo-yun was doing rather well for herself, too.

Do-won must have been quiet a little too long with his ruminations because Ye-jun set down his chopsticks, slurped up the rest of his kong guksu, and didn't even bother to wipe his mouth.

"Oh, you've got it bad," Ye-jun stated, his lips still glistening from the cold soy milk broth.

Do-won handed Ye-jun a napkin. "I have no idea what you're talking about." Just then, he heard the beeping and whirring of his studio door and Jae-sung strolled in. "Does no one knock around here?" he griped.

The rapper threw him a sheepish glance. "Ran into Katie on her way out and she mentioned something about hyung buying lunch." Jae-sung shrugged in his off-white oversized Fear of God T-shirt and ran a large hand over his short buzz cut. While his friend often grew out his hair for DOYEN promotions, in between, he would shave it off because he preferred the ease and freedom of it. "It's alright if I join you both, right?"

Ye-jun and Do-won both agreed readily and Jae-sung joined Do-won on the couch to hunch over the food splayed out on the coffee table. As much as there were times Do-won was sick to death of them all, there was an unmatched level of comfort when he hung out with DOYEN members in any configuration. They were more than his family. They were the very beat of his heart.

"What were you guys talking about before I came in?" asked Jae-sung as he grabbed a new pair of chopsticks and then the naengmyeon from Do-won.

"Nothing," said Do-won at the same time Ye-jun said, "Katie."

Jae-sung raised a curious brow. "Oh? What about Katie? Do-won's producing her new album, right?"

"Is that what we're calling dancing provocatively in the dark nowadays? I can never keep up with the slang," Ye-jun deadpanned. He was so full of shit. Thanks to his nonstop gaming habit, the man was the most up-to-date on all the slang save for Soo-min.

Jae-sung laughed at Do-won's clear dismay. "Is our Wonnie finally making a move on Katie?" He high-fived Ye-jun and turned to high-five Do-won, only stopping when he realized that Do-won hadn't lifted his hand. "Did hyung interrupt your attempt?"

Do-won glared at the two older members. "Hyung didn't interrupt anything other than a dance tutorial. Noona is prepping for some dance challenge and though she was better than both of you, she wasn't great."

Ye-jun just sighed as he continued eating. "You should go for it. As long as you talk to Hiro about it, he'll be fine."

"Or he will be, anyway," added Jae-sung. "After all, he's seeing people. Didn't he go out with that dancer a few times?"

"Does noona know that?" Do-won asked. He often worried that Katie was still in love with Akihiro and that, more than anything, was what held him back. He deserved to be someone's first choice.

"I don't know that it's Katie's business," Jae-sung broke gently, "and what does it matter that she knows? They broke up over a year ago."

"Well, Aki moving on doesn't mean he's okay with me dating his ex," countered Do-won, hastily adding, "not that I'm trying to date Katie noona."

Ye-jun smirked into his kimchi fried rice. "So you're just trying to get into her pants. I thought your feelings for her were more than that, but I don't judge."

"That's not what I said," snapped Do-won. Jae-sung and Ye-jun exchanged amused glances and Do-won felt played by his own reactions to his friends' needling. "Look, I'm not saying I wouldn't jump at the chance to date Katie noona. She's ridiculously talented, kind, and genuinely cares about me and other people. Plus, she's funny and already knows you idiots."

Jae-sung snorted. "Yeah, and she's hot as fuck. Don't forget she's really fucking hot."

"Noted," Do-won said dryly.

"So, what's the hold up?" Ye-jun pushed.

Do-won sighed. "I don't think she's over Akihiro," he answered, "and don't I deserve better than being a rebound?"

Jae-sung looked at him with sympathy. "Ah," he said. "You do, Wonnie. You deserve someone who wants you wholeheartedly."

This time, it was Ye-jun who snorted. "Well, don't wait so long you miss your window. She can't stop gushing about you every time she comes over, and I have to remind her how I'm just as — if not more — awesome and talented as you are. Not to mention handsome!"

Do-won cracked a smile. Though Ye-jun often played the daft fool, Do-won knew he wielded that persona both as a weapon and as a shield.

It was Ye-jun's way to both make his point and apologize about provoking Do-won regarding his feelings for Katie.

"How could she forget, hyung?" he joked back. "You never give anyone the opportunity."

"Awww, with a face like hyung's? How dare she not talk about how great you are when you're right there in front of her!" added Jae-sung fondly as Ye-jun sniffed balefully. "Now, please regale us with tales of your babies."

"Hmph, I came to work to escape my babies, not spend all my time talking about them," grumbled Ye-jun dramatically. "Oh, did I tell you that Soo-mi started smiling already? Mina noona says it's most likely gas since she's too young to smile, but I think she's a genius and, obviously, her father is an idol, so of course she's an early smiler. As for Soo-hwan, well, he'll get there. He might be older by a few minutes, but he's just being a considerate oppa and letting Soo-mi get all the glory for now."

Do-won and Jae-sung obediently stared at the pictures of Ye-jun's smiling (gassy) daughter and dutifully cooed at Soo-hwan gumming his tiny fist. It didn't matter that Ye-jun had already texted the story and these very photos in their group chat. Some things were better experienced together.

September 2024

Akihiro heard a knock on his hotel room door but was too tired to answer. It was a rare day off on their tour where he didn't have to travel, didn't have any official schedule, and didn't have to perform.

He figured if it was a fellow member, they'd take the hint and leave him to sleep.

The knock came louder this time. More insistent.

Shit. Maybe it was a manager hyung.

Akihiro dragged his naked body out of bed, wrapping a flat sheet around his waist for some semblance of modesty. He cracked his door open with eyes half-opened.

"Hey," Katie grinned. "Happy Birthday, Hiro."

Akihiro was surprised because technically, his birthday wasn't for another three weeks. In fact, he was so surprised he dropped the sheet as he threw open the door. Then he yelped and slammed the door closed. He could hear Katie's hysterical laughter in the hallway.

When he was decent, he opened the door again.

"You okay?" she asked, amusement still in her voice.

Akihiro threw her his haughtiest expression. "Of course. Never better."

Katie tilted her head in acknowledgment. "Can I come in?"

He swept her in and watched as she brought in a large rolling suitcase and her travel backpack. "Are you planning a long stay?" He didn't want to hope, but he hoped.

"Sorry, Hiro-yah. The large suitcase is full of ramyeon and snacks. Your managers asked me to schlep over some hard-to-get foods, and the rest are Taiwanese goodies for Junie oppa." At Akihiro's crestfallen face, she kissed him on the cheek. "I can only stay a few days. I'm sorry I can't stay longer. The only reason I could even get away at all is because the show isn't filming this week because of Mid-Autumn Festival."

Akihiro started as he realized it was close to the Japanese moon-viewing festival of Tsukumi. Without being in Korea and all the reminders of Chuseok, he'd completely forgotten. He eyed her bags again. "That's not enough clothing for a few days' stay," he said carefully.

"Oh," she batted her lashes at him. "I don't plan on wearing much."

Katie startled awake in the mostly dark hotel room, her heart beating wildly, a scream stuck in her throat, a small mercy for which she was grateful. She could barely grasp the remnants of her dream, its awful tendrils evanescing away in the night. Though her nightmares had dropped to a few times a month, they'd started ramping up again ever since Mattie's wedding. Something about seeing her father — smug and strutting without any remorse, eating up the attention as the father of both the groom and an international singer — had smashed something inside her that she hadn't even known she'd had to protect.

She wasn't stupid; she'd known it was going to be difficult.

She'd never told Mattie or her mother about what her father had blackmailed her into doing, and she'd certainly never told them about what Tony had done to her. Of course, her father would be at her brother's wedding. Of course, he would be front and center of the activities, making her brother's event all about himself. She had considered it a victory when she'd made it through the weekend without exploding at anyone.

Thankfully, both Mattie and her mother knew that Katie and her father were often at odds. Because no one wanted to make a scene during such a happy occasion, she'd successfully avoided speaking to her father much at all. Katie strongly suspected that Alton had made leaving her alone a condition of paying off her father's debts.

She would never finish owing Alton no matter how long she lived.

When Katie's heart rate finally lowered, she rolled over on the hotel mattress and stared at Akihiro's sleeping form in the sliver of light coming from the bathroom. She hated sleeping in total darkness and always left the bathroom or hallway light on in hotels. Not only was she less likely to stub a toe or trip on the way to the bathroom, the light helped to orient her when she was startled awake like she'd just done. It reminded her that she wasn't still trapped in a Hong Kong apartment, desperate to escape by any means necessary — even death.

She returned her attention to Akihiro and his soft snores. He was so pretty even without makeup that she often wondered if she was dreaming. She couldn't understand how someone as perfect as Akihiro would chain himself to someone with as much baggage as herself. It didn't matter that they'd been together for over a year at this point. Katie couldn't help but feel as if the other shoe would drop eventually.

One glance at her phone confirmed that though her body thought it was time to be awake and get moving, it was still in the middle of the night where she was. She gamely closed her eyes and tried to fall back asleep, listening to Akihiro's breathing. Katie briefly thought to cozy up to him and pull his arm over her so that he cradled her with his body, but she hated how hot he ran. His heat and her lying on her right side would annoy her more than any comfort she'd receive from the position.

Katie grabbed her phone to check the time again and grimaced at how barely fifteen minutes had crawled by. Her screen showed a disappointing 3:17 a.m. and she knew without a doubt that no more sleep was left for her tonight.

She sat up and got out of bed, careful not to disturb Akihiro. He did not stir, and she breathed a silent sigh of relief. She stretched, cataloging her body's various aches and complaints, thankful she was already naked so that she didn't have to make more sounds than necessary.

She wanted to think her intention was to not accidentally wake him, cognizant of how tired he was from welcoming her on tour as thoroughly as he'd done, but she knew it wasn't really the case. Of course, Katie didn't want to wake him, but she knew the years of being with Tony and the ingrained caution were still pervasive in every moment of her life.

Perhaps Katie had been away from Akihiro too long. Her body had forgotten his safe harbor and had returned to its baseline. She despised that being afraid of Tony was still her default after all these years.

She padded softly to the joining ensuite and turned on the water, waiting for the mirror to steam up. She felt a twinge of fear deep in her gut and though her heartbeat stuttered, Katie angrily forced herself to step into the tub and dragged the white, waffle shower curtain closed. Under the hot spray of water, she used a washcloth to vigorously scrub both the sex and travel off of her body.

She hated how Tony was on her mind so much lately. She idly wondered if it was because this September marked three years since she'd returned to Seoul and if so, how a body could know how many years had passed and still retain the physical imprint. It seemed patently unfair.

Katie finished rinsing herself off and stood directly under the hot stream of water pounding directly at the nape of her neck. She closed her eyes and let her wet hair hang over her face as she tried to relax her body, even as her ears were still closely attuned to any sounds from the bedroom.

As the water continued beating down her back and stung her skin with heat, she squeezed her eyes even tighter and held her breath as long as she could. She tried to subsume her fury and despair, to drown her thoughts in the water splattering on her body. She only had a few days with Akihiro; she refused to let her past ruin them.

Akihiro woke up to the smell of food and the sounds of tinkling silverware and low laughter, mixed with a sharp cackling he recognized as belonging to Dae-jung and Soo-min filtering through the closed bedroom door. He groggily swiped his face and turned on the metal lamp on his bedside table.

He wasn't sure why he was disappointed that Katie hadn't stayed in bed with him. He was sure he'd told her about wanting to wake up and make slow love to her first thing in the morning. He immediately scolded himself for his unreasonable response even as another part balked and wondered why she'd felt the need to have breakfast with his bandmates.

Akihiro hated feeling petulant and jealous. It made him feel small and stupid. He resolved to move past it, but even as he tried to adjust his attitude, he felt his lingering resentment infect all his attempts. Part of him wanted to blame Katie, insisting that he wouldn't feel this insecure if she'd spent more time with him and prioritized their relationship. Another part of him wanted to stomp out to the sitting area and drag her back to bed, his friends' presence be damned.

Instead, Akihiro opted for a third option: he chose to be grateful that Katie had flown in to surprise him and then hunted for his discarded boxer briefs. He pulled them on and walked out of his bedroom to greet his members.

"Get out," Akihiro growled at Dae-jung and Soo-min even as he stooped over behind the couch to kiss Katie on her head. She smelled of the hotel's shampoo and he tried not to miss the scent of the grapefruit shampoo she'd been favoring right before she'd left for tour.

Seated in one of the desk chairs he'd dragged over to the coffee table, Dae-jung tossed his permed, brown locks and smirked in complete disregard for Akihiro's feelings. "But I'm eating," he whined.

"You're eating my breakfast," Akihiro retorted.

"Untrue," Soo-min, still clad in the basketball shorts he'd slept in and a hoodie, pouted from his spot on a light cream armchair, as only the youngest of their group could get away with. "Noona ordered enough for all of us."

Katie leaned her head back against the matching sofa and beamed an indulgent smile back up at him. She was clad only in a loosely tied robe and Akihiro itched to see if she was naked underneath. He wasn't sure if he was annoyed or aroused that she was wearing barely anything around Dae-jung and Soo-min and decided he could be both.

"I got you extra bacon and an omelet with some fruit," she said, reaching for her cup of tea. "Come sit with us," she added, patting the spot next to her.

Akihiro could not help but notice how the top of her robe gaped open a little wider with her movement and how he could catch a glimpse of her breast. Katie was most assuredly naked. From the amused looks on his friends' faces, they'd also caught an eyeful.

He rounded the sofa and sat next to Katie, trying to keep a scowl off his face. Judging from her raised eyebrow as she passed him a covered plate with what he presumed was his order, he did not succeed.

"You alright?" Katie asked softly, her hands pulling down the folds of her robe so that they sat more flush against her body. "You seem grumpier than usual."

"Don't worry about Aki," Dae-jung observed slyly. "He's just mad we're cockblocking him."

Soo-min snorted an inelegant laugh. "Listen, if the rest of us aren't getting any, you should suffer, too."

"Well, that's not strictly true," Dae-jung teased. He took a bite of his waffle and then continued, "Just because you have no game doesn't mean the rest of us have your problem."

"Liar! Who? And when?" queried Soo-min as he shoved an entire breakfast sausage into his mouth.

Dae-jung merely mimed locking his lips with an imaginary key and throwing it away. Katie laughed and gazed fondly at Akihiro's best friend. "Take it easy on Soo-min, Dae. You know he's a good and faithful boyfriend to Myung-ok. I'm sure if he was single, he could give you a run for your money."

There was a pause, and then everyone, Akihiro and Soo-min included, burst out laughing.

"That's a good one, noona," giggled Dae-jung. "Imagine our baby Soo-min being a player." He gasped, holding onto his belly. "Shy boy Soo-min who blushes when a pretty woman even half looks at him."

"Hey! Myung-ok is pretty and I don't blush when she looks at me," protested Soo-min.

Dae-jung's eyes lit with glee. "Need I remind you of how you used to stutter and hide when Myung-ok would visit me and Akihiro?"

Akihiro smiled as Soo-min blushed and sputtered, trying to recover his dignity. If Akihiro recalled correctly, Myung-ok had really been more of Dae-jung's friend in school, but she had been kind to Akihiro even when his Korean was extremely limited. Dae-jung was the only reason Akihiro even had friends at school for the first six months after he'd immigrated to Korea. Granted, they'd been trainees together at the same small company, but Dae-jung had gone above and beyond to take care of him.

Akihiro had struggled with going from the top of his class in Tokyo to constantly feeling stupid in Seoul. And while most of the students had been nice enough, some boys definitely had been cruel to him. Without Dae-jung's boxy smile and natural ability to befriend anyone — even the cruel boys he'd made apologize to Akihiro — Akihiro would have felt so much lonelier.

Some of Akihiro's irritation leached away. At any rate, it was hard to stay mad at his bandmates. Katie glanced happily between him and his members and suddenly, Akihiro's earlier jealousy surged back with a vengeance. Why did she have to seek out his friends for company? Why couldn't he have been enough for her?

"Why didn't you wake me?" Akihiro interrupted suddenly.

Soo-min and Dae-jung exchanged a weighted glance while Katie's eyes flashed in exasperation before disappearing into a familiar blankness. He hated that careful look she affected whenever he expressed any displeasure. It made Akihiro feel like she was comparing him to Tony — like he was someone from whom she had to hide. It made him feel as if he was a monster.

He pouted as he tried to affect a teasing tone, but even he could hear how an edge bled through. "You're here for so little time, I just wanted to spend more time with you, that's all."

"I booked the earliest flight I could as soon as my schedules were done, Hiro," Katie replied evenly, her gaze going from blank to hard in a matter of seconds. "I skipped out on our family's Harvest Moon dinner with my grandfather and aunts so I could see you. Nothing I do is ever good enough for you," she spat.

Akihiro was surprised she'd even said as much in front of other people. "I don't know why you're sounding so defensive about it — I didn't say you didn't try your best," he snapped back.

Dae-jung's dark brown eyes radiated concern and Soo-min looked distinctly uncomfortable. Soo-min chewed on his lip before saying, "Sorry, hyung. I'd heard from manager-nim that noona was visiting and I texted her this morning and invited myself over for breakfast because she couldn't sleep."

"And I tagged along because I saw Soo-min coming to your suite as I was heading back to my own," Dae-jung shared soothingly. "I figured I could eat first then go to bed."

"Pretty sure you were coming from a bed already," muttered Soo-min under his breath.

"Anyway, we thought you'd sleep longer than you did," Dae-jung said. "You know how you barely get out of bed until the early afternoon on our days off." He finished the last of his waffle and got up to set his plate back on the room service table.

Akihiro couldn't stop his mouth from moving. "I likely would have, but you guys woke me up." He heard Katie sigh and internally berated himself for killing the morning mood.

Soo-min rolled his eyes and stood up, grabbing his plate and his Coke Zero. "It was good to see you, noona," he said. "I hope I get to see you again before you head out."

"We'll see if I'm allowed to," Katie sniped sarcastically. Akihiro merely gritted his teeth.

She half-rose to hug Soo-min and Dae-jung while they left, and Dae-jung — that little shit — purposely held Katie a little too long to be considered decent and left a lingering kiss on her cheek. Then, he had the nerve to flip Akihiro off on his way out.

As soon as the door closed, Katie rounded on him. "What the fuck, Aki? What the actual fuck?"

He held out his arms placatingly. "I'm sorry, Katie, I was an ass," he admitted. "I don't know what came over me."

"Your stupid dick is what came over you. Just say you're mad that you didn't get a morning fuck like you wanted and threw a tantrum," Katie spat. "You're such a child."

Akihiro stewed in his guilt and sadness as he watched her clear the dishes from the coffee table to the room service one. The plates clanked loudly as she worked her anger out onto the inanimate objects.

"I'm sorry, Katie. I just missed you so much," he apologized, pitching his voice in his most convincing aegyo.

He noted how Katie sighed again and gave the impression of succumbing to his all-out cuteness assault. He didn't quite believe her, but he also wanted to take that olive branch for what it was. Akihiro took his cue and moved so that he wrapped around her from behind, hooking his chin over her shoulder.

"Come back to bed and let me apologize properly?" he breathed in her ear, feather light.

This time, Katie really did melt convincingly into his embrace. "Fine," she grumbled. "But I'm just going to lay there and do nothing at all."

Akihiro chuckled. "Like that's any different," he teased and then nipped the curve of her neck.

Katie was true to her word and made him work for it, but judging by the sated glow on her skin when she left a few days later, she'd accepted his apology.

August 2026

Produced entirely by 1DEL1GHT (given name Jung Do-won) of K-pop band DOYEN, the latest Katie Wu album "Jubilee" (SB Entertainment, 2026) surprises listeners with the inclusion of not one — but two — songs that are exuberantly happy. "7x7+1" and "Happy" are produced to great effect by Wu's labelmate, who also created the powerful and grimy beat to "A Near Thing" and wrote the haunting topline to "There Are Still Bad Days."

Wu is notorious for writing all her own music and lyrics, trusting only certain SB Entertainment producers for her albums. It speaks much for 1DEL1GHT's talent and abilities — which were already evident on DOYEN albums — that Wu relinquished control over her entire album to her colleague and friend. 1DEL1GHT showcases Wu's incredible voice, broadens Wu's musical palette, and elevates Wu's already heady genius.

"Jubilee" explores what it means to be free, what it means to be happy, and even in its raw honesty, delivers moments of unrestrained joy. Magical.

- South China Morning Post, August 2026

How we doing, Jezebelle CHIMERA?
                        - Koreaboo Twitter post, August 2026

[1] 7x7+1 [1:49]
[2] The Only Way Out Is Through [3:07]
[3] A Near Thing [4:23]
[4] There Are Still Bad Days [3:39]
[5] We Were Not Freed, We Freed Ourselves [2:46]
[6] Indemnification [3:42]
[7] Happy [3:21]
  - Track List, "Jubilee (Prod. 1DEL1GHT of DOYEN)"
                        (SB Entertainment, 2026)

Forget the neverending calculus
Follow the order of operations
Remember who we are
Even if it's beyond our imagination

Here we lay fallow
Here we lay free
Here we rest and return
Here we can be, we can be, we can be

We've come home
You're my home
At last, I've come home
Declare the Jubilee

- "7x7+1 (Prod. 1DEL1GHT of DOYEN)" (SB Entertainment, 2026)

To my younger self.
- Album dedication, "Jubilee (Prod. 1DEL1GHT of
DOYEN)" (SB Entertainment, 2026)

"Hyung, why are you hiding in the corner?" Akihiro asked Do-won as he and Dae-jung surrounded him at Katie's album release party.

The rooftop hotel bar was lit in happy, twinkling lights, and attractive people (both famous and not) milled about or mingled in tiny clumps around tall round tables. Servers in tuxedos wound among the attendees with platters full of hors d'oeuvres and flutes of champagne. The hot, balmy air made Do-won feel flush and uncomfortable. He didn't know how the servers were surviving in their uniforms.

"It's embarrassing," he admitted. "It's Katie's album, and yet, the focus seems to be all on me. I don't want my presence to overshadow her."

"No offense, Wonnie," commented Jae-sung as he joined their discussion, "but you could never overshadow Katie. At best, the two of you are twin stars in the same system."

"Uh, right," replied Do-won, not really understanding what Jae-sung was going on about. "She opened up so much of herself to me during the album writing. She risked so much on me — I can never repay her."

Akihiro paused, eyeing him discreetly. "You were a good friend to her when she needed you, hyung. You were as much of a support to her as she was to you." He cleared his throat. "I'm — I'm grateful she had you."

Do-won saw the sadness in his old roommate's eyes. Guilt glanced through him even though he hadn't done anything deserving of it. He reached out and gently squeezed Akihiro's arm.

Do-won had witnessed firsthand how Katie had struggled after her EMDR sessions this past year, how sometimes, she would just show up in his dim studio and lay on his couch, staring at his ceiling for hours as he worked on his own music around her. Occasionally during the album-making process, she'd even confided in him some of what she'd gone through with Tony and her father, shedding new light on herself and all her music. It had made him wonder all the more about her.

Katie had transmuted her pain into art — and what art it was. She was a marvel. She was also exceedingly gracious.

"You're the one who came up with the concept in the first place, Won-nie," she said later when he thanked her. "I'm just glad I got you before you could no longer squeeze me in."

Do-won smiled shyly. "I only told you to try a happier sound — I had nothing to do with the concept."

Katie was also right, though. His inbox had an influx of love calls from artists or their reps who wanted 1DEL1GHT to produce their next track. He was really excited and cautiously optimistic.

"You're the reason I thought of the concept," Katie said, looking deeply into his eyes. "You're the reason the album sounds like my vision — but is even more than I could have ever imagined."

"But it's your words and your voice — your essence that allowed me to produce the tracks, noona!" insisted Do-won.

"But you're the reason that stupid 'A Near Thing' dance challenge went viral — and also why I didn't end up looking like a sad, middle-aged woman!"

"It's both of you, you idiots," Woo-jin said as he joined the conversation with Alton following close behind. Do-won glowed as he observed the two older men together.

"Besides, if Katie didn't want everyone to celebrate you," continued Woo-jin, "she wouldn't have insisted on the 'Producer 1DEL1GHT of DOYEN' as part of her album title."

"Well, the SB Entertainment marketing department insisted on that, oppa," Katie chuckled softly. "I would have just bolded his name in the credits or something subtle. Maybe tagged him in my Instagram stories."

"Seems like adequate crediting," mused Woo-jin.

Alton wrapped his arm around Katie's waist and kissed her on the forehead. Then he directed his intense gaze to Do-won. "Wonnie, I know I already told you," he said in his much improved Korean, "but you did such a fucking amazing job on Katie's album. It's not only very her, it's also very you. You two make a great team."

Do-won flushed at Alton's praise and Katie might have preened a little, too.

"Ah, hyung," he said even as Alton automatically said, "Call me, 'Alton,'"

"Don't make Wonnie uncomfortable, Alton," Katie said, leaning into him. "How many times do I have to say this? When in Seoul and all that."

Alton gazed at her fondly. "As you wish, Mei."

"I want some champagne," she said, stepping toward an approaching server.

Woo-jin looked a bit concerned, as if he wanted to say something, but Alton pressed a reassuring hand in the small of his back.

Katie's sharp eyes missed nothing. "Alton," she cooed, "are you fucking Woo-jin?"

Do-won was so glad his friends had found him tonight. He had been waiting for her to put it all together.

All the concern melted off Woo-jin's face as he morphed into a predator. "I'd say it's more that *I'm* fucking *him*, hmmm?"

Alton, good man that he was, colored only slightly. "Tonight, anyway," he said, voice low and scratchy.

Katie double-fisted Alton's very expensive shirt and tugged him close. "When. Did. This. Happen."

"Uh, you might want to ease up on hyung a bit, noona," murmured Do-won. "People are watching."

Katie let Alton go and smoothed his shirt with both hands, some hurt evident on her face.

"I would have told you, Mei, but it's really new and you've been dealing with so much —." Alton seemed uncharacteristically flustered. "And I — I had to come to terms with what it meant. You know what it's like in Singapore and with our elders."

"I would have supported you. I know I was struggling with stuff, but I would have listened," she whispered.

Do-won felt a little bit as if he were intruding, but Woo-jin wasn't moving and, at the very least, Do-won felt as if he should support his hyung.

"Wait, you're not surprised I'm also into men?"

Katie shrugged. "I mean, I am a little, but Woo-jin is my bias for a reason, Ge." Woo-jin smirked, and she glared at him and then Do-won. "Don't think I don't have any strong words for you — we're supposed to be besties!" she growled. "And Wonnie knew this whole time!"

Do-won and Woo-jin cried out "DOJIN!" and fist-bumped.

"Too soon?" joked Do-won, trying to defuse the tension.

"I didn't even know you had each other's contact information," commented Katie.

Woo-jin took a sip of his whisky. "He got it when we were working on the DOYEN branded suites for Alton's project in Seoul a few years ago."

"He seduced me over his vast knowledge of interior design," quipped Alton quietly.

"Of course he did. Well, that explains how your Korean got better so fast." She embraced Alton, squeezing him with all her might. "I'm so happy for you, Alton. Woo-jin is the best of people and so are you." And then, pitched much lower so that Do-won almost didn't catch it, she ordered in English, "Tell me everything. I must know about Woo-jin's tongue technology."

Alton broke out into a loud, open laugh and, just like that, everything seemed to reset.

"Well, now I'm going to get wasted," Katie declared. "We're going to celebrate everything!"

And thus, surrounded by his favorite people, Do-won proceeded to get incredibly drunk.

When Do-won woke up the next day, mouth tasting sour and wretched, he wasn't quite sure where he was. It looked like a hotel room? And then, Do-won was acutely aware that he was not alone.

He looked over in the bed and found Katie passed out next to him.

Do-won took quick stock of his shirtless state and looked under the covers to see if he was wearing underwear. When he noted that he was indeed clad in Balenciaga boxer briefs, that reassured him very little. After all, he didn't remember anything after a certain point last night, and he certainly did not remember heading to the hotel suite — least of all with Katie.

Katie was wearing his undershirt, so that buoyed his spirits a bit. The odds of them fucking and then putting their clothes back on after getting shit-faced seemed unlikely. Do-won got up to check the trash cans for used condoms — just to make sure — and was even more relieved not to find any. There was still the option that he fucked Katie raw, but he really didn't think that was the case.

Do-won was reasonably confident he was too fastidious a person — even drunk — to do something that irresponsible.

Not that he thought she'd make it weird. He knew Katie well enough to know that she was a very compartmentalized person. Plus, Do-won wasn't new to sleeping with the occasional friend and keeping everything casual.

He would be lying if he claimed the idea of having sex with Katie was displeasing, but that wasn't quite the same as wanting to have sex with her while blackout drunk.

No, the only potential wrinkle was that she was Akihiro's ex, and Do-won was pretty sure she was still hung up on Akihiro. Well, that and the minor detail that Do-won wanted Katie to want him with her whole self in the same way he could see himself wanting her.

He decided that he would shower first and then deal with it. Everything always seemed better after getting cleaned up and presentable.

Katie was still asleep when he was done, so Do-won picked up his clothes from yesterday and folded them neatly. He wasn't particularly eager to get back into his clothes from last night and thus, he also collected Katie's dress, hung it in the closet, and arranged her heels by the door. He didn't notice a bra or panties, so he figured she was still wearing her underwear (another relief) and now that he thought about it, her dress hadn't allowed for a conventional bra.

Do-won promptly shook his head to rid himself of all of Katie's breast-supporting possibilities. It was too early in the day for this line of thought.

He decided to order breakfast and ordered some for her as well. Do-won was actually surprised at how good he felt considering how bombed he was last night. But then he vaguely recalled downing several bottles of a hangover cure, so he was grateful that at least drunk Wonnie had common sense.

Do-won scrolled through his phone and checked his socials, commented on CHIMERA posts in their fancafe, and texted Woo-jin. He figured Woo-jin likely had an equally late night with Alton, but his hyung had a much higher alcohol tolerance and likely would have a better read on how Do-won ended up in a hotel bed with Katie.

Hyung, he texted, *do you happen to know why I woke up with noona next to me in a hotel bed?*

If you have to ask, you likely weren't that memorable. Woo-jin was infuriating. *You really don't remember?*

If I remembered, I wouldn't be asking. Do-won was getting more annoyed by the second. He was getting hangry.

Woo-jin's response didn't make him any less annoyed. *Is she naked? Are you?*

No to both, he replied. *You're the worst.*

Disappointing.

Well???

Do-won could practically hear Woo-jin's exasperated sigh. *Obviously, you were completely drunk and Katie got you to her suite so that you wouldn't embarrass yourself in public.*

So noona wasn't drunk? That was also a relief.

Oh, I didn't say that, replied Woo-jin. *But she was a helluva lot more sober than you were.*

All signs were pointing to a night of platonic drunkenness and no sex. Do-won sent a belated *thx* to Woo-jin. He decided to do some stretches and light exercises as he waited for breakfast or for Katie to wake up, whichever happened first.

He staunchly avoided that tiny bubble of disappointment in the distant corner of his mind. Do-won was not at all fit to dive into what it could mean — especially when he'd yet to consume breakfast.

December 2024

"What do you mean you're not coming back to Seoul for Christmas?" asked Akihiro.

Like in his home country of Japan, Christmas in Korea was more for couples, and he had been looking forward to the romantic holiday. Though he wanted to sulk, he was trying to sit very still in his seat for the coordi-noona currently touching up his makeup. Akihiro and the rest of his members were on set to film a commercial for a soju company and currently taking a break in the greenroom.

"I thought your show just ended? I already booked that fancy hot springs spa in Busan. I don't think I can cancel without paying a hefty fee."

Woo-jin, who was sitting in a chair nearby, shot him a sympathetic look. Akihiro knew it was bad form to take a video call in a room full of people without using headphones, but he'd left his at home and he hadn't talked to Katie all day. Besides, it was mostly just his members and their long-time managers and staff. He supposed Katie wouldn't appreciate their business being on blast to everyone, but she was also used to how impossible it was to keep secrets in their line of work.

"My ah-gong is really sick, Aki-yah," Katie replied. He could tell she was stressed even through the tiny screen. He couldn't quite tell where she was but it wasn't her Taipei residence. "He was actually sick during the Harvest Moon Festival, but it wasn't as worrisome. But lately, his condition has deteriorated a lot."

"Oh," he said, feeling like an asshole. "Did I know he was sick?"

Katie tried to hide a sigh of irritation. "How am I supposed to know if you knew?"

Akihiro's face heated at her harsh tone, acutely aware of how everyone could hear how she was speaking to him. But he was pretty sure that over the last three months of his world tour's first leg, Katie hadn't mentioned anything about her grandfather being sick or otherwise. Had he just been too self-absorbed and forgotten in the midst of work, or was it one more thing she hadn't told him?

"I guess I mean, did you tell me about your ah-gong being sick?" Akihiro clarified. He didn't know why he was digging in, except that with so many people listening in, he didn't want to seem like Katie was walking all over him.

The makeup artist put on the finishing touches and left him to work on Soo-min.

"Why would it matter if I told you before?" Katie retorted, her pretty face screwed into impatience. "The point is he's getting worse now. They don't know how much longer he'll hold on."

"I didn't realize you were that close to him." Shit. If he hadn't known he fucked up from Katie's sharp inhale, Woo-jin palming his face would have clued him in. Akihiro immediately apologized. "I'm sorry, Katie. That was a super shitty thing to say."

Akihiro could tell she was fuming. He could practically hear her pulsing with fury.

"I'm not that close to him," Katie seethed, her voice loud in the sudden silence of the greenroom.

Akihiro didn't know whether he was grateful or not when the managers and staff started to discreetly leave. He noted that his members stayed put, likely anticipating needing to comfort him.

"It's somewhat difficult to be close when you grow up in a completely fucking different country and your grandfather is super old school Taiwanese and barely speaks Mandarin and you don't speak Taiwanese," she continued.

"Katie, I really am sorry," Akihiro said, voice soft and contrite.

"I have to go."

"Wait — will I see you before I head out on tour again?"

"I guess it depends on how quickly my ah-gong dies, doesn't it?" Akihiro winced at Katie's acidic tone. "I'll be sure to tell him that you're on a schedule."

It took Akihiro several moments before he realized Katie had ended the call without even saying goodbye. He stared stupidly at his screen until Ye-jun put a comforting hand on his shoulder.

"When I piss off Mina noona that badly, I usually send something expensive and sparkly right away to make amends," the older man said, "along with prints of my ugliest pictures."

Woo-jin scoffed. "That seems like it would just make her madder," he observed.

"Oh, it absolutely does — it doesn't help at all," chuckled Ye-jun, "but I do it anyway because it also makes her laugh. If I can make her laugh, she's more than halfway to forgiving me."

"Not everyone has your face, hyung," Jae-sung said absently while typing busily on his phone. It was his common refrain to Ye-jun whenever the eldest member gave advice that hinged upon his fantastic face.

"Well, that's not my fault," protested Ye-jun, "but Hiro isn't terrible looking and I'm sure Katie doesn't mind his looks." He paused to think and then added, "Maybe you should send pics of your abs, Hiro. I know she's weak for those — Mina has told me on more than one occasion. Like abs are hard to get or something."

Normally Akihiro would have laughed, but there was a dull pressure behind his eyes and an ache in his throat and he couldn't bring himself to do so.

"I'm sure she'll come around. It was obvious what you said came out wrong," Jae-sung continued, this time catching Akihiro's gaze from across the room. "You'd never say something that cruel on purpose. You don't have it in you."

Akihiro didn't know if that was true anymore. Lately, Katie seemed to bring out the worst in him. He didn't know if it was the months apart or if the distance merely exposed the worst of the cracks they couldn't mend with proximity and sex.

"I seem to keep fucking things up with Katie," he finally admitted. His members murmured in commiseration, waiting for him to disclose more if he wanted to. "I can't seem to do anything right, and I never know if she's going to lose her temper or give me the silent treatment for days."

Do-won looked at him with gentle compassion. "That sounds really difficult, Aki," he said. "I hate it when Ae-cha is upset at me when we're on tour. It always feels particularly impossible because we're apart and can't read each other's body language or hear our tones over text."

As much as Akihiro wanted to appreciate Do-won's insight and attempt at relating, he couldn't. He'd seen his hyung with Ae-cha — and Ae-cha and Katie were nothing alike. If he was honest, Ae-cha was sweet and fun, if not a bit shallow and dim. Of course, it was always possible that she was hiding trauma underneath it all, but Akihiro didn't think she was.

"Thanks, hyung," Akihiro said, trying to end the conversation with his noncommittal response. They wouldn't understand — not even Dae-jung, to whom he told almost everything.

Thankfully after over a decade together, his members sensed that he wanted to change the subject. Ye-jun went into some ridiculous story about how on their days off last week, he'd spent the entire time binge-playing his favorite game, only surfacing to eat and grunt at Mina noona, who'd merely wrinkled her nose and demanded he bathe.

Akihiro latched onto the rise and fall of his hyung's familiar voice and focused on trying not to cry. He didn't want to ruin all of the coordi-noona's hard work just because he couldn't keep his stupid mouth shut.

Katie didn't respond to his texts or calls for the next few days, and when she finally started returning them, she just acted as if nothing had happened.

Akihiro spent most of Christmas crying in Dae-jung's arms. No matter how Dae-jung tried to convince him that it wasn't entirely his fault, Akihiro didn't know why he kept fucking things up with her.

November 2026

"Come on, noona," whined Do-won. "Let's gooooooooo already. We're going to be late to the movie, and the morning showings are the easiest to attend incognito."

"Just go without me," Katie protested. She was jet-lagged, still in bed, rumpled and very grouchy. She was absolutely adorable.

"You're going to be jet-lagged forever if you stay in bed," scolded Do-won lightly.

He rummaged through her closet and chose a pair of her most stylish joggers, a long-sleeved tee, and her thickest sweatshirt, laying them out on the far side of her bed. Then, he threw the blankets off Katie and dragged her up.

"Don't make me dress you like you're an actual baby, noona," he threatened.

Do-won attempted not to blush when Katie started changing right in front of him after she went to the bathroom. He noted that she didn't even bother putting on a bra. She merely swapped her pajama top for the long sleeve over her camisole, put on the sweatshirt, and then swapped her pants.

"No socks?"

"Fuck socks. I hate socks." Katie ran her fingers through her hair in an attempt to straighten it and then gave up, grabbing a hat and scarf.

"Your feet will get cold," he observed.

She rolled her eyes at him as they headed toward her front door. "I'll wear my boots with the shearling lining."

"With your sweats?" Do-won was horrified.

Katie grabbed her purse and baby blue winter puffer jacket, opening the door. "Yes."

Do-won was seriously reconsidering being seen in public with her.

"Are you coming or not?" she hollered from down the hall.

Do-won sighed, closed her door, and followed. "You're treating," he said.

"Of course," Katie replied. "I'm your noona."

A bloom of warmth burst through his veins. He decided to push his luck. "Can I drive your Porsche?"

Katie just sighed and tossed her keys at him. "I'm making you pay if you fuck up the gears, Wonnie."

Do-won merely grinned in response. It was going to be an amazing day.

After the movie, Katie and Do-won ended up spending the rest of the day together. She accompanied him as he dropped by all his favorite shops to get an early start on shopping for Christmas presents. Though she complained and wondered why he couldn't shop for gifts online like regular people, she still held his numerous shopping bags, insisting that their bodyguards were not there for him to use as overqualified porters.

When they returned to Katie's apartment to drop off her purchases, Do-won invited her to join him for dinner with his parents. Katie scolded him about the last-minute notice, worrying that she didn't have anything to give them. She was darling.

"Noona, don't worry about it," assured Do-won. "You see my family all the time. They won't care if you don't bring anything."

It was true, too. At some point during their album-making process, Katie had started tagging along to Do-won's monthly family dinners. Though his sister teased him about it when Katie was out of earshot and his mother sent him way too many hopeful glances, Do-won wouldn't trade her presence for the world.

"I can't go meet your parents empty-handed!" Katie sounded offended. "I would never! We at least need to stop for a bag of oranges — I am Chinese after all."

"Oranges are fine, noona. There's a place on the way to their house and we can pick up some tangerines or something." Do-won smiled. "I'll even drive, that way you can drink!"

That seemed to mollify Katie and she, finally satisfied, followed Do-won to his BMW, got in the passenger side, and promptly pulled out her phone to scroll through her socials as he drove.

No, it wasn't good for his heart how seamlessly Katie slotted into his daily routines, and yet, he couldn't bring himself to pull back and find someone else. She had ruined him for all others.

"Don't worry, imo," Katie said. "I'll drive Wonnie home. I didn't drink very much even though he was supposed to be the responsible one tonight."

Do-won's mother smiled and patted her cheek gently. "Thanks, Katie-yah. You are too good to our Do-won."

"He makes it easy," Katie beamed. "Come on, Wonnie," she cooed. "Let noona take you home. Your sister's family already left, and you should let your parents rest."

"Okay, noona," Do-won said, dutifully hugging his parents goodbye. He leaned heavily on Katie as they left, all the while humming some nonsensical tune as he staggered down the hallway. "You're so pretty, noona," he trilled. "You always take such good care of me."

Katie chuckled to herself. Drunk Do-won was always extra affectionate. He was so red and cuddly. He really couldn't hold his liquor at all, though he'd improved since they'd first met.

"Well, don't you forget it, Wonnie. Only the best for my favorite producer," Katie said.

"I thought your favorite producer was Woo-jin hyung," he frowned. "You don't have to say that just to make me happy, noona."

She patted him comfortingly. "I'll let you in on a secret, Do-won," she whispered conspiratorially. "I don't always like Woo-jin oppa's work. You're the one I trusted for my album, not oppa. Now, I don't want to hear any more arguments about it!"

They reached Do-won's BMW and Katie clipped him into the passenger's side, drove Do-won to his building in Hannam-dong, and hauled him to his penthouse. She helped him change into his pajamas (which were really just him in his black Balenciaga boxer briefs), knowing how much he also hated having outside clothes on his bed. She even managed to ignore all that golden skin covering his flat chest and belly and his wiry arms.

"Stay, noona," Do-won mumbled into his pillow. "This way, you don't have to drive my car back tomorrow."

"Alright," Katie replied.

She found a T-shirt and sweats in his very organized walk-in closet and slid into bed next to him. Do-won — likely out of muscle memory from when he was dating Ae-cha — tucked her into the curve of his body and she allowed herself to yield to his embrace.

"I love you, noona," he whispered as he inhaled her scent, his arm tightening around her for a second before he dropped into sleep.

Katie, however, was wide awake.

March 2025

Katie's ah-gong passed away at the end of January, right before Lunar New Year. Akihiro would have tried to attend the funeral, but Katie hadn't asked him to attend. The multi-day event involved paid mourners, a lot of sitting, keeping vigil, and traveling back to her family's ancestral village. Even if she had asked, Akihiro's touring schedule had already resumed.

Akihiro had apologized, had tried to ask where he could send wreaths and money for her grandfather's soul, but Katie had continually brushed him off. "It's fine," she would say. "Alton is coming with his entire clan. He'll take care of me."

It had stung. Akihiro hadn't been sure if she'd meant to imply that he wasn't taking care of her, but he'd felt it all the same.

Katie had turned so mean, and it'd felt so similar to when she was changing her medication. When Akihiro had asked if she was remembering to take her pills, the frigid silence emanating from her end of the phone had been breathtaking in all the worst ways.

He hadn't known what to do. He still didn't.

When Dae-jung had again asked him if he was happy with Katie, Akihiro had only replied that it seemed like a dick move to break up with her when her grandfather had just died. The tight line of Dae-jung's mouth had told Akihiro all he'd needed to know.

After her grandfather's funeral arrangements, Katie joined Akihiro on the Asia leg of DOYEN's tour. There hadn't been any fights so far — which granted, they had spent the first few weeks fucking — but it wasn't working.

It didn't matter that they increasingly filled the time with his members so that they hardly spent any time alone together. Everything felt fraught and fragile.

Akihiro had thought there was nothing worse than being apart from Katie, but it turned out there was.

"Katie, we need to talk," Akihiro said one night after he'd done a joint livestream in Soo-min's room to chat with his fans after their concert in Bangkok. He'd wanted to fill himself up with the energy and well wishes of CHIMERA before he did the inevitable.

"Alright," Katie said warily. She closed the book she'd been reading and rearranged herself on the couch as he sat across from her at the other end.

Akihiro scooted closer so he could easily reach out and hold both of her hands. He felt somewhat sick to his stomach. "I can't do this anymore."

Katie made her face blank.

"You can't do what anymore, Aki-yah?"

Akihiro hated the way her voice trembled. He supposed she deserved specifics. "This. Us. Everything. We're toxic together."

"Ah," she breathed. "Toxic." Katie looked so dejected. It seemed as if she'd shrunk between those two tiny words.

"You're not toxic, Katie. But us together? We're toxic. For each other."

"I've been trying to be better," she said, her voice so very small.

Akihiro nodded to give Katie credit. She had been on her best behavior lately, but it was too little, too late.

"I'm so exhausted, Katie." He couldn't bring himself to see her face. "I'm so tired of trying to decipher your moods based on your microexpressions and body language alone."

"You could just ask me," Katie said reproachfully. She withdrew her hands and placed them carefully in her lap.

Akihiro coughed a bitter laugh. "I could just ask you," he repeated.

Dae-jung couldn't understand why Akihiro couldn't just ask her either. But Dae-jung didn't know how she could get.

"I don't think you quite realize just how impossible that is," he added.

"Ah," Katie sighed. "I see."

"Do you?" Akihiro asked. "I'm not an idiot. I know it has to do with your father or Tony." He plowed on despite seeing her recoil. "You say I can just ask — but I can't. Not really. Not when you suck all the oxygen out of a room. Not when I ask what's going on and you freak out or lose your temper or completely check out and ignore me."

Katie was trembling and Akihiro wondered if she realized her hands were clenched.

"You can't even talk to me about it without spiraling into panic attacks." Frustrated, he ran a hand through his hair. "I don't even know if this conversation will trigger one."

"I can't help that," she objected. "It's not as if I haven't tried. It just — I — I can't help it if I get panic attacks!" Tears streamed from her dark eyes.

"I know," Akihiro said, trying to soften his tone. "I know, baby."

Katie looked away and stared at the bland flower print hanging on the wall of his hotel suite. Her fingers dug into her wrist and worried the old scars.

"I want kids, Katie. But how could we possibly have any?" Akihiro knew he was hurting her, but he was hurting, too. He had been hurting for months, perhaps years. "I don't want them to constantly walk on eggshells around you like I do. I don't want them to live constantly in fear of your moods, worrying about what will kickstart a panic attack or you disappearing for hours."

Akihiro snuck a glance at Katie, but immediately averted his gaze. He couldn't bear the heartbreak spread all over her face.

"I love you and I'm trying, Akihiro," she begged. "I don't know what else you want me to do. I go to therapy. I take drugs. I —," Katie abruptly cut off as if she remembered herself. She stood. She spoke the last bit to the floor. "Give me fifteen minutes and I'll be out of your room, Akihiro-ssi."

"Katie, I can get another room. You shouldn't have to —"

Katie waved him off. "All I need is fifteen minutes," she said and promptly turned to gather all her things. She was very thorough and very fast, so much so that she was at the door in eight minutes.

It was shocking, really.

He hadn't meant to kick her out. Akihiro admittedly hadn't considered the logistics all the way through. He didn't mean to be petty, but still, he thought that it was typical of Katie to exit so efficiently from his life.

Akihiro moved to hug her but she balked so harshly that he froze in his tracks. "I do love you, Katie. Please know that."

He didn't know why he said that. It seemed cruel, even for him — to twist the dagger in Katie's heart after he'd stabbed her.

Katie's face was like stone. "You said you were safe," she bit out. Accusatory. "You said it was okay to trust you, that it was okay to be real with you."

Akihiro reeled as if hit, and now he was pissed. "But you didn't trust me, did you?" he yelled. "You were never real with me! You never even gave me a chance to be safe!"

He was crying now, and he hated how messily everything was ending. Why couldn't Katie see that she was still such a confounding mystery — that she was laden with hidden booby traps, and if he stayed, he would sink along with her?

Katie opened her mouth as if to tear into him, but then she shut her mouth with a click. She opened the door and left.

He did not see Katie again for months. When he finally did, he didn't expect her to act as if nothing had happened, but that's exactly what she did. Katie treated him with the same tolerating affection that she had used to before they'd dated.

It was as if the two years with Akihiro had never happened.

March 2027

"Akihiro, do you have time to talk?"

At the familiar voice, Akihiro looked up from the slate gray couch in the SB Entertainment artist lounge. Clad in a fuzzy, oversized red sweater and cream leggings, Katie was still so fierce and beautiful it made his heart ache. He noted that he hadn't seen her lately, but Akihiro had a gut feeling that she'd been avoiding him since her album release party.

He plastered as friendly a smile as he could muster. "Sure," he said. It had been almost two years to the day since their breakup. They'd talked in passing plenty of times. He could do this. "Do you want to talk here or somewhere else?"

He watched as she pretended to consider his question even though he knew she already had a location picked out.

"Is my studio okay or do you prefer a more neutral ground?" Katie asked.

"Are we gearing for war?" Akihiro joked nervously, worrying his lower lip between his teeth.

Katie shrugged. "I don't think so, but you might think differently."

"Let's go to your studio," Akihiro said practically. "Fewer eyes on us."

She nodded. He followed her to her studio and chuckled. Katie really was such a creature of habit. Her space hadn't changed much since the last time he'd been there. She still had the framed Batman logo on the wall along with a Prince Zuko print. She still had books and instruments everywhere.

Katie's bookshelves were still crammed full of textbooks and thick tomes of fantasy. Her mini baby grand piano still had pride of place next to her recording equipment, and one wall was still covered with hanging guitars and basses. The far corner of the room was still stacked with her cases of stringed instruments — it looked as if she'd collected some more — and her coffee table was still littered with notebooks, Korean novels, and colored gel pens. The teal couch's upholstery was decidedly worse for wear, but he was happy to see it was still quite comfortable when he sank down into the cushions.

Akihiro waited as she seemed to quietly gather her courage.

"Thanks for agreeing to talk with me, Aki-yah," she started finally.

He wasn't sure if it was a good idea yet, but he nodded politely anyway and found that he was glad he'd agreed.

"I — I miss you." Katie's voice wavered and he wanted to tell her that it would be okay, but Akihiro knew better than to make empty promises.

"I miss you, too," he said. Once again, out of politeness, but again, he found that he meant it as soon as it was out of his mouth.

"I've been doing a lot of thinking lately," she said, "about your reasons for breaking up."

Shit.

"And I want you to know that I'm so sorry, Akihiro. I'm sorry I took out all my trauma on you. You deserved so much better. I treated you terribly."

Akihiro had not quite expected the conversation to go this way. He wasn't exactly sure how he'd thought it would go, but it wasn't this. He nodded stiffly. "It's okay, noona."

Katie met his gaze earnestly. "No, Akihiro. It wasn't okay. It wasn't your fault that I didn't tell you about my PTSD and its triggers," she shared. "I had thought I was dealing with it — and I guess I was doing the best I could at the time — but I've since done a ton of work on myself and am a lot better now."

"I'm sure I could have dealt with it better, too, noona," Akihiro said. "I was far from perfect." He paused. "I'm glad you got the support and healing you needed."

He meant it, too. He'd also done some thinking, especially after he'd gone through a slew of brief and torrid affairs after her. He knew a lot of their relationship difficulties stemmed from his inability to state his needs and face his fears about Katie's possible reactions. Akihiro knew he shouldered his fair share of blame. He was also happy to hear that she was doing better. He'd never wanted her to suffer.

"I've processed the worst of the trauma — I haven't had a panic attack in at least a year — and I can even talk about what happened to me without spiraling. I'm so much better now, Hiro-yah," Katie said. "You can test it out — ask me whatever you want!"

"That's great, noona," he said as his heart twinged. Akihiro couldn't shake the feeling that Katie was seeking his approval, and that broke his heart. Had she been doing all this for him?

She was crying now, and Akihiro didn't know why or what to do. Katie wiped her eyes with a tissue, her watery breath shuddering.

"Ah, fuck," she laughed shakily. "This is probably not doing much to convince you that I'm better. But I promise I am. I can get my doctors to explain to you if you want."

"You don't have to do that, noona. I believe you and am happy for you." Akihiro paused again. "I've already forgiven you for what happened between us, noona. You don't have to say you're sorry."

"Oh," Katie breathed as more tears leaked from her eyes.

Then she stared at him, with her heart on her sleeve, and Akihiro had a sinking feeling he knew what she was going to say next.

"I still love you, Akihiro," she said softly. "Do you think — do you think you'd be willing to give me another chance?"

There it was.

"Oh, noona," Akihiro said as gently as he could. "I will always love you, but I don't love you like that anymore. And —" He hesitated and tried to think of a way to be as kind as possible. "I don't think it would be good for me to give it another try."

"Ah," Katie said.

Katie was always so devastating with her "ahs." He appreciated how she didn't press him.

"I've done a lot of thinking over the years, too," Akihiro continued. "I'm sorry, too. I'm sorry that I didn't know how to love or support you the way you needed. I'm sorry my insecurities and fears made healing so much harder for you."

"Oh," Katie repeated. "My trauma response wasn't your fault, Akihiro."

"It may not have been my fault, and I'm still sorry. I'm sorry I wasn't honest with you about what I wanted or needed. I'm sorry I didn't know how to care for you."

Katie nodded, the tiny flyaways at her hairline floating in the air, making her look softer than she was in reality. "I forgive you, too, Akihiro," she returned.

They sat in silence for a few more moments, trying to collect their individual emotions.

"I should go," he said as he got up. "Unless you have something else to add?"

"No, nothing else to add," Katie said as she also stood. "Thanks for hearing me out, Akihiro. I — I appreciate you."

"Would it be alright for me to hug you?" Akihiro asked. At her assent, he wrapped his arms around her, willing his love and hope to seep into her. "I love you, noona. We're going to be okay, alright?"

Katie's breath shuddered, and she nodded against his shoulder.

He kissed her on the crown of her head and left, feeling both heavier and lighter at the same time.

CHAPTER 9

March 2027

Do-won was heading to Katie's studio to see if she wanted to grab lunch when he saw Akihiro leaving her studio. Katie had mentioned wanting to talk to Akihiro a few days ago about getting back together, and he surmised that that was what had just transpired. From the look on Akihiro's face and the fact that he was leaving and not staying for some epic makeout session, Do-won guessed Katie was likely inconsolable on the other side of the door.

Do-won's brain buzzed and the next thing he knew, he was speaking. "What did you do?" he accused.

Akihiro startled at Do-won's unusual intensity and threw up his hands instinctively. "Nothing, hyung. She — she wanted to get back together and I said, 'No.'"

"And you just left her there? Is she okay?" The buzzing in Do-won's brain got louder.

Akihiro examined Do-won curiously. "I think so? I —"

"You think so? Goddammit, Aki — she's been doing so well! You have no idea what she's been through!"

Do-won vaguely noted pain flashing across Akihiro's features, but he didn't care. All he could think of was Katie sobbing alone in her studio, in distress because of Akihiro's rejection.

"I — you don't think she'll hurt herself?" Akihiro blanched. "I don't think she'll hurt herself...do you? She said she was better."

At Akihiro's words, Do-won only saw red. He grabbed fistfuls of Akihiro's shirt and slammed him against the wall. "You better fucking hope she doesn't."

"What the fuck, hyung?" Akihiro shouted.

He was pretty sure Do-won was going to punch him in the face. Although Akihiro had enough training in martial arts to block it (as well as to get out of this situation), it was more upsetting that Do-won was going to punch him in the face.

"The fuck is going on?"

Akihiro had never been so relieved to hear Jae-sung's voice. He was vaguely aware of a whole slew of studio doors opening up and down the hall. Do-won seemed to come back to himself and loosened his grip on Akihiro's shirt, backing away.

"Wonnie?" Katie said from her doorway at the same time Jae-sung asked, "Akihiro, are you alright?"

"I'm fine," Akihiro gruffed out, noting that Katie's concern was first for Do-won and not for himself. "Just a minor difference of opinion," he added, wondering when that switch had occurred. He was annoyed at himself for the twinge of sadness he felt at no longer being her person.

He had made his choice. He would live with it.

Do-won gave Akihiro a curt nod and rushed to Katie's side. Akihiro only caught a murmured "Are you okay, noona?" before Jae-sung ushered him into his studio.

"What was that all about?" his leader asked.

He should have known Jae-sung would go into leader mode ASAP. Akihiro and his members had gotten into their share of fights over the years, but rarely had they almost come to blows.

He sank into the sturdy sectional Jae-sung had against a wall and sighed. "Noona asked if I wanted to get back together," Akihiro explained. "I declined, and when Wonnie hyung found out, he threw me against the wall."

The older man pursed his full lips and seemed to make a mental note. "Are you okay?" Jae-sung asked again.

Akihiro was a little bit shaken but he was fine overall. "I think hyung was worried about noona," Akihiro said. He slid the sleeves of his shirt over his palms, his fingers gripping the soft cotton for comfort. "Did, uh, something happen between them, and no one told me?"

"Not that I know of." Jae-sung gave Akihiro a sidelong glance. "I just know they got really close when she was making her last album, and then Wonnie ended up producing it."

Akihiro threw a casual glance over the shelves full of Jae-sung's KAWS figurines and settled his gaze on his leader's favorite fiddle-leaf ficus. It always amused him that the rapper had enough fiddle-leaf ficuses to have a favorite.

"He's in love with her, isn't he?"

Jae-sung just hemmed and hawed. "I, uh, I actually have no idea. You would have to ask him yourself when you work this shit out." His friend's expression took on a stern quality. "You will work this shit out," he ordered more than asked.

Akihiro rolled his eyes and tugged his denim bucket hat lower over his eyes. "Yeah, yeah, we will."

"Katie's my friend, too, and I get it. Relationships and exes are tough to deal with, but I can't have you and Do-won fucking it up for the rest of the team," Jae-sung admonished. "You're all adults. Please, for the love of god, act like it."

"I heard you loud and clear, hyung. No brawling in the hallways over a girl — check."

"No brawling at all — hallways or otherwise."

Jae-sung sighed the bone-weary sigh Akihiro recognized from all their years of living and working together. He knew he was being a bit of a smart-ass, but from the morning he'd just had, he felt he was entitled to it.

Akihiro knew he and Do-won were long overdue for a conversation, but he was not looking forward to it. It probably didn't seem like it, but he understood where Do-won was coming from. Katie was easy to fall in love with. It was the living with her that was hard.

"Are you okay, noona?" Do-won asked Katie again.

"Of course, I am," she said, arching her brow at him. "Want to tell me what that was about?"

Embarrassed, Do-won merely shook his head. "I may have overreacted a bit."

"I suppose Akihiro told you?" Katie avoided looking him in the eyes, fussing instead with the random notebooks on her coffee table. "It was a stupid thing to hope for," she said resignedly.

Do-won wanted to scoop her up into a hug, but judging from her body language, Katie did not seem as if she would want such a thing. He supposed he could just ask.

"Do you want a hug?"

Katie looked up and was silent, as if contemplating his question deeply. Then, she nodded.

He was glad he'd asked. Do-won crossed her studio and enveloped her in a full body embrace. "It wasn't stupid," he said, his voice slightly muffled in her hair.

Katie's breath hitched against him and before he knew it, she was sobbing onto his shoulder. "Akihiro knew me so well — and he doesn't want me — said I wasn't good for him —," she bawled. "Who's going to want me, Do-won?"

All of a sudden, Do-won realized that he did. He wanted her. He wanted her so much that he ached with the wanting.

Do-won rued his poor timing.

Instead, he tenderly said, "But Akihiro didn't know you, noona. He knew how you behaved, but he didn't know why. Don't you think the 'why' makes a big difference?"

"He knew enough," Katie said, her voice quavering. "He said we were toxic together."

He backed away from her and cupped her face between his hands. "He called you toxic?"

"Just us together. He made sure I knew it wasn't me," Katie said, eyes slick with tears.

Do-won nodded, reassured. "Just because you and Akihiro weren't good for each other doesn't mean you're not good for someone else — or good enough on your own."

"I don't want someone else," she whined.

"I know, noona. I know. But you will eventually," he mentioned softly. He couldn't decide if he wanted to laugh or to cry.

"How can you be so sure?" Katie's lip trembled. Do-won would have given anything to make her happy again.

"You're gonna have to trust me on this one." At her dubious face, he added, "After all, I'm your delight." He paused just like he was at a concert. "You're my delight." Do-won paused again and his spirits lifted at her tentative smile. "I'm one —" He held a fake mic out to Katie.

"Delight!" she replied, sounding happier but still somewhat forlorn.

Do-won tucked some of Katie's loose hair behind her ears. She was so fragile yet strong. His heart hurt to see her in pain. "You'll be okay, noona," he said with more confidence than he felt.

He pulled her into another hug and Katie melted into him. "Okay," she whispered. "Thanks, Wonnie."

"Of course, noona," he replied. "You know I love you, right?"

Katie nodded into his chest. "I love you, too, Wonnie," she said, voice muted by his shirt. "I love you, too."

It was surprisingly easy for Do-won to avoid Akihiro over the next few days considering they were all supposed to be working on a new album, but Do-won supposed there was no real hurry. Their fans had waited this long, they would be fine with waiting a little bit more — or if they weren't, that was fine, too. DOYEN would take all the damn time they wanted.

But in the end, Do-won couldn't put off talking with Akihiro any longer. One, because Jae-sung was on his dick about it. And two, Akihiro was currently sitting on Do-won's leather sofa.

"You wanna tell me what the fuck that was all about the other day?"

The singer, dressed in a thin white tee, dark wash jeans, and a black, metal-studded moto jacket, looked like he was expecting another fight. Do-won felt comparatively underdressed in his bright yellow sweatshirt and loose cargo pants. Akihiro was apparently not fucking around.

Do-won felt a little ridiculous. He couldn't believe how little he'd trusted Katie and how much he'd overreacted. "I, perhaps, got a little carried away," he admitted. "I'm sorry, Aki-yah. That was uncalled for."

Akihiro examined Do-won so long that he wanted to squirm, but he didn't want to give the younger man the satisfaction. He hated how his old roommate knew exactly how to read him.

"She's easy to love, hyung," Akihiro said eventually.

Do-won nodded. "She is."

"You weren't there, though," Akihiro continued. "You were wrapped up in Ae-cha. You saw us together, but you weren't in it with us, hyung."

"You think I don't know that?"

Akihiro pulled on the sleeves of his leather jacket. "Loving her was killing me." He cleared his throat. "I loved her so fucking much, hyung. But it wasn't enough. Love itself is never enough."

Do-won pretended not to see a tear spill down Akihiro's cheek.

"Noona's different now, Hiro. She actually talks about what happened — and she doesn't spiral anymore," said Do-won.

"Maybe noona's changed, hyung, but that isn't the same as her being good for me."

"If you'd just give her another chance, you'd see that she's so much better. You didn't see her work through everything with this new therapist. She was so brave."

"You think I don't know she's brave? You think I don't constantly wonder 'What if?'" Akihiro's voice cracked, as if he'd held years of pain inside him. Do-won supposed he had. "What if I had been braver and just asked noona all the questions I'd kept inside? What if I had been a better boyfriend? What if I could have taken all those late nights worried about where she was and if she was safe? What if I could have taken her freezing me out for days at a time? What if I hadn't felt so alone even when we practically lived together for two years?"

Akihiro roughly palmed the tears off his face. Do-won crossed the room and sat next to his friend, reaching out a hand for him. Akihiro gripped it as if it were his only life preserver.

"But then I wonder: what if I pushed her too hard and she made another attempt on her life? What if I asked her questions and I couldn't handle her answers? What if she dragged me down with her?"

Do-won felt like an asshole. "I'm sorry, Aki-yah. I should have known you would have thought it through. We've been friends long enough for me to have known better."

Akihiro just nodded, focusing on trying to get his emotions back in line. Do-won let go of Akihiro's hand and just sat with his old friend and bandmate in silence. He wondered if he would have fared any better than Akihiro if he'd been Katie's boyfriend during those same years, if he would be making the same decision that Akihiro did now.

After some moments wandering down his own what ifs, he stopped. It was no use imagining what he would have done in Akihiro's place. He wasn't Akihiro. He was only himself.

"You know what I don't understand, hyung?" Akihiro's words cut into his ruminations. "Why do you insist I give noona another chance when you're in love with her?"

"I —," Do-won stuttered. There was no use denying him — Akihiro knew him inside and out. Do-won glared at Akihiro and his infuriating smirk, then looked away. "I just want noona to be happy," he said at last. "She deserves to love and be loved."

Do-won could feel Akihiro examine him some more. "So do you, hyung. So do you."

He shrugged, not knowing what to say. "I suppose we all do, Aki-yah," he belatedly said. "Are you talking to a therapist about what happened between you and noona?"

"You think I should?" Akihiro asked as he fiddled with the empty water bottles lining Do-won's workstation. "Sometimes, I think I made the whole thing up. I think that maybe I was too sensitive. Maybe I was too much for her."

"I know I was a dick to you, Akihiro," Do-won said, throwing his arm around the singer's shoulders, "but I do believe you. It might help to talk to someone and process whatever lies snuck in during your relationship."

"Dae-jung says the same thing."

"Well, maybe you should listen to your soulmate then," joked Do-won, then added on a more serious note. "Helping someone deal with trauma can be taxing. You deserve to be taken care of, too."

Akihiro cast him a soft glance, full of affection. "Thanks, hyung."

"I love you, Hiro-yah," Do-won said, voice unexpectedly full.

"I love you, too, hyung," replied Akihiro.

It wasn't enough. "And I am so sorry."

"I know, hyung. I know."

Akihiro pulled Do-won into a hug and leaned into his chest. The two of them just sat, content to hold and be held.

July 2027

Wu's latest full album "Tesseract" (SB Entertainment, 2027) is brain foreplay, sinking its teeth into the meat of your soul, lighting up your pleasure centers long after the afterglow passes.

"Tesseract" explores the cosmic questions of our place in the universe with a backdrop of love found, love lost, and love renewed. The album opens with the ethereal "Stardust" and Wu's topline floating over 1DEL1GHT's dreamy delivery. KJ (formerly King Ja$e) and his verse is right at home with Wu's slinky

vocals on the sublime intellectual breakup song, "Orthogonal Lives" — the pairing of music's two most erudite lyricists a match made in heaven.

On "Jumpspace," 1DEL1GHT's production frames Wu's first foray into rap in sparse, atmospheric beats, never overpowering and always illuminating her rapid-fire flow. "Tesseract" closes with the Lambent-produced "Gravity," a lush track full of surprising beat change-ups, orchestral swells, and heartbreaking lyrics.

- Consequence, July 2027

Not to beat a dead horse, but Katie Wu is a musical and lyrical genius. This album is filled with a veritable powerhouse of features and producers. Save for a few, "Tesseract" puts all other albums this year to shame.

- Paper, July 2027

[1] Stardust (feat. 1DEL1GHT of DOYEN) [2:34]
[2] I Marvel at Your Universe [3:12]
[3] Eyes Wide Open [3:36]
[4] A Small Step [2:39]
[5] When Is an Acceptable Time for Wrinkles? [2:50]
[6] Orthogonal Lives (feat. KJ of DOYEN) [4:16]
[7] Time Travel and Other Interstellar Adventures [3:08]
[8] Jumpspace (Prod. 1DEL1GHT of DOYEN) [2:47]
[9] Gravity (Prod. Lambent of DOYEN) [3:21]
- Track list, "Tesseract" (SB Entertainment, 2027)

How can we both be right
If it all turned out so wrong
Proof bearing our cross was for long
Intersecting at this point, so brief

Should I be glad instead
We didn't have parallel lives
Existing side by side
Never the twain to meet

Oh, isn't it better to have squared up
Met each other head on
Crashing headlong
Than yawning from eternity to eternity
                    - "Orthogonal Lives" (SB Entertainment, 2027)

To my future self.
        - Album dedication, "Tesseract" (SB Entertainment, 2027)

Do-won popped his head into Katie's studio. "Noona, you wanna grab dinner later? My treat."

Katie looked up from her mindless guitar strumming and shot him a bashful smile. "Ah, I can't tonight, Wonnie. Ye-jun oppa set me up on a date with one of his actor friends. He says it will be good for me."

"Oh," Do-won said, surprised she had time to date even in the midst of new album promotions. He was going to have to talk to his eldest hyung about sticking his nose where it didn't belong.

"Raincheck?"

"Sure. How about lunch tomorrow so you can tell me all about the date," Do-won joked and made at being lighthearted despite feeling anything but.

Katie sighed. "Oppa already had the same idea. He wants to debrief and give me pointers." She made an annoyed face. "Oh!" she said, face brightening. "You should come, too!"

"What? I don't want to impose, noona."

"Nonono! This is a great idea! This way, you can distract Junie oppa if he gets on my case — as if this were 'Pygmalion' — really, the nerve — anyway, yes! Please join us tomorrow and save me from oppa. He's really the worst. I don't even know the name of the actor he's setting me up with."

"Hyung didn't tell you?" asked Do-won, finally cramming in a word edgewise.

Katie waved a careless hand in the air. "Oh, he did. I just forgot. Clearly, the actor can't be all that famous if I did."

Do-won started to tune Katie out as she chattered, clearly nervous and needing to babble at someone, that someone being him. He wanted to kill Ye-jun — his hyung knew he was into Katie and still had set her up. If this was some weird psychological strategy to goad him into action, Do-won couldn't promise not to exact some sort of very public and very humiliating revenge.

The next day, Do-won reluctantly joined Katie and Ye-jun for lunch at Heiwa.

"Alright, Katie," said Ye-jun as he slid into his seat, "how was your date?"

Do-won ignored the smirk his hyung tossed his way and sipped on his freshly ground matcha tea, grimacing only slightly. No matter how much he tried to enjoy the beverage, it always tasted like grass. He longed for his regular iced Americano.

"Oppa, I know the man is your friend, but he is so boring," Katie complained. "It's a good thing he's attractive because that was about the only thing going for him."

"What do you mean? Why didn't you like Ju-ho hyung?" Ye-jun's smug face dropped into concern.

Katie's eyes took on a sly gleam that had Do-won preparing for trouble. "Oh, that was his name?"

Do-won honestly tried not to laugh at Ye-jun's exasperated face, but it was a lost battle from the start.

"Katie, Lee Ju-ho is super famous. How do you not know who he is?" Ye-jun seemed as if he wanted to tear all his hair out.

"I mean, he looked familiar?" she shrugged. "Look, you know my memory is for shit."

Ye-jun sighed with his whole body. "Why was he unacceptable to you? He's a very nice person, you know."

"I'm sure he is, oppa," Katie appeased. "But he didn't understand my latest album at all. He asked me if it was about the Marvel Universe. I mean, there's that tongue-in-cheek song about it — but it's 4-dimensional geometry and a literary device in science fiction and fantasy for fuck's sake! Like, how can I even have a conversation with this man?"

"To be fair, noona, I didn't understand your latest album until you explained it to me." Do-won didn't know why he was defending Lee Ju-ho, but he was a fair person and he really hadn't gotten the finer points of her album until she'd explained it.

"I can't express it right. He just doesn't spark joy."

Do-won hadn't been too keen on crashing this lunch debrief, but now, he didn't seem to mind so much. "I'm sorry he didn't spark joy, noona," he said.

"It's okay, Wonnie. I still fucked him," Katie said blithely. "That part wasn't so bad."

"I —," Ye-jun just shook his head. "I really don't want to know about this part."

Katie grinned. "Well, if you ever change your mind, just ask unni. I told her all about it this morning. His dick was really pretty."

"Katie!!" Ye-jun sank his head in his hands. "I do not want to hear about hyung's penis."

"I always forget most South Korean men are uncut. It's like a little turtleneck."

Ye-jun flagged down a waiter and asked for two bottles of soju. "Make great haste, please," he begged.

Do-won was torn between the pang in his heart at hearing of Katie's sexual activities with men who were not him and amusement at Ye-jun's chagrin. "Are you going to see him again?" he asked.

"Maybe? I suppose if I keep his mouth occupied, he won't bore me to tears." Katie shrugged some more. "Oppa, do you have any other actor friends?"

Ye-jun made a sound that could only be described as extreme dismay. Do-won decided he would laugh because the alternative was too depressing.

October 2027

"Katie-yah, I refuse to introduce you to any more of my friends," complained Ye-jun.

The singer was sitting next to Woo-jin across the table from Do-won and Katie. They were once again at Ye-jun and Ye-sung's restaurant Heiwa because they were guaranteed privacy, and Katie had a weakness for the steamed meat.

"At some point, they're going to figure out that you've slept with all of them."

"I didn't sleep with all of them," Katie corrected primly because she loved accuracy perhaps a little too much. She sipped on her hot sake. "Some of them just ate me out."

Woo-jin hollered his amusement, his cat-like eyes creasing into happy crescents. "You should see her spreadsheet, Junie. Alton and I are constantly amazed at all the categories she considers. The joy rating is particularly dismal on them all. She even has pivot charts."

"I don't even know what a pivot chart is," exclaimed Ye-jun.

Katie glanced over at Do-won and he seemed to share Ye-jun's confusion.

"I don't know what it is either, but Alton and Mina noona both praised them to me on separate occasions so it must be important," said Woo-jin while shoving a shockingly large piece of beef into his mouth.

"Don't forget the color coding, Woo-jin," Katie preened as her eyes danced.

"I confess, I don't quite understand the color coding," he admitted with his mouth full.

Katie rolled her eyes. "Well, it's no fun if I explain it," she moped. "It should be obvious. I want to see at a glance how many Kims, Lees, Parks, Jungs, and Chois I've collected."

"You color coded them by family name?" Do-won asked incredulously.

"I have a different color for each of the top five surnames in Korea."

"You may as well have sorted them by hometown," Do-won complained.

"I thought about that," she mused. "But Wonnie, if you think I'm gonna ask a man about his hometown while his dick is in my mouth…"

"YAH!" cried Ye-jun as Do-won and Woo-jin cracked up.

"Please ask if my distribution curve is similar to the percentages of surnames in the South Korean population." Katie practically vibrated.

"Do you even have enough of a sample size?"

"Wonnie, first of all, I'm so proud of you for knowing enough science to ask about the sample size." Katie winked at him. "However, I must say that I am still disappointed that you think I wouldn't be thorough in my data collection."

"A simple 'yes' would suffice," Do-won groused.

"Full disclosure, this chart isn't just from the last few months," Katie clarified. "I was very bored one day and cataloged all my sexual partners. Well, all of them except for Tony, anyway," she added as an afterthought. "What's the point of having a bar so low that it skews my data and pulls all my averages down?"

"We wouldn't want that," agreed Woo-jin seriously. Katie loved how invested he was in her spreadsheet. She would turn him into a data guy yet!

"Of course, I didn't include non-Koreans in the data for the surname distributions, but it is indeed very close!" Katie clapped, obviously very pleased with herself.

"I just want to make sure you're having fun and not being an asshole to my friends," said Ye-jun in full big brother mode, his face drawn and serious.

It was sweet how concerned he was acting, but it wasn't necessary. It wasn't as if Ye-jun's friends didn't enjoy themselves. Besides, how else was Katie supposed to make up for lost time now that her trauma wasn't hindering her dating life?

Ye-jun was still frowning. "They're actual people, you know, not just a collectible or notch on your belt."

"I can do both!" Katie stuck out her tongue at Ye-jun. "Stop being such a stick in the mud, oppa. I know they're not interchangeable cogs. I just enjoy data."

"Oh, okay," trilled Woo-jin, "is that what you're calling dick?"

"You think you're so fucking funny, oppa," Katie shot back. She didn't have to explain herself to them. She deserved to play the field; if men were willing to be had, why shouldn't she have them?

"It's been months and you've gone on countless dates, noona," Do-won observed, "and to a one you've complained they haven't sparked any joy. I don't think the phrase means what you think it means. Isn't it supposed to apply to possessions you declutter?"

Katie cut her eyes at Do-won. He was normally so supportive so she didn't quite understand his change of heart. He was seriously annoying.

"Don't take things so literally, Wonnie," she justified. She picked up some of the steamed kabocha slices and set them on her plate before grabbing some more fried octopus. "I'm applying Kondo's theories across disciplines."

"I suppose it's the little things in life that spark joy," he replied, "and if the men only sparked joy as data points on your spreadsheet, I guess that's good enough for me." Katie didn't quite trust Do-won's sudden change in opinion, and her suspicions were justified when the rapper said thoughtfully, "I just wonder if you would even recognize joy if someone did manage to spark it."

Ye-jun and Woo-jin burst into laughter and high-fived the younger man much to Katie's dismay. She knew what she was doing — even if all that dating was already growing a bit tiresome.

Do-won was seriously annoying.

December 2027

"Are you okay, noona?" Do-won asked over lunch in the SB Entertainment cafeteria. "You haven't pestered Jun hyung about setting you up with his friends lately."

Do-won didn't know why he was asking except that he was a glutton for punishment. Better he constantly remind himself of Katie's unavailability than to give in to the human urge of fantasizing a future with her — a future full of laughter, love, and maybe tiny people who looked like her and him mixed together.

Woo-jin raised a judgmental eyebrow and said, "That's because she's moved onto bothering me or Alton — although Alton's suggestions don't help her with collecting the top five surnames of Korea."

"Mina noona says Katie has a different set of color codes for Chinese surnames," Ye-jun piped in helpfully. "What are those again, Katie?"

"Wang, Lee, Chang, Liu, and Chen," Katie replied automatically, grinning saucily at the older man. "I am wondering just how many Lees in total I will collect by the end of this grand experiment."

"I haven't checked in a while. What are you at so far?" asked Woo-jin curiously.

Katie laughed. "I think last count was eleven?"

"You've fucked eleven Lees since July?"

"I didn't sleep with them all, but even if I did — don't slut shame me, oppa," Katie said cheerily as she slurped up ramyeon noodles. "I spent all my hot years in college being a conservative Christian." She sighed and propped her chin on her hand. "All my hotness wasted on a white boy named Gary!" She cringed intensely. "Although to be fair, it would have been wasted on any college boy. Men are so worthless."

"Hey!" Do-won chorused with Ye-jun and Woo-jin in their mutual indignation.

"Oh, don't be like that. I'm sure you all were terrible at sex in your late teens and early 20s — assuming you even had time to have any."

Ye-jun and Woo-jin exchanged a sly look. Oh, no.

"Hyung," Do-won started at the same time Ye-jun said, "You know, Wonnie here was legendary in his early 20s."

Katie's eyes widened. "Oh, really?"

"Guys, this isn't necessary."

Woo-jin smirked. "He made more than one girl cry."

"I think crying is an understatement. Wailing is more accurate."

Katie leaned forward conspiratorially. "Tell me everything."

Do-won desperately wished for the floor to open up and swallow him whole.

"I think that was during your dom phase, wasn't it?" Woo-jin asked solicitously, as if he were verifying for maximal accuracy versus humiliation. "Didn't you order them to call you 'Daddy' and 'Sir'?"

Katie was choking. "Oh my god," she gasped. "No!!" Tears were trickling down her face from laughter. "It's always the straight-laced ones!"

Do-won's soul was actively leaving his body. He was going to have to move to a different country and find a new occupation altogether. Except he really was only good at rapping and dancing, so he was totally fucked.

"You're the reason Soo-min is so corrupted," Ye-jun observed. "It was just a passing phase for you, but your hooks sank into Minnie and he's never been the same." Ye-jun tsked and shook his head regretfully.

"Minnie is a pervert, too?" Katie asked, horrified. "I'm surrounded by deviants!"

Woo-jin giggled. "You forget, Alton has told me all your secrets."

"Noona, too," agreed Ye-jun. "You're no angel."

"I need new confidants — although I should have known there are no secrets from spouses," Katie complained. "At least let a girl have her illusions!"

Do-won was grateful no one mentioned Dae-jung and just how much he knew about Katie and Akihiro, though he was pretty sure Katie knew exactly how intimately acquainted Dae-jung had been with her sex life. Do-won just listened with half an ear as she and his hyungs gossiped about their respective partners.

"So, why did they cry?" Katie asked long after Do-won thought the subject had veered onto other things.

A shit-eating grin broke over Woo-jin's face. "Why don't you tell her, Wonnie."

Do-won felt heat rush to his face and muttered, "This really isn't necessary, hyung."

"Were you that bad?" Katie asked kindly. "It's really okay. You shouldn't let us tease you like this. You were so young. A spring lamb. A newborn babe. I'm sure you're much better now." She patted his hand reassuringly. She could be so condescending.

Now Ye-jun and Woo-jin were crying and Do-won was super annoyed.

"Noona, why do you keep assuming they cried because I was bad?" Do-won asked.

Katie shrugged. "There's no shame in it. I was terrible at the beginning. Actually, I might still be terrible now. I fully cop to the fact that I'm a bit of a pillow princess." She straightened her posture and flipped her long hair over her shoulder.

"They cried because I fucked them so hard and so well that they couldn't bear to come anymore." Do-won was not too proud to take satisfaction in watching Katie's pupils blow out.

"It's true. The way those poor women would stagger out in the morning all bow-legged," added Ye-jun helpfully.

"That doesn't sound like fun at all," Katie said starchily. "In fact, it sounds like a UTI waiting to happen." She sipped her hot tea as if she wasn't interested in the topic, but she obviously couldn't resist knowing more. "How come they stopped crying?"

"I changed tactics. The other members were complaining too much so I started using gags." Do-won flashed a wicked grin. "And I never said they stopped crying."

Katie choked.

Do-won decided he liked the way his lunch conversation turned out after all.

March 2028

"I'm sick of my clothes, Wonnie," Katie declared as she stomped into Do-won's studio. She swept a glance around the dimly lit room. "Oh, hi, Hiro," she added when she saw Akihiro sprawled on Do-won's leather sofa. "Why is it always so fucking dark in your studio?"

"Vibes," both Do-won and Akihiro replied simultaneously. Akihiro laughed and leaned over to give his hyung a high-five.

Katie shuddered. "That was way too creepy. Seriously, it's been years since you've lived together. Why are you guys like this?"

Akihiro shrugged while Do-won replied, "We've been with each other more than we have any other person in the world. It would be weird if we didn't know each other as well as we do."

"Yeah, noona," Akihiro said slyly. "The real question is: why don't you know this when you're the one Do-won spends the most time with outside of us members." He took great pleasure in the choking sound coming from Do-won's side of the couch. He had zero qualms continuing. "Have you not been paying enough attention?"

If Katie noticed the death glare Do-won was currently sending Akihiro, she had to be willfully ignoring all the signs that Do-won had it bad for her. It was amusing for Akihiro to witness. Surely, he hadn't been that obvious when he'd liked her.

"Do you want my help right at this moment? Or, like, you want to go shopping?" Do-won asked in a desperate bid to change the subject back to safer waters. He was no fun at all.

"You know I hate shopping," Katie said, "so definitely not that."

"Then I'm not sure how I can help?" Do-won asked.

Akihiro cracked up. He was experiencing just the right amount of secondhand embarrassment as he watched his ex and friend circle each other in a bizarre mating ritual. He grabbed his phone and started texting Dae-jung frantically.

You are missing it, he wrote.

True to form, Dae-jung texted back *???* almost immediately.

Katie noona told Wonnie hyung she was sick of her clothes and it was so obvious hyung immediately pictured her naked, he typed. When he received an *Oooooh, spicy!* in reply, Akihiro giggled to himself.

"I need a fashion makeover," Katie stated as she huffed in indignation at the idea. She stomped to Do-won's Embody chair and sat down far more forcefully than she needed.

"And you're asking hyung? You're like polar opposites in terms of fashion! He's all loud and 'look at me' and you're all 'do not perceive me'! Plus, you'll definitely cry when you see the final bill," Akihiro observed, laughing even more at the image of Katie aghast at the damage to her bank account. "What's got you all in a lather?"

"Someone called me an ajumma today!" she whined. "Me! An ajumma! Excuse me for hating the sun and protecting my face with a giant hat! The fucking nerve of these pestilent little shits!"

"Did you babysit Ye-jun hyung's kids this morning?" cracked Do-won, clearly happy to have the attention off himself.

"See if I ever help Ye-jun oppa out last minute ever again," Katie complained. "He has all this money and a whole fleet of nannies, yet he bothers me to watch his wretched offspring. As if I don't have better 'young people things' to do than to chase after his horrible children!"

"Go easy on them, noona," suggested Akihiro, unsuccessfully suppressing a grin, "they're not even 2 yet."

Katie was not remotely done being worked up. "What happened to respectful terms like imo or gomo? YAH! This new generation!"

"I'll buy you something young and fun before I head to Los Angeles, noona," Do-won promised. Akihiro could already see the gears turning in his hyung's head. He wondered what sort of garish atrocity Do-won would pick for Katie. "I have just the thing in mind. You'll love it."

Akihiro was back to hysterical giggling. "Oh, no. Noona, you're gonna hate it. I can't fucking wait."

"You didn't have to pick me up from the airport, noona. I'm sure one of my managers could have done it," Do-won said as the mob of photographers and obsessed fans pressed from behind his bodyguards.

In an effort to blend in with the surroundings, Katie was sitting in the driver's seat of one of SB Entertainment's ubiquitous SUVs instead of her own Porsche 911 Turbo. Wearing a plain black face mask, low-slung black cap, and black Ray-Bans, she fervently hoped she looked like any of Do-won's managers (albeit, a bit slighter). She didn't know why it was so important for her to pick Do-won up from the airport when he and his staff could have all ridden in the same car, but she had insisted anyway.

"Don't worry about it, Wonnie," Katie said as she pulled away from the curb. "How was your trip? Did the tracks turn out the way you wanted?"

"Yeah, it went better than expected."

"Did you get a chance to see Ellie? And did you give her my presents for her and the rest of the girls?" She smiled as she thought of her old college roommate and their mutual friends.

Do-won grinned, wide and indulgently. "Yes, noona."

"Did you and Ellie get reacquainted?" Katie raised her eyebrows up and down suggestively.

"Not in the manner you're implying, noona, but yes. We grabbed dinner in K-town."

Katie snuck a glance at Do-won and thought she could see a hint of pink rise in his cheeks. When Do-won had hooked up with her old friend at one very memorable KCON LA years ago, it was all Ellie had been able to talk about for months. Katie had begged off on the specific details, but that hadn't stopped Ellie from mentioning Do-won at every opportunity.

She couldn't help but wonder if Do-won and Ellie had rekindled any sparks. Her friend had recently separated from her husband and Katie wouldn't blame Ellie if she'd taken advantage of the situation — even if the thought made her want to squirm. Katie decided she would call her old roommate soon and catch up.

"I should get the real story from her," Katie teased in an effort to fluster Do-won simply for the pleasure of it. "Find out if you made her cry."

"You never asked?"

"Oh my god — NO," she replied, only slightly horrified.

After a bit of a pause, Do-won asked, "How come? I was under the impression you talked a lot about your sex life with your friends."

Katie shivered as a chill rolled down her spine. "First of all, you were an infant then."

"I was 24 —"

"Not your confusing Korean ages —," she interrupted.

Do-won sputtered. "I'm only six months younger than you!"

"You were 22 international, and if noona says you were an infant, you were an infant!"

"Well, Ellie didn't mind," Do-won smirked.

Katie rolled her eyes, checked her blind spot, and changed lanes. "No, Ellie didn't mind. You were her bias and she was very pleased to make your acquaintance. She's the reason I even knew about DOYEN."

"I recall you mentioning this a few times," he said, leaning back and closing his eyes in the passenger seat.

"That's because it's worth repeating," Katie retorted, taking comfort in the familiarity of the banter. "And two, you were my colleague. I really did not need to be regaled with how amazing your stroke game was or how you fucked her into the mattress." Her traitorous mind flashed to images of Do-won doing hip thrusts on stage, hair sweaty and matted.

"I mean, all the rumors are true." Do-won sounded too smug for his own good.

Katie laughed, a deep, throaty thing. "I'm sure they are, Wonnie. I'm sure they are." Woo-jin's voice detailing Do-won's sexual exploits in the SB Entertainment cafeteria came to her mind unbidden.

"What changed, then?"

"Hmmm?" she murmured as she shook herself of salacious thoughts about her friend.

"What changed between KCON and you dating Akihiro? He was younger and a colleague, and yet you slept with him," he asked.

Katie was quiet for some time. "I guess by the time I was 30, it didn't really matter as much."

"Ah," replied Do-won.

"And by then, most men my age were dating younger women," Katie continued. "The dating pool for women shrinks dramatically the older you get. That's why now it's all divorced men or permanent playboys trying to get it in."

"Does it bother you?" Do-won always asked the questions she'd rather he not ask, but in the end, she always answered. She supposed she appreciated his curiosity and willingness to learn about her.

"Not really. I'm not trying to keep them out." Katie chortled again though she wasn't really that amused.

"You don't want to settle down? Get married and have kids?" he pressed.

She stared ahead on the road as if the cars in front held all the answers. "If it happens, it happens," she replied. "But no one I want to shoot their shot is shooting, so I guess, we'll see."

Do-won was silent for a few moments before asking, "What's your type, anyway, noona? What kind of man are you looking for?"

Without even meaning to, Katie thought of Do-won. He was a good man, and he seemed to be secure enough in himself that he wasn't threatened by her past. She didn't know what to do with this revelation and why Do-won was asking.

"I don't know, Wonnie," she replied softly. "Maybe someone like you."

Her words hung between them, heavy and full of intent. And for someone who rarely shied away from asking Katie uncomfortable questions, Do-won was strangely quiet. Their conversation petered out as he murmured an acknowledgement and drifted off into a jet-lagged sleep. Lost in thought, Katie wondered if she actually wanted Do-won — if he could be the last Jung on her spreadsheet — or just someone like him, but not him in specific.

May 2028

Who knew Katie Wu was a romantic? "Blooming" (SB Entertainment, 2028) is gorgeous.

- IZM, May 2028

Tender and sweet without ever wandering into maudlin territory, Katie Wu's latest album is the dawning discovery that the love of your life has been in front of you all along.

Title track "Soseol (First Snow)" is bound to be the wedding song for years to come. The title references the popular belief that if you confess your love or are with the person you love on the day of the first snow, you will stay together for a long time. Stunning in its quiet realization of love, "Soseol" showcases Wu's maturity and musicality.

In perhaps the bookend to "Soseol," "Come Back to Me on the West Wind" features labelmate Akihiro of DOYEN and is produced by longtime collaborator, 1DEL1GHT of DOYEN. The captivating ballad lets go of past love and wishes for a future where healing will allow a joyful reunion.

- The Korea Times, May 2028

Superlative.

- Rolling Stone Korea, May 2028

[1] Blush [1:49]
[2] Arms Wide Open [3:02]
[3] In Sleep We Meet [3:18]
[4] Sunbursts and Rainbows [3:46]
[5] Look Again [2:27]
[6] Solstice [3:19]
[7] Melt Water [4:22]
[8] Soseol (First Snow) [5:20]
[9] Your Smile Is My Heart [3:21]
[10] Come Back to Me on the West Wind (feat. Akihiro of DOYEN, prod. 1DEL1GHT of DOYEN) [4:05]
[11] Amaryllis [3:36]

- Track list, "Blooming" (SB Entertainment, 2028)

Here I was, waiting so long for spring
When all this time, you'd been waiting for snow
I have been a fool
Even the sun shines in winter
                - "Soseol (First Snow)" (SB Entertainment, 2028)

To my delight.
                - Album dedication, "Blooming" (SB Entertainment,
                                                                    2028)

"They're in," Katie said, entering Do-won's studio with a stack of pale pink albums. Even from where he sat, he could see that she had on the tiny flower charm necklace he'd given her a few weeks ago. He was inordinately pleased by this revelation.

"There's only one version?" he asked. "I thought you were going to have multiple versions."

Katie shrugged as she sat next to him on his sofa. "I changed my mind at the last minute. We just made the photobooks extra thick."

"After being so involved on your other albums, it feels weird that I was only on one track this time," observed Do-won. "I am very pleased with how your duet with Hiro turned out though."

"Don't be greedy, Wonnie," Katie quipped, her shoulder nudging his companionably. "You already have your own group."

"But you didn't even let me hear the other tracks!" he protested. He wondered why she suddenly seemed so jumpy, but he attributed it to new album nerves. "Gimme it!" he cried, gleefully grabbing at her hands.

"YAH! Show some respect for my child," Katie griped as she handed him an album.

Do-won used his teeth to rip open the plastic shrink wrap and cackled at her huff of disgust. "Oh, noona, you are so soft and pretty," he murmured as he flipped through her photobook. "I didn't even know you could be this soft!"

Katie blushed a fetching shade of rose he rarely saw on her. He decided then and there that he would do whatever he needed to bring this about more often.

"I'll pull up the tracks on my phone," she said.

Do-won spent the next few moments happily perusing Katie's physical album and all its fun extras. K-pop-related albums were always way more tactilely satisfying than regular albums, and he was glad she had chosen to make albums that followed in their K-pop leanings than that of whatever genre she was in instead.

He was surprised at how smitten the opening notes of Katie's album sounded, but that's what he liked about her. She was always trying new things. Do-won looked at the track list for the song title and "Blush" seemed totally fitting.

He paused to listen more intently to the lyrics and found himself swept into a love story so gentle and kind he almost teared up. He exhaled a deep sigh of longing and wished that the song was about him.

When it was done, Do-won beamed at her. "Noona," he breathed. "It's beautiful."

Katie merely nodded and sat on her hands. The next song was about to play automatically when Do-won interrupted.

"Wait, noona," he said. "I want to listen while looking at the lyrics. But let me find my name in the credits first. That's the best part!"

Katie smiled and waited as he scanned the credits, briefly noting that all the song titles were uncommonly romantic for her and crowed when he saw his name. Then he flipped the lyrics booklet to the front and noticed the dedication. *To my delight.*

He stilled.

"Is your album dedicated to delight in general or to me, noona?" he asked quietly, afraid of what her answer would be.

Katie swallowed, and he followed the movement of her throat with his eyes.

"I suppose it depends on who's asking."

"Me," Do-won said. "I'm asking."

"It's for you," Katie said. "The album is for you."

"Why?" he asked. He really, really needed to know why.

"Just listen to it. And if you're still not sure after, I will tell you."

Do-won listened. He closed his eyes, leaned against Katie, and listened with his whole heart. He heard her love in the brash and joyful tracks as well as the tentative and questing ones. Katie's voice was leading him down a path of love and he followed, hopeful and expectant.

And then, he heard her plaintive confession.

Here I was, waiting so long for spring / When all this time, you'd been waiting for snow / I have been a fool / Even the sun shines in winter

Do-won's eyes flickered open, and he sat up, staring at her. Katie peered at him, eyes brimming with hope and desire.

"Noona?"

"I love you, Do-won," Katie said, voice trembling. "And I think you might love me, too?"

Do-won only nodded, unable to speak.

"I think you've loved me so well for a long time now. I'm sorry it took me so long to catch up. I'm sorry it took me so long to tell you that I love you, too."

"It's not a race, noona." He cupped Katie's face and slid his thumb across her cheek. "However long you took is however long you needed."

This time, it was she who nodded.

Suddenly, he grinned. "I never pegged you as a romantic." Do-won reached out and booped Katie's nose.

"I — I am no such thing."

"Are, too."

Katie groaned. "I'm never going to live this down, am I?"

"Nope! I can't wait to brag to the guys — my love for noona turned her into a soft, mushy Squishmallow of love."

"No."

Do-won pinched Katie's cheeks. "A squishy. Mallow. Of love."

"I'm canceling the album."

Do-won threw his arms around Katie. "It's too late! I'm sure they've already shipped and have been distributed! Everyone's going to know you're nothing but a big softie."

Katie sighed. "You're the actual worst," she fussed endearingly.

"You forget, I've loved Woo-jin hyung even longer, and I'm used to these useless declarations."

"Did you just compare me to Woo-jin oppa?" she asked incredulously.

Do-won cackled again. "Of course! You're practically the same person!"

"I — we're not — I'm —"

"I think it's best if you get used to losing your words, noona," Do-won said, his voice dipping low.

"And why's that?" Katie responded huskily.

He leaned in close and whispered into her ear, "Because I'm going to fuck them all out of you."

"Oh," she gasped, mouth parted.

Do-won tenderly ran his thumb over Katie's lips and said, "I'm gonna kiss you now, noona."

At Katie's tiny nod of permission, he slotted his mouth over hers, eager to finally taste her. She was so wet and warm and open, he had to force himself to slow down and take his time. A woman such as she deserved to be slowly unfurled, the enjoyment in the careful unwrapping.

He dipped his tongue into Katie's inviting heat and, at her whimper, swept himself in and out of her mouth in a rhythm as old as time.

Katie bloomed.

Chapter 10

Later that night, after Do-won had texted all his bandmates in the group chat and taken Katie out for a celebratory ice cream, she invited him up to her place as he was dropping her off.

"Did you want to come in?" Katie asked as they stood by her front door. She was busy inputting the code for her door and trying very hard not to let the tremble in her fingers show.

Do-won grabbed her fingers and kissed them sweetly. "I don't have to come in if you don't want me to. You seem really nervous, noona."

"You can come in — I — I'm not —," Katie bit her lip, conflict clear across her face. She was enchanting.

Do-won leaned in, tucked her hair behind an ear, and cradled her face. "Noona, I love you and I know you love me, too. I don't have to come in. I won't be offended or hurt, I promise."

Katie looked up at him through lowered lashes. "I want you to come in."

"Okay, then I will." Do-won smiled, imbuing it with as much gentleness and care for her as possible.

Katie finally opened her door and let him in. He followed her through her penthouse as she dropped off her things and then headed into the kitchen. "Do you want me to make you dinner? I know we just had dessert, but I — I got a new knife block." Katie smiled tentatively. "I think I still remember how to cook."

Do-won's heart swelled with joy. "I'd love that, noona."

"You can just call me Katie, you know. If you want," she said softly. "I don't mind."

"I don't mind calling you noona, either," he replied. "But I do like the option to call you Katie sometimes."

She smiled and he sat at her counter, watching as Katie carefully took out baby bok choy, tofu, chicken, garlic, wood ears, shelled edamame, and salted duck eggs. It was simple food, but the fact that Katie had never cooked for him before — the fact that she could even have knives in her home — seemed both significant and deeply vulnerable. He was inexplicably moved.

Do-won had to admit, he was surprised at how efficient Katie was while cooking, cleaning as she went. Granted, it wasn't as if she had a lot of ingredients, but still. There was something incredibly sexy about Katie making him easy dishes her mother had made for her as a child.

"If it's terrible, just lie," Katie quipped as she set down freshly stir-fried bok choy and a dish of everything else. She handed him a bowl of rice and kept one for herself.

Do-won dug in and was happy to find that he didn't have to lie at all. "It's great, noona. Thank you for making dinner."

Katie beamed and returned to eating. Do-won sipped at his Sprite that she'd handed him at some point, and she sipped her hot tea. It was lovely.

"Why were you so nervous?" he asked when dinner was almost over.

She flushed. She looked so soft that Do-won wanted to squeal and hug and then kiss her, but he did not.

"I — I haven't been in a relationship for years — and the last one really didn't turn out well." Katie fiddled with her tea cup. "I don't want to hurt you, Do-won. I don't want to make you feel like I made Akihiro felt. He

— I loved him so much, Wonnie. And I made his life hell for two years." A tear slipped down her cheek.

"Oh, noona." His heart felt too small to contain all of his love for her. "I also haven't been in a relationship for years. We're probably going to hurt each other because we're human." He grabbed her hand and held it, stroking her idly. "I've watched you fight so hard to heal — and you have. You have trusted me through so much of the process. I have learned so much from you about what it means to be vulnerable."

"Oh," Katie breathed.

"You've done the work."

"But Akihiro said —"

"I'm not Akihiro. I love him, and I know that you love him." At her protest, he held up a finger to stop her. "You two weren't good for each other. Maybe in a different universe, under different circumstances, you two would have worked out."

"I know you're not Akihiro, Do-won. I hope you know that — that I'm not comparing the two of you. I — I'm just so afraid." Katie peered deep into his eyes. "The way I feel about you is just so big. It's so big that I feel as if I will burst from all that feeling, and I don't know what it means. If I hurt you or break you, I don't think I could live with myself."

"Hey, none of that now. You won't break me — or if you do, I'll heal and move on. I can't guarantee that we'll be forever, noona. I can't guarantee that we won't really fuck up with each other occasionally." Do-won reached for her other hand until he had both of hers in his. "I see my future with you, Katie. I see babies and grandbabies and a lifetime of love and healing with you. I don't know if that will happen, but I sure as fuck want to try."

Katie swallowed thickly. "Okay, Wonnie. I want that, too. I want that so much it hurts."

Do-won had a wicked idea. "We can get started tonight, noona. I can fill you up with all my babies."

"Oh, my god. No." Katie looked aghast. "Please, please don't have a pregnancy kink."

"Don't kink shame, Katie."

Katie's face remained pained. "I — I'm really boring Do-won. I hope you know this. My favorite position is missionary because all I have to do is lay there and get fucked."

"Then what was with the spreadsheet?"

"I don't *not* do other things, I just prefer to lay down and have a man just wreck me." Katie's voice was hoarse and rough and Do-won felt that last bit in his gut.

He grinned. "What a coincidence. I am very good at wrecking women. Some might say legendary."

"Hmmph. I'll believe it when I see it," Katie scoffed.

Do-won leaned in over her kitchen table. "That can be arranged." He paused. "You sure you wouldn't be open to me saying shit like, 'Want all my little Wonnies to find your eggies?'"

"Oh. My. God. WHY."

He cracked up as he got up to help Katie clear the table. "Let me do the dishes, noona," he offered.

Katie sighed happily. "You really are the perfect man, Wonnie." She kissed him on the cheek and then whispered in his ear, "Want to stay the night?"

He turned and kissed her on the mouth, slow and sweet. "Most definitely, yes."

"You ready to admit I'm a legend?" Do-won chuckled in her ear. Katie was currently panting after her third orgasm — or was it fourth? Do-won had lost count.

"Never." Her gaze was unfocused, and she closed her eyes. "But maybe we can take a breather?"

"Sure. Water break?"

Do-won got up from the bed and headed to her kitchen, getting Katie a mug of hot water — sometimes she was such an old Taiwanese woman — and a glass of cold water for himself.

When he got back to her room, Katie was sprawled out and completely asleep. Do-won laughed softly to himself and tucked around her, pulling up the covers. He couldn't wait to tease Katie for passing out before he even got to come — but he also wasn't too upset. There was all the time in the world.

September 2028

"You should have seen her, Do-won," laughed Katie's elementary school friend Danny.

Do-won sat in a cushioned patio chair on Danny's back deck, bathing in the buttery sun of a hot California afternoon. The table was set with pitchers of sangria, pink lemonade, and water, as well as a few platters of charcuterie, cheeses, nuts, and summer fruits. He reached out for some salted almonds and relished their satisfying crunch.

He and Katie were in the Bay Area visiting Katie's mother (who had told him to call her Auntie Grace), and Katie had taken the opportunity to visit Danny and his wife Emily. Do-won only vaguely recalled meeting Danny when the man and a few other friends had visited Katie in Seoul right after she'd debuted, so Do-won appreciated the effort Katie was making to integrate him more into her life. Besides, he knew Katie was also trying to do better at keeping her old friends updated about her life, too.

Danny briefly set down his wine glass and picked his phone up from the patio table to check on their napping toddler. "Katie looked like a drowned rat," he said after assuring himself that his daughter was still sleeping.

"Unkind," Katie huffed good-naturedly into her lemonade. "You know how I don't believe in water."

Do-won stared at her. "Maybe my English isn't as good as I thought it was. Did I hear you say you don't believe in water?"

"I'm surprised you don't know this, Wonnie. I hate water," she said.

Emily laughed, absently patting her pregnant belly as she did so. "Like, the liquid?" she clarified. "I guess it's good I prepared other drink options."

"Katie hates large bodies of water especially. She hates the pool, the ocean, lakes, the beach — which includes the sun — something she also hates," teased Danny.

Do-won could clearly see the affection between the two old friends. It made him smile to see that even after all these years, they were people Katie could depend on.

"Good thing you no longer live in California much," Emily mused as she got some salami and cheese.

Katie frowned fetchingly. "It's just so wet!" she insisted. "And it's not just that I can't swim; I would totally die and as a rule, I try to avoid death."

Danny's face clouded over. "Katie," he choked. "I — I want you to know that I'm so glad you're here. That you're still here."

"Danny," Katie said, her voice suddenly broken.

Do-won reached out and squeezed her hand as both she and Danny wiped tears off their faces. Emily went inside the house and came out moments later with a box of tissues.

"I know you hate this sentimental shit," Danny said after blowing his nose, "but I am so sorry I wasn't there for you. And I'm so glad you got the support you needed."

"It wasn't your fault, Danny," Katie assured her old friend. "I shut everyone out. If you had known, I know you would have tried to help."

Danny nodded earnestly and Do-won once again felt a surge of happiness that Katie had more and more people she could rely on.

"I totally brought the mood down, didn't I?" her childhood friend rued as Emily kissed him on the cheek.

Katie laughed, watery and damp. "Just a little bit."

"I need you to know that I love you. That you matter to me — even if we don't talk all the time. I've known you since the third grade when you showed up in my Chinese school class one Saturday morning and then never left. You are a light in my world."

Danny flashed an embarrassed smile and Do-won could see why Katie had been in love with the man in high school.

Katie had said it had been twenty years and water under the bridge — but sometimes, sometimes, she wondered. She wondered what would have happened if she had just been an ordinary girl. Do-won had protested that Katie could never be ordinary. She had just rolled her eyes and said, "Cheesy."

"Aiyah," Katie protested, clearly flustered. "Tell me all about being a father and how it hasn't ruined everything."

Do-won tried to follow the conversation as best as he could, interjecting every now and then. But mostly, he was content to soak in who Katie was in contexts outside of Korea, to see her navigate in her native language. Not that her Korean wasn't proficient, but Do-won never noticed just how intently Katie listened and focused when speaking in Korean until he witnessed her among her friends in America.

She was so loose and light, as if some ballast had been cut.

He wondered if Katie would wish to move back to America at some point, and if so, what that would mean for them. He both wanted to be a tether, and yet, did not want to tie Katie down if she wished to return to her homeland.

Later, when they both were leaving, Do-won overheard Katie whisper "I love you, too, Danny" as she hugged her friend fiercely. "Let me know if you go to Taiwan or anywhere in Asia and I'll try to meet up."

Do-won shook Danny's hand and hugged Emily, who blushed heavily, much to Katie's amusement.

"Send me pictures of the new baby, okay?" Katie said when it was her turn to hug Emily. "I wish you a healthy and safe delivery."

Do-won waved to them again and joined Katie in the front seat of her mother's Tesla. "I didn't know she was a CHIMERA," he observed.

"Oh, she isn't," Katie said. "You're just incredibly attractive."

Do-won grinned. "Glad to hear I haven't lost my touch with the noonas."

"Maybe when we get back to my mom's house, you can touch this noona."

He cackled. He couldn't wait.

When they finally pulled into the driveway of Auntie Grace's house, he idly wondered how quickly he could get Katie from the garage to her room without being rude to her mother. With those happy thoughts in mind, Do-won trailed Katie into the house and through their kitchen, staring mostly at her ass and wanting to bite it.

He was so lost in his thoughts that he almost did not stop in time when Katie suddenly stopped at the edge of her family room. Only when Do-won tried to step around Katie did she move, holding her arm out to keep him behind her.

"Daddy?" she asked, voice small and questing.

He looked up and saw a huge bear of a man with graying hair and wire spectacles sitting next to Katie's mother on their couch. Even if Katie hadn't identified him, there was no mistaking who this man was. Thomas Wu looked like an older, male version of Katie, and though he was seated, he looked like a giant compared to Auntie Grace.

"Hello, wá," Thomas said as he rose from the deep, forest green sofa. "Did you miss me?"

Though Katie's mind was busy cataloging the fastest exits, as well as calculating how physically close her mother and Do-won were to her father, she was rooted in place, trying to comprehend how her family home had so quickly become a trap. Bodyguards had accompanied the couple to America, but Katie had given them a semi-vacation once they arrived, not thinking they'd be necessary during her personal time at home. The home she had grown up in had seemed safe.

She held back a frustrated scream when Do-won not only stepped around her to stand by her side, but he actually placed himself slightly between her and her father. Do-won was brave and strong, but her father had at least seventy-five pounds of muscle on him. She did not need Do-won to protect her; she needed him safe and alive.

"What are you doing here?" she asked in English so Do-won could understand — could be a witness — trying to buy time, trying to figure out threat levels and what her father wanted. "You know the conditions Alton laid out."

"Alton's not here, is he? Besides, I missed you, bǎobèi, and I wanted to meet your new boyfriend," her father replied, smiling and congenial. He always knew how to put on a good show. "Kǎi Tíng, come and give your baba a hug." He stood up from the couch and took a step forward.

Katie took a step back, dragging poor Do-won with her.

"Mommy," Katie directed to her mother, ignoring her father's order. "Why is he here? You know I'm not speaking to him."

Katie's mother huffed, her face long-suffering and annoyed. "I've indulged you long enough, Kǎi Tíng-ah. You've always been too spoiled and

American for your own good. Baba is your father. Say you're sorry and get over it," her mother said from her seat. "I'm tired of your childish grudge inconveniencing everyone in the family."

"No," Katie said, clenching her hands. She willed her heart rate to slow down. She would not lose it in front of Do-won. Not when they'd just started. She would be better than she had been with Akihiro. "I will not."

"Don't think you're too famous for us to scold in front of your boyfriend," her mother hissed in Chinese. "I raised you better than this."

Though her mother's words stung, Katie tried to tell herself that it was only because she didn't know what her father had done to her. Surely, surely if her mother knew what her father had made her do, her mother would be on her side.

"He left me to die, Mama," Katie said in English, her voice shaking. She vaguely registered Do-won reaching for her hand and squeezing. "He sold me to the Laus."

Both her parents scoffed. "I'm sure it was so terrible for the Laus to get you those movie roles and brand deals," her father said acerbically in Chinese. "You think you would have gotten them on your own? There's no way. You're a terrible actress and not nearly pretty enough."

"Tony almost killed me," Katie seethed. "He cracked five ribs and bruised my face and body so badly that I couldn't leave the apartment for at least a month." Hot tears rolled down her face without her permission. "All because you were stupid and tried to fuck over the wrong family."

Her father smiled condescendingly as if she were crazy. "Bǎobèi, I heard you got rid of Tony's baby," he said in English, as if wanting to make sure Do-won knew. "Don't you think any real man would be angry enough to hit you if you killed their child? I'm sure you're exaggerating your injuries."

Katie heard Do-won inhale sharply, but she still refused to look in his direction. She did not want her father to notice him any more than he had to. Her mother looked horrified.

"You knew?" Katie asked. She hadn't known her heart had any more pieces left for her father to break. "You knew that whole time? You were across the river and never tried to help me?"

Her father shrugged as he sat back down casually. "Someone had to teach you obedience. If your mother had done a better job at it in the first place, you wouldn't have gotten hurt."

Katie took another step back. "You're a monster," she said as evenly as she could muster. She absently rubbed her wrist, adding, "You didn't care that the Laus were threatening Mommy and Mattie. All you cared about was your money, your —"

"No, Katie," her father cut in. "You're the one who didn't care. You would have left me to deal with the Laus myself. They had to threaten your mother and Mattie before you would even do your duty. You're the one who only cared about money — as if Tony didn't help you make it all back."

Katie floundered. Maybe she really was the selfish one. She'd been ready to leave her father to deal with it on his own, except that didn't seem right, either. Katie did not dare look back at Do-won.

"Now, sir. I think you know that is not true," Do-won interjected. "Forgive me, my English is not that good," he continued as he wrapped an arm around her and held her close. He was solid and Katie wanted to sink into his strength. "I think you know that Katie noona and Alton hyung saved you, that you owe them your life," he continued in the clipped tone he reserved for his most scathing criticisms. "You're her father, you know. You are supposed to protect her — not the other way around. You should be ashamed of yourself."

"How dare you," her father cried, rushing up from his seat. "I don't care how famous you are, you are still in my house. Get out."

Alarm crossed her mother's face as she also stood, as if poised to keep her father from doing something he'd later regret.

Katie's heart dropped. She had to get Do-won out of her house and to safety. "Do-won, please. He's not worth it. Let's just go."

Her boyfriend turned to her, his face still calm and steady. "Alright, noona," he said and then turned to her mother. "Thank you for your hospitality, Auntie Grace," Do-won said and bowed. "I hope to see you again under better circumstances."

Do-won gently led Katie out through the kitchen and garage until they were standing on her mother's driveway.

"Let's take a walk, noona," he said softly.

It was his softness that ultimately unmade her. Katie burst into tears.

"I'm so sorry, Do-won," she wept into his chest, clinging to his warmth and the sturdy beating of his heart. "I'm a mess — my whole family is a mess. I don't want to drag you into this."

"Shhhhh, noona. I knew what I was getting into," he said. "You've told me enough of your family for this to not be surprising."

She hugged him even tighter. "It's one thing to know in theory, it's another altogether to experience in person." She shivered. "I'm so sorry."

Do-won kissed the top of her head and tilted her chin so she faced him. "You have nothing to be sorry for. Let's check into a fancy hotel or something and come back later for our stuff."

She looked up at his face and searched for the lie that would give his true feelings away, but found only kindness and sincerity. She leaned upward and kissed him gently on the mouth.

"Okay, Do-won. Okay."

It wasn't as simple as saying it, but it did end up being okay. After Katie had booked them a suite at The Ritz-Carlton in San Francisco, Do-won called their bodyguards and asked the men to accompany them to her parents' home and gather their things.

He could tell Katie burned in shame as more people witnessed the brokenness of her family life. He tried to assure her that their longtime guards wouldn't judge her — if anything, they knew what she'd gone through and would want to keep her safe. At any rate, her parents hadn't been home, and they were able to pack their luggage and leave in peace.

They'd finally settled into their suite at The Ritz, so Katie went to shower and Do-won ordered room service. After Katie finished, Do-won took his own hot shower to wash off the day's fatigue. When he finally emerged in just a fluffy towel wrapped around his waist, Katie had already rolled the room service cart by the bed and was curled up under the covers.

"You alright?" he asked.

She looked up at him, her baby hairs still a little curled on the edges from the dampness. Her eyes held a world of sadness.

"Is it stupid of me to have hoped that my mother would have chosen me?" Katie asked, sniffling a little as a tear escaped her dark eyes.

Do-won discarded his towel, hung it over the back of a chair, and crossed the room to slip into bed next to Katie. "I don't think it's stupid to hope your mother is on your side, noona." He opened his arms and she crawled into them, resting her head on his bare torso. "And who knows? She just might surprise you."

Katie shook her head. "It's easier not to hold out any hope," she murmured.

Do-won hummed his understanding and stroked Katie's arm absently as she lay still, her breath tickling his chest. He was about to doze off when Katie began placing light kisses all over his skin.

"Katie?" he mumbled sleepily.

Katie's kisses became more insistent. "Make me forget, Do-won. I don't want to think tonight."

Do-won shifted down the bed so that Katie could more easily kiss his mouth. They made out lazily for some time, Do-won getting lost in the sheer pleasure of her lips on his, her weight half thrown on him.

"You're so beautiful," he gasped, "can't believe you let me kiss you whenever I want."

"You can do more than kiss me, you know," she complained, the pout evident in her voice.

He chuckled at her eagerness. "So can you," he teased, "I'm certainly not stopping you." She nipped his lower lip and he laughed at her obvious ploy to rile him up. "I'm on to your tricks, Katie. I'm not the impatient one in this relationship."

"Fine," she sighed. "I'll make you regret it though."

With that, Katie broke off their kisses and shifted her body down until she slipped her wet and warm mouth over his cock.

"Can't say I regret anything," Do-won joked as he sank his fingers into her hair, tugging slightly at her roots.

Katie glared up at him but didn't pull off of him as he half expected her to. Instead, she proceeded to suck him light and shallow, not letting him thrust fully into her heat. She added her hand to the base of his shaft and began to bob slowly over him, all the while neatly twisting her palm as she stroked him.

Do-won felt his blood heat from a low simmer to a relentless boil as Katie expertly worked her mouth in tandem with her fist. When Katie finally removed her hand and gave him full access to her mouth, he took as much as he could without hurting her. He fucked her mouth as slowly as he could stand it and relished the slick sounds of his dick sliding in her spit.

"Fuck, baby," he panted, his body all ravening demand.

Do-won allowed himself a few more indulgent thrusts, grateful that all his years of training enabled him such tight control over his body. Then, when the coil of desire in his belly started to near the point of no return, he pulled out and dragged Katie back up to kiss her hardworking mouth.

"You're so good to me, noona," he rumbled as he shifted her onto her back. "God, I love your fucking mouth."

He slotted his lips against hers and methodically began to fuck his tongue into her waiting heat. All the while, his hand snaked down and slipped up her sleep shorts to stroke Katie over her damp panties. The moan she let out gratified him more than any orgasm, and he teased his fingers over her sex until she was begging him to do more.

"Shhhhh, noona," Do-won crooned in Katie's ear as she arched into him. "You don't want the neighbors to hear, do you?"

He licked up her neck, delving his tongue into the hull of her ear in an imitation of fucking, and her whimper shot straight to his throbbing cock. Katie's ears were always so sensitive and one day, he was going to see if he could make her come from them alone, but today was not that day. Today, he was going to see how long he could occupy her in this overpriced penthouse.

"Wonnie, please," Katie whined. "Need you. Want you."

"Oh, Katie," he snickered darkly. "We've barely even started."

He kissed down her throat, swirling his tongue here and there to taste her and brand her with irregular blooms. He slowly unbuttoned Katie's light flannel shirt and continued his tasting menu along the valley and swells of her breasts, the ridges of her ribs, and the soft round of her belly.

It had been months of learning the map of her body and still, Do-won knew he would never grow tired of her. Katie was it for him. Katie was his person and he hoped to the gods that he was hers.

Do-won nipped the tender flesh of her thighs and pulled off her shorts and underwear, then spread her before him like a banquet. He could feel her tremble as she anticipated his tongue; instead, he continued to knead her ass and kiss everywhere but her dripping entrance.

"Wonniiiiie," Katie whined.

"All things come to those who wait, noona," he replied as he sank his teeth into her inner thigh and Katie sobbed a broken cry.

He continued his slow, sensuous torture until finally, Do-won decided he had made her wait long enough. He dipped his tongue into her core before sliding his wet muscle through her folds.

"Oh, fuck," she sighed as she buried her fingers into his hair.

He swirled around her hooded clit and Katie bucked into his mouth, trying to press his face harder into her cluster of nerve endings. He allowed it as he flattened his tongue and began to actively eat her out. She was juicy and ripe, and he wanted to devour her.

Do-won fluttered his tongue over her clit, and Katie shoved a fist into her mouth as she whimpered and writhed under his ministrations. He thrust a few fingers into her wet core and pumped as quickly as he could, all while lashing her clit with his tongue. When he sensed Katie tensing, clenching her thighs tighter around his head, and grinding her center deeper into his face, he suddenly backed off.

"Oh —," Katie cried, her wail muffled by her hand.

"Not yet, noona," Do-won said as he flipped her over and pushed her ass up.

Do-won lined himself up, wound some of her hair around his fist and yanked slightly. He held Katie in place by the base of her neck and slid into her slippery heat.

"Fuck," Katie gasped as the air whooshed out of her lungs.

Do-won forced himself to body roll as he rocked into her with controlled restraint. He watched as the globes of her ass bounced and jiggled. He couldn't help but give an experimental slap.

"Shit," Katie panted.

"You like that?"

"I think I like the idea of it more than the reality of it," Katie admitted, "but I don't mind if you want to slap me again."

Do-won grinned. He slapped her again. "Love your ass, noona," he growled. "Wanted to bite it today. Love how eager your body is for any bit of me — even if it's a slap."

He plowed into her, his grip still in her hair. He continued rolling into her sweet, gushy pussy as Katie attempted to push back onto his cock. The sound of his balls slapping her cunt and his thighs slapping her thighs resounded in the hotel room. What a fucking sight she was.

But then, as before, when her moans grew in volume and he could tell she was close, Do-won pulled out.

"Do-won," Katie scolded, "if you do not fucking make me come soon, I will never let you fuck me again."

He laughed. "Threats only work if you mean them, Katie." Do-won flipped Katie back onto her back and settled between her legs. "Wanna see you when you come, baby."

"You don't deserve it," Katie complained.

He reached for a dusky nipple and tweaked a little harder than she normally liked, gratified by her hiss. "I think you like it when I'm a little mean to you, noona. I think you like the idea of me taking you however I want as long as you get to come."

Katie tried to squeeze her thighs together, puffing in frustration as his body obstructed her. "Wonnie, please," she begged this time. "Want you to fuck me full."

Do-won slid himself back into her cunt and nuzzled into her neck. "As you wish, noona," he said and proceeded to fuck the everliving shit out of her.

Katie bit down on the meat of his shoulder, that tiny flare of pain goading him on as he pummeled into her. Her broken cries of pleasure were punctuated by lewd squelching, and Do-won lost himself in the rhythm of fumbling toward ecstasy.

"Fuck," Katie gasped as her fingers dug into his back. "*Fuckfuckfuck-fuckfuck*," Katie keened, arching her back off the mattress.

"Shhhhhhh," he admonished as he shoved his fingers in her mouth. Katie sucked and he was gone, shooting his load into her as her cunt fluttered around his shaft. "I love you, I love you, I love you," he mouthed into her hair. "I love you, Katie."

Katie started to shake and gulped huge mouthfuls of air. Shit.

"You okay, love? Did I hurt you?" Do-won peered closely at Katie as she struggled to keep herself together. He slowly swept her face of flyaway baby hairs. "Shhhhhh, noona. You're okay. I've got you, baby."

Next thing he knew, Katie crushed him with an embrace so hard that he felt like his ribs were cracking. She broke into stupid, incoherent sobs. Somewhere in there, Do-won thought he could make out tiny "love yous" and "fucks" and "love you so muches." He murmured sweet nothings to her as she blubbered into his chest. He knew it had been a hard day, and he hoped that this bit of physical intimacy would be enough to stop the churning of her anxious thoughts.

When Katie finally calmed down enough to throw him a watery smile, Do-won smothered her face with butterfly kisses, her tears and sweat blending into a salty mix on his lips.

"You okay, love?"

Katie nodded. She cupped the nape of his neck and drew him in, kissing him with a passion and tenderness that Do-won could not recall her ever kissing him with. He lost himself again in her mouth and relished the way she opened herself to him.

"I love you," she whispered into his mouth. "I love you so much I don't know what to do with myself."

He kissed Katie a few more times and as his cock softened and slipped out of her, he whispered back, "I told you I made women cry on the regular."

A few days later as Katie was about to take her daily birth control pill, he heard her utter a quiet "fuck."

"What's wrong, noona?" he asked.

"I don't understand how I can be so off on the days. I think I skipped one? Maybe two?" Katie frowned. "It's not as if I've never traveled while taking the pills before. I don't understand."

"Is it that big a deal?" asked Do-won. "You've been taking the rest — it should be fine, right?"

Katie shot him the most scathing look. "Is it that big a deal?" Katie repeated. "I don't know, Wonnie. Is getting pregnant a big deal?"

Do-won gulped. "What are the odds though?"

"I got pregnant when I was on birth control just from barfing and diarrhea." Her voice pitched higher and more strident. "I think the odds are pretty fucking high."

Do-won mentally calculated all the times he had come inside Katie since they had arrived in America. It was a lot.

"Oh, shit."

"I'm keeping it if I am," Katie said, her voice shot through with steel. "You don't have to acknowledge them or raise them. But I am keeping it."

Do-won wrapped himself around Katie from behind. "Noona," he said, nuzzling her neck. "Why wouldn't I acknowledge our baby? Why wouldn't I claim a person we made with love?"

"But your reputation —," her voice wobbled.

"I am a grown-ass man in his 30s."

Katie shook her head. "I'm no good for you, Do-won."

He nipped her ear. "Are you an overzealous fan, trying to manage my life now? I didn't think you had it in you."

"I thought you liked it when I got bossy," Katie parried back weakly. "Sorry for bringing the mood down, Wonnie. We'll worry about it if we need to." She turned around in his embrace and kissed him lightly on the lips.

He leaned back to get a better look at her and smoothed her hair back. "Noona, I mean it. I love you. Whatever happens in our lives, I want to go through it together."

Katie nodded and let him crush her into his chest.

October 2028

"You sure you don't want me to help, noona?"

"I'm pretty sure I can manage to piss on a stick."

"Okay, but I'll be right next to you while you do that," Do-won said loyally. "You're the best pee-er on sticks."

Katie laughed and opened the packaging. She rolled her shoulders back, taking in a deep breath. She peed on two tests as Do-won stood in the doorway. She flashed back to a boutique restroom in Hong Kong and though Katie knew her memories could no longer hurt her, it still thrilled her when they did not.

Her body was filled with uncertainty about the future, yet Katie also felt reassured that she had at least healed from this bit. She had survived hard things, and she would continue to survive hard things.

It helped that Do-won was by her side. It helped a fucking lot.

Katie held the two tests horizontal in her hands despite the instructions telling her to place them on a flat surface. She did not know if she would be more disappointed if the tests came back positive or negative. Do-won hovered behind her, hooking his chin over her shoulder while he wrapped his arms around her.

Katie was safe. Katie was always safe with Do-won.

When two pink lines appeared on both tests in short order, Katie exhaled a quiet "Oh" as tears leaked out her eyes. Do-won whooped in joy and grabbed her, lifting her in the air.

"We're going to have a baby, noona!" he hollered, his eyes brimming with happy tears. "My little Wonnies found your eggies!! This is the best day ever!"

Katie was so endeared she couldn't even bring herself to cringe.

"I love you, Katie," said Do-won. "I love you so fucking much."

Then the love of her life dragged Katie out of her bathroom and proceeded to show her just how much he loved her. If she'd thought he'd be more careful with her body because of her pregnancy, she'd have been wrong. Do-won was at once tender and a beast. Katie wasn't sure if it was the pregnancy hormones or the adrenaline, but he played her body like a finely tuned machine, and she was a more than willing instrument.

February 2029

Singer Katie Wu seen sporting a baby bump while out on errands...

- Soompi, February 2029

SB Entertainment will neither confirm nor deny Katie Wu's alleged pregnancy.

- 38JieJie, February 2029

[+ 210,726, - 729] When is Katie Wu going to learn how to wrap it up? Once is a mistake, but twice? Twice is a lifestyle.
                              - Internet user, Pann, February 2029

Slut just can't keep her legs closed. Johnny dodged a bullet.
                              - Dcard user, February 2029

Singer Katie Wu refuses to disclose the father of her baby...
                              - South China Morning Post, February 2029

Who cares who fathered Katie's baby? As long as it's not one of our boys, we cool.

                              - X user, February 2029

The past few months had been a whirlwind of doctor appointments and meetings with SB Entertainment, and Katie was constantly exhausted. Do-won watched as she dealt with the pregnancy taking so much out of her. Whenever he checked in on her, she repeated that she was just grateful the baby was healthy. He could tell Katie was trying valiantly not to complain.

Under the care of Dr. Im, Katie slowly weaned herself off the anti-anxiety medications with the understanding that the instant she felt off or a spike in anxiety or depression, to notify Dr. Im immediately. Katie even made a few more appointments with Dr. Choi to work through the events of her father's surprise visit. Thankfully this time, tapering did not wreak as much havoc on her body and brain chemistry as much as it did when Katie had tried before.

Do-won didn't know whether it had to do with all the pregnancy hormones coursing through her body, her better mental state, or just a stroke of fucking luck. Whatever the reason, he was disinclined to look a gift horse in the mouth.

His parents and her mother were ecstatic and pushed for them to get married as quickly as possible. Katie, on the other hand, was not keen on marriage for the sake of a baby. It wasn't that Katie didn't want to marry him — it was just that she didn't want their parents to dictate when. She repeatedly said she wanted to make sure that if Do-won married her, that he wasn't pressured into it.

It didn't matter how often he reassured her, Katie dug in her heels.

Sometimes, he thought her reluctance to get married was because her relationship with her mother was still so tenuous. Though Katie had reached out a few times to her mother to discuss her father, Auntie Grace adamantly changed the subject to safer topics and circumvented her attempts neatly. Katie always ended the conversations frustrated and bewildered. Thankfully, her brother Mattie had been far more understanding, immediately refusing to speak to their father as well. Plus, he was beyond excited about the baby, and the two of them were constantly texting and chatting.

He was also comforted when she busied herself with reading as much as she could about pregnancy, openly indulging herself in imagining a future with Do-won and his children. She thought of names that would fit in Korean, Chinese, and English, and for some reason, that helped settle him.

He learned right quick to not push Katie anymore and shielded her from the majority of their parents' efforts to conspire against her. His heart swelled when his fellow bandmates and their partners closed ranks around Katie, keeping her in the protective bubble of their love and support.

Alton even gifted Katie his penthouse as a baby shower present.

"Hyung," complained Do-won. "I can buy her all the penthouses!"

"I know, Wonnie. Let me do this for my favorite little sister, okay?" Alton said, steering Do-won out of her earshot before he continued. "I'm not trying to step on your toes, Do-won. But I want Mei to know that she has a way out if she ever needs one — and before you protest, I *know* in my bones that you would never hurt her. It has nothing to do with you and everything to do with her." Alton pinned him with a terrifying stare. "And if I ever find out that you laid a finger on her or your children, I will make sure you never touch her again. I don't care if you are Woo-jin's bandmate and beloved the world over. You will disappear in an extravagantly painful way."

Do-won gulped.

However, when Katie asked him about it later, he just adroitly side-stepped it. The less he wondered about what had really happened to Tony and how much she knew, the better. Plausible deniability was one way he could choose to protect her.

March 2029

Is Katie Wu getting soft in her middle-age? Beautifully con-templative and sweet.

- Liberty Times, March 2029

Katie Wu's latest mini-album "Love Without Fear" (SB En-tertainment, 2029) gives lie to the belief that good art is only born from pain. Her latest proffering is a thoughtful discussion on hubris, on the fear of finally being happy and waiting for the gods to yank it all away. Gentle and hopeful, Wu's prowess has matured, proving that her last album was not a fluke of joy.

All K-indie guitars and cafe-friendly tunes, "Love Without Fear" is surprisingly free of rap and hard-hitting beats. And yet, the album doesn't feel lacking in any way. The sound is cohesive, lovely, and incredibly chill, all the while not singing about the typical K-indie topics of love lost and found.

"Looking Over My Shoulder" sets up the problem of happiness perfectly, firmly confronting her anxieties, all the while challenging the notion that doom is around the corner. "I Chose You and I Choose You" is a steadfast declaration of love, of romance in the continual choosing of the same person yesterday, today, and tomorrow. The album closes with "Bright Child," a compassionate song from Wu's inner child granting Wu permission to give herself fully to jubilation, to find freedom in hope.

- Rolling Stone Korea, March 2029

[1] Looking Over My Shoulder [4:37]
[2] I Chose You and I Choose You [3:45]
[3] Unknown Quantities [4:26]
[4] A Soft Place to Land [3:51]
[5] Bright Child [4:30]
- Track list, "Love Without Fear" (SB Entertainment, 2029)

I dreamt of you last night
So long since I last saw you
Broken on the bathroom floor
Wondering if he'll come back for more

You kissed me on my sweating brow
You hugged me close and whispered
There is a seed in you so bright
Endure just a bit then fight with your might

Your halcyon days are ahead not behind
Fear not, for I am with you, alright
I am you and you are me
And together we will shine so brightly
          - "Bright Child" (SB Entertainment, 2029)

To my baby.
    - Album dedication, "Love Without Fear" (SB Entertain-
              ment, 2029)

Though not common for singers to promote while knocked up, Katie banked on the controversy of her unplanned pregnancy to book her on various programs and garner support for her latest album. Nothing like outrage marketing to drum up views and listens from the curious. The reviews were kind and her fans appreciated her mellowed sound, and Katie was thankful for her loyal Jezebelles and the general public.

Despite Do-won's numerous protests, Katie continued to weather all the internet speculation alone — not out of some misplaced martyrdom as he originally feared, but because she wanted to keep him to herself just a little longer. She did not want to open their relationship — let alone their baby — to his fandom or hers.

"Let me be selfish, Wonnie," Katie whispered as he kissed her belly and rubbed cocoa butter on her ever-expanding middle. "Just give me a little more time."

"You said that last month," he whined. "I want everyone to know you're mine. That I'm proud to be your partner and the father of our child."

"You know as soon as it's announced, people are going to be assholes about it — like even more than they are now," Katie said.

"I can handle it, noona. I'm used to it."

"But I don't want you to, Wonnie," Katie said gently. "You're my sunshine and I can't be held responsible for what I will do to people if they're mean to you."

Do-won laughed into her belly. "You hear that, baby girl? Your eomma is a warrior and will protect appa from all the mean internet people. We're both so lucky, baby."

"You're going to be the best appa," Katie said, pulling him up for a kiss.

Do-won's hands wandered over her fleshy curves, thumbing her sore nipples. Katie hissed in pain.

"Sorry, love. I forgot," he murmured. "Wanna see if I can get you any more pregnant?"

Katie groaned into his mouth. "You really do have a breeding kink, don't you?"

"Shhhhhh, just go with it, noona." He sucked on her neck and the sensitive part right behind her ear. "Can't wait for you to have my baby so I can fill you up with more."

"Do-won," Katie objected even as she pressed herself more into him. "Let's have this baby first, okay?"

"Want to make you my wife, noona," he panted later as his fingers sank deep in her cunt.

"You are not proposing while knuckle-deep in me."

"I am," he insisted. "You won't say 'yes' even when I ask properly."

Her core clenched around his agile digits as Do-won plunged them in and out of her. "It means that much to you?" Katie gasped.

"You mean everything to me, noona." He sucked more bruises on her throat. "Marry me."

"Okay," Katie breathed, and she came, wet and sloppy and perfect.

When people asked later how Do-won proposed, Katie always blushed prettily before spinning some bullshit about a romantic dinner. It pleased him how not a single one of his members believed the official story.

They were all in Jae-sung's studio one day, discussing the concept for DOYEN's next album when suddenly, Akihiro jabbed him in the ribs with a well-placed elbow. "You asked her while fucking, didn't you, hyung?"

Surprised, but also greatly amused, Do-won answered, "A gentleman never tells."

"That's a confirmation if I've ever heard one," cracked Ye-jun. He held out his palm. "Pay up, motherfuckers."

Do-won watched as Jae-sung, Dae-jung, and Soo-min — the three romantics of the group — opened up KakaoPay and each sent the other members an obscene amount of money.

"This is so disappointing," mused Do-won. "It's like we didn't live together for almost a decade at all."

"What's disappointing is this desecration of love and all that it means," Jae-sung lamented.

"We all work to our strengths, hyung," Do-won retorted. "And my stroke game is unparalleled."

"Yeah, yeah, we get it," griped Woo-jin as he threw a half-empty water bottle at him. "You're a fucking sex legend. You're welcome for helping you plant that idea in her mind, by the way. I never received my appropriate thanks."

"Thanks, hyung."

"Hmmmph," the older man grunted.

"I know we already celebrated, but me winning all this money really calls for another celebration," Ye-jun gloated as he went straight to where Jae-sung hid his best liquor.

Though Jae-sung could not have possibly thought they didn't know all his secrets, the man still gamely protested a loud and indignant, "Hey! I was saving that — have you been snooping when I'm not here?"

"Don't be an idiot, Jae-sung-ah," cried Ye-jun, who was in fine form today. "I taught you everything you know — I raised you on my back! This is the least you could do to thank me!"

Everyone laughed and Do-won was filled with so much fond affection he was practically bursting.

Later, Akihiro pulled Do-won aside and embraced him tightly. "I'm so happy for you two, hyung. You're good together and good for each other."

"Thanks, Aki-yah," replied Do-won, tearing up only a little bit. "It means a lot to me that you think so."

"Of course, hyung," Akihiro said fiercely. "We're brothers to the end."

"To the end," Do-won repeated. "To the end."

June 2029

It is with great pleasure and joy that we announce the safe and healthy birth of Katie Wu's baby girl. We ask for fans and the media to respect her request for privacy for herself and her family. Welcome to the world, baby!!

- @Katie_WuWuWu, X, June 2029

I'm an appa! I love you, yeobo. You and our perfect girl are my universe.

- @1DEL1GHT, Instagram, June 2029

Congratulations to @Katie_Wu_SBEnt and our 1DEL1GHT on her marriage and baby! We love Eun-mi so much already!

- @doyen_twt, X, June 2029

Surprise, it's a girl! DOYEN member 1DEL1GHT and singer Katie Wu welcome their new baby!

- allkpop, June 2029

DOYEN 1DEL1GHT stuns everyone! Married to singer Katie Wu and a new baby girl!

- Soompi, June 2029

What a slut. She'll never be good enough for Wonnie.
                                        - X user, June 2029

Get her name out of your mouth. Fuck solo stans.
                                        - X user, June 2029

AAAAAAAAAAAHHHHHHHHHH!!! WONNIE + KATIE!! JEZEBELLE CHIMERA RISE!!!!
                                        - X user, June 2029

OMG WAS TO MY DELIGHT TO WONNIE
                                        - X user, June 2029

Katie had not expected Do-won to announce her marriage and the birth of Jung Eun-mi in quite the way he had, but in the end, she supposed he'd held out as long as he could. Frankly, he'd lasted much longer than Katie had thought he would, but she didn't want to puff up his ego anymore. He was such a stereotypically proud father that Katie couldn't help but love him more.

She was slowly recovering from a C-section and obediently eating all the seaweed soup that Do-won's mother brought over daily. Her mother had also taken over her kitchen and made Katie a bunch of Chinese herb concoctions that Katie could not identify, but just thanked her while she ate.

Katie and her mother were still delicately dancing around the issue of her father. Her mother seemed to truly be making an effort to figure things out for herself, so Katie allowed it. She was tentatively hopeful that wanting to protect Eun-mi would be the deciding factor for her mother. Even if the logic didn't really make sense, Katie clung to that hope.

Her mother and father's marriage wasn't the only thing she was avoiding thinking about. Katie studiously ignored the internet and social media entirely. Everything was making her cry and she knew she wouldn't be able to keep it together if she saw even one mean thing about Do-won or Eun-mi. Katie didn't care so much if she personally got internet hate; she was used to it. But Do-won or her precious baby? She would scorch the entire earth if anyone came for the two most important people in her life.

"You should be sleeping, yeobo," chided Do-won as he came into her room holding their daughter.

Katie glared at him from the bed. "I'm only going to allow you 'yeobo' for another week, Wonnie. I can't do it. I just can't." She softened her expression as Do-won handed Eun-mi to her.

"But you're my wife," he whined as he sat in the easy chair near the bed.

She leaned over and buried her nose in the crook of her baby's neck. "What's wrong with what you were doing before? Call me by my name," Katie retorted, "or call me 'noona,' but I swear to god if you call me 'yeobo' or 'jagiya' one more time, I will throw something at you."

Do-won pouted. "You're so weird, noona."

"Did you think I would change after you married me?" Katie teased. Eun-mi burbled and Katie immediately cooed back, delighted.

"I hoped that you would on that front, anyway." This time, it was Katie's turn to pout. "Don't pout, love. You'll still let me call you that, right?"

Katie nodded and to her horror, fat tears slipped down her cheeks.

"Oh, noona, don't cry," Do-won soothed. "I was just kidding — I love you the way you are. I love you so much, Katie-yah."

"I know," Katie sniffled, holding Eun-mi closer to her. "I don't know why I'm crying."

Do-won climbed into bed with Katie and hugged them both tightly. "It's all the hormones flooding your body, baby," he said. "Do you need a cheeseburger?"

"Oh my god, Wonnie," Katie sobbed. "Yes! Yes, I need a cheeseburger with avocado and extra pickles and fries and a milkshake. I love you more than any person in the world, except Eun-mi — even if she can't order me American food yet. But one day, we will teach her to properly respect her elders."

Do-won laughed and ruffled her hair though he knew Katie hated it. Katie didn't comment on it only because he was going to order her a cheeseburger.

"You're the best mother ever, love," he said, his voice full of love.

Katie's eyes got round and filled with even more tears. "She's so little, Do-won," she said as she peered at Eun-mi's perfect little face. "What if I break her?"

He kissed Katie on her temple. "You won't, noona." He kissed Katie again. "Will you fuck up? Of course. But you will do everything in your power to raise our babies in an emotionally healthy and loving environment." He squished her even more. "You put in the work, and I have no doubt you will seek help the moment something triggers you."

Katie closed her eyes and let herself bask in the warmth of Do-won's love. She breathed him in and let his love wash over and through her, filling in all her crevices.

"Thanks, Do-won," Katie whispered.

"Alright, now let me order you that cheeseburger."

"Oh, thank fuck."

EPILOGUE

August 2059

"Where did we go wrong, Wonnie?"

"I don't know, love," Do-won replied, frowning. Even after all these decades, nothing struck fear (and if Katie was honest, a tiny bit of arousal) in her as much as the sight of that triangle mouth.

From her spot at the round table in the Chinese restaurant, Katie stared at her four children who were sitting at the various kids' tables spread around the private room and sighed. "It breaks my fucking heart."

"What are you talking about, noona?" laughed Akihiro from across the table. "Your kids are amazing. Every other parent would be so proud. You have a tax attorney, an accountant, an electrical engineer, and a software developer." He leaned back, his arm casually draped around his wife.

"They were in the top of their classes, too, right?" added Soo-min.

Katie sighed again. "But they're so boring."

"I knew we should have tried for one more after Eun-ju," mused Do-won, wincing imperceptibly after Katie pierced him with her furious gaze. "Eun-mi wouldn't even let me dance at her wedding. Me! DOYEN Dance Leader 1DEL1GHT!"

Alton, who was seated to Katie's right, couldn't stop cracking up. "Eun-ju's an actual genius, though. She's fielding offers left and right from the top development companies, and she's rejecting them all to come work for me!" he exclaimed rapturously.

"I don't even know why you would need her talents," Katie griped. "You're just taking her away from me."

"You love Singapore," Alton cajoled. "Don't be mad, Mei."

Katie sulked. Do-won, fantastic partner that he was, also sulked.

"You two are ridiculous," scolded Woo-jin as he sipped his Kavalan whisky. "You don't see Mina noona and Ye-jun complaining about their boring children."

"Hey!" protested Ye-jun as Mina just looked on tolerantly. "My kids aren't —"

"Oh my god, you're right," Katie interrupted. "I can't believe you made not one but two actuaries."

Ye-jun's ears burned bright red. "They're the top actuaries in the field! They make a shit ton of money!" he sputtered. "They're highly sought after by pretty much every fucking company in Korea!"

"But at what cost, hyung?" replied Do-won mournfully. "At what cost?"

"Fuck you all, you motherfuckers! See if I come to the next family reunion."

"It's literally at your house next month, hyung," quipped Jae-sung as he pulled up a chair from a neighboring table to sit with them.

"Don't try to get out of it. I know your door code," added Dae-jung, who up until this point, had been quietly minding his own business.

Akihiro clapped delightedly. "We all know your door code!"

All of a sudden, Do-won smacked his forehead. "Oh, shit. We forgot to get a cake, Katie!"

"You forgot the cake, Wonnie," Katie chuckled. "Akihiro brought one because he's the cake fairy."

Do-won breathed a sigh of relief. "Good man, Hiro-yah!"

"Awww, hyung!" Akihiro blew her husband a flying kiss.

Katie pecked Do-won lightly on the cheek and blushed at the exaggerated whistles from her friends and groans from her kids. "Idiots," Katie muttered fondly. "Now sing me my song so we can eat cake!"

Katie leaned back and gazed at her family and friends as they gathered to serenade her with a surprisingly off-key rendition of "Happy Birthday." They were all a bit older, many with graying hair and a few more wrinkles on their familiar faces, but they'd obviously all been former idols. They were all still trim, handsome, and dressed to the nines. Do-won was the worst — he was still as energetic as he had been in his youth. Truly, it was annoying.

Except she couldn't be too mad. Here she was, 66 years old and still lucky enough to be surrounded by so many people who loved her — and loved her deeply.

Katie teared up, squeezed Do-won's hand, and blew out all sixty-six candles.

It was a good life.

The End (of this timeline).

Acknowledgments

First of all, this book would be in shambles were it not for the talents and eagle eyes of the following amazing women:

Jacquelin Cangro, your enthusiasm and professionalism taught me so much about writing a book. Your developmental edit improved my craft, and I am forever grateful.

Diane Park, your brilliant, strategic mind and friendship have saved me from looking culturally incompetent on main. Thank you for the cultural edit and ensuring I depict the beautiful Korean culture as accurately as possible.

Melody Ip, thank you for tightening my blatherings, curbing my misuse of em-dashes, commas, "bemusement," and overuse of "froze" and "shuddered." You were one of my first friends at Mochi Magazine, and I am so happy to have a fellow GenX in the trenches with all the infants.

Joyce Park, I'm so thankful for your art, your creativity, and your work. I can't imagine any better person to translate my words into visual art. Who would have thought a random comment about OSC would spawn a friendship over K-pop, Two Dots, and theology?

To the Boba Ramen Crew: Rose Nieh, Andrea Siu, Patti Chang, and Amy Lee. What would I do without any one of you? You all saw me through early motherhood, teaching our kids Mandarin Chinese, and all the shenanigans in between. I love you, and I love us. Thank you for including me in the commune even though I am not nearly as useful or helpful.

Cindy Chiang, you are the badass of all badasses. If I could eviscerate terrible logic and awfulness as thoroughly and as completely as you could, I would rule the world. You are my fiercest protector, my biggest cheerleader, and one of the most generous and giving people I know. It is an honor to be your friend and to know you.

To the VEJ chat, I love you both so much. Jessica Robinson, your love and support mean the world to me. This entire series wouldn't exist without you. Thank you for always being there to listen to me as I scream "what if" and help hash out plot points. It's also your fault this book is part of a multiverse, so thanks for that. You are the best reader and friend. I live for your voice recordings. E, the writer you are!!! The way you evoke such emotion and evocative description — I could never write the way you do. What a joy it is to read your words, to be a part of your life and love. Being on this writing journey with you has fed my soul.

To my fellow Degenerates, Hasina Rashed and Blessing Gana, you both sustain me. I love you both so much. The way you two are so brilliant, clever, beautiful, and funny, I couldn't ask for better friends. Thank you for always entertaining my ideas seriously, for being so down for whatever, and for loving me and mine almost as much as I do. Hasina, you really are the original multi-hyphenate. I honestly cannot believe you're real. You inspire me with your generosity, kindness, competence, and absolute sexiness. Blessing, to have even a fraction of your incisive strategery, cracking good humor, and agile mind! You make me so proud to know you.

Erica Howard, you are a rock in my life. You love me, check up on me, love my babies, and unstintingly care for my whole person. I love you. You taught me how to be the kind of friend who checks in and says "good morning" and "hello." Thank you for enfolding me into your life and for sharing your world and loved ones with me.

To the Uncreepy Accountability Buddies, I love you! Most especially, Stella Won and Marsha Ungchusri, thank you both for being such steady presences in my life. Stella, your incisive mind and ability to word better than I ever could continually speaks life into me. Thank you for sharing your joys, sorrows, and beautiful family with me. You make me think that I can do the impossible. Marsha, you taught me so much about keeping boundaries, consent, and how to be a good friend. Over the years, our weekly writing sessions kept me sane and on deadline. Thank you for introducing me to Pedro Pascal and for joining the stan life with me.

I could not write if I didn't have a support system in place. Jenn Yoo, Nancy Lin, Sophia Lai, Emily Lai, Sandi Francioch, Cathy Barger, Jessica Klugman, Sarah Poon, Jie Gao, Po-wen Chen, Vicky Tai, and countless other friends: thank you for your friendship and for being part of that support system. It takes a village to raise children and mothers, and you are my village. Without your love and support, I would not have become a good mother. Thanks to you, I never have to worry that my kids are loved, have friends, and are educated.

Chris Wong, you are the first Asian American I knew personally who pursued art wholeheartedly, come what may. Your genius, musicality, deadpan humor, and friendship have carried me through so many decades. I am forever thankful for how you paved the way for me and so many others. You made me think art and craft were possible.

Joe Chang, I'm so happy to see you pursue music again after so many years. Together, we can figure out what it means to be Asian American artists who create art that is not only art, but can only be made by us. Our conversations sustain me. Thank you.

Lizz Porter, my eternal roommate and cornerstone. Without you, would I even have any friends? All my best and most meaningful relationships from blogging are because of you. Thank you for showing me the way for over 30 years, for your generosity of spirit, and for being the reason I could imagine a different life at all.

Brandi Riley, I adore you. Your expansive heart, your care, your wisdom, and your fantastic mind amaze me. I can't believe you are my friend and love me! Thank you for believing in and encouraging me. You saw me as I could be and made sure I could see it, too. I love you!

Katherine Shorter, my gorgeous and kind friend. Our (almost) daily Zoom co-working sessions saw me through the pandemic. Thank you for your steadfast love, your steady humor, and your willingness to spend hours recording reaction videos with me. You breathed life into me.

Jeff Harry, my nemesis and Bay Area food buddy, you always ask me the tough questions. Thank you for always making me re-examine myself, for not accepting the status quo, and for consistently making sure I don't talk myself out of what I really want. You are a joy, a riot, and a fellow troublemaker.

Damion Taylor, you are just so kickass. I'm so grateful for 25 years of friendship, laughter, and tomfoolery. I love your strategic, analytical, and ambitious mindset, how you use your talents to uplift and carry your friends, and how you shine so bright. Thank you for making me believe I can do big things.

Anita Jackson, thank you for your unwavering belief and support. Watching you actively choose to be bold in your life allowed me to also be bold in mine. The love and encouragement of you and your beautiful family will always warm my heart.

Susanna Stroberg, thank you for your friendship, your unending enthusiasm and positivity, and for bringing my K-pop hair aspirations to life. You make the impossible possible.

Thank you to all my Possums, current and alumni. I love our trash heap dumpster haven. Thank you for all your encouragement, love, and partnering in thirst. I never knew a writer community could be so safe, loving, supportive, and unabashedly kind. I have learned how to be a better human from all of you. Most especially, thank you to Rei, Grid, sahmfanficbts, and Em. Thank you for listening to me plot, whine, and moan about writing. Thank you for allowing me to be in your lives and do writerly things with you.

Leslie Hartje-Dunn, I'm so thankful for our friendship. You see the world so differently from me and the way you are so generous with your thoughts and emotions, I am just in awe. I love your heart.

Jenny Park, I can't believe you recognized me in the bathroom at a concert even though we were strangers. Thank you for always making me feel like a rockstar. Your friendship, love for my writing, and general attitude bring me so much joy. You're the coolest!

To the Barricades or Bust group chat, thank you for your friendship and for being some of my earliest readers. I can't believe it's been five years since I randomly joined a chat off of Reddit. What a ride it's been! Thanks especially to Xtal and ASIW — Candimatters forever! Xtal, I'm grateful for the way you fiercely love and defend my characters, and are so thoughtful and conscientious. ASIW, thank you for letting me steal your life for my stories, our marathon phone conversations, and for never agreeing on anything musically related except for our greatest loves. SURPRISE!

To the Unnies Afterlife group chat, thank you for being a global sisterhood that is truly supportive and sweet. I am so happy to have met many of you in person, and my life is all the richer for having you all in it. Most especially, I want to thank Tiina Paldán and Carmie Zhang. QUEEN Tiina, I adore you! You are the reason our little band of misfits have all fit together and have lasted so long. Thank you for loving me and for being such a meaningful part of my life. Carmie, my default concert buddy and videographer! I love you!! You are so fun, so talented, and so kind. You make my life shine so bright and I'm so lucky to know you.

To the Kpopcast podcast and Slack group, thank you for your most thorough K-pop education, the comradery, and the great discussions. Most especially, DJ Peter Lo and PD-nim Michaela. You two are such a joy. Thank you for your friendship and our many hours of hilarious and informative conversation.

Giannina Ong, thank you for your leadership at Mochi Magazine and your friendship in general. You have taught me so much about community, allyship, and tenacity of spirit. You are so generous and supportive, I'm so lucky to know you!

Jessica Rosenberg and Maxine Liming, thank you both for your generosity. I could not have gone this self-publishing route without the benefit of your experience and wisdom.

BTS, thank you for existing. You eased my sorrow, gave me courage, and slaked my thirst. May you all be happy and healthy all the days of your life.

To my mother Sarah Huang, I love you.

To my baby brother Alex Duan, I adore you. Sometimes, I think you're actually the older sibling because you take care of me, check in on me, and in general, love me and mock me in equal parts. Thanks for being my oldest friend.

And finally, I am grateful to my husband James and my ridiculously good-looking children Cookie Monster, Gamera, Glow Worm, Sasquatch, and Kitsune. Jimmy, without your good humor, stable job, steady personality, and support, none of this would be possible. Thank you for loving me. Kids, thank you for teaching your mama just how high and how wide, how deep and how long my love can be. I love you from eternity to eternity, from this life to the next, and beyond the boundaries of time.

GLOSSARY

Aegyo (애교): acting cute or childish by pitching the voice higher, and changing speech patterns, facial expressions, or gestures to seem cute. Common among K-pop idols for their fans.

Ah-gong (阿公): Taiwanese for grandfather

Ajumma (아줌마): Korean for a married or middle-aged woman

Appa (아빠): Korean for dad (informal/casual)

Bàba (爸爸): Mandarin for father

Banmal (반말): informal spoken Korean, generally used with close friends or people who are younger

Bǎobèi (寶貝): Mandarin for treasure, darling, baby

Chaebol (재벌): in South Korea, a large conglomerate owned by a family, usually very rich individuals or family

Dongsaeng (동생): younger sister/brother, what Koreans of any gender call a younger person if they are close or related

Eomma (엄마): Korean for mom (informal/casual)

Gēge (哥哥): Mandarin for big brother, can also be used as a term of endearment

Gomo (고모): Korean for paternal aunt

Gyopo (교포): term for the Korean diaspora, sometimes used in a derogatory manner

Hyung (형): older brother, what Korean males call older males if they are close or related

Imo (이모): Korean for maternal aunt

Jagiya (자기야): honey, darling, baby, an affectionate name for your significant other in Korean

Maknae (막내): the youngest member in a group of people (e.g., family, friends, K-pop groups)

Mèimei (妹妹): Mandarin for little sister, can also be used as a term of endearment

Nǎinai (奶奶): Mandarin for paternal grandmother

Nim (님): roughly translated as Mr./Mrs./Miss/Ms., adding "-nim" after a proper noun is the most formal honorific to show politeness and respect to people when in formal or professional settings

Noona (누나): older sister, what Korean males call older females if they are close or related

Oppa (오빠): older brother, what Korean females call older males if they are close or related

PD: Producer-Director, can be used in film and television as well as music production

Sajangnim (사장님): Korean for boss, CEO, president

Shú Gong (叔公): Mandarin for paternal granduncle

Soseol (소설)/Xiǎoxuě (小雪): Korean/Mandarin for "little snow"

Ssi (씨): roughly translated as Mr./Mrs./Miss/Ms., adding "-ssi" after a proper noun is an honorific to show politeness and respect to people/strangers who are generally the same age or social status, less formal than "nim"

Unni (언니): big sister, what Korean females call older females if they are close or related

Wá (娃): Mandarin for baby, child, son or daughter, doll

Yeobo (여보): honey, Korean term of endearment used only by married couples

About the Author

Virginia Duan is an Asian American author who writes stories full of rage and grief with biting humor and glimpses of grace. Her debut novel "Illusive" is a steamy and evocative behind-the-scenes story set in the K-pop industry. Part of the Her Multiverse series, the books will follow pop singer Katie Wu and K-pop boy band DOYEN through multiple timelines, exploring how Katie's tough choices drastically change her future.

Based in the San Francisco Bay Area, Virginia lives with her husband and five children. (Yes, five.) She spends most of her days plotting her next book or article, shuttling her children about, participating in more group chats than humanly possible, and daydreaming about BTS a totally normal amount.

Join Virginia's mailing list to receive sneak peeks, bonuses, and updates on her latest stories at https://virginiaduan.com.